# The Girls from Mersey View

# Lyn Andrews

# The Girls from Mersey View

HEADLINE

First published in 2020 by
HEADLINE PUBLISHING GROUP

1

Cataloguing in Publication Data is available from the British Library

ISBN 978 1 4722 6967 6

Typeset in Janson by Avon DataSet Ltd, Arden Court, Alcester, Warwickshire

Printed and bound in Great Britain by Clays Ltd, Elcograf S.p.A.

MIX
Paper from
responsible sources
FSC® C104740

Headline's policy is to use papers that are natural, renewable and recyclable
products and made from wood grown in well-managed forests and other
controlled sources. The logging and manufacturing processes are expected to
conform to the environmental regulations of the country of origin.

HEADLINE PUBLISHING GROUP
An Hachette UK Company
Carmelite House
la Embankment
ı EC4Y 0DZ

eadline.co.uk
achette.co.uk

For my great friends Margaret McMahon, Sharon Devaney, Jackie Kneem and Liz Meredith, who with myself constitute the 'Ramsey Ladies Wine Appreciation Group', which meets once a month in the excellent 'The Other Place Brasserie' in Ramsey for lunch and – of course – wine-tasting (otherwise known as 'Fun Friday')! An occasion that quite often turns into, shall we say, a rather boisterous event; although extremely enjoyable. All our thanks go to the proprietors Mark and Alison for their good-humoured patience and Mark's fabulous food.

# *Acknowledgements*

---

During my time working on this novel there has been quite a number of people who contributed in no small way to its completion. Firstly, I would like to thank Dr R Peshin, Consultant Rheumatologist at Nobles Hospital, and Dr A Neel, my GP, for all their assistance in helping me manage my osteoporosis so I am able to continue my writing career. Mere words are insufficient repayment for their kindness and medical expertise.

I would like to thank my agent, Anne Williams of the Kate Horden Literary Agency, for all her wonderful support, advice and encouragement. I know I can always trust her judgement, for, in all the years I've known her (at first as my editor), she has never been wrong where characters or storylines are concerned.

Also to Jennifer Doyle, Rosanna Hildyard and all the team at Headline Publishing Group for their hard work on my behalf, especially under the difficult circumstances that have faced us this year with COVID-19. You are all consummate professionals and I respect and admire you all.

# Chapter One

Liverpool,
1935

'Why is it called "Mersey View" when you can't even *see* the river from here?'

The question was uttered in a slightly argumentative tone that fifteen-year-old Monica Savage wasn't sure she liked very much. The girl facing her was part of the new family that had moved into the street yesterday, and she looked to be about the same age as herself. She was taller and thinner, though, and had very dark brown – almost black – hair swept back from her forehead, her dark eyes animated and fringed with thick sooty lashes. She wasn't what you would call pretty, by any stretch of the imagination, but she was, Monica had to admit, what Mam would term "striking". Why she was taking this belligerent attitude she didn't know.

Monica shrugged in response to the girl's question. 'I don't know why they called it that. I've lived here all my life and I've

1

never heard anyone else ask that before. I suppose the Council or whoever is in charge of these things thought it sounded more . . . interesting than just such-and-such a street. Anyway, you actually *can* see the river if you go to the end and peer around the corner of the last house.' Monica shrugged again. 'And why would you want to be bothered looking at the river at all? It's not called the "Mucky Mersey" for nothing – in summer it stinks to high heaven!'

The other girl considered this. 'Oh, I just thought me mam might have moved us all here so she could actually see the river. You see, me da goes away to sea. Nothing fancy, like; not on the big liners. It's just a cargo ship and he's in the engine room.' Her tone had softened slightly as she spoke of her father and then she grinned, transforming her features entirely. 'What's your name?'

Monica grinned back; maybe she wasn't too bad after all. 'Monica Savage, what's yours?'

'Joan. Joan Copperfield. We moved into number ten yesterday. Mam, me and our Charlie. He's me brother, he's twelve and a holy terror, so me mam is always saying. He needs me da to keep him in order but, well, Da's hardly ever here so he's not much use in that department.'

Monica nodded her understanding. In this city half the male population had chosen 'going away to sea' as a job if not a career. She leaned back against the end wall of the house nearest to them, which had been warmed by the rays of the setting sun now cascading over the dark slates of the roof-tops, and stared up the street, her arms folded. Maybe Mrs Copperfield *had* expected to be able to see her husband's ship as it came upriver to the docks but if so she would be disappointed. As the girl said, you couldn't even see the Mersey.

Joan followed Monica's example, crossing her arms over her chest and looking up the street. This wasn't bad, she mused to herself. Much like the one they'd left – but then nearly all the streets in the working-class areas of Liverpool looked pretty much the same. Two- and three-storeyed narrow terraced houses with yards at the back which housed the privies and the ashcans. Some were in better condition than others but all were old and blackened by the soot that poured from countless chimneys both domestic and industrial. They had no gardens, of course, and in this part of Everton the streets were very steep, the houses looking as if they were clinging desperately to the side of St George's Hill. In winter these streets were treacherous to both man and beast, or so she'd heard; that's why they all had railings for people to hang on to. There was a small shop on the corner where Mersey View joined Northumberland Terrace and on the opposite corner was The George and Dragon, the obligatory public house.

Surreptitiously Joan had quickly taken in her new acquaintance's appearance. About the same age, a bit on the plump side and not as tall as herself, but with light brown hair which seemed to wave naturally, and very blue eyes. Her green-and-white cotton dress and matching green hand-knitted cardigan were definitely better than the faded print dress she wore herself. 'So, you'll have to tell me who lives where in the street and who has the shop. That's really important – me mam will want to know that, so she can see about getting a bit of credit, like. Do they let you put things on the slate?'

Monica nodded. 'Once Ethel knows you, and if she thinks

you're reliable. Come on, we'll walk down there and I'll introduce you to her. Mrs Ethel Newbridge is her proper name, and Mo Clancy has the pub – not that me da goes in there much, and we'd be skinned alive if we set foot over the doorstep. Mo's name is Maurice Clancy really but everyone calls him "Mo".'

They fell into step as they walked slowly up the narrow, steep cobbled street with Monica pointing to the various houses. 'We live there, number fifteen. Me da works on the railways. He's a guard and he's based at Lime Street. There's Mam and me, of course, and our Eileen, me sister. She's the same age as your Charlie and she's a real pain in the neck. We just don't get on, never have done. When we were younger, Mam made me take her everywhere with me and she was always whining and lagging behind. I *hated* it!'

Joan took in the pristine lace curtains of number fifteen, the scrubbed and 'donkey stoned' step, the polished brass door knocker, and a small frown creased her brow. The Savages appeared to have more money than most people in the street, judging by the outside of the house. But with Mr Savage a guard on the railways, it was only to be expected. That was a very secure and much-sought-after job; a job for life, and with a pension too at the end of it. 'That place looks a bit run-down. Who lives there?' she asked, pointing to a very dilapidated-looking house a few doors further on.

Monica cast her eyes skywards. 'All sorts; at least that's what Mam calls them. Every room's rented out – and you never know from one month to the next who is living there, what with all the comings and goings and moonlight flits and that.' She laughed. 'It drives Mam mad; she does like to know what's going on in the street. She thinks it's her "duty", but privately me da says she's just nosey!'

'Then she's just the opposite of my mam; it's like trying to get blood out of a stone getting any gossip out of *her*. Now me Aunty Lil, she's a different kettle of fish. She's Mam's sister but they're not a bit alike. I suppose Aunty Lil's more . . . sort of "outgoing", probably because she's always worked in the theatre.'

Monica was surprised; she'd never known anyone who had such an exotic occupation. 'Really? Is she an actress or something?' It would be very exciting to know someone related to a real-life actress!

Joan grinned but shook her head. 'No, she works in the wardrobe department at the Empire. But she's quite glamorous, which me mam definitely is not. You'll meet her, she comes round sometimes.'

This was really interesting, Monica thought; she'd look forward to encountering this Aunty Lil.

'So, who lives next door to us, then? We've not heard a sound since we moved in, although maybe that's because of all the noise our Charlie was making last night, supposedly helping Mam and me to unpack and get the beds up.'

'That's Mr Garswood – and you probably wouldn't have heard a sound anyway. He's very quiet, he keeps himself to himself. He does go out to work, but we don't know what he does exactly – another mystery for Mam.'

'Hasn't he got any family? Does he live in that house all by himself?' Joan queried. It seemed to her it was quite big just for one person. In fact, it was the biggest house in the street.

'Mam said when she was young his mother was alive, but

then she died after I was born and there's been no one since. He doesn't seem to have any family or even relatives or friends.'

Joan frowned. 'Bit odd that.'

'I don't suppose many folk think about it; we don't. Oh, he's pleasant enough if you see him on the street. Always says "Good evening" or some such,' Monica replied and then decided to change the subject. Her new friend would find out all about the rest of the neighbours in time. 'When we've been to the shop, why don't you come home with me and I can introduce you to Mam. And perhaps if there is anything we can do to help . . . ? After all, we're going to be neighbours and maybe . . . friends?' Monica suggested tentatively.

Joan smiled. 'Oh, definitely friends. I do hope Mam decides to stay here. She's a great one for upping sticks and moving – I don't know why half the time – but it gets to be a nuisance. I just seem to make friends, then we're off again.'

'I hope you stay too,' Monica replied, for she'd taken to Joan Copperfield. But, she wondered, did they have much in common? Well, no doubt she'd soon find out.

Ethel Newbridge, a small wiry woman with sharp grey eyes that missed nothing, and a shrewd business head on her thin shoulders, had been encouraging after Monica's introduction. Joan felt relieved she'd be able to inform her mother that their financial situation – always precarious owing to her da's job – would be eased by the fact that credit would more than likely be extended. The shop had been just like all the other corner shops she'd experienced. Small, dark, crammed to the rafters with every commodity you could think of, the floor space an obstacle course of sacks containing coal and potatoes, small bundles of wood known as 'chips', as well as brooms and shovels. It was obviously a meeting place for the local house-wives and she was glad her new friend Monica had been on hand with the introduction, which always helped in a new area. She'd learned that much over the years.

She felt a little uneasy when Monica ushered her into the kitchen of number fifteen, which she quickly ascertained was far better furnished and more comfortable than the one in her home. The range gleamed from regular applications of black lead and elbow grease; on the mantel above were two black-and-white Staffordshire dogs, a fine clock and a brass spill holder. There were clean rag rugs on the floor, the table boasted a blue-and-white checked-cotton cloth – spotlessly clean – and the curtains and the cushions on the chairs all matched. Not like the hotchpotch of soft furnishings and bric-a-brac that graced their kitchen. There was an appetising smell of something cooking in the oven in the range, which made Joan realise that she hadn't had anything to eat since her breakfast – it was now almost six o'clock.

'So, *you're* the new neighbours,' Nelly Savage remarked, wiping her hands on her apron as Monica introduced Joan. 'How is your mam managing, girl? Is there anything I can help her with, like? It must be a bit of a nightmare moving house, although I've never done it meself. I've always lived here; me mam – God rest her – had this house before me and Arthur.'

Joan managed a smile. 'Ta very much, Mrs Savage, but me mam's moved house that many times I don't think it's much of a bother to her now.'

Nelly frowned and studied the girl. She seemed likeable

enough and was clean, tidy and polite, but why would anyone keep on moving house with all the upheaval and stress and expense of it? 'Why on earth does she do that, Joan?'

'I don't know, and that's the truth. I've asked her and all she says is "itchy feet". Maybe it's got something to do with me da being away at sea so much.'

'Has he been away long this time?' Monica asked, wanting to divert her mother from the interrogation as to why the Copperfields moved so often.

'A couple of months – that's usual. He's due home in about four weeks, according to Mam.'

'Would you like a cup of tea and a biscuit, Joan?' Nelly offered, thinking she might get more information out of the girl about the family. 'I don't suppose you've had much, what with the upheaval of it all.' She suspected their moving so frequently was down to their financial situation. It usually was the case.

'Oh, yes, please, Mrs Savage.'

Monica smiled appreciatively at her mother and began to take down the cups from the dresser. She was glad Mam seemed to like her new friend, though she was fully aware Mam wouldn't be satisfied until she'd found out all there was to know about the Copperfields.

Once Joan had gratefully drunk her tea and eaten the shortbread biscuits that had been offered – a real luxury – she settled down to find out more about her new friend. 'Have you left school yet, Monica?'

'No, I leave at the end of next term. Mam insisted I stay on so I'll have the chance of a better job,' Monica replied, casting a rebellious glance in her mother's direction.

'There's no use pulling a face like that, miss! It's for your own good. With a bit of luck you'll get something in an office,' Nelly retorted sharply as she gathered up the dishes.

Joan raised her eyebrows. 'I left at the end of last term, but all I could get were just temporary jobs, mainly in shops, and the pay was terrible. Sometimes I think I'll go into service, at least that's steady.'

'Oh, I wouldn't do that, luv. You'd be just a skivvy – and the pay and hours are far worse than in any shop, so I've heard,' Nelly advised.

'Then I suppose it will have to be a factory,' Joan replied, downheartedly.

Before the subject could be discussed further there was a loud knocking on the back door and Nelly, taking off her apron, went to see who it was. She came back with a woman in tow who was obviously Joan's mother, judging from the way Joan hastily rose from the armchair.

Olive Copperfield glared at her daughter. 'So this is where you've got to. I've been up and down the street looking for you, Joan. Charlie and me have been trying to get the dresser sorted out but it's well and truly wedged in the kitchen doorway and we can't shift it!'

Nelly felt sorry for the woman; it was no picnic trying to move house on your own without a man to help. Obviously Olive Copperfield was a capable woman, but some things were just beyond her abilities.

'Just you sit down there, luv, and get your breath and have a cup of tea. You must be worn out. Don't try to shift that thing by yourself; you'll do yourself a serious injury. When Arthur gets home I'll send him in – he's on a regular shift

9

today – and Monica, you can go down and ask Ethel if her Harry will give a hand too. Heaving furniture isn't women's work, Olive.'

Gratefully, Olive sat down in the chair Joan had vacated and sighed heavily. She'd introduced herself when Nelly had opened the back door to her, and she was thankful for the help offered.

As Nelly poured the tea she studied her new neighbour. She was tall and slim, and Joan resembled her; both mother and daughter were striking-looking with their dark, almost black, hair and eyes, and that quite remarkably fine bone structure. And Olive Copperfield didn't have a single grey hair despite, Nelly was sure, being of a similar age to herself – and her own once light brown hair was now liberally sprinkled with grey. Over the years she'd put on weight too. 'Joan says your husband's at sea,' she remarked as she passed the tea over.

Olive nodded and took the cup and saucer from her with thanks, noting that the china matched. 'He is. Oh, nothing very grand, he's a stoker on a rust bucket called the MV *Adventurer*. If you ask me, that ship is ready for its last "adventure" – to the breaker's yard!'

'Has he always gone to sea? 'Nelly persevered.

'Aye, from when he was eighteen. He seems to like the life – God knows why!'

'It's not much fun for you, luv.'

Olive looked thoughtful. 'Oh, I don't know, Nelly. You get used to it after a while. You get used to managing and to not having him under your feet all day and night.'

'There's something to be said for that, Olive. At least Arthur has his pigeons to keep him occupied in what spare time he has, although I won't go near them. Smelly, dirty things! I hate that corner of the yard where he keeps them!' Nelly shuddered.

Monica cast Joan an amused glance and stifled a giggle. Her mam's views on her da's pigeons were known the entire length of the street – she sometimes thought he made them an excuse to get out of the house for far, far longer than was necessary. He even had a battered old chair in the small loft he'd constructed for the birds. She decided to change the subject before her mam really got going on the subject of the pigeons. 'Joan was telling me that your sister works at the Empire Theatre, Mrs Copperfield.'

Nelly was so surprised she nearly dropped the tea caddy she was holding. 'She's not on the stage, is she?' she asked in a rather restrained tone. She had always thought there was something not quite 'proper' about people who worked in the theatre or the music halls. 'Racy' and 'fast' and usually unreliable was how her old mam had always described them.

'Lord, no! She's in the wardrobe department; in fact she's Wardrobe Mistress,' Olive replied, casting a reproving glance at her daughter. 'And she's not a bit like me either. I tend to keep my business . . . private, like. Our Lily's got a mouth like a parish oven! All gush, gab and affectations, she is. That's our Lily!'

Nelly nodded as she spooned fresh tea into the pot. 'It wouldn't do for us all to be the same.' She turned to her daughter. 'Now, Monica, while Olive and I have a quiet cup of tea, you go and find your sister and bring her home. She was going to play with Lizzie McBride from York Terrace. They'll have been out in the street so she's bound to need a good wash before her tea. And call into Ethel on the way.'

'Joan, you go with her so you can see a bit more of the neighbourhood – and if you see Charlie, tell him I'll be in in a few minutes,' Olive instructed her daughter.

Monica began to protest but her mother quickly silenced her with a look. There were a lot more questions she wanted to ask Olive Copperfield, for she'd never met anyone quite like her before and she'd certainly never known anyone with a relative who worked in the theatre. She wanted to find out all she could.

# Chapter Two

———◦•❖•◦———

The two girls made their way slowly down the street towards the corner shop, Monica bemoaning the fact that she always had to go and bring her sister home when Eileen was more than old enough to get home on her own.

Having relayed Nelly's request to Ethel, who had readily agreed to send her husband along when he got home from his work, they had reached the corner of York Terrace when Joan suddenly let out a startled cry.

'What's the matter?' Monica asked.

'Would you just look at the state of him?' Joan was glaring and pointing at a small boy coming towards them. Decidedly grimy and scruffy-looking, he was hanging firmly on to an equally scruffy-looking dog by a length of rope tied around its neck. 'Why aren't you at home? And what are you doing with that . . . that animal?' she demanded.

The lad peered up at her through a thick fringe of unruly dark hair. 'I got fed up waiting for Mam, and he's mine. I found him wanderin' around all on his own and 'e likes me. I've called him Rags.'

'Well, I wouldn't bother giving it a name; you won't have it that long! Hasn't Mam got enough to put up with, Charlie Copperfield, without you bringing flea-bitten mutts into the house? You know what her feelings are about dogs.'

The lad scowled at her. He had no intention of giving up his new pet without a fight. He'd always wanted a dog. And last time he was home, his da had said he would see about getting him one after he'd complained vociferously about all the times they'd moved house and the fact that he never had his mates for long. A dog could move with them and be his permanent 'mate'.

'Where *is* Mam?' he asked, to divert Joan's attention away from Rags.

'She's having a cup of tea with Mrs Savage, Monica's Mam.'

'And you're to leave the dresser alone. My da and Mr Newbridge from the shop will come and shift it later,' Monica supplied. She bent down and scratched the dog's ears; she was fond of animals, but her mam's views on animals were no doubt the same as those of Charlie's mother. 'If I were you, I'd try and tidy him up a bit before your mam sees him.'

'No amount of "tidying up" will make that thing look more presentable. Oh, get home with you, Charlie, but leave the animal in the yard! Don't take it in, God knows what it's got crawling in its fur!' Joan instructed, aware of the battle of wills that would surely follow.

Monica's mood wasn't improved when, further down York Terrace, she finally set eyes on her younger sister, sitting with her friend Lizzie McBride on the edge of the kerb. They were playing 'grid fishing', a pastime which involved suspending a magnetised pin on a piece of string, between the metal slats of the grid in the gutter – hopefully to retrieve any coins or other useful bits and pieces that had fallen into it. They had been quite successful, although they had also become quite grubby in the process.

'Oh, would you look at the state of the pair of you! Mam will kill you, Eileen Savage, for playing in the gutter!' Monica exclaimed. 'You're filthy and you can catch all kinds of horrible diseases poking down grids! You're to get home and get washed before tea, and before Mam sees you, if you know what's good for you!'

'Who's she?' the younger girl demanded, ignoring her sister's annoyance.

'I'm Joan Copperfield from number ten, and you're as bad as our Charlie. Don't either of you ever even *think* about what a mess you look? And that it doesn't look well for your mam and all the efforts she makes to turn you out clean and tidy?'

Eileen scowled; this one was as bad as Monica, and she had no idea who Charlie was, but she did know there was always someone intent on spoiling what bit of fun you might have after school.

'Oh, they make a pair all right,' Monica added darkly before turning away, leaving her sister to follow reluctantly at a distance.

It was after eight o'clock before Arthur Savage and Harry Newbridge, accompanied by Nelly and Monica, finally went to the Copperfields' house, Nelly having said it would be best to leave Olive to get the meal over and done with first. Monica wondered how the appearance of Charlie's new friend Rags had gone down. Seeing the dog tied up, lying contentedly on a piece of old matting and with a battered tin bowl of water beside it, she guessed Joan's Mam hadn't hit the roof after all.

'Well, you're a fine guard dog!' she laughed as the animal watched them – four strangers – walk up to the back door without uttering a sound.

It was Joan who let them in – she'd been washing the dishes in the scullery.

'Go on through, Mam will be glad to see you, we've had a right job trying to squeeze around that dresser,' she informed them.

'I see your Charlie got his way about the dog,' Monica whispered as the adults went into the kitchen.

Joan raised her eyes to the ceiling. 'Sometimes he can twist Mam around his little finger. If you ask me, Mam's just so worn out with everything, she just gave in. He's promised to take it for walks and clean up after it and everything – although how long that will last, I don't know.'

Monica automatically took the tea towel from its hook on the wall and started to dry the dishes, one of her regular chores at home.

'Thanks,' Joan muttered, before she sighed. 'I suppose I'd better make a start soon to see what jobs are available. Mam could do with the money; Da's allotment isn't much.'

Monica was curious. 'Is that how he's paid? I thought they weren't paid off until the end of each trip?'

'They're not, but they can leave what's called an "allotment" for the family to live on while they are away. It's deducted from their wages, of course, but God knows what we'd do without it. Mam would have to get a job, I suppose, as well as run the house and look after us, but she wouldn't be happy about it. It would look as if Da couldn't keep us, and his pride and his standing with his mates would be ruined. She wouldn't do that to him, no matter how much she needed the money – and she's got her pride too.'

Monica nodded her understanding. Although many women, forced by circumstances, did work, she thought the way Mr Copperfield was paid wasn't very satisfactory at all. Her da got his wage packet regularly, every Friday evening, and her mam had her housekeeping money on Saturday mornings, so everyone knew exactly what budget they had to work to. 'I'll help you, if you like,' she said. 'Da always brings home a copy of the *Echo*, so we'll look in the jobs pages.'

'Thanks, that's great. There might be *something* I can do that isn't too awful and pays a bit more than a pittance.'

The girls continued chatting while they dried up and tidied the pots away. Then, while the girls were poring over the pages of the newspaper, fetched from number fifteen, Olive made a pot of tea for her neighbours, as a small 'thank you'. The dresser had proved to be obstinate and it had taken all Arthur's and Harry's strength, aided by Charlie, to shift it.

'That's a sturdy piece of furniture all right, Olive,' Nelly remarked, accepting her steaming cup as they all sat round the kitchen table.

'It belonged to a great-aunt so I suppose you could class it as "antique". It's the only decent thing I've got, not that I'm complaining. There's a lot more worse off than me in this city.'

'That's very true, luv,' Nelly agreed, sipping her tea.

'Still, it must be a great comfort for you to have a good job, Arthur – and you too, Harry,' Olive added. She'd been informed that Ethel's husband worked as a foreman in a local factory, another steady job. She could understand why Ethel continued to live in this area because of the shop, but not Nelly. Surely with a job like Arthur's – a guard on the railways, no less – they could afford to live in a much nicer area? Tentatively she voiced her thoughts.

Nelly looked surprised. 'Why on earth would I want to move from here, Olive? I've lived in Everton most of my life, it's not a bad area, the people are great on the whole – there's always a few wrong 'uns, of course – the kids were born here and we've got everything we need at hand.'

Olive smiled at her. 'Oh, it was just a thought, Nelly. Don't mind me.'

Joan looked up from the newspaper, having been listening to the conversation with one ear. 'Do you think we'll stay here, Mam?'

Nelly thought Olive looked a little furtive at this question; she hadn't been able to get much information about the woman, or her background, so far.

'We might, we'll have to see how . . . things go,' was Olive's non-committal reply.

'How will your husband know where to find you all when he gets home?' Nelly persevered; it was something that had been puzzling her.

'Oh, I'll just go down to the shipping office next week, they'll tell him.'

'He doesn't write, then?' Nelly asked, wondering if Billy Copperfield *could* in fact write; many of these seafarers couldn't.

'Not very often,' Olive answered a little sharply, rising to collect the cups.

'For heaven's sake, Nell, the man's stuck down in the engine room for most of the trip. He probably doesn't see much daylight, let alone find the time to be writing letters home by the minutes,' Arthur put in, aware of his wife's overly curious nature and noting that Olive Copperfield was looking a bit put out. He liked what he'd seen of her; she seemed a very handsome and capable woman indeed.

'I suppose you're right, Arthur. Well, we'd better be getting home. Monica, are you staying?'

'Just for a bit longer, Mam. We're looking to see if there's a job in here for Joan.'

Olive smiled at the two girls. 'I hope there is, it's about time she made her way in the world. At fifteen I'd been working for three years and our Lily for four. Mam was more than glad of our wages.'

Joan smiled back at her mother. 'I'll get something, Mam – I'm looking forward to getting a steady job.'

Monica spread the paper out on the table; she too hoped they could find something for Joan. She also hoped Mrs Copperfield would decide she liked this street and stay.

But after half an hour's close scrutiny of the 'Situations Vacant' both girls were despondent. Oh, there were enough adverts, but nothing that Joan felt the slightest bit inclined to pursue.

'None of them are at all interesting. It looks as if I'll just have to take any job I can get, and in any factory,' Joan announced glumly. 'Although I suppose I should have realised by now I'm not really fit for much else.'

'Some of the local factories look pretty grim, but perhaps Mr Newbridge could put a word in for you where he works?' Monica suggested. 'It's the way a lot of people get jobs.'

'Would he?' Joan looked more hopeful. At least Tate & Lyle's Sugar Refinery sounded better than 'animal feeds' or the rope or match works.

'I'll have a word with Mam, she's known Ethel and Harry for years and years,' Monica promised, thinking now that maybe it had been worth it, staying on at school, if it meant she didn't have to work in a factory. She couldn't imagine anything worse.

'When do you think I might know something?'

'I don't know. In a couple of days, I suppose. Well, I'd better be getting back or Mam'll be complaining about me staying out – and if I need her help, I don't want to annoy her. I'll see you tomorrow; at least it's Saturday so there's no school for me.'

Joan nodded as Monica got to her feet and folded up the newspaper. She needed a job and she was grateful for any help.

Arthur looked up from the copy of J. Kilpatrick's *The Racing Pigeon* he'd borrowed from the library as his elder daughter appeared and handed back his newspaper. 'Seems like a decent family, and she's a nice girl. Did you find her anything?' he smiled.

Monica sat down on the small sofa beside her mother, who

was knitting a new school jumper for Eileen. 'No, she's got no qualifications or experience, except for a bit of shop work. I said I'd have a word with you, Mam, about asking Mrs Newbridge if her husband could help.'

Nelly laid her knitting in her lap and looked thoughtful. 'I wouldn't hold out too much hope there. He might be a foreman now but Harry Newbridge hasn't had that position for long – and I think he's still feeling his way around with his colleagues, if you know what I mean.'

'I . . . I feel as if I need to help Joan, Mam. It can't have been easy for her at school, moving around like that all the time. Heaven knows how many schools she's been to.'

'I don't suppose it was. I really can't understand why that woman feels the need to keep moving, but I couldn't get any kind of a sensible reason out of her.'

Arthur looked thoughtful; he too wanted to help the Copperfields. 'Perhaps I could have a word with Bert Harrington, one of the usual drivers on my route. His sister has some kind of a good job at Crawford's Biscuit Factory. If Joan's got to work in a factory she might as well work in a decent one, and they're one of the best. It will be clean work and not too heavy either, I don't suppose.'

Monica brightened up. 'Would you, Da? Oh, I bet Joan wouldn't mind working there.'

Arthur nodded as Nelly resumed her knitting.

'It's not exactly on the doorstep, is it – Binns Road? Joan would have to get two trams,' Nelly reminded them both. 'And it's got such a good reputation, I don't think it will be all that easy to get a job there. I wouldn't go giving the girl high expectations, Monica.'

21

'But you *will* try, Da?' Monica pressed, ignoring her mother's pessimism.

Arthur smiled fondly at her. 'Of course I will, luv.' He was already putting feelers out about possible jobs in the offices of the London and North Western Railway Company for her, and if he could help young Joan Copperfield too, he would.

# Chapter Three

It was almost a week later when Arthur came home with the news that Ada Harrington had actually managed to get Joan an interview at Crawford's, reputed to be one of the best employers in the entire city, offering decent wages, clean, safe conditions, health care and even a sports and social club for their workers. They employed a lot of girls and women in the manufacture and packing of their biscuits, and Ada apparently was in charge of the entire 'piping' room. Not that a new girl would be involved in that skilled process. She would have to work up to it – and it took years, or so Ada informed Joan when she presented herself for the interview.

Joan felt very nervous, for she badly wanted this job – whatever it entailed. She wore her best dress and had borrowed a hat from Monica, for no decent girl went for an interview without a hat. This was her one chance of getting work that she might actually enjoy and, from what she'd seen of the place so far, it was unlike any factory she'd ever come across. Usually they were grim, dark dirty places with little or no thought given to the working conditions or health and safety of employees, but this was light, bright, clean and very modern, and it smelled of the delicious aromas of baking and jam and chocolate. All the girls and women she'd seen so far had been smartly dressed in a light green overall coat which covered their clothes, a matching turban over their hair, and they all seemed to be in fine spirits; she'd not seen a glum or bored face at all.

All the way on the tram – and it was a fairly long journey from Everton to Binns Road in Fairfield – she'd wondered what she could say that might possibly help her cause; she hoped she'd concocted all the right answers.

'So, you've not much experience of work, Miss Copperfield?' Ada Harrison remarked, scrutinising the young girl in front of her. She looked tidy enough and seemed polite but you never could tell; they were always on their best behaviour at interviews, though she prided herself on her ability to judge people. And of course the girl had Arthur Savage's approval.

Joan bit her lip. 'Er, no, Miss Harrison. You see, due to . . . family circumstances we . . . we moved around rather a lot and that didn't help with my education.' She'd worked all this out on the tram.

'I see,' the older woman replied, nodding. The girl spoke well for herself, despite the lack of education. 'I take it you *can* read and write?'

'Oh, yes! It's just that I didn't do well in the other subjects and of course I never matriculated or took a leaving certificate. You see, my father is a seafarer and it's not a job that is . . . steady. After each trip he has to sign on again – if there's work for him, that is – sometimes there isn't and we . . . we've never really settled anywhere for long,' she explained, hoping it sounded reasonable. It was, after all, the truth.

'And now you are living in Mersey View, near Mr and Mrs Savage?'

'Yes, Miss Harrison, and I really do hope we stay there. I've made friends with Mrs Savage's daughter Monica. They are a really nice family.'

Ada nodded. She'd met both Arthur and his wife a few times. 'You won't object to the distance you will have to travel?'

'Oh, no! Not at all! Crawford's has a great reputation, and I know I'd be really fortunate to get work here,' she added earnestly.

Ada Harrison smiled at her. If she'd judged correctly, Joan Copperfield would be a quick learner, for she seemed intelligent. 'Well, then, I can offer you a job on one of the lines, assembling the custard creams, and we'll see how you get on. It's a bit repetitive and fiddly, but it's a start. The wage for a girl your age is ten shillings a week and the hours are eight o'clock until six with a break for lunch. You'll get a small raise when you're sixteen. There is a canteen and the food is subsidised; overalls and turbans will be provided but you must launder them yourself and they *must* be clean at all times. We are producing and handling food and therefore hygiene must be of the highest standard, you understand?'

Joan nodded vigorously, overjoyed at her good fortune – and ten shillings was more than she'd ever earned before.

'Fingernails must be kept short, clean and free of varnish, hair must be completely confined under your turban, shoes must be polished and no face powder, rouge or lipstick may be worn. When can you start?'

Joan beamed at her, unable to contain her delight. She didn't mind the regulations, and she never wore make-up or nail varnish anyway – she couldn't afford them – and besides, Mam would have had a fit. 'Whenever is convenient for you, Miss Harrison.'

'Then we'll say on Monday morning. You will of course have to work a week "in hand" but you will be paid the following week. You will receive your wages from the clerk each Friday afternoon and must sign for them. You will clock in at eight in the morning and off at six; your clock card will be in the rack on the wall with everyone else's, and I must stress that it is a sacking offence to either clock on or off for someone else, or have them do it for you.' Then she smiled warmly. 'Now, Joan, is there anything you'd like to ask me?'

Joan shook her head. 'But I really would like to thank you, Miss Harrison. This will be the first decent job I've had, and I won't disappoint you. I'll work hard and I won't be late or be staying off sick.'

'Good. I think you'll fit in very well here. Oh, and as an added little "perk" of the job, once a week you will be allowed to buy misshapen or broken biscuits for a few pence a bag. We can't sell them to the shops but, to save them being wasted, we give our employees the opportunity to buy them. It works well.'

'Even the chocolate ones?' Joan asked, amazed when Miss Harrison indicated that was the case. They were the most expensive of all biscuits, something the Copperfields only ever had as a treat at Christmas, and not always then. It was indeed a 'perk'. It seemed everyone was right that William Crawford was one of the best employers in the city, and she was determined to do well.

When she got back to Mersey View, Joan was surprised to see Monica waiting for her at the tram stop.

'Well, how did you get on? Did you get a job?'

Joan grinned at her as she linked arms. 'I did! And straight after I've told Mam, I'm coming to thank your da. I'd never have got in there without his help.'

'You'll have to wait, I'm afraid; he won't be home until later. He's on the run to Crewe today. But I'm so glad for you, Joan, really I am.'

'You wouldn't believe how clean and modern it is, Mon! The pay is good and there seem to be heaps of benefits – we even get to buy the biscuits they can't sell to the shops, for a few pence a bag. Our Charlie will think he's gone to heaven; he can have biscuits every week now!'

'Really?' Monica queried. She'd never heard of such a thing before.

'Of course, I won't finish work until six and by the time I get home, I won't get to see as much of you as I do now,' Joan continued. 'That's the only fly in the ointment that I can see.'

'There's the weekends – and don't forget that after Christmas I'll be working myself, I hope. I won't be finishing much before six either.'

Joan brightened up. 'That's true. And, just think, this Christmas I'll be able to buy some decent presents. I'll be able to save up for them.'

'And you'll be able to buy your own clothes, choose what

you want, instead of having to have what your mam thinks is "suitable" – and which is usually something awful! That's what I'm really looking forward to when I get a job,' Monica confided, opening up an entirely new field of thought for Joan too.

Olive was as delighted as her daughter at the news. Of course, she wouldn't take all the girl's earnings, that wouldn't be right. Joan would need money for fares and lunches, and a bit of money to spend on herself; but the extra money would certainly come in handy.

As Joan had predicted, Charlie couldn't believe that they'd have fancy biscuits every week – even chocolate ones. Never had he known such luxury. With a spring in his step, he got ready to take Rags on an extended walk with three lads he'd palled up with from school who lived further down St George's Hill. This stroke of luck would no doubt make him quite popular.

'Don't you be too late back, Charlie! The nights are drawing in now and I'm not having you and that animal running around the streets in the dark,' Olive called after him, before turning her attention to the girls. 'I really must go along later, Monica, to thank your da for his help. When would be most convenient?' Olive enquired as she finished sweeping the kitchen floor, prior to putting the rag rugs back down.

'Well, he won't be in until well after six tonight, then we'll have tea . . . I suppose any time after that would be fine,' Monica replied.

'They're not planning on going out, then, it being Saturday?' Monica shook her head. 'No. They don't often go out. Da will occasionally go for a pint with Mr Newbridge, or they'll all go if it's Mam or Ethel's birthday. They sit in the snug, as Mam doesn't really think it's "proper" for a decent woman to go drinking in pubs – the ones around here aren't posh enough to have Lounges.'

Olive raised her eyebrows. 'Oh, I see. Well, I suppose on special occasions, it's different.' She herself liked a night out. She preferred the music hall or the theatre to a pub – particularly if Lily could get cheap tickets – and when Billy came home they usually went out to celebrate, providing Billy had the money to pay for their entertainment. She thought privately that Nelly Savage was a bit of a killjoy. But she wouldn't say so for the world – after all, Nelly and Arthur had both been very helpful – but on Arthur's wage they could certainly afford the occasional night at the Empire or the Royal Court or the Everyman. The latter two might be a bit too upmarket for Nelly's tastes, of course, but there were usually good turns onstage at the Empire and the numerous music halls in the city. There were hotels too that had Lounge Bars open to the general public, all very respectable and indeed quite fashionable – if you had the money for the fancy drinks they served in them. She was quite happy with a port and lemon, she always told Billy, whenever he'd urge her to try something a bit different.

Olive left it until after eight before she tidied herself up and went along to see Arthur and Nelly. She'd left Joan and Monica calculating how much a week Joan could save from the money left after she'd given her mother her 'keep'. The dishes from the evening meal had been washed and put away but, to Olive's annoyance, Charlie had managed to slip out again after dinner without her noticing. 'When our Charlie finally gets in, tell him to get a good wash, Joan. I'm going to have to take that lad in hand; I'm not having him roaming the streets after dark. I don't care that his excuse is taking that dog for its last walk. He doesn't know this area very well yet, and I'm not going out looking for him!'

'Oh, he won't get lost, Mam. He's not that daft,' Joan replied scathingly.

'Anyway, Rags will know his way home, you can be sure of that,' Monica added, her mind more on the fact that, after Joan had paid her tram fares and bought her lunches, there wasn't going to be a great deal of money left over to save.

Over at the Savages' house, Olive was made very welcome by Nelly, who ushered her into the parlour. Arthur followed, leaving Eileen sitting at the kitchen table with a colouring book and some wax crayons.

'We usually sit in here on a Saturday evening and listen to the wireless,' Nelly informed her neighbour. 'Arthur likes to drink his glass of stout in a bit of comfort,' she added, as if it were a huge treat to be using this room.

Olive smiled politely. Hardly anyone who was fortunate enough to have a parlour ever used them on a regular basis – which she thought was such a waste, as it was usually the best furnished room in the whole house. If she had good furniture like this – a fine big rug, nice crewel-work cushions and frosted-glass lamp shades – she'd certainly make good use of her parlour. 'I just wanted to thank you, Arthur, for putting in a word for our Joan. She'd never have been taken on at that place otherwise. She'd never even have got an interview with your workmate's sister, so we're both really, really grateful.'

Arthur nodded and smiled back at her. 'Oh, there's no need, Olive. She's a nice, polite girl and I'm sure she'll do well. Nelly, do you think this calls for a small glass of sherry for you and Olive? It *is* good news – and we can't have me drinking alone, can we?'

Nelly raised her eyebrows but said nothing, crossing to the small side table where a plain glass decanter and half a dozen sherry glasses were set out on a tray. They were her pride and joy, even though the sherry was seldom drunk, for she only took a drink at Christmas.

'I'm looking forward to meeting your Billy, when he gets home,' Arthur remarked as Nelly handed Olive the small glass. 'I'll bet he's got a wealth of tales to tell about all those foreign places he's been to. It must be an interesting life, if a hard one.'

Olive sipped the rather sickly-sweet drink and smiled a little ruefully. 'Oh, don't get him started, Arthur! He'd go on for hours on end about places in Portugal and Spain and South America and all the islands in between. But I bet you've been to some interesting places too; do you often get to London? I'd love to go and see all the sights.'

'Aye, not that we actually see much of the place, let alone the sights. Usually, it's just the inside of Euston Station – and there's nothing remotely exotic or even interesting about that!'

'So, when does Joan start this job, Olive?' Nelly asked, for this topic of travelling held no interest for her at all.

'Monday, and from what she's told me it sounds almost too good to be true. They have medical care, subsidised meals and a sports and social club somewhere in the south end of the

31

city. Mind you, I can't see girls of her age being allowed to attend functions there. I've left her with your Monica working out how much she'll be able to save. And she *will* save, will our Joan. She likes nice . . . good things, so she'll save for them. She gets her extravagant tastes from our Lily.'

'Well, being a saver is a very good trait, Olive,' Nelly remarked; she was about to enquire about the 'extravagant tastes' but was cut short by Eileen's appearance. 'What's the matter with you?' she asked curtly.

Eileen was disgruntled at having her pastime interrupted. 'Nothing, but our Monica's come home and she said to tell Mrs Copperfield she's to go home at once, it . . . it's important. It's about your Charlie.'

Olive finished her sherry quickly and stood up. 'Oh, Lord! What has that lad done now? I can't leave either of them alone for five minutes without *something* happening. Did she say anything more about Charlie?'

Eileen shook her head. 'But she looked a bit . . . shocked, like,' she volunteered.

Arthur too got to his feet. 'I'll come with you, Olive. I might be able to help.'

'Well, if you're sure. I don't want to be imposing on your time, Arthur. You've been working all day. I can usually deal with whatever he's been up to – I've had plenty of practice,' Olive finished grimly, wishing for once that her husband had a job that kept him at home.

# Chapter Four

―◦‣◦―

Olive hadn't quite bargained on seeing a large police constable standing in her kitchen, eyeing her errant son with some disfavour, and she gave a startled little gasp.

Arthur put a supportive hand on her arm. 'What's he done, Constable?' he asked quietly, taking in the lad's white face and dark fear-filled eyes.

'I take it you are his parents? Well, you'd do better to be staying at home and keeping an eye on your family than gadding about.'

Pulling herself together, Olive drew herself up defensively. She didn't take to his preaching attitude. 'I'm his mother, Constable, and I was only a few doors away on a matter that I considered important. I was *not* "gadding about". So, what's he done?' she demanded curtly.

'He was caught with three other lads, trying to enter by the back alley the premises of Mr Harold Solomon – or "Uncle", as I'm sure you know he's usually called – the pawnbroker. The other three are well known to us and will no doubt end up in borstal if they don't mend their ways, but I've not seen your lad before.'

'That's because the family only moved here just over a week ago, Constable. Mrs Copperfield's husband is away at sea, so I've come along to give her moral support,' Arthur informed him. 'I'm Arthur Savage from number fifteen. Mrs Copperfield is a friend of my wife and was visiting us – albeit briefly. I'm a guard with the London and North Western Railway.'

Constable Oates studied him. He knew him by sight, of course, just as he knew most people on his beat, and the man had a reputation as a solid, respectable citizen. He could see that, like many other women in this city, Mrs Copperfield was trying to bring up her family virtually on her own, which was no easy task.

'He's never ever done anything like this before, Constable, I swear. Oh, he gets into scrapes, as most lads do, but nothing like . . . *this*!' Olive pursed her lips in temper. She'd kill Charlie! What was he thinking of, running with a pack of young reprobates, breaking and entering – obviously intent on vandalism or even theft! To have this happen now and in front of Arthur Savage – who would of course have to tell Nelly – it would be all over the neighbourhood in a matter of hours.

'The lad has obviously got in with a bad crowd, but I think he's probably now learned his lesson,' Arthur added grimly.

'What . . . what will happen to him?' Olive asked. 'Will he be charged?' Her voice suddenly dropped to a whisper on the dreaded word.

Charlie began to cry. He hadn't ever thought he'd be *arrested* and he certainly didn't want to go to borstal! The lads had made a fuss of him after he'd told them about the biscuits, said he could be part of their 'gang'. He'd only gone along with them because he thought it sounded like a bit of excitement. He hadn't meant to do anything wrong. In fact, he'd only helped Jimmy and Ronny to climb over the wall because the back gate was securely locked and bolted. He hadn't even gone into the old man's yard. And this had only happened because when he was giving Tommy a leg-up, Rags had suddenly decided to try to get free from the ashcan he'd been tied to and had started barking and making a terrible noise as he pulled the ashcan over. Then they'd been caught. 'I didn't mean to do anything wrong, Mam! I didn't, I promise! I just gave them a leg-up!' he sobbed.

Olive shook her head and went and put an arm around his shaking shoulders. Angry and upset though she was, she knew there was no real badness in her son. 'Charlie Copperfield, you'll be the death of me! What'll your da say when he gets home? And he'll blame me!'

Joan, silent during all this, could see how upset both her mother and brother were. Yes, she was furious with Charlie for being such a fool and for causing all this trouble, but he was only twelve, and she was sure he shouldn't be accused of a serious crime and made to suffer such dire consequences. He hadn't really known what he was doing. 'Mam is right, Constable. Our Charlie has never ever done anything like this before; he's been led astray by that lot! They're older than him. He never even skives off school – you can ask his headmaster at St John's, our old school. He never missed a day in a whole year.'

'I will,' Constable Oates replied firmly and looked

meaningfully at Arthur. 'If the lad is telling the truth, then from what I understand he didn't actually go into the yard.'

'Well, surely that must count for something, Officer?' Joan pleaded.

'Oh, please, sir, don't bring him before the magistrate at the juvenile court?' Olive begged, fighting down her anger and pride and flushing with shame.

Arthur turned to the lad. 'Now, Charlie, what you told the officer was the truth, wasn't it? This is very important, but don't be afraid. We want no lies.'

Charlie nodded. 'I didn't tell you no lies, sir! Honestly!'

Constable Oates considered everything. It was still 'aiding and abetting' but the lad was genuinely shaken and sorry, his mother was obviously a decent woman, and the families in this street were – in the main – respectable and law-abiding. He made up his mind. 'If you promise not to get into any kind of trouble again, lad, and give up hanging around with delinquents like those three, then this time we'll take it no further. But be warned, I'll be keeping a close eye on you.'

Olive could have kissed him, she was so relieved, but instead she reached out and took his hand and shook it. 'Thank you, Constable. Thank you so much. I'll make sure he doesn't step out of line again, you can be sure of that.'

Joan added her thanks, as did a still-tearful but very relieved Charlie, until Constable Oates began to feel rather embarrassed. 'Well, I'll be going, then.'

'I'll keep my eye on the lad until his father gets home,' Arthur promised as he showed the officer out. Charlie needed something to do to occupy him after school and he wondered if he could think of something that would keep the lad out of mischief. Maybe he could help in cleaning out the pigeon loft? Perhaps the lad might even show an interest in the pigeons? They'd have to see, but it was a thought.

He'd barely returned to the kitchen, where Charlie had his arms around Olive's waist, swearing to be on his best behaviour for the rest of his life, and Joan was filling the kettle, knowing her mother needed a cup of strong tea, when there was a loud knocking on the front door.

'Oh, Lord, he's not changed his mind, has he?' Joan cried, and both Olive and Charlie looked fearful.

'I'll go and see,' Arthur volunteered. He knew it wasn't Nelly or any of the other neighbours come to see what was wrong; they'd use the back door.

He was astonished to find a woman on the doorstep; a very attractive woman. Tall and slim, with shiny blonde hair partly covered by a small but very smart hat, and wearing a coat that would have had Nelly green with envy, although he doubted his wife would have worn such a bright shade of blue. Her eyes were very dark brown and fringed with dark lashes, and there were hints of blue eyeshadow and rouge; she wore bright red lipstick. Her dark eyes sparkled with curiosity and some amusement. 'Don't tell me our Olive's taken to "entertaining"?' she laughed.

Arthur was embarrassed. 'No! Er, no. I'm Mrs Copperfield's neighbour, Arthur Savage. And you are . . . ?'

'I'm Lily. Lily Cooper. Olive's sister.'

'You'd better come in, then, er . . . Mrs Cooper?'

Lily flashed a smile at him; he was a bit on the stuffy side, she thought. 'It's "Miss". I never bothered taking that trip down the aisle, never found a man I wanted to spend my life with – unlike our Olive, although she really doesn't see much of him,' she replied as she followed Arthur down the lobby, taking in the rather faded wallpaper and scuffed paintwork.

'What on earth are you doing here, Lil, and on a Saturday night?' Olive greeted her elder sibling with some surprise and not a little annoyance. She could do without Lily right now, having just been so badly shaken by Charlie's behaviour.

'It's my Saturday night off, Olive. I *do* get one off a month, you know, and I did the matinee, so I thought I'd come and take a look at this place. From what I've seen so far, it's a bit better than the last one.'

Arthur decided it was time he went home, for Nelly would be eaten up with curiosity. 'Well, I'll leave you to it, then,' he nodded. 'Goodnight.'

Olive smiled at him. 'Thank you so much, Arthur. Tell Nelly I'll be in to see her tomorrow.'

When he'd gone, Lily stared hard at her sister, taking in the frown and Joan's grim expression as well as her young nephew's tear-streaked and still-ashen face. 'What's going on, Olive? You all look as if the bailiffs are about to descend. Is it something to do with that copper I saw leaving as I came up the street?' Suddenly it seemed to dawn on Lily that there could be something really seriously wrong; the Police didn't come calling otherwise. 'Oh, God! Olive! It . . . it's not . . . Billy?'

Olive shook her head. 'No, it's nothing to do with Billy, thank God!'

'It's our Charlie, Aunty Lil,' Joan supplied as she poured the tea and her aunt sat down in the armchair by the range and took off her hat. Despite still feeling upset and annoyed, Joan couldn't help but notice how smart and fashionable her aunt looked. That coat must have cost a few guineas, she thought, as had the hat. Lily had gloves and a small black leather clutch bag, and she wore silk stockings and black leather shoes with high heels.

'So, what's he done now?' Lily asked.

Joan handed both her mother and aunt a cup of tea. 'Got into trouble with the Police,' she supplied, glaring at her brother.

'Nothing serious, I hope?' Lily seemed unperturbed.

'Serious enough. Caught – with three other local hooligans – trying to break into the pawnbroker's. Fortunately – or unfortunately – they were caught. But as meladdo here was only giving them a leg-up over the back wall, the constable decided to give him another chance – thanks in part, I'm sure, to Mr Savage. Honestly, Lil! I could murder him! Making a complete show of me like this, and us having only been here a week. What will the neighbours think of us – of *me*?'

Lily sipped her tea and raised her expertly plucked, arched eyebrows. 'I've told you before, Olive, you worry too much about what the neighbours will think. Who cares? Who are they, after all?'

'*I* care, Lily! I'm not like you. I've responsibilities. I've to see that these two grow up respectable . . . and people see us as a responsible family.'

Lily slowly nodded her assent. Olive did have a point. But in her opinion Billy Copperfield had totally abandoned *his* responsibilities, leaving her sister to cope with things on her own, and no one said a word against him. Oh, he was providing for them, wasn't he – as a man should? But in her eyes that didn't exempt him from his 'duties'. If his kids did not turn out to be respectable and responsible citizens, Olive would be blamed, not him. No matter that women had the vote and things were so much better, far more 'liberated' now, it was still a man's world.

'The good news, Aunty Lil, is that I've got a job, and a decent one at that,' Joan informed her, feeling she should lighten the atmosphere. 'I start at Crawford's on Monday. I'll be paid ten shillings a week – and there are so many other benefits.'

'One of which being at the bottom of meladdo here getting into trouble – don't worry, I'll explain later,' Olive added, seeing her sister's puzzled expression, which quickly faded.

'Oh, that's really great, Joan, luv. And no doubt the pay will increase as you get older and more experienced. They've got a good reputation.' Lily scrutinised her niece. 'The first thing I'd do, Joan, is get your hair cut in a decent salon. You'd look far better – far more stylish – with a good cut. You've lovely thick hair and great bone structure, like your mam. Like us all, in fact; we've inherited it from Granny Cooper. A decent hairstyle will do wonders for your appearance.'

'Won't that cost a small fortune, Lil? Ten bob a week is not that much,' Olive reminded her.

'I can save up for it, Mam,' Joan said earnestly. If that's what her aunt really thought then she'd do it. There was no one quite as stylish as her Aunty Lil, especially not in Mersey View, and the one thing Joan was aiming for was to be like her aunt.

Olive sighed as she sipped her tea. 'What a day it's been, Lily. I'm fair worn out with it all.'

'Well, you will keep on moving – and let's face it, luv, you're not getting any younger.' Lily cast a knowing glance at her sister, fully aware of the reason Olive felt the need to move so often. 'When will Billy be back?' she asked to change the subject.

'In three weeks, so I should have this place looking decent by then. Do you think you might be able to get us some cheap tickets for a Saturday night at the Empire for when he's home?'

Lily smiled fondly at her. 'I don't see why not, I think by then you'll deserve a bit of a treat. Now, Joan, tell me more about this job of yours?'

By the following afternoon Nelly had got over her initial shock at the fact that young Charlie Copperfield had managed to get himself into trouble with the law barely a week after arriving in the neighbourhood. 'I thought they were a decent family, Arthur, but now I'm beginning to wonder,' she'd said grimly after her husband had returned home that evening.

'Oh, they are, Nelly! The lad's just been led astray, I'm sure he'll stick to the straight and narrow from now on,' Arthur had protested.

Nelly had pursed her lips and looked doubtful. 'I still think there is something not quite *right* in that family.'

'It's just because Billy Copperfield goes away to sea, Nell, and Olive manages on her own. It's a different way of life, that's all it is. We've not had a seafarer living in the street for a long time, you have to admit that.'

She'd agreed, but was very surprised on Sunday afternoon when she spotted Charlie in the yard with her husband. 'What's all this, then? What's Charlie Copperfield doing in our yard?' she asked Monica, who was sitting with Joan leafing through an already well-read fashion magazine, left by Lily for her niece the previous evening.

'Oh, Da thinks it will do Charlie good to have something to occupy him, help to keep him out of trouble,' Monica answered, offhandedly.

'So, what's he going to do, then?' Nelly persisted, peering through the kitchen window at the lad. This was the first she'd heard of it.

'He's going to clean out the loft twice a week, and I think Mr Savage is hoping he might take an interest in the pigeons. It might keep him out of mischief, at least. Charlie seems keen and so Mam's delighted,' Joan informed her with a smile.

Nelly frowned. 'She won't be very delighted to have him coming home smelling of pigeon muck!' she replied tartly. Arthur had said nothing about this to her, yet it appeared that Olive already knew. She wondered if Arthur had promised to pay the lad? This was something she'd have to sort out later, she mused, as she picked up her knitting. Even though it was Sunday, and therefore a day of 'rest', there was never much rest for wives and mothers. It seemed as if she'd no sooner got the lunch over than it was time to start with the tea, without having other issues put on her plate.

The two girls were engrossed in the pages of the magazine and an article giving tips on how to 'Pluck and Pencil for Perfect Brows'.

'You've already got perfect brows, Joan,' Monica commented. 'Mine are so fair you can hardly see them.'

'They only need a bit of pencilling in,' Joan advised. Her dark brows were far from perfect in her opinion and always seemed to need plucking to keep their shape. Her aunt had shown her how to do it months ago and had even bought her a pair of tweezers for the job.

'I suppose so, although I never seem to get it right,' Monica complained. 'Are you really going to get your hair cut in a fancy salon in town?' she asked, for Joan had already relayed her aunt's suggestion to her friend.

'Oh, yes. I'll have to save up for it, though, Aunty Lil says that somewhere like Marcel's in Dale Street will cost at least six shillings.'

'That's more than half a week's wages!' Monica was scandalised – a good hairdresser must be able to earn a fair amount of money if they charged prices like that.

'I know, but Aunty Lil said it will be more than worth it, and I believe her. She's really stylish, Mon. She had this gorgeous bright blue wool coat on – Cobalt Blue she said it was – with a matching hat. She'd got them both in Lewis's in Ranelagh Street, and that's not a cheap shop by any means.'

Monica was impressed. 'How much does she earn, then?'

'I don't know exactly, but I don't think it's a great deal, so Mam says. She lives in theatrical digs – and because she's lived there so long, she doesn't pay much in the way of rent. Buttons, so Mam says, although she did say she wouldn't fancy living there – apparently, it's not up to much. The house is in Lord Nelson Street, so it's very handy for the theatre, but she just has one small room, so it's all rather cramped and pokey and dark, according to Mam. I've never been there.'

'And she's never been married or engaged?' Monica found Aunty Lil's circumstances a little strange.

'I think she was engaged once but nothing came of it. He

lost his job, or didn't have a good enough job, or something like that. She says that now she prefers her own company, her independence, and she also prefers to spend what she earns on herself. I suppose she's happy enough; she does seem to go out quite a lot with friends – theatrical friends.'

Monica nodded. Joan's Aunty Lil did appear to have the perfect life. She herself couldn't wait to start work and earn her own money. Maybe she'd have her hair styled in a good salon and wear stylish and fashionable clothes. It was a shame the circumstances of Lily's visit hadn't exactly been favourable, or she might have met her, but the last thing Joan's mam would have wanted last night was a neighbour trailing in to be introduced to Aunty Lil. All Monica could hope was that she'd come back another day.

# Chapter Five

—◦‣•◦—

The recent weeks had seemed to fly past, Joan thought, as she waited for the tram one early October morning. She'd settled in so well at Crawford's. Although that first day, when she'd watched the girls on the assembly line nimbly sandwiching the two halves of a biscuit together with a cream mixture and then moving quickly on to the next without getting sticky or messy from the cream, she'd never have believed she could do it so deftly. But she could – and what's more, now she could hold a conversation as she did so. Not that that was really encouraged – you were supposed to concentrate on your job – but the supervisor didn't mind, as long as you didn't natter the whole day long. She had marvelled at the delicately piped cream and icing on special biscuits and hoped one day to progress to this level of work, for the pay was far better.

She enjoyed her lunches in the canteen, taken in the company of her newfound friends Nora and Jenny, who were a bit older than she was. Because they all lived in different parts of the city, they generally only saw each other at work, although sometimes on a Saturday afternoon they went into town to window-shop. Of course, all three were too young for the functions held at the social club, you had to be eighteen for that. She, Mam and particularly Charlie all benefited from the weekly treat of the 'rejects' bag, and now that Charlie was helping Mr Savage to look after the pigeons and being paid threepence a week pocket money, he'd settled down a lot.

Mam had gradually unpacked everything and given the place a good clean from top to bottom, and it was looking more like home. Usually, Monica came in after tea for a few hours to catch up on all the news. Her friend had finally met Aunty Lil and had been quite captivated by her. And, at last, Joan had saved up enough money to have her hair done and Lily had booked an appointment for her at La Belle Coiffure just off Bold Street, Liverpool's equivalent to London's Bond Street, as Lily had emphasised. She was going straight from work this afternoon and so would look very smart and grown-up after her appointment – she hoped – for today was special. Her da was due home that morning. Mam and Charlie were going down to the Bramley Moor Dock to wait for the MV *Adventurer* to come in, and she knew that Mam had tickets for the Empire this evening for herself, Da and Mr and Mrs Savage – and of course Aunty Lil would join them after the show for a drink. Joan, Monica, Charlie and Eileen had all been promised a bottle of lemonade and crisps, as they were to spend the evening in Olive's house.

Nora and Jenny had decided to accompany her into town after work; they'd have a look in the shops, maybe buy something in Woolworths in Church Street while she was in the hairdresser's, then they'd meet her in Bold Street later on.

Joan's very first visit to a posh salon was quite daunting, and for a brief instant she wished her aunt had accompanied her. Taking a deep breath, she pushed open the frosted-glass door which opened on to a small reception area, decorated in shades of pale blue and cream, so light, bright and modern. Monica had told her to note every single detail so she could relay it all back. The reception desk was behind a glass screen, the centrepiece of which depicted a dancing lady – the very height of Art Deco fashion – and at the desk sat a young woman dressed entirely in black – but on her it looked anything but funereal. Her blonde hair was taken up and pinned in a chic French pleat at the back of her head and dangling, drop marcasite earrings emphasised her slender neck. Joan had never seen such long fingernails; they were painted a bright scarlet and the whole effect was sheer elegance, she thought in awe.

Joan was asked her name and appointment time and then shown through into the salon itself. Gazing around, she realised it was a single large room divided off into separate enclosed cubicles, each with a wash basin, chair and foot-stool, with linoleum on the floor and a large mirror above the basin. She was ushered into one of the cubicles and swathed in a pale blue cotton gown, which in turn was covered by a large blue fluffy towel, then she was seated in a chair, facing the mirror.

Her stylist was a girl called Madeleine who looked to be in

her early twenties. She appeared friendly enough, Joan thought, relaxing a little. There didn't seem to be many girls of her age here – in fact, there were none. All the other customers – at least those she could actually see – seemed quite old.

'Now, how would you like your hair styled, miss? I have to say, it's lovely, so thick.'

Joan smiled politely at the girl. 'I . . . I really don't know. You see . . . er . . . Madeleine, this is the first time I've ever been to a proper hairdresser's. Mam's always cut it in the past,' she confided. 'But my aunt persuaded me to come – she's the wardrobe mistress at the Empire, so she knows all the modern trends.'

'Is she really? I wish I had an aunt who was in the world of theatre.' The girl smiled and bent down so her mouth was on a level with Joan's ear. 'Sometimes it's a bit like that here. Actually, my name's Mabel, but they like us to sound as if we're French,' she whispered.

Joan relaxed and grinned back at Madeleine in the mirror. 'Then I'll leave it to you, but I really do want to look stylish.'

'And so you shall, I promise.'

After having had her hair washed, followed by half an hour of snipping and pin curling, her hair was covered with a net. She was seated under one of the hairdryers and given a magazine to peruse – but she could hardly read it, she was so eager to see the result when her hair was unveiled. She prayed it wouldn't be a disaster but then bolstered her spirits by remembering how much it was costing – surely it had to be a success? – and by admiring the other clients' finished hairdos.

When, finally, Madeleine had combed out all the pin curls and arranged her hair around her face, Joan was delighted with the result. It was far shorter and softer than anything she'd had before, but it did make her look older. 'Oh, it's gorgeous! I love it!' she enthused.

'It certainly makes you look more sophisticated,' Madeleine nodded, smiling. 'And I just wish I had cheekbones like yours. With a bit of make-up and a nice pair of earrings you'd look like a film star.'

Joan giggled. 'It would take more than that, but thanks, Madeleine.'

The girl nodded. 'You'll soon get used to managing it. If you pin curl the front after you've washed it, it should hold its style. It's the cut that really matters. I hope we'll see you again.'

'I hope so too, but I'll have to save up,' Joan confided.

As she paid the receptionist and left, Joan felt as if she was walking on air. She turned the corner into Bold Street and noticed a few people glance towards her with admiration. Oh, Aunt Lil was right. It was money well spent – she really did feel grown-up and sophisticated. It was a bit of a laugh that all the people employed in that salon had to assume fancy names, but maybe it was something all the big posh salons insisted on. She'd have so much to tell Monica.

Nora and Jenny were equally admiring of Joan's new image and hung on every word of her glowing descriptions of the salon and stylists as they made their way to their various tram stops. Joan was impatient to get home; she was certain her da would have been paid off and the family would be home by now. It seemed so long since she'd seen him, but she'd got used to that. And she knew he wouldn't be home for long either. He couldn't afford to be, he always stated. He didn't get paid if he was 'idling' his days away. She smiled to herself as the tram came into view. He nearly always had a little gift for each of them. Nothing expensive, just cheap little souvenirs of the places he'd been, but they added a bit of colour and interest to the place and reminded her of him – as, no doubt, they did her mam. She doubted Charlie missed him very much, but Mam was determined that Charlie was not going to follow in his father's footsteps by going away to sea. She knew her mam wanted better for Charlie, maybe even an apprenticeship, but that was probably beyond their reach. She patted her new hairstyle as she found a seat on the tram. She really hoped her da would like his grown-up daughter.

Joan smiled to herself as she opened the back door, hearing her father's familiar voice followed by her mother's. For a couple of weeks now it would be a proper home; they would be a family again.

'I'm back! Oh, Da, it's great to see you!' she cried as she hugged her father tightly. He looked just the same as always; a bit more tanned maybe, and the sun had bleached his hair blond, but he was her da and she loved him and he was home.

'Good grief, I hardly recognise you, our Joan! You've grown up,' Billy remarked, holding her away from him. She did look older, he mused, and that made him feel strangely old himself. It was unsettling, and even a bit depressing, to realise that he was middle-aged now.

'And I've got a great job too, Da. Did Mam tell you that? All thanks to Mr Savage, Monica's da.'

'She's been filling me in on everything, but she didn't tell me what a real stunner you've turned into, lass.' Billy meant it. Joan looked just the way Olive had when he'd first met her – and she'd been considered the best-looking girl in the neighbourhood, after Lily, and therefore quite a catch. 'You'll have to keep your eye on her, Olive, luv. You'll have the lads fighting to take her out.'

Olive laughed a little ruefully. 'I know, and I sometimes wish you were at home more often, Billy. Now they're getting older, the problems and the worries don't go away, they just change.'

His smile faded. 'Let's not go into that now, luv. But I would have thought things would be a bit easier as they grow up.'

Joan shot her mother an enquiring glance, wondering if she had informed her da of Charlie's recent misdemeanour. 'Well, now I'm working, that will help Mam out a bit. And as for lads . . .' Joan shrugged. 'Well, there's time enough for that. The right one will come along one day, I'm not in a rush to get to the altar.'

Olive smiled at her. 'I have to say, our Lily was right, Joan. That salon was money well spent. Your hair is gorgeous, and it does make you look older.'

Joan smiled back, cautiously patting the soft curls that framed her face. 'Thanks, Mam.'

'Why don't you go in and show Monica? She'll be dying to see it! I'm going to get your da a decent meal. He'll have had little better than slops while he's been away, I'm sure.'

Billy nodded his agreement as he settled himself down at the table, rubbing his hands together in anticipation. 'I've been looking forward to your cooking for weeks, Olive. Give me a good steak and kidney pie any day of the week. And then we're off on a night out tonight. Oh, aye, there's a lot of advantages to being home!' he enthused.

And in a week he'd be getting restless again, Olive thought, as she set to cooking the dinner. She'd hoped, as he'd grown older, he'd have started to think about maybe getting a shore job so they would be able to spend more time together, but obviously not. Would he ever settle at home? she wondered. Not from choice, she was sure of that. Still, he was here now and they'd all enjoy the time together.

When he'd finished his meal, Billy leaned back in the chair. 'That was really great!'

Olive smiled at him. 'And we'll have a great night out too. Do you think that maybe we could go out somewhere again next Saturday? It's not often I get to go beyond these four walls, apart from shopping for food, and you're away for so long.'

He stared at her hard but looked a little uncomfortable. 'It's not like you to complain, Olive.'

'I'm not! It . . . it's just that I sometimes feel a bit lonely.'

Billy frowned. 'How can you be lonely with the kids, your Lily and all these new neighbours in and out by the minutes? It's me who should be feeling lonely. I hardly see anyone, stuck down in that engine room. And besides, well, we can't afford to go out more than once this trip. I'm a bit short in my pay.' He stood up, turning away from Olive, and took a paper spill from the container on the mantelshelf to light his cigarette.

'Short? How do you mean, Billy? They pay you the same amount each trip, don't they?' A little shiver of mistrust ran through her. A few times before, he'd admitted to being short of money at the end of his trip and then he'd fobbed her off with various excuses, mainly about having to lend some to one or other of his shipmates for reasons that were never fully explained. Quite often, it was money she could have done with. At the back of her mind were the circumstances of their early days together, when she'd been head over heels in love but unsure of the depth of his feelings for her. He'd always sworn she was the only girl for him and always would be, so how could she not trust him? But in a city like this people often made remarks about seafarers and what they got up to when they were away – although she'd always tried to ignore such remarks and her own misgivings. Not all seafarers were the same, she'd told herself firmly. Billy always swore he had neither the inclination nor the money for such goings-on, and she was inclined to believe him.

He shrugged. 'Sometimes it does sort of . . . vary. It's a bit of an uncertain job. I've told you before, Olive, it all depends on the type of cargo, how much they can charge for carrying it or for selling it, and how much they have to spend on things like loading cargo, coal, maintenance and wages. It's not just straightforward – at least that's what they tell *us* – so this time it probably wasn't as profitable. There's not a lot anyone can do about it.'

Olive frowned, trying to take this in. It was something he actually hadn't mentioned before. It did seem plausible but still she was doubtful – and just how short were his wages? She sighed as she began to clear away the dishes. There was no use her going on and on about it; he'd class that as nagging and say she was spoiling his time at home. If there was no money to spare, to go out more than once, then that was that. There was no use arguing or complaining about it, but it had sort of put a damper on things.

# Chapter Six

Round at the Savages', Monica was full of enthusiasm and praise for Joan's new hairdo. Even Nelly remarked that you could tell the cut was very 'professional' – and so it should be at those prices, she added.

'I think I'll go there before I get a job interview,' Monica remarked, glancing hopefully at her mother. 'I'm sure I would look much smarter.'

'You can go there after you've got a job and can pay for it, miss,' Nelly replied flatly. Her mind was on just what she was going to wear for this evening's outing to the Empire Theatre, followed by a drink in the Lounge Bar of The Bradford Hotel where they were going to meet up with Olive's sister. She wasn't used to frequenting such places but obviously Olive was – when Billy was home – and of course, from what she could gather, her sister Lily's life seemed to revolve around them. She still hadn't met Olive's sister, but Monica had, and had pronounced her 'so glamourous she's a bit like a film star'. Nelly sincerely hoped the evening would be a success and that she and Arthur would get on with both Billy Copperfield and Lily Cooper, though she supposed neither Billy nor Lily would be around much in the future – Billy didn't seem to spend much time at home at all, and Lily didn't visit her sister on a regular basis.

At the kitchen table Joan was describing in great detail her 'salon experience', as she called it, and Monica was clearly very impressed.

'It all sounds so interesting. The place sounds just gorgeous. If you work there, you must meet all kinds of different people. And they actually had a girl just doing people's nails?'

'They did, and it looked to be a far more involved process than just painting them too,' Joan replied, for she'd watched the manicurist with fascination.

'Fancy that! And what was *she* called?'

'Francine, I believe,' Joan giggled. 'Probably she's really Frances. What would you call yourself if you worked there? I'd have to be Joanne, or maybe Jacqueline.'

'I suppose I'd be Monique. It certainly sounds better than just plain Monica, I've always hated my name. I don't know what possessed Mam! I mean, Monica Winifred, it's frightful . . .' She paused thoughtfully. 'You know, I'd never even thought about working somewhere like that.'

'You mean as a receptionist?' Joan queried, thinking of the elegant young woman in black.

Monica considered this. 'No, you know I think I'd prefer to be a hairdresser. I'd earn more, and it's classed as a profession.'

'Stylist,' Joan corrected. 'That's what they're called in posh salons. You'd have to train, and I don't suppose you'd get paid very much while you're doing that. Anyway, I thought your mam wants you to work in an office?'

Monica pulled a face. 'She does, but it sounds so . . . boring, especially compared to somewhere like La Belle Coiffure. Just think, Joan, I could be "Miss Monique", with elegantly styled hair and long painted nails.'

'Well, I wouldn't go saying that to your mam,' Joan advised.

Monica nodded. She supposed her friend was right. But still, the more she thought about it, the more she quite fancied the idea of becoming a hairdresser. It was far more glamorous than being a clerk, surely?

Nelly had enjoyed the evening's performance at the Empire, and the seats hadn't been too bad – at least they weren't way up in the gods. She'd particularly enjoyed seeing and listening to Florrie Ford, whom she'd admired for a long time. She hadn't quite made up her mind about Billy Copperfield yet. He seemed a pleasant enough man, obviously quite handsome in his youth, but he was a bit 'loud' for her tastes, although Arthur seemed to be getting on well with him. She'd been quite surprised by Olive's appearance, for she usually wore clothes similar to her own – plain dresses or skirts and sensible blouses, hand-knitted jumpers, and all in muted colours – but tonight her new neighbour wore a bright red, smartly tailored two-piece costume with a black taffeta blouse underneath and a matching red-and-black hat with a single black feather. Nelly felt totally eclipsed in her 'safe' dark green coat and hat. When she'd commented on the fact, Olive had smiled and whispered that her outfit only came out for high days and holidays and that she'd had it for years and years, and Lily said it was now very outdated. Goodness knows what Lily would think of her own staid get-up, Nelly thought.

As they entered the Lounge Bar of the hotel, Nelly looked around speculatively. It was fairly crowded, as you would expect on a Saturday night, but everyone was very well dressed so she could only guess what the prices of the drinks would be. Still, she didn't get to go to places like this very often, and she knew Olive didn't either – though whether Billy did on his travels, she didn't know.

'There's our Lily over there, she's managed to save us some seats,' Olive informed them, and Nelly looked closely at the woman waving to them from the other side of the room. Well, Monica had been right, she thought. This one was indeed very glamorous, and she was unattached; she'd have to keep her eye on Arthur. Obviously the hair was bleached, but it wasn't at all 'brassy', falling in soft waves around Lily's face, and she was definitely wearing make-up. The expensive bright blue coat and hat suited her, and she was attracting quite a few admiring glances from the male customers in the bar. Although she smiled as Lily was introduced, Nelly began to feel rather like a sparrow, dull and dowdy. This family were all a bit too exotic for her tastes, but she cheered up considerably when Lily passed her a folded notelet.

'Our Olive said you were a fan, so I thought you'd like this,' Lily smiled.

Nelly smiled back. 'Oh, thank you! This is very kind of you ... er ... Lily.' It was Florrie Ford's autograph. 'I've admired her for a long time and never thought I'd get to see her, let alone have her autograph.'

The drinks were ordered and Billy and Arthur were soon in

conversation about the places Billy had visited over the years, leaving Olive, Lily and Nelly to their own conversation.

'I really appreciate the autograph. Is she as nice off stage as she appears on it?' Nelly asked.

'She's better than a lot of them, I can tell you, Nelly. You wouldn't believe how rude and bad-mannered some of them are,' Lily confided.

Nelly had been hoping for some more specific information on the stars, though it was interesting to learn that some of these famous people had feet of clay. She'd have loved to have known more.

Lily sipped her pink gin. 'So, how long is he home for this time, Olive?' she asked.

Olive shrugged and sipped her own drink, a small port and lemonade, the same as Nelly's. 'Who knows, Lil? When he gets fed up or else has spent up, he'll be off again, and apparently this trip hasn't been very profitable so . . .' She shrugged and smiled at Nelly. 'It's a bit of a strange life, Nell. I'm weeks . . . months on my own, well, with just the kids, and then he's home and life changes utterly! Suddenly there's more money and he insists we spend it. I try to put good meals on the table because I know the food on those ships is terrible, and then . . . then he's gone again and it's back to the usual grind.'

Nelly nodded slowly, it certainly was a very different life to her own; she didn't think she could put up with it. It must be lonely, and Olive had to shoulder all the responsibilities of family life single-handed. 'I suppose it'll be a worry for you too, Olive, I mean his safety, you hear such terrible things. And then, he's with you and Joan and Charlie when he's home, but what does he do while he's in these foreign ports?'

Lily's eyebrows rose slightly, realising what the woman was implying. In her opinion her sister had quite enough to contend with, without the likes of this rather sour-faced neighbour adding to her woes. For the millionth time she wondered why her sister had chosen to tie herself to a man like Billy Copperfield, who was basically totally selfish and – like most men, in her view – untrustworthy. And for the millionth time she wondered why on earth Olive couldn't see this. She looked across at Billy and frowned. 'No doubt he goes and gets drunk and passes out, like the rest of them, Nelly,' she replied curtly.

'I heard that, Lily!' Billy interrupted, a little irritably, aware that Lily had no time for him and that the feeling was mutual. 'And I don't, Nelly. Oh, I'll go and have a drink, but it might surprise you to know that quite often I go and take in the sights. What's the point of just staying around the docks?'

'Really? Where's your favourite place, Billy?' Arthur asked.

'Lisboa – Lisbon, Portugal. It's a lovely city, built on seven hills, like Rome, and with big elegant squares and magnificent churches. But the Alfama district is my favourite. It's the old part of the city, with lots of narrow, twisting streets, quaint little white-painted houses all with orange-tiled roofs. The people who live there aren't well off by any means, so the houses are small and . . . humble, I suppose you'd call them. But the best views of the city are from the castle – São Jorge, they call it, St George – then there's the flea market, Feira da Ladra, by a beautiful big church, you can get great bargains there.'

'So that's where you get all those bits and pieces you bring home, then?' Olive remarked, although there had been none this time, and for obvious reasons. 'A flea market – and I bet you bargain for them too?'

'Of course I do, that's half the fun,' Billy laughed.

Arthur was curious. 'Do you speak Portuguese, Billy? You don't seem to have any trouble pronouncing the names of those places?'

'Not fluently, but you do pick up a bit of the lingo, especially if you go to the same ports regularly, and we're often in Madeira, the Cape Verde islands, Recife and Manaus in Brazil, and they're all Portuguese colonies,' Billy replied, frowning. 'But things are changing in Lisbon and Portugal, now that Salazar is in power, and some say not for the better.'

Arthur too became serious. 'The whole world seems to be changing, Billy. There seem to be dictators in power every-where now. Franco in Spain, Hitler in Germany, Mussolini in Italy, and this Salazar in Portugal. It makes you wonder where it's all going to end.'

Lily finished her drink. 'Oh, for heaven's sake! We're supposed to be enjoying ourselves, not worrying over the future of the world. Shall we have another drink before we all have to head off home?'

Billy grinned at her cheerfully, his good humour restored. 'You're right, Lil! Same again, everyone?'

Everyone agreed, and as he went to get their drinks Nelly reflected that it had been an interesting evening and that perhaps she had misjudged Billy Copperfield – he was more serious-minded than she'd thought at first. Fancy him visiting places of interest and culture – not just dockside bars – and even being able to speak a few words of a foreign language! They were proving to be an unusual family all right.

# Chapter Seven

———◆◦◆◦◆———

As Christmas approached, along with the end of her final term at school, Monica began to think more and more about her future. One Saturday afternoon, as they waited for a tram in town, she confided all her hopes to Joan.

'I know that Da is trying to get me an interview for some kind of clerical job in the railway offices but I've decided that I really *don't* want to do that. Surely I have *some* choice? It's my future.'

'It will be a secure job, Mon, and I don't suppose the pay is too bad,' Joan reminded her friend, thinking that really neither of them had much say in their futures. They'd been looking for little gifts for their respective families but before she'd met up with Joan, Monica had gone and stood opposite La Belle Coiffure salon and watched the wealthy clients leaving, looking confident and smart. It was something she'd done a few times before, trying to envisage herself working there.

'But the railway offices will be so boring, Joan! I don't actually know but I'm sure it will be all train timetables, ticket prices, station rules and regulations and stuff like that. No, I've made up my mind. I want to be a hairdresser.'

Joan shrugged. 'So, when are you going to tell your mam? You'd better do it before your da actually manages to get you an interview. He'd look such a fool if he had to then turn it down – and you don't want that, Mon, do you?'

'Lord, no! Oh, you're right, I suppose I'd better tell them when I get home and get it over and done with.'

'Do you know how you actually go about it? I mean, do you just walk into a salon and say, "I want to learn to be a hairdresser, please"?'

Monica looked a little perturbed. 'I don't know. I'd not thought about that.'

'Then the first thing to do is to find out. Why didn't you go in and ask them this afternoon?'

Her friend shrugged. 'I don't know. I just didn't think about it but I *will* find out. I suppose you write in, like you do for most jobs.' Monica wasn't relishing the thought of breaking this news to her parents, but Joan was right; the sooner the better, and she certainly didn't want to embarrass her father. She decided to change the subject, remembering that Joan's father had gone away on a short trip a couple of weeks ago. 'When exactly is your da home?'

Joan smiled happily. 'In two days' time and we're all excited. It's the first time he's been home for Christmas in three years. His trips are usually longer but he had to take what was going, so he wasn't going anywhere tropical this time, just "tramping" around Germany, Holland and Denmark, which he's not keen on at all this time of year. He's hoping to get something much better for his next trip. Still, it will be great to have him home.

Finally we can have a real family Christmas,' she added happily, gazing out of the window at the darkening streets still busy with people and traffic. A few of the shops had even begun to put up their festive decorations.

When Monica got home it was to find her mother mixing the ingredients for the Christmas pudding and her father and young Charlie Copperfield out in the yard with the pigeons.

'That smells good, Mam. It's really Christmassy,' she greeted Nelly, taking off her coat, hat and scarf.

'I was saying the same thing to Ethel when I bought all this stuff. It wouldn't be Christmas without a "plum duff", as my mam, God rest her, always called it. And it's always better if you make it early and let it mature, like. I know Joan's mam was doing hers today too, she was in Ethel's shop at the same time as me.'

'Well, Mr Copperfield's home in two days, Joan says – he hasn't been home for Christmas in ages,' Monica informed her.

'I know, and at least that might keep young Charlie at home. He's getting as bad as your da, he's so taken with those damned birds.'

Monica grinned. 'Or maybe it's the threepence Da pays him he's taken with.'

Nelly tutted as she transferred the thick, sticky mixture from the earthenware bowl into a large pudding basin into which a muslin cloth had been placed. Then she neatly tied the top and gently lowered it into the pan of hot water already simmering on the range. 'There, that will take hours to cook.'

'Shall we have a cup of tea, Mam? There's something I

want to talk to you about . . .' Monica suggested a little hesitantly. It was better to get this over with now, she thought, as she filled the kettle.

Nelly had gathered up all the utensils and dishes and moved them into the scullery to be washed. 'Right, then, what's all this about, Monica?' she asked bluntly as she returned to the kitchen and sat down at the table. She knew her daughter well and she realised there was something on the girl's mind.

Monica made the tea, passed her mother a cup and then sat down opposite her.

'I'll be leaving school in just over a week, Mam.'

'I know that, girl, and we're hoping that we'll have everything settled before the holiday. Your da –'

'Mam, I don't want to be a clerk! I don't want to work in an office!' Monica blurted out. 'Oh, don't think I'm not grateful that Da is doing his best to get me a decent job, I am. But . . . but it's just . . .'

Nelly was frowning. 'Just what, then? Surely you don't want to end up like Joan, sticking cream into biscuits all day long, glad of a job in a factory, however clean and modern it is? Good God! You don't want to do that too, do you? It's not what we want for you, Monica.'

'I know, Mam, and I don't want to work at Crawford's. But . . . but I've decided that I want to be a hairdresser.'

Nelly was astounded. 'A *what*?'

'A hairdresser, Mam. I want to get all properly trained, with an apprenticeship. It . . . it's classed as a profession now.'

'Well, not in my book it's not! It's not like being a doctor or a lawyer, or even a teacher or a nurse!' Nelly got up and went to the back door and opened it. 'Arthur! Will you come in here now, please? There's something our Monica has to tell you!' she shouted. 'And send that lad home,' she added. She had no wish for the family's affairs to be broadcast to the neighbourhood, although doubtless her daughter had already confided in Joan.

Arthur looked puzzled and a little annoyed as he came in a few minutes later, wiping his hands on an old bit of towel. 'What's the matter now?'

'Missy here doesn't want you to help her get a decent office job. Oh, no! She's decided she wants to be hairdresser of all things. We don't have to look far to see where she's got that idea from! This is all to do with that Lily Cooper urging their Joan to go to that posh salon to get her hair cut. Putting ridiculous ideas into both their heads!'

'She didn't, Mam! I . . . I thought about it by myself. I'd meet so many different people; do different things each day, things I'd enjoy. I've been and looked at that salon a few times and I . . . I'd really, really like to work somewhere like that.'

Arthur sat down and looked hard at his daughter, surprised and perturbed. 'Have you thought long and hard about this, Monica? Do you know exactly what it entails? Do you know what educational qualifications you'll need – if any? How long is the training? I suppose you will have to train? You need to think properly before you make a decision like this.'

Nelly nodded her agreement with her husband, but Monica shook her head. She couldn't answer all these questions. Unless she got her da on her side, her dream would surely be quashed by her mother. 'All I know, Da, is that it's something I'd like to work at and something I think I'd be good at too. I can find out all about it. Oh, please, please, I *know* I'll be good at it – and maybe even, one day, I might be able to have my own salon.' She'd never even dreamed of that but it sounded good, if not very realistic.

'And pigs might fly!' Nelly snapped, seeing Arthur thinking about Monica's suggestion. 'Oh, what on earth are we going to do with her, Arthur? People like us don't end up owning businesses like that.'

'Mrs Newbridge has a business,' Monica reminded her mother.

'That's not the same thing at all!' Nelly shot back. 'It's a corner shop.'

'I'd *hate* being a clerk, Da! I really would,' Monica persisted, ignoring the looks her mother was giving her.

'I have to agree it's not the most interesting job in the world, but it's steady, secure –'

'I know all that, but surely hairdressing is just as steady and secure? There will always be people who can afford to have their hair done professionally. Please, please, just let me *try*?'

Arthur sighed. He naturally wanted to see both his girls in decent jobs and earning a wage – at least until they got married and had a husband to provide for them – but maybe trying to get both his daughters jobs in the offices of the L&NWR would be a bit much? When it was Eileen's turn, maybe she would stand a better chance if her sister was employed somewhere else? And was it fair to make Monica take a job she was unlikely to enjoy if her resolute expression was anything to go by. 'I'll have to talk to your mother at length about this, luv,' he finally replied, looking meaningfully at his wife.

Nelly gave a little gasp of exasperation as she got to her feet. Well, she for one wasn't at all happy about this. Monica had seemed quite content to be looking at office work until a couple of months ago; she laid the blame for all this nonsense firmly at the feet of Lily Cooper. She felt the woman was no example for impressionable young girls like her daughter and Joan, with her bleached hair, make-up, fancy clothes and independent ideas – and no suitable man in sight.

The next few days in the Savage household seemed rather fraught, so Joan thought. She was unaware of Monica's mother's disapproval of her Aunty Lil's involvement, and she had heard from her friend that her ambitions hadn't gone down well at all, although Monica was hoping her da would come round to the idea. She was disappointed too that when her own da had arrived home from sea, two days earlier, he'd looked decidedly down and disgruntled.

'Oh, it's great you'll be home for Christmas, Da!' she'd greeted him, glancing enquiringly at her mam, who was rolling out the pastry for mince pies.

Olive had just shrugged. But when Monica arrived, later that evening, Joan had taken her friend into the front room, feeling the need for some privacy.

'I know it's freezing in here, we only have a fire in here on high days and holidays, but I wanted to talk to you without the rest of them all earwigging,' Joan explained as Monica stood shivering before the empty grate.

'Well, the atmosphere in our house isn't much warmer,' Monica confided. 'I just wish they'd make a decision. Get it over with – one way or the other. I want to *know*.'

Joan nodded, pulling her cardigan tightly around her as she sat on the edge of the battered sofa which was the only item of furniture in the room. 'Have you no idea at all?'

'No. Mam goes around with an expression on her face as if she's sucking a lemon and won't say a word. Da looks harassed, and as for our Eileen, she's her usual self – an utter pain! Keeps going on and on about what she wants for Christmas, as if I care!'

'Well, it's really not much better here. I don't know what's the matter with Da; I've never seen him like this before. He's usually happy to be home – well, at least at first – but he's in a right mood about something and won't say what. Even Mam doesn't know what's wrong with him, although she thinks it might be something to do with work. That trip was only short so there's not much money – they're not even going out for a drink tonight – so maybe he's worrying about not being able to get a decent ship next time. He wasn't happy working on that last one; he hates cold weather.'

'Don't we all?' Monica replied, grimly glancing around the cold, bare room.

'And then our Charlie's got his heart set on getting a real leather football for Christmas.'

'A "casy"?'

Joan nodded. 'It's all he keeps going on about, and Mam hasn't got the money for one. I know she's spent more than she can really afford on all the Christmas food and trimmings, what with Da being home, and it . . . it's as if he really doesn't care about Christmas at all.'

Monica could see Joan was upset. 'Maybe it's because he's not used to being at home for the holiday? I don't suppose they make as much of a fuss on a ship that's at sea. I suppose it's like any other working day for them, while for us it's . . . special, like.'

Joan brightened a little. 'You know, Mon, you might be right about that. He hasn't been used to all the fuss and bother.'

Monica smiled at her, glad she'd thought about that as an explanation. 'I bet he changes his tune later on, when he's been home a few days and it gets nearer the time and when all the decorations go up and everyone's in a happier mood. At the moment all the women are getting into a right state of nerves about the shopping, the cooking, the preparations, the expense. It's always the same, and then on the day everyone has a great time.'

'You're right. Well, at least Mam won't have to worry about the biscuits this year, we all get a big box of the best Christmas Assorted along with our wages on Christmas Eve; and just think, maybe next year you'll be getting tips from customers in your posh salon.'

Monica bit her lip. 'Oh, I don't know, Joan. I just wish they'd make up their minds and tell me, otherwise Christmas is going to be a right miserable affair in our house.'

Joan privately thought that if Monica's parents were so dead set against her being a hairdresser, then indeed her friend's Christmas wouldn't be a happy one. In fact, if her own da didn't cheer up, neither would her or her mam's. She was finding the whole situation very upsetting.

Olive too was far from happy with the situation. There was something bothering Billy, and she hoped to find out what before the holiday was ruined. She'd gone over to the pub and

Mo Clancy had filled the jug she'd taken with ale.

'Just a bit of a treat for him to have with his dinner, Mo,' she'd enlightened the landlord, although it was something she really couldn't afford, not on top of everything else.

'What's this in aid of, Olive?' Billy had queried as she'd set the jug and a glass down in front of him.

She sat opposite him. 'Well, I'm hoping it will cheer you up, Billy, for I'm getting a bit sick of seeing you looking so dour and miserable. What in God's name is the matter with you? We all thought you'd be delighted to be home for Christmas, but you don't seem to be – far from it – and it's making the kids miserable.'

Billy shrugged but poured himself a glass of ale and took a deep swig. 'I don't know, Olive, and that's the truth! Maybe it was that last trip . . . I hate short trips, and to bloody dark, freezing cold places. It's downright miserable.'

Olive chose her words carefully. 'Do you think that you are getting fed up with the sea?' He wasn't getting any younger for the harsh conditions and heavy manual work in the engine room of various small cargo ships and trampers. It would certainly help if he were to get a steady shore job.

Billy took another deep swig of ale and shook his head. 'No, it's definitely not that! Maybe it's a combination of things – that trip, the uncertainty of getting a decent ship and decent pay next time, and just getting older. I . . . I just hate the thought of getting old, Olive. It's bloody depressing, that's what it is.'

Olive managed a wry smile at this. He'd always been so proud of his good looks, and he was still a handsome man. 'Well, Billy, that's something that none of us can do anything about. We're all getting older, and there's no use getting depressed about it.'

Billy refilled his glass. 'No, I suppose there isn't, but I still hate it.'

She nodded. 'I know, but let's not allow it to spoil the holiday. And with luck you'll get a trip on a decent ship next time. Cheer up and enjoy that ale.'

Billy managed a smile. 'Aye, let's hope I do get something decent.'

# Chapter Eight

―◦―◦―◦―

At last, just a few days before Christmas, Monica had her answer. It was with some trepidation that she followed her father into the parlour when summoned. Nelly appeared to be totally engrossed in supervising Eileen, who was decorating the Christmas tree which stood in a large pot under the window. This added to Monica's unease, for usually she and her sister undertook the task together, and her mother never became *that* involved unless there was an argument brewing. She bit her lip as she sat down on the edge of an armchair opposite her da, fearing the worst.

'Well, luv, your mam and I have talked this whole thing over and while she's far from happy about you going in for hairdressing, I've persuaded her that we should let you try, seeing as how you seem so set on it.'

Monica jumped to her feet, excitement rushing through her, ready to embrace him, but he motioned her to sit down again. 'I've looked into it all very thoroughly and you'll need to serve a three-year apprenticeship, followed by two years as what they call an "improver" before you are fully qualified. That's five years in all, Monica; it's a long time, and on a pittance of a wage to start with. You'll be a young woman of twenty by the time you do qualify.'

Arthur had actually gone to the salon and made an appointment to see the owner and had been somewhat perturbed by what he'd learned. 'But that's not all, luv. We have to pay them for you to be indentured – to learn your trade – and it's far from cheap. And then there's all the equipment you will need and which we have to supply you with.'

Monica's heart, which had been racing with excitement, began to slow down and thump dully in her chest. She'd had no idea there would be such costs involved. 'Oh, Da! I didn't know!'

'So you see, Monica, you have to be absolutely sure that this is what you really do want to do as a career. There can be no changing your mind halfway through.' Arthur didn't want to dampen her hopes and dreams but the amount of money involved was a fairly substantial amount for working-class people like themselves to find. Nelly had been horrified and absolutely scandalised that they would have to pay the salon owner to actually train their daughter. In her opinion – which she had voiced in no uncertain manner – they should be grateful to have a decent girl willing to work for them for mere shillings, never mind having the cheek to ask *them* for money.

Slowly Monica nodded. It was a serious commitment, and for five years of her life. What if she didn't like it? What if she got fed up with the low wages? And she was sensible enough to realise that she would be allotted only the most menial tasks to start with. It would probably be years before she would be let loose on real clients' hair. Doubts began to creep into her mind. But then, as she envisaged days, months and years spent in a stuffy office doing repetitive tasks – or worse, a factory – her resolve strengthened. 'I'm sure, Da. It's what I really, really want to do and I won't let you down. I promise. And, maybe one day I *will* have a salon of my own.'

Arthur nodded and smiled at her. He'd been sure this would be her answer. And it didn't hurt to have ambitions, even if this particular one would more than likely never be realised. 'Then I don't begrudge paying for your indentures or all the other stuff you'll need – if they'll take you on, that is. When I saw the owner he was non-committal.'

Monica looked perturbed. 'So, he didn't actually say he would?'

'It's all subject to an interview with this Mr Claude Eustace. He's the owner. And Miss Helen Marshall, the senior stylist, who apparently has the final say as she will be the one supervising you.'

Monica relaxed and beamed delightedly at him, and her da smiled back as he got to his feet. 'Right, we'd better start the ball rolling. You will need to write a formal letter of application, and then they will reply giving you a date and time for an interview, hopefully. But I doubt it will be before Christmas now. They're bound to be extremely busy – everyone is at this time of year.'

Monica hugged him. 'Oh, Da, thank you! Thank you! You've really made my Christmas a very special one! I'll write that letter now.'

Arthur disentangled himself gently. 'Well, go on into the

kitchen and thank your mam first. She's taking it all very hard, luv. She wanted you to get office work and thinks this hairdressing lark is all a waste of money.'

Monica sighed. 'I know, but I'll make you both proud of me, I promise!'

Nelly was still handing the coloured glass baubles to Eileen when her elder daughter rushed into the room and hugged her.

'Oh, Mam. Thank you! I . . . I know it's hard for you, and Da has explained about all the costs, which I didn't know about, but I promise I'll work hard and stick at it. And you've got to admit, I will have my uses – in time. Just think, you'll have free perms and tints and cuts for years to come!'

Nelly nodded and managed a grim smile. 'The cuts and the perms I won't mind, but I'm not one for having my hair dyed.'

'If it's professionally tinted, Mam, no one will even notice,' Monica informed her, but Nelly was still sceptical.

Eileen had been watching and listening to all this with interest. 'Well, she's definitely not going to be experimenting on *me*! You won't go letting her loose on your hair with a pair of scissors either, Mam, will you? She'll make a right mess of it!' It hadn't escaped her notice that her parents had been very concerned about something to do with her elder sister these past weeks, and now she knew what. Oh, why was there always such a big fuss about whatever Monica wanted to do? She couldn't see what was wrong with working in an office, it sounded far better than just messing with people's hair; less tedious than just brushing up and holding hairpins, which was probably all her sister would be doing for months.

Monica glared at her. 'Don't be stupid! I'll have to learn how to cut hair properly first.'

Seeing an argument brewing, Arthur intervened. 'Why don't you go in and tell Joan your good news?'

Monica nodded. 'I will, Da. It might cheer her up too. She thinks her da's getting a bit fed up with all the fuss and bother and is missing being away at sea.'

Nelly raised her eyebrows. 'A pity about him, then! I don't see him doing much about the place to help Olive, even though he's at home all day.'

Arthur retired behind his newspaper and Monica grabbed her jacket from the hook behind the door, leaving her mother and sister to continue decorating the Christmas tree.

Just as she'd expected, Joan was delighted by her news. Even Mrs Copperfield remarked that it was great, and that she should be very grateful she had parents who would – and more importantly *could* – pay for her indentures.

'Will your mam go with you when you go for the interview?' Olive queried.

'I don't know. I'd not thought about it,' Monica replied.

'You didn't come with me, Mam,' Joan put in.

'This is different, Joan. Nelly will be paying good money to these people. If it were me, I'd want to know just what I was paying for and what kind of people they are.'

Joan shrugged but Monica looked concerned. She could see that Mrs Copperfield had a point, but she wasn't sure she wanted her mam sitting there looking like thunder and asking innumerable, possibly awkward, questions. She pushed the thought from her mind. 'Where's your da and Charlie?' she asked Joan, realising there was no sign of her friend's father or brother, which was unusual, for it was nearly teatime and the winter darkness was falling rapidly on the street.

'Our Charlie's out with the dog and Da's gone to the pub with him from next door,' Joan replied offhandedly, concentrating on pressing the collar of her factory overall which she would need for next day.

Monica was very surprised. 'You mean he's gone with Mr Garswood? I didn't know they were that friendly.'

'They're not. But when Mr Garswood called, he said it was the least he could do, seeing as how Mam had been so good as to ask him to come for his Christmas dinner.'

Monica's eyes widened, this was something unheard of in the street. Mr Garswood always kept himself to himself. 'Did she really?'

Joan nodded.

'And he actually agreed?'

'Why not? Where else has he got to go?' Olive put in. 'He's nice enough, and I couldn't see the poor feller sitting in there on his own on Christmas Day. He's given me a hand with things around the house over the months.'

'Well, I didn't know that. Him coming for Christmas dinner is a real turn-up for the books!' Monica stated, wondering what her mam would say about it. Nelly had invited him many times over the years, but he had declined all the invitations and she'd eventually given up. Nor had Joan's mam mentioned that her neighbour had been helpful on occasion, for she was sure her mam would have said something about it.

'I don't think me da was very keen on the idea to start with, but he's coming round to it. Maybe if he gets pally with him next door, like, it will cheer him up a bit,' Joan stated.

'Has he said any more about going away again?' Monica asked tentatively, lowering her voice and casting a surreptitious glance in Joan's mother's direction.

'He goes on about nothing else!' Joan hissed back emphatically but with a note of disappointment in her voice. She also cast a sideways glance at her mother, who was peeling potatoes. 'It's getting me mam down, I know. I think she's getting to the stage where she wishes he was away, even if neither me nor our Charlie do.'

'Oh, he'll be all right at Christmas, Joan, and then let's hope he gets a decent trip in January,' Monica mused, thinking it must be very strange to actually want your husband to be away.

Joan hung up the finished overall. 'Oh, let's forget about all that. Tell me all you know about this new job of yours – sorry, your "career".'

Monica brightened up. 'There's not much to tell yet, but I'm hoping to get an interview soon after Christmas and maybe start in the New Year.'

'So, you'll be Miss Monique, then, by the time 1936 comes around,' Joan laughed.

Monica, raising her eyes to the ceiling, laughed with her. If that was the case, she couldn't wait.

Nelly was more indignant than surprised when her daughter returned home with the news that the Copperfields would have an extra guest on Christmas Day.

'Well, that's nice, I must say! And after all the years he

refused us! And he's taken Joan's da to the pub?' Nelly cast a searching glance at her husband, who just shrugged.

Monica nodded, going into the scullery to fill the kettle.

'I told you, Arthur, that one's a dark horse!' Nelly muttered to her husband while Monica was out of the kitchen. 'She's deep. Oh, there's more to Olive Copperfield than meets the eye. I've said all along that there's something not quite *right* in that family.'

Arthur shook his head. 'Now, Nell, luv, there's no good jumping to conclusions about the woman. Billy's been away a lot and there must have been times when she's needed a man's help about the place. Charlie's still a bit young to handle some jobs.'

'Aye, but she could have asked you or Harry Newbridge,' Nelly replied firmly, determined not to be swayed.

'But he's only next door to her, Nell.'

'And has never been known to cross any doorstep in this street other than his own, and so seldom does he frequent The George and Dragon that I bet Mo Clancy got a right shock to see him!' She didn't continue the conversation, as Monica had returned.

'Will I make a fresh pot, Mam?'

Her mother nodded curtly. What puzzled Nelly more than anything was why Frederick Garswood had accepted when he'd refused her invitations so often in the past. Maybe he found Olive Copperfield more attractive than herself, she mused, and of course Billy was away so much. Or maybe on one of his visits he had encountered the glamorous and unattached Lily Cooper and hoped to see her again, for hadn't Olive told her that she always had her sister to lunch on

Christmas Day? It was all a bit of a mystery.

She sighed heavily as she took the cup from Monica. What a day it had been! She'd be glad when the holiday was over and things returned to something like normal. But then she remembered that in the New Year her elder daughter would be starting work – and in a job of which she heartily disapproved.

Monica had mentioned briefly that Joan's mam had asked if she was going to accompany her for the interview. She hadn't intended to but the more she thought about it, the more determined she became that she would indeed go. Providing, of course, that there would be an interview. But as for charging for indentures, she'd never heard anything like it in her life – and if she got the opportunity, she'd tell them so.

Christmas Day dawned bright but very cold. There had been a heavy frost overnight and the cobbles glistened and sparkled in the weak sunlight, belying the treachery of the steep pavements. There was even ice on the inside of the window panes, Monica noticed, shivering as she hurriedly got dressed, ensuring she stayed on the rag rug beside the bed – the lino was bound to be freezing.

As usual, Nelly was up, dressed, and had the fire going, so the kitchen was warm by the time the girls came down. The girls had set the table the night before, and she already had the goose in the oven and the vegetables in bowls of cold water in the scullery, ready to be transferred to the pans. She smiled to herself. She had everything under control – and she needed to, as it was one of the few days in the year when they all walked the short distance to the big red-brick church of St George that crowned the hill and from where, on a clear day like today, you could see the whole city and the river spread out below. The only other time they went to church was Easter – and of course for funerals, weddings or christenings. Most people in this area of the city were Protestant, as they were themselves, but they were not what you would call a 'devout' family, by any means.

When Arthur joined them, having washed and shaved, ready to start the day, the girls excitedly opened their gifts, Monica exclaiming in delight at the beautifully enamelled powder compact, a complete surprise. 'Oh, it's gorgeous! I'll take such good care of it – and keep it *forever*!' she cried, tracing the design of a full-blown rose with the tip of her finger.

'Well, we thought that seeing as how you'll soon be starting work and will be mixing with smart people, you should have something smart of your own,' Nelly informed her, smiling.

Eileen had a beautifully bound copy of *Black Beauty*. She was fond of all animals, but particularly horses, and always begged a carrot or a bit of apple to give to the milkman's horse when it was tethered to a lamp post while its owner was inside someone's house having a cup of tea.

'Mam, can I go along and see Joan before we go to church?' Monica asked, as she carefully folded the wrapping paper.

'No you can't, there won't be time. And I suggest that you leave going until everyone's had their dinner – late this afternoon would be best. Olive will have a houseful, what with her sister and Mr Garswood and Billy and her own two kids.'

Monica pulled a face. 'Oh, Mam! I've got her a lovely pair of earrings! Only from Woolworths but really nice.'

'Well, they'll keep – and when we get back from church there'll be more than enough to keep you busy here, miss.'

Monica shrugged but knew better than to argue. Very probably her mam was right. It was bound to be hectic in Joan's house; Mrs Copperfield wasn't nearly as organised as her mam. She'd see her friend later on, when both Mr Garswood and Joan's Aunty Lil would most likely have gone home, and Joan would have the time and opportunity to relay any gossip. She'd just have to wait.

# Chapter Nine

To both Monica and Joan's disappointment there had been no real Christmas Day gossip to chew over. It had been pleasant enough, Joan informed her friend. Aunty Lil had been in fine form after a few glasses of sherry and even Mr Garswood had become quite chatty, although he had seemed a bit in awe of her aunt. Da had been more like his old self, and Charlie had been over the moon with his new football – which he'd given up all hope of getting – and had spent the afternoon out in the street kicking it against the wall of the house, despite the freezing cold weather. Joan had received a lovely bangle from her mam and da – hollow and only silver-plated, of course, but still, it looked like real solid silver. Aunty Lil had bought her a Yardley lipstick – her first – in a gorgeous shade of deep orchid pink, which really suited her, and she had been delighted with the clip-on earrings that had been Monica's gift.

'They'll go great with my new coat,' she remarked to her friend, peering at her reflection in the mirror over the fireplace, turning her head from side to side to see the earrings to their best effect. She'd saved up hard for her coat and was very pleased with it. She'd bought it in T. J. Hughes, one of Liverpool's less expensive shops, and though it wasn't cut from what you could call 'good quality' matcrial, it was brand new and a bright cherry red that suited her colouring and made her feel smart.

'And by all accounts you're going to need a warm coat like that in the months ahead, Joan,' her mother had remarked grimly, refilling her glass with the last of the sherry. She wasn't looking forward to the long, cold, dark months ahead; Billy was bound to be away at sea, leaving her with just Joan and Charlie for company. Unlike her daughter, Olive couldn't say she was relishing the prospect of 1936.

Joan's Mam had been right, Monica thought, as she trudged along beside her mother towards the tram stop late that January afternoon. Overnight there had been a light fall of snow and on top of the ice already on the pavements, it made getting about even more hazardous. She had pulled the collar of her best black-and-white-houndstooth coat up around her ears and was glad of the warm black scarf and gloves knitted by her mam. She knew she'd have been warmer if she'd worn the knitted hat that matched them, but it wasn't smart enough and, determined to look her best for this interview, she'd borrowed Joan's best black corduroy beret. She glanced sideways at her mother and smiled to herself. Mam had made an effort with her appearance too: under her neat chocolate-brown wool costume she wore her best cream crêpe de Chine blouse, and to keep out the cold she'd even borrowed a coat from Lily, at Olive's suggestion. It wasn't real fur, just fake, but it was a good imitation, and it looked well on her, as did the matching small close-fitting hat.

All the way in on the tram, Monica felt nervous, and she knew her mother, sitting next to her, was apprehensive too, for Joan had described in great detail the interior of the salon to her and Nelly had marvelled at such luxury. Monica had also been going over in her mind the answers to the questions she felt would be asked, and was determined not to stammer and make a fool of herself; she wanted to sound and appear confident.

When they finally stepped through the doors of the salon, glad to escape the freezing January air, Nelly felt as though she had stepped into another world, taking in the carpeted reception area and the elegant young woman seated behind the ornate desk. On either side of the desk were glass-fronted cabinets containing cosmetics and perfumes in coloured glass bottles.

'May I help you?' the receptionist asked, smiling pleasantly.

'We have an appointment to see Mr Eustace and Miss Marshall,' Nelly informed her curtly.

She consulted her appointment book. 'Ah, yes. You must be Miss Savage and . . . er . . . Mrs Savage? If you would take a seat, I will inform them you are here.'

They sat down on the delicate gold-painted chairs and Monica looked through into the salon beyond, where two of the cubicle doors were open. In one a girl about the same age as herself was on her hands and knees, washing the marble-effect linoleum, and in the other a girl was cleaning the mirror above the wash basin. They were both wearing the same pale blue overall with the letters LBC embroidered in gold on the pocket.

Nelly too was surreptitiously looking around, wondering who on earth could afford to come to a place like this just to get their hair done? She certainly couldn't.

After a few minutes, the receptionist returned with another young woman whom she introduced as Miss Marshall, the senior stylist.

Monica rose and held out her hand, smiling. Helen Marshall was a small, slim young woman of about twenty-five with dark auburn hair worn in a very complicated upswept style of waves and curls. What make-up she wore was lightly applied and her nails were short and free of varnish. She too was dressed in the smart, fitted pale blue overall, but hers sported a black trim on the collar and cuffs. 'I'm delighted to meet you, Miss Marshall. This is my mother.'

Nelly inclined her head.

'Would you both like to come with me, please? Mr Eustace is waiting for you in his office.'

They followed her through the salon and into a small room at the far end, carpeted and furnished with a desk, three chairs and a filing cabinet. A very smartly dressed middle-aged man sat at the desk. Nelly noted his receding slicked-back dark hair and dark eyes, which seemed to take in every aspect of their appearance. His pale grey suit was immaculately cut and he wore a pink carnation in his buttonhole. A heavy gold Albert watch chain with an ornate fob adorned his waistcoat. To Nelly he appeared slightly foreign-looking, and she wasn't sure if she liked him, but his manners were impeccable as he rose, shook hands and bade them sit down.

'Now, Miss Savage – Monica, an unusual name – would you like to tell me why it is you wish to become a hairdresser?'

Monica swallowed hard, hoping she had prepared her answer well. She managed a smile. 'It is something I've been thinking about for quite a while and also a trade I'm sure I will enjoy. Of course I don't have any experience at all, but I can manage my own hair quite well and I'm very willing to learn. I also notice how other ladies wear their hair, and if it suits them or not, and whether maybe a different style would enhance their appearance. I know that this is a high-class salon, as my friend came here to have her hair cut and she was very impressed.'

Mr Eustace leaned his elbows on the desk and steepled his fingers, nodding slowly. 'She made an excellent choice – it is a little unusual for a very young girl to be a client. Do go on,' he encouraged.

'Oh, her aunt recommended her and made the appointment. Miss Lillian Cooper, she's the wardrobe mistress at the Empire Theatre.'

He smiled. 'Ah yes. We do get such recommendations. Now, I assume your father has informed you of the length of time your training will take and the long hours and . . . meagre remuneration for the first years. It is hard work.'

Monica nodded. 'I won't mind all that.'

He continued. 'You will receive a very thorough training, a complete grounding in all aspects of hairdressing.'

Helen Marshall had remained silent throughout this exchange but now she smiled at Nelly who, she could see, was not as enthusiastic as her daughter. 'Mrs Savage, are you quite happy with all this? We do realise that it's a long training period and that it's quite an outlay for you.'

Nelly pursed her lips; now was her opportunity. 'It most certainly is expensive, Miss Marshall . . . and it's something we hadn't anticipated. In fact, I've never heard of such a thing before. Apprenticeships, yes – but not *paid* indentures.'

Monica quailed and bit her lip. Oh, she just hoped Mam wasn't going to get on her high horse and ruin everything.

Claude Eustace looked far from pleased as he glanced from Nelly to her daughter. He had invested a great deal of time and money into his highly successful salons and he didn't take kindly to what he suspected was the questioning of his business practices. 'I can assure you, Mrs Savage, it is the norm in the world of hairdressing. It is necessary to ensure we do not end up with an overcrowded profession filled with half- or badly trained girls. If we did not charge for indenturing, what do you think would happen? Many girls think it is a very glamorous profession, without having any idea of the work and dedication involved, and therefore get disillusioned and leave halfway through their training. They then try to set up on their own or go to work in a shop – I refuse to call them salons – where they are not particular about their staff being properly trained. I can assure you that, in the past, there have been some terrible accidents involving girls unused to the certain types of permanent wave solutions and bleaches and tints. Girls who have not had the proper training but have just been guessing have caused injury to their clients. It gives the profession a bad name, and that is something we all wish to avoid. It will not *do*, Mrs Savage!'

Nelly said nothing, rather taken aback by these revelations.

'But I'm sure, sir, that nothing of the kind has ever happened in good salons like this,' Monica added, for she could see he was annoyed.

He smiled at her, good humour apparently restored. 'Of course not, Miss Savage. Now, Miss Marshall will continue with the interview – I'm a very busy man.' With that he stood up and walked briskly out of the room.

Monica smiled back at him, relieved.

Helen Marshall took the seat he had vacated and smiled across the desk at Monica. She liked her – despite the obviously interfering and disapproving mother – and knew that Mr Eustace wished to offer the girl a job. 'I'm delighted to tell you, Monica, that we'd like to offer you a position as an apprentice. You appear to have the right temperament and a good attitude to the work and hours et cetera. When would you be able to start?'

Monica's cheeks flushed with pleasure. 'As soon as you would like me to, Miss Marshall. I left school before Christmas.'

'And with excellent results in her leaving exam,' Nelly added, determined that they should know her daughter was probably better educated than the usual apprentice.

Helen Marshall ignored her. 'Good, then shall we say next week – Tuesday? We are closed on Mondays. You'll need to go to Osbourne and Garret in School Lane – the hairdressing wholesalers – to purchase everything on this list. I realise there is rather a lot but . . . well, you'll need it all in time.' She passed a handwritten list across the desk and Monica quickly scanned it. It seemed endless, and she knew Mam would not be happy, but she didn't care. She'd got the job she wanted! She'd taken the first step on the road to becoming a hairdresser! 'Oh, thank you, Miss Marshall!' she beamed, almost overcome with excitement.

The young woman rose and extended her hand to Nelly. 'I'm sure she will do well, Mrs Savage, and Mr Eustace will be in touch regarding the formalities of the indentures.' She turned to Monica. 'I'm delighted to welcome you to La Belle Coiffure, Monica – I'm sure you will be an asset to the salon.'

'Thank you, Miss Marshall. I'll do my very best. And I'll be here – prompt – on Tuesday morning next.'

Helen Marshall showed them back to the reception area where the elegant young woman – whose name, Monica ascertained from the senior stylist, was Anna – sat at her desk. She rose as they emerged and ushered them towards the door. 'Will we be seeing you again?' she whispered to Monica, one eye on Nelly who still looked full of disapproval.

'You will, next Tuesday! Isn't it great? I'm so looking forward to starting here!'

Anna grinned at her. 'Congratulations! You'll have the weekend to think up a name for yourself. Did she tell you the salon policy?'

Monica shook her head. 'No, but my friend Joan did. I've already decided to be called Monique.'

'Oh, I like that. It sounds very classy. I'm really just plain Anne, and you can't do much with that. See you next week then, Monique.'

Nelly raised her eyes to the ceiling but said nothing until they were outside.

'Well, that's that, then! I hope you know what you're doing,

Monica,' she said grimly as they walked towards Bold Street.

Monica was determined not to let her mam's attitude spoil the moment. 'Oh, I *do*, Mam! I really do!'

To Monica's surprise, Joan was waiting at the tram stop – despite the fact that, now that it was dark, the temperature had plummeted. 'Joan, you must be freezing! How long have you been standing here?'

'Oh, not long, only about ten minutes. When I got off the tram I thought, what's the point in going home? I might as well wait, as you probably wouldn't be long, and I'm dying to hear your news.' Joan linked arms with her friend as Nelly walked on ahead. 'So, how did it go? Your mam still doesn't look very happy.'

Monica grinned. 'She's not, but I don't care. As of next Tuesday I will officially be an apprentice hairdresser at La Belle Coiffure! Oh, Joan, it's all so exciting! Even Mam was impressed by the salon, it's gorgeous! I can't wait to start work there; Miss Marshall, the senior stylist, is very elegant, but friendly too, and the girl on the reception desk seemed really nice.'

Joan smiled back. 'Let's hope you still think like that after six months.'

'I will. Can you come into town with me tomorrow afternoon? I've got to go to the wholesalers for everything I'll need, and I know Mam really doesn't want to come with me – she thinks it's all a terrible waste of money.'

'I'll meet you after I finish work at lunchtime. What do you need?'

Monica paused under a street light and handed her friend

the list that she and her mother had scrutinised on the tram home.

Joan scanned it and gave a low whistle. 'Lord above, I can see why your ma's not terribly thrilled! "Two pairs of scissors – never to be used on anything other than hair – a pair of thinning scissors, a cut-throat razor also for thinning and tapering, two steel combs – one heavy, one light – a tail comb, clippers, two sets of waving irons medium size B or C, four coloured hairnets, six packets of clips, six packets of straight pins and three overalls,"' she read aloud. 'I would have thought they'd supply you with the overalls – Crawford's do,' Joan finished. 'You'll need me to help you carry this lot!'

Monica nodded. 'I know. It does seem a lot. But I suppose if you are careful, it will all last.'

They walked on towards the corner of Mersey View but before they turned into the street Joan stopped. 'I've a bit of news meself. Da's leaving, early on Monday morning. He's signed on the MV *Hubert*, that's the Booth Shipping Company, and it's a decent line too. He's going back to South America.'

'How long will he be away?' Monica asked, knowing her friend really didn't want her father absent again for long periods.

'About three months; he should be home early April. It's not too bad, and Mam says he's never happy when he's home under her feet all day . . .' She paused and sighed. 'And I don't suppose there's much money left now from his last trip. Not after Christmas.'

'Maybe one day he'll be happy to get a job ashore,' Monica suggested.

Joan shrugged. 'I can't see it being any time soon, Mon, but let's look on the bright side, you're starting work, I've got a job I like – and before we know it, it will be spring again.'

'And I should really have settled into my apprenticeship by then,' Monica added happily as they followed Nelly up the street.

# Chapter Ten

It was the first week in February when the first really heavy snowfall almost brought the city to a halt. Trams and buses were infrequent, the services were erratic, and people struggled to get to and from work, having to walk long miles through bitterly cold streets over hard-packed snow. Along the eight miles of docks the hauliers struggled to get cargoes to and from the ships where dockers worked in freezing temperatures and increasingly dangerous conditions.

For Monica it quite often seemed a pointless waste of time to undertake the arduous journey into the city centre and back, as the clients who managed to keep their appointments were few and far between, and all she seemed to do all day was clean cubicles that did not need cleaning, practise pin curling and finger waving on one of the other apprentices or herself be the subject of their ministrations, and sit delving into the pages of her copy of *The Art and Craft of Hairdressing*. As the cold snap continued, everyone grew more bored and tempers became increasingly frayed.

Thankfully, Crawford's managed to keep to their production schedules – although deliveries were difficult, so Joan informed her friend. The two girls sat as close to the fire in Olive's kitchen as they could get without actually burning themselves.

'We're not like you, Mon. If we can't work, there's no money at the end of the week, so I'm glad we've kept going,' she said.

'I know, but I get next to nothing on a regular basis, apart from the odd tip for washing someone's hair, and there've hardly been any clients in all week. I wish *I* earned ten shillings a week, Joan.'

Joan shivered. 'You can't blame them for not keeping appointments. Just thinking of washing my hair in the scullery sends shivers down my spine.'

'Isn't your da well out of it? Lucky him in the sunshine,' Monica mused. According to the Journal of Commerce, the MV *Hubert* was due to dock in Brazil where, no doubt, it would be hot.

'He is, isn't he? Still, let's hope this weather doesn't last much longer,' Olive put in, trying to keep her mind off whether or not the pipes in the scullery would freeze again tonight. 'If it does, I'm going to ask our Lily if she wants to move in for a week or two. I know she's got a lot of spare time on her hands now. Audiences are down so they cancel shows – people don't want to venture out again once they've finally got home from work, and you can't blame them. I know that room she's got is convenient for the theatre, being just around the corner, but I'll bet it's downright freezing – and she *must* get a bit lonely at times, especially when she's not at work!'

'Do you think she will, Mam?' Joan pressed; she liked the idea of having her aunt to stay with them.

'All I can do is ask her. Now, who on earth is that at this time of night, in this weather and at the front door?' Olive asked irritably as the sound of the door knocker echoed loudly down the lobby. None of the neighbours would use the front door, and as Charlie wasn't in yet with that blasted dog, she felt uneasy.

'I'll go and see, Mam,' Joan offered reluctantly, loath to leave the fireside.

Both Olive and Monica stared in amazement when Joan came back into the room accompanied by a waif-like girl of about twelve. She was thin and pale, with huge dark eyes and long dark hair that curled over her shoulders but was tangled and matted. She was shivering violently, dressed only in a very grubby cotton dress, a thin jacket, with no stockings, and just a pair of broken-down canvas shoes.

Olive was filled with alarm at the sight of her. 'Who on earth is she, Joan?' she asked, getting to her feet and folding up the evening paper. She was concerned at how very pale and shocked her daughter looked.

'She . . . she's foreign, Mam. She says her name is Annabella and she's come from Portugal looking for her father – Billy Copperfield!'

Olive uttered a strangled cry and sat down suddenly, the colour draining from her face, her hand going to her throat as she stared in horror at the girl. 'She . . . she can't . . . *he* can't . . .'

Joan passed over the folded piece of paper the girl had thrust into her hand on the doorstep. 'It's some kind of certificate, Mam.'

Olive unfolded it and scanned it, quickly biting her lip, the colour slowly returning to her cheeks but her hands visibly shaking. 'It . . . it's a Baptismal Certificate. I . . . I can't understand all of it but . . .' She shook her head in disbelief. Oh, God! How could Billy do this to her? It stated clearly, in a neat but cramped script, that the girl's name was Annabella Maria Copperfield, that her mother was Maria Isabella Ferreira Silva and her father . . . William George Copperfield!

Joan was staring at her mother in horror. 'Is she . . . is she . . . ?'

Olive managed to nod before she covered her face with her hands, unable to speak. But should she really be so surprised? she asked herself. She was shocked and bitterly, bitterly hurt, yes. Oh, definitely both those things, but hadn't she always had small, nagging doubts about Billy when he was away? Especially after their early years together? Hadn't Lily said often enough that she personally wouldn't trust him as far as she could throw him? She'd always, always pushed those doubts away, as far to the back of her mind as was possible, for she didn't want to believe he was capable of such betrayal, but now she couldn't ignore it any longer. This child was the proof.

Monica stood up, just as horrified by these revelations as her friend. 'I'm going for my mam, Joan! Your mam's in shock, and you can't cope with all this on your own.'

Joan looked at her helplessly, feeling she was in a state of shock herself, while the girl looked from Joan to Olive, and then Monica, in confusion and fear.

'Bring her over here to the fire, Joan, she's frozen stiff – and she's little more than a child,' Monica instructed, before turning and leaving.

Ignoring the icy pavements, it took her only a few minutes to run home. 'Mam, Mam, you've got to come at once! Something . . . something's happened at Joan's!' she cried, bursting into the kitchen.

Nelly got to her feet, knowing immediately by her daughter's face it was something serious. 'You go on ahead of me, Monica. I'll get my coat, it's freezing out there.'

'No, I'll wait for you, Mam,' Monica replied, for she wanted to apprise her mother of the whole situation before they got back to Olive's house.

When they arrived at number ten, Nelly took charge, seeing the state Olive and Joan were in, though she also felt sorry for the poor little waif sitting by the fire still shivering with cold and obviously terrified. 'Right, where's Charlie?'

'Out with the dog,' Joan replied, twisting her hands helplessly together.

'Well, that's something. Go and get a blanket to wrap that child in, Joan, and then when Charlie gets in, tell him he's to go straight to bed – the last thing your mam needs is him asking all kinds of awkward questions. Monica, stir yourself and make a pot of tea, everyone needs a cup.' She crossed to the table and sat down as the girls moved to do as they'd been instructed.

Olive looked at her neighbour, feeling dazed and confused. Her eyes were bright with unshed tears.

Nelly took both her hands in her own. 'It's all right, Olive. You cry, luv. You're entitled to, you've had a real shock.'

Olive slowly shook her head. She really didn't want Nelly Savage here, not now. 'I . . . I just can't . . . cope with it!'

'Of course you can't, that's why I'm here . . .' She paused, sensing something Olive wasn't telling her. 'You've no need to worry, Olive,' she said gently. 'I know I've a reputation for being a gossip, but I can keep my mouth shut when I have to, and this is definitely one of those times.'

Hesitantly Olive pushed the girl's Baptismal Certificate across the table and Nelly scanned it, sighing deeply. 'So, it's true? She's his child?'

'I can't believe it! I don't *want* to believe it, Nelly!'

'No, luv, I don't suppose you do. But why is she here? Where's her mother? How the hell did she get here, and how did she know where to come to find him?'

Olive shrugged, dashing a tear from her cheek. 'I don't know!' Suddenly she felt completely overwhelmed by the situation and abandoned all caution regarding Nelly's reputation. 'Oh, Nell, how could he do this to me? Look at her; she's probably eleven or twelve years old. When . . . when Joan was just a toddler and Charlie only a tiny baby, he . . . he must have been . . .' Olive broke down.

'Hush, luv! Hush now!' Nelly urged, casting an anxious glance at Joan while getting up and putting her arms around Olive. 'We'll get it all sorted, luv, don't worry,' she said, thinking it best not to make things any worse than they were for poor Joan.

Monica quietly handed around the mugs of tea. Joan nodded her thanks, sitting down beside the girl she now was beginning to realise must be her half-sister, and who still looked terrified, although she took the mug of tea gratefully and began to sip it.

Olive was trying desperately to pull herself together, mainly for Joan's sake, but the more she thought about it all the worse it became. 'Joan, do you think, luv, you can ask her . . .'

'Ask her what, Mam?'

It was Nelly who replied. 'Why she's here? How she got here? She . . . she doesn't seem to be frightened of you, luv.'

Joan nodded and managed a weak smile. At least the girl had stopped shivering. 'What . . . what happened . . . Annabella? Why did you come here?'

'Bella, everyone call me just Bella. I live with *minha mãe* – my mother – in a house by Castelo de São Jorge, in Alfama – in Lisboa. My *mãe*, she get sick and she . . . *morto*.' The girl's dark eyes filled with tears which trickled slowly down her thin cheeks.

Without really thinking, Joan took the girl's hand and squeezed it, and for the first time the look of fear disappeared from Bella's eyes.

'But before that . . . she find something in my *pai* – my papa's – sea bag when she goes to look for his clothes to wash. A little book with an address, this place here and sums of money.'

Olive nodded slowly; it made sense to her. The woman had found Billy's Discharge Book, which was both a seaman's passport and a record of his trips, conduct and pay.

'My *mãe*, she tells me if anything bad happens to her while he is away, I must come to Liverpool, to this place, and I will find him. She write it down for me, see . . .' From the pocket of her thin jacket she produced a crumpled ball of paper.

'So you've come all the way from Portugal?' Joan asked incredulously.

101

The girl nodded.

Olive was feeling a bit calmer now. None of this was the girl's fault, all the blame lay with Billy, for no doubt the girl's mother had trusted him too. But she couldn't think about that woman now. It was all too raw, too sudden, but she recognised the names of the places the girl had spoken of. Billy had mentioned them often enough – and now she knew why.

'How?' Monica asked quietly, smiling encouragingly at Bella and thinking it was a blessing at least that her English was quite good.

'I have little money but not enough for fare. So, I go to docks and find a ship and when all is quiet I go aboard and I hide.'

'You stowed away?' Monica was astonished and knew that everyone in the room felt the same way.

Bella finished her tea but kept tight hold of the still-warm mug. 'I . . . I had to get to Liverpool. I . . . I did not want to go to the nuns, and I have no money and no family.'

Joan gently prised the mug from her but then put her arm around her shoulders.

'You were very brave.'

At her words the girl began to cry softly, and Joan looked across at her mother for help.

Olive couldn't bring herself to make any remarks, comforting or otherwise.

'When you arrived, what did you do, Bella?' Monica asked, sensing both Joan and her mother were at a loss for words.

Bella wiped the back of her hand across her cheeks and

sniffed. 'I very afraid but I hide and I wait. I wait until everyone leave the ship, then I too leave, but . . .'

Joan could only imagine the terror the girl must have felt leaving that ship alone, in the dark and in a foreign city, where everything would appear alien to her, most of all the weather. 'How did you find your way here?' she coaxed.

Bella smiled. 'I meet a good man. I show him the paper and he take me to tram stop and ask the man in charge of the tram to help me find this street.'

'And he did, the conductor on the tram?' Joan pressed.

Bella nodded. 'Good men, both kind. So, I find you but not my *pai* . . .'

'No. He . . . he's away.' Again Joan looked across at her mother. 'So, Mam, what are we going to do now?'

Olive, who was still clinging to Nelly's hand, looked at her neighbour in some confusion. 'I . . . I . . . can't, I don't . . .'

Nelly took a deep breath. 'Well, you can decide that later on, Olive, luv. But you've got to agree that we can't turn the child out on to the streets at this time of night, and in this weather, not after all she's been through.'

Olive nodded silently.

'First of all, I'd say she needs some food inside her, then a good night's sleep. Which is something I'd say you all could do with,' Nelly suggested. She was about to continue when Charlie, accompanied by Rags, burst into the kitchen.

'Mam, can Rags sleep by the fire tonight, it's freezing out there?' he cried, before looking around in some confusion.

Joan quickly got to her feet. 'No, he flaming well can't, Charlie! Put him in the scullery as usual!'

'And then get yourself to bed, meladdo! I'm sure it's way

past your bedtime, and you've school in the morning. Your mam has enough on her plate at the minute,' Nelly instructed him firmly.

'Who's she?' Charlie asked, unperturbed, staring hard at Bella.

'You'll find out soon enough, now get that dog out of here!' Joan cried.

With very bad grace Charlie complied, and when he'd gone Joan put what was left of the scouse on the range to heat up and cut two thick slices of bread, while Monica put a bowl, plate and spoon on the table.

Nelly stood up, patting Olive's hand. 'I'm just nipping home, luv. Our Eileen's about the same size as Bella here. I'll see what I can find – she'll have to have something warmer than that frock – and she'll need something to sleep in too. I won't be long, and I'll bring a drop of something stronger than tea too. I think you need it, Olive, and then we can . . . talk.'

# Chapter Eleven

As Bella greedily ate the scouse and bread, Joan – on Nelly's instruction – put two bricks into the range to heat up. She'd wrap them in flannel and put them in the bed she'd share tonight with her half-sister, for the bedroom was cold, there being no heating upstairs in the house. Two hours after the shock of Bella's arrival, it seemed things were slowly taking on a more normal feel. Her mam seemed to have pulled herself together and was gathering up the dirty dishes. Charlie had gone to bed in high dudgeon, outraged at the fact no one would tell him what was going on and who the strange girl downstairs was. Joan herself was trying to push to the back of her mind all thoughts of her father, his betrayal of them all, and the deep hurt that caused. She'd have to face all that at some time, but just not now. Not until they'd got some practical things settled – like what they were going to do about Bella.

Within the space of fifteen minutes, Nelly was back, carrying a big hemp bag which she placed on the table.

Bella was once again sitting by the fire with the blanket wrapped around her, staring around the unfamiliar room but looking less afraid and more relaxed.

'There's a couple of skirts and jumpers our Eileen's grown out of. A few bits of underwear, a pair of thick stockings, a flannelette nightdress and a dressing gown that's much too short, I was going to unpick it,' Nelly informed them all, taking all the items out of the bag one by one. Nelly was always practical and never wasted anything. Clothes that were too short or too small were unpicked and the material used again, even if only for backing quilts or rag rugs.

'This is very good of you, Mrs Savage,' Joan said, picking up the nightdress and taking it over to Bella.

'Well, needs must. I'm afraid there's no coat, though, and she'll need one if she's not to freeze, poor lass. Maybe, when things are a bit more settled, you can go to Paddy's Market and get something second-hand,' she suggested to Olive. Everyone knew Paddy's Market. It was officially Great Homer Street Market, a favourite haunt of foreign seamen, who were often to be seen staggering back to their ships laden down with bundles. Clothes there were second-, third- or even fourth-hand, and laid out in piles on the floor for people to rummage through, but sometimes, if you had the time and inclination to rummage, you could get a really good bargain for a few shillings or even pence. Olive could get the girl a good warm coat and a pair of serviceable boots there, she was certain.

But Olive didn't respond to Nelly's suggestion; her mind was still in too much turmoil, aware only that her neighbour was being kind, sympathetic and practical, and for that she would be endlessly grateful.

Nelly could see that the poor woman was still distracted. 'Right, then! Joan, I suggest you get yourself and Bella here up to bed. She for one must be absolutely worn out, and you've work in the morning. Monica, get yourself off home. Olive and I need to talk . . . and we'll need privacy.'

When all the girls had gone, Bella somewhat hesitantly, Nelly sat down opposite Olive at the table and again took both her hands. 'That's them settled for the night, Olive. Now, we're going to have to decide what to do with the girl.'

'I know, Nelly, but I just don't seem to be able to think straight! I've always prided myself that I can cope with any situation, manage any problems that come my way – I've had to in the past – but . . . but . . . *this*!'

Nelly nodded her understanding; if she could get her hands on Billy Copperfield she'd kill him! 'Do you feel you can take the girl in, give her a home, luv? Or would it be best for you turn her over to the authorities? No one would blame you if you did; she's not your responsibility by any stretch of the imagination.' And she would be another mouth to feed on what she suspected was the very meagre allowance Billy left.

'I don't know. She . . . she's so young, she's clearly known awful grief, and she's travelled so far, Nelly.'

'It can't have been easy for her, having her mam die and *him* away, and with no one to turn to. I suppose that when she said she didn't want to go to the nuns, she meant a convent orphanage.'

Olive bit her lip. 'How can I now send her to an orphanage here? Because that's where the authorities will put her.'

Nelly agreed, before delving into the bottom of the bag.

She brought out the small bottle of brandy she kept strictly for medicinal purposes and took two glasses from the dresser. 'And God knows what she suffered getting here, she must have been terrified; all that way and on her own, poor lass.'

Olive took the small glass of brandy and sipped it slowly. 'It doesn't bear thinking about.' She sighed heavily. 'I'll let her stay, Nelly. I can't turn her away after what she's been through.' She sipped her drink again, feeling it burn her throat but warm her at the same time, bringing a tiny spark of her usual determination back. 'After all, *she's* done nothing wrong.'

'No, she hasn't, but you're going to have to decide what you're going to do about *him* too.'

'I know, but I'll need time to sort that out in my mind. Decide what's best for us all.' She took another sip of brandy. At this moment in time she really didn't know what she was going to do about Billy. 'The Lord alone knows what our Lily is going to say about it all, though. Very probably, "I told you so!" She never really liked him.'

Lily Cooper was a good judge of men, then, Nelly thought, although she kept this opinion to herself. 'Oh, never mind your Lily. That does give me an idea, though.'

Olive showed a slight interest in Nelly's words. 'What?'

'She's your sister, so what if people thought you had another sister? One who'd got married and gone to live in Portugal with her seafarer husband? She's just died and, with him being away so much, he can't look after the girl, so you've taken Bella – your niece – in to bring up with your own two.'

Olive actually managed a brief smile. What her friend said

108

made sense. 'I would never have thought of that, Nelly.'

'Well, you'll have to explain her sudden appearance, and she'll have to go to school, she's too young to work . . .' She paused. 'I don't want to pry, Olive, luv, but will you be able to manage on what he leaves you?'

'I expect so, I'll just have to economise, but I'm used to that,' Olive replied wearily. Now she knew where those missing pounds of Billy's wages had gone, the money he'd told her he'd never received or had lent to mates! 'What am I going to tell our Charlie? He idolises his da.'

'As little as possible – but still the truth, luv. It's no use trying to hide the fact that she's his half-sister. He'll just have to keep his trap shut. Billy's got a lot to answer for . . . to all of you.'

Tears again welled in Olive's eyes, but inside she felt utterly drained of all emotions. She couldn't – *wouldn't* – think of Billy now. Suddenly a terrible, shattering thought hurtled into her mind and she gasped. 'Oh, God! Nelly! No!'

'What? What's the matter now?' Nelly cried, startled by the expression in her neighbour's eyes and the fear in her voice.

'What if . . . what if there are . . . more?'

Nelly's eyes widened and she clutched her glass tightly. 'No! Surely to God, Olive, there . . . can't be! You'd know, wouldn't you?'

Olive tossed back the last drops of the brandy. 'I didn't know about this one, Nelly! You know what people say about sailors having "a woman in every port". Our Lily comments on it often enough – and fool that I am, I refused to listen!'

Nelly was still trying to get her mind around this latest

fear of Olive's. She hated to even think about it, but Olive could be right. She'd known nothing at all about Maria Isabella and her daughter. Billy had kept that quiet for all these years. What if, indeed, there were more women and children? He seemed to call regularly into other ports. But no, she couldn't let her friend torment herself with this prospect. She had to nip Olive's fears in the bud – just in case, in her distress, she blurted them out to Joan and Charlie. 'No, let's be sensible about it, luv. God knows, financially he couldn't possibly afford to support more families or keep quiet about them, no matter how far away,' she stated firmly. She didn't think even Billy Copperfield was that stupid or heartless, and he certainly didn't earn the kind of money he'd need to keep such a harem. She knew what she'd have to say to Billy Copperfield when he showed his face again! Poor Olive, it just didn't bear thinking about. She was very thankful that her Arthur was a decent, steady, faithful if rather dull husband . . . whose only other interest in life apart from his family was pigeons.

Joan could see Bella was almost dropping with exhaustion as she helped her pull the nightdress over her head and climb into bed. She was painfully thin and shivering again in the cold air that filled the room, but she managed a smile as she felt the warmth of the brick against her feet. Joan smiled too as she smoothed the dark curls from the girl's forehead and tucked the quilt around her chin. She should probably feel bitter and resentful about Bella, but strangely she didn't. A few hours ago, she hadn't even known she existed, but now, she felt . . . protective. Bella was far from clean after her experiences, but to give her a bath would have involved far too much effort. And what if Charlie had come back downstairs in the middle of it? No, a good wash was all Bella had been subjected to for now.

Joan climbed in beside the girl and lay staring at the outline of the window where a beam of bright moonlight found its way through a crack in the curtains, foretelling yet another night of hard frost and worse conditions in the morning. There seemed no end yet to this cold snap, but that was the least of her worries. Her da would have a lot of explaining to do when he got home in April. How could he have been so disrespectful to her mam in taking up with Bella's mother? Didn't he love her? And how could he have cared so little about herself, Charlie and even Bella? And how had he lived a lie so easily for so many years? Oh, they were all questions to which she wanted answers – but would those answers cause her more pain than she was feeling now? Could the family ever get over it? Could any of them ever trust him again, especially her mam?

Suddenly, she realised Bella was crying softly. She thrust all her doubts and anxieties to the back of her mind and put her arm around the girl's thin shoulders. 'Hush, hush now, Bella. You're going to stay with us, I'm sure of it. We'll take care of you,' she soothed, for she couldn't countenance the idea that her mam would turn the girl out. Bella would always be a constant reminder of her father's betrayal, and they would never be a close, loving, trusting family again, but she knew her mother would never take it out on Bella.

'I glad I can stay, Joan,' Bella sobbed. '*Obrigada!* Thank you, but I . . . I can't forget . . .'

111

'Forget what?' Joan asked cautiously, wondering if there were more revelations about her father yet to come.

'The man. The man on the ship . . .' The girl's sobs increased and Joan sat up and gathered her into her arms.

'What man? What . . . what did he do, Bella?'

'He find me. He bring me food but . . . but he try to do . . . bad things . . .'

Joan held her closer. 'Oh, God!'

Bella raised a tear-stained face, her eyes filled with terror. 'But I scream and scream and kick and scratch and . . . other men come. They hit him and take him away and then take me to see the *Capitão*. I hope I safe then from the man, and I was . . . but I pray, always I pray . . . and am afraid, until I get to Liverpool.'

Joan stroked the tangled dark curls. Oh, the poor girl! What a terrible experience she'd suffered. It must have been bad enough for her stowing away, trying to exist in some dark, cold, damp cupboard or such like, hungry, thirsty and terrified, but then . . . 'Hush now, Bella, luv. You're safe with us now. Nothing and no one is going to harm you, I promise.'

'You so kind, Joan. You my . . . sister?' The girl was clearly intelligent and, despite all the traumas she'd suffered, had realised that her father obviously had another family. That must have been a terrible shock for her too.

Joan smiled at her. 'Yes, Bella. I'm your sister.'

'That I like, I . . . I miss my mama so much, Joan.'

Joan stroked her hair. 'I'm sure you do, but you've got us . . . me now, and I'll look out for you.'

Bella smiled back. 'I happy now, Joan.'

'And safe. Now, go to sleep, Bella,' she urged.

It was a long time before she finally closed her eyes. But when she did, she had determined one thing. And that was that no man was going to use her the way her mam, Bella's mother and Bella herself had been used, hurt and humiliated.

# Chapter Twelve

———◆◆◆———

Gradually, in the days that followed, Olive began to feel like she was no longer walking in a dream. She'd made her decision – hard as it had been – and as there were practical things she needed to attend to, it was something of a relief. The child was still wary of her, and of Charlie, although she seemed more at ease with Joan. She'd discussed with both her daughter and Nelly how she would explain things to Bella and was relieved once she'd heard what Joan had to say.

'Mam, she already realises Da's my father too, as well as Charlie's, and that she's our half-sister,' Joan informed her mother. 'I told her we're her new family and that Liverpool is home now, not Lisbon. What she thinks about it all, I don't know. She's said nothing, but she seems to have accepted it – although she hates the cold weather, and I can't say I blame her.'

'And she understands that . . . he . . . Billy won't be home for a while yet?' Olive pressed.

Joan nodded, uneasy with the whole matter. 'She does, and

114

I hope by the time he gets home she'll have settled in more.'

It was Nelly who continued the conversation. 'And when Billy gets home, does the girl realise that there will be . . . problems?' She cast a knowing glance at Olive, thinking there would be fireworks, never mind 'problems' – and the child would be at the centre of everything.

Joan shrugged. 'I don't know . . . but I don't think so.'

'We . . . we've got time to sort that out, Nell,' Olive said, although she was loath to even speak about him.

'Then first things first: she'll have to go to school, or you'll have the School Board down on you because *someone* round here is bound to stick their oar in. Even if she can't speak much English, let alone write it, they'll want her at school. I'll come along with you, luv, to see them at St George's Juniors – if you want me to, that is,' Nelly offered.

'I'd be grateful of that, Nell. I just hope she doesn't start acting up about it. I don't think I could cope with any tantrums!'

'Surely, she'll have been at school back in Portugal? Joan, you'll just have to make her understand that she's got another two years at least at school here. We'll have to get her tidied up a bit first; she looks like a little ragamuffin.'

'That's not her fault, she'll look fine once she's had a good bath and puts on those clothes you brought for her, Mrs Savage. Do you think Monica could do something with her hair?' Joan urged, a little annoyed at Nelly's remark. 'It curls naturally, but at the moment it's just so tangled and matted it's a real mess. No wonder though; it's probably not had a comb through it for weeks.'

So Bella had been given a bath in the tin tub in front of the kitchen fire – and Monica had patiently and painstakingly combed the tangles out of the long, dark curly hair before washing it – and gently towelling it dry. Then she'd combed it again and plaited it. She smiled at the girl, passing over a hand mirror. 'There, you look lovely now, Bella.' And she did too, she thought, dressed in a bright cherry-red knitted jumper and a red-and-navy-plaid skirt, colours that suited her. She no longer looked like a little waif.

Bella stared hard at her reflection. 'I not look like me!'

'You look much tidier, Bella, and it will be easy to comb out now. They won't let you wear it loose for school,' Monica informed her, mouthing the word 'nits' to Olive and Joan.

'And that we can do without! I have to sleep in the same bed!' Joan commented.

True to her word, Nelly accompanied Olive to see the headmistress of the girls' section of the local junior school. After Olive had explained, somewhat cautiously, how Bella had come to live with her, it was agreed that she should start the following Monday. She would be in the same class as Eileen Savage, they being of a similar age and, more than likely, aptitude. The headmistress had expressed some doubts as to Bella's level of education, which she'd found Olive to be very vague about.

'Oh, her English is good, Miss Forshaw,' Olive impressed upon the teacher.

'And so are her manners,' Nelly added.

'Maybe, but can she read and write in English? I doubt it, and we don't know what her arithmetic is like . . . and I assume you have all her papers, birth certificate, passport et cetera?'

'Not yet, Miss Forshaw,' Olive replied carefully. 'Things

were all rather . . . confused at the time she left. But we've got the matter in hand.'

'Although heaven knows when they'll finally get here. That country is having serious problems at the moment, what with that Salazar feller,' Nelly added, having heard this from Arthur, who took an interest in world affairs.

'I'm well aware of what's going on in the world, Mrs Savage. Well, we shall have to see how Bella progresses,' were the headmistress's final comments, and with that they had to be content.

Eileen wasn't very happy about the fact that she would have to take Bella to school and introduce her to the other girls in the class and show her around. 'Why do I have to do it, Mam?' she complained to Nelly, the morning Bella was to start school.

'I thought you would have been pleased to do it. Miss Forshaw wants to see how she settles and just what kind of education she's had in Lisbon. And I'm sure it would help Bella if she had someone to help her find her way around.'

'And I bet there isn't another child in that entire school who speaks two languages or who has travelled so far on their own!' Monica remarked, before she'd left for work.

Eileen pulled a face at her sister while Nelly's back was turned and went to call for Bella, thinking, however, that her elder sister was right. Bella might prove to be something of an attraction, with her dark foreign looks and accented English. Being able to show her off might add to her popularity at school, given she was Bella's friend and neighbour. That thought cheered her up a bit as she negotiated the still-icy pavement to Olive's house.

\* \* \*

Bella had gone off to school without any complaints or tantrums, for which Olive was extremely thankful. She could see the girl was very apprehensive – even scared – but she hoped she'd settle down fairly quickly. Young Eileen Savage had promised cheerfully to look after her and make sure she was included in the games at playtime, and she really did hope that Bella wouldn't have too traumatic a day. At least the girl was now dressed for the weather, for she'd gone to Paddy's Market on Saturday afternoon with Joan and Bella and they'd found a good-quality coat in a dark green wool that obviously hadn't had much wear; it fitted the girl well and only cost a shilling. Nelly, who was always knitting, had provided a scarf, mittens and tam-o'-shanter in a bright red, so now Bella was warm and looked well too.

She had accompanied Nelly down to the corner shop when the older girls had gone to work and Eileen, Bella and Charlie had gone off to school. As usual, after the weekend, they both needed groceries. Ethel Newbridge had been given the same story about Bella as all the neighbours and Miss Forshaw, and had expressed her sympathy at the demise of Olive's fictitious sister. She was obviously a little suspicious about the whole story. But not having known Olive for very long, and knowing next to nothing about her family or background – something unusual in this neighbourhood – she decided to give her the benefit of the doubt and accept that Bella was her niece.

They had almost reached the top end of Mersey View when Nelly caught sight of Lily Cooper making her way carefully towards Olive's house, obviously coming from the tram stop. 'Looks like your Lily's having a bit of bother with the pavement in those heels,' she remarked.

Olive grimaced. 'She should have more sense and wear something sensible! She'll fall, and where will she be then? I was going to ask her to come and stay for a week or so, until the weather gets better, but now . . .'

Nelly nodded her understanding. 'I'll leave you to it, luv. How do you think she'll take the news?'

Olive pursed her lips and frowned. 'Oh, she'll have plenty to say all right!'

Nelly raised her eyes to the leaden grey sky. 'Go in and get the kettle on, she's bound to be frozen,' she urged, not envying her friend the task that lay ahead.

Olive did exactly that when she let herself and her elder sister into the kitchen. Thankfully, she had enough coal for the range, so at least the room was warm, she mused; while Lily shrugged off her imitation Persian lamb coat, draping it over the back of a chair as Olive took the cups from the dresser.

'I wish to God this weather would improve. I've that much time on my hands, it's driving me mad. We've washed, pressed, sponged and repaired every single garment and item in the entire theatre wardrobe. It's all in pristine condition now. Oh, it makes life easier when things are running normally, but dear God, it's boring!'

'I wish I'd had time to be bored,' Olive replied, pouring the tea and sitting down and preparing herself for what she now must tell her sister.

As Olive told her tale, Lily listened in silence, her eyes wide with astonishment and her scarlet-tinted lips pursed tightly in disapproval as Olive detailed everything that had happened in the last week.

'So you see, Lily, what choice did I have? I couldn't turn

the girl away, not after all the poor child had been through!'

'I can see that. But her mother did. Fancy telling the girl to come here, to a foreign country, and with no money! And surely she must have had some inkling that he would have family here – sisters, brothers, parents at least – and that the child might not be welcome?' Lily shrugged. 'Well, I suppose the woman was half out of her mind as to what to do about the girl. That's understandable in the circumstances.'

'I know, don't you think I've been over it all in my mind a hundred times?'

'So, what will you do now? What will you do when he finally gets home, or will you write to him?'

Olive sipped her tea and shrugged. 'I've decided not to write. I seldom do anyway, but I . . . I don't think I could put just how hurt and angry, shocked, betrayed and humiliated I feel into words.'

Lily reached across the table and patted Olive's hand. 'I don't suppose you can, and I don't think it would be wise to warn him. After all, if he doesn't know the girl is here in Liverpool, once he's face-to-face with you, he can't go making up all kinds of excuses.'

'Just what kind of excuses could he make, Lily? She's *here*! She's got proof, and the worst part is knowing that he . . . he's been carrying on for *years*! She's twelve, the same age as our Charlie! Oh, I should have known, Lily! I should never have believed all his lies about him loving only me and never being unfaithful! I should have known better, with his past record! I should have *known*, Lily!'

Lily tutted. 'He always did think he was God's gift to women! Fancied himself as a bit of a Casanova, as Mam used to say. You were too good for him, Olive. You were the best-looking girl in our street – in the neighbourhood – you could have done better, and you know it. And then there was . . . !' Lily's voice trailed off, knowing her sister knew only too well what lay unsaid between them, although in fact she herself had often been described as the better-looking of the two attractive sisters.

'Oh, Lily! Don't go dragging all that up again! I know full well Mam couldn't stand him, and why –'

'That's an understatement!' Lily interrupted, bubbling with fury at the way her sister had been treated.

Olive looked down, her eyes welling up with tears. 'But I . . . I loved . . . love him! I always have done.'

Lily was incredulous. 'Even after this? Lying, cheating and leaving his other daughter for you to bring up? No thought about how you'd feel!'

Her words were like daggers in Olive's heart, but she soldiered on regardless. 'But no one knows she's his daughter. Nelly came up with the story that she . . . she's my niece. That I had another sister who lived in Portugal but who died, so –'

'Oh, that's really worthy of a fairy story! Do people actually believe it?' Lily demanded scathingly.

Olive nodded. 'So far they do. She . . . she must take after her mother because she certainly doesn't look like Billy.'

'Then I suppose they'll all think she's my niece too! God, Olive, what a performance! I just hope that when he gets home you'll give him the length of your tongue and show him the door! But make damned sure he provides for that girl, as well as you and the kids. She's not your responsibility!'

Olive didn't reply. She wasn't sure what she would do when

she finally came face-to-face with Billy. Despite everything she did still love him – and what would the consequences be if she refused to have anything more to do with him? They'd starve, or near enough. He was the breadwinner, no matter how erratic his earnings might be, and she depended upon him completely. They all did, and now so did Bella. Oh, it was fine for Lily to get on her high horse and tell her to throw him out; her sister was an independent woman without the responsibilities of children, and able to earn her own living. The fact that her family had never liked or approved of Billy Copperfield had never bothered her, until now. But then, she'd known nothing of the double life he'd been living for all these years, until Bella had turned up on her doorstep and turned her world upside down.

# Chapter Thirteen

T he weeks that followed were tense for everyone in the Copperfield household as they all tried to adjust to the new situation and Olive struggled to come to terms with what Billy had done to her. To her relief Bella settled well in school. She was a bright child and eager to learn all she could, especially about her new city and country, and seemed to be happy living with them; she was particularly attached to Joan.

Nelly reported to Olive that Eileen had said that Bella was very quick at arithmetic and that her manners were much admired by all the teaching staff.

'And at least that should keep that Forshaw woman happy,' Nelly commented as she and Olive were walking back from the corner shop one cold morning in early March, chatting about how Bella was getting on.

'Let's just hope it takes her mind off the missing documents,' Olive replied, although thankfully no further mention had been made of them so far. The authorities appeared to accept that

Bella's parentage was British enough for her to be schooled here.

Nelly shifted her shopping bag to her other arm as she clutched her coat tightly around her, for a chill, blustery wind was scouring the streets of Everton Brow. 'Lord above, I thought by now this weather would have improved! I'm sick to death of it, and that poor little lass must feel it more than we do,' she added.

Olive sighed. 'She does, but she'll get used to it, in time – and anyway, in a few weeks, it should be getting warmer.' She refused to let herself even think that, next month, Billy was due home, so she changed the subject. 'I was very surprised, Nelly, to learn that Bella can sew – and sew very well.'

'Really?' her companion remarked, eyebrows raised in surprise.

'Yes, the hem of one of our Joan's overalls had come down and she was trying to mend it, and making a right mess of it, I might add – she was never a great one with the needle and thread. Bella was watching her and she took the overall from Joan and had the hem sewn up in no time – and such small, neat stitches. Our Joan was amazed, I can tell you, and so was I.'

'Did her mam teach her or did she learn at school, do you think? There's very few around here who can sew decently. I was fortunate; my mam taught me the basics. Nothing fancy, mind, you'd need to serve your time as a seamstress for that.'

'I asked her that, Nelly, and from what I can gather, her mam showed her to start with and then the nuns at school taught her the finer sewing and how to embroider.'

Nelly was impressed. 'She can do that at her age? I don't

know anyone who can embroider, our Eileen certainly can't. I might ask Bella to teach her, it would give the pair of them something to do on these long evenings.'

They had reached Nelly's house and the two women paused.

'You know, Olive, she might even be able to earn her living at it when she's older. I know the big expensive shops in town all employ women to do alterations, as well as some fancy sewing.'

Olive looked interested. 'I'd never thought of that, Nell, but I'll bear it in mind, thanks. She's going to have to work at something when she leaves school.'

'Have you time for a cup of tea, luv? That wind has me frozen to the bone,' Nelly enquired, and gratefully Olive accepted.

Bella's ability to sew was also the subject of discussion between Joan and Monica. Now that the evenings were getting both lighter and slightly warmer, they took it in turns to wait for each other at the tram stop at the top of Northumberland Terrace after work and would then walk home together.

'You mean she really can do embroidery? She's not just saying it?' Monica queried.

Joan nodded. 'She can, Mon, honestly. Oh, we haven't got the proper thread but she did a little design on the corner of a hankie in plain black sewing cotton, and it was really lovely.'

Monica looked thoughtful. 'Do you think if we bought some "silks", as I think they're called, between us she could embroider designs on things like the collars of blouses and dresses? To dress them up a bit, like? Make them look more expensive.'

Joan nodded eagerly. 'I bet she could.'

'But would she?'

'I don't see why not, she likes doing it – or so she says.'

'Well, I'll go into Lewis's in my lunch break one day and see what they've got in their haberdashery department and just how much these silks cost. And then – in return, like – I'll trim Bella's hair. I've just started to learn how to trim hair – today, in fact,' Monica informed her friend proudly.

Joan grinned at her. 'You've certainly improved in confidence, Mon – and in style – since you started there. I'd never have thought of asking our Bella to dress up some clothes for us.'

Monica grinned back. 'Do you know, Joan, that's the first time I've heard you call her "our" Bella?'

'Well, she *is* my half-sister.'

'And not half as much of a pain in the neck as our Eileen is, and she's my "full" sister,' Monica laughed.

Joan said nothing as she left her friend and walked the remaining distance home. She had accepted Bella – she liked her and felt sorry for her – but she hadn't . . . couldn't accept what her da had done. It made her feel somehow less of a person than she had been before she'd known about Bella, less 'special'. Not only was she no longer her da's only daughter but in some way she couldn't fully understand, she felt humiliated. She was also aware he was due home in a matter of weeks, and then all hell would break loose. And that was something she just didn't want to think about at all.

\* \* \*

The following week, Olive was tidying up the kitchen. She'd washed up the breakfast dishes and put them away, moved the blouse Bella was embroidering for Joan and the three skeins of embroidery silk to the cupboard in the bottom of the dresser for safety, swept the floor and brought more coal in for the range, when Nelly appeared, bringing a cake tin which she set on the table. 'That's just a little something, Olive, to thank Bella for the lovely job she's made of our Monica's best blouse. It could have been done professionally; I've never seen such fine work done by a child.'

Olive wiped her hands on her apron and smiled. 'That's good of you, Nell, but there's really no need. She enjoys it. In fact, she takes great pride in it. I intend to show the blouse she's doing for Joan to our Lily next time she deigns to call in.'

Nelly seated herself at the table and nodded as she glanced around the kitchen. 'That's a good idea. Your Lily might be able to do something to help – when the time comes.' She frowned and then gazed intently at the range. 'There's some very odd noises coming from your range, Olive,' she remarked. She shivered. 'And it seems a bit chilly in here.'

'I'd noticed that myself, Nell. I'll put more coal on and see if that makes a difference.'

Nelly watched as her friend and neighbour stoked up the fire in the range, but after a few minutes it was clear that the extra fuel had made no difference.

Olive stood back, staring at the range, perplexed. 'Isn't that all I need now, Nell? Something wrong with the damned range – and in this weather too.'

Nelly got up and poked tentatively at the fire with the brass poker. 'I'd say it's the back boiler, luv.'

Olive threw up her hands in despair. 'If that goes, Nell, I'll really be sunk! I'll have no hot water, no fire, no nothing!'

Before Nelly could reply, there was a bang and then a hissing noise and a huge cloud of steam issued from the range, followed by a rush of soot-coloured water which effectively doused the flames and trickled down the front of the oven and on to the hearth. 'Looks like it's gone, luv! What a flaming mess! And Arthur's on an early shift, so he's not here to help.'

'I'll have to go and see if Mr Garswood has gone to work. I just hope he hasn't; sometimes he goes in a bit later.'

Nelly nodded and sat down again. Maybe Frederick Garswood would still be at home, and maybe he could help, but she doubted it. A broken back boiler wasn't easy to sort out. It looked as if Olive would need to get hold of the landlord and get him to replace it – the boiler was his responsibility, after all. But it would all take time, and in the meanwhile . . . well, as Olive had said, no fire, no heat, no hot water, no cooking!

Slightly to Nelly's surprise, Olive returned a few minutes later with Frederick Garswood, who was looking just as perturbed as her friend.

'Well, let's have a quick look at it, Mrs Copperfield. From what you've said, it definitely sounds as if the back boiler's gone. It's probably been on the blink for a while; over time, and with the intense heat of the fire, the metal wears thin until finally a hole develops.' He probed the now-soggy black mess of coal, ash and water with the poker, and nodded. 'Yes, that's it. There's a fairly large hole there.'

Olive sank down beside her friend at the table and covered her face with her hands. 'Oh, I really, really could do without this! Now I'm going to have to go and see the landlord to get it repaired, and God knows how long that will take!'

'Don't fret, luv, I'll come with you. And I'll help you clean up the mess and then we'll try and sort something out,' Nelly offered, before turning to the man standing beside the range. A man she'd known for years and yet really *didn't* know at all. 'How come you're such an expert on boilers, Mr Garswood?'

'Because it's what I do, Mrs Savage. By trade I'm a plumber. I have a business, employing a few men, and we're often called on in cases like this. I operate from an office at the back of a small workshop and yard in Butler's Court, at the bottom of Everton Brow.'

Nelly was taken aback. Although there had always been much speculation between herself and Arthur as to just what Frederick Garswood did for a living, she had never expected him to have a plumbing business. That would be a lucrative enterprise, even if he did only employ a few men, so he wouldn't be short of money. But still he lived in this street. Another mystery.

He'd turned his attention back to Olive and smiled at her reassuringly. Over the months, he'd come to admire her greatly. She was a fine-looking woman, impressively self-sufficient, and managed her household well. She was always pleasant and made him very welcome whenever he came in to help with some task or other, and now she'd even taken in her niece, so he'd heard. He was glad to be of assistance. 'There's no need for you to have to go trailing down town to see the landlord, Mrs Copperfield. I'll send one of my men and the lad around, either this morning or this afternoon, and they'll have it all fixed up in no time, and then I'll just invoice your landlord with the costs.'

Olive beamed up at him, relief flooding her face, delighted that it would be fixed today and she would suffer so little inconvenience. 'Oh, would you, Mr Garswood? Would you really do that for me?'

He smiled back, his cheeks reddening a little. 'Of course, and I think it's time you started to call me Fred. We are neighbours, after all,' he added a little shyly.

'Oh, I couldn't! But I could call you . . . Frederick,' Olive replied, thinking that sounded more appropriate, for after all she didn't know him very well, despite him having been in the house to help out on previous occasions. She thought back to Christmas, and how well he and Billy had seemed to get on. She wondered fleetingly what he would think of Billy now if he learned the truth about Bella.

'That will do fine – and may I call you Olive?'

'Please do,' she urged, still smiling and trying to ignore the mess the filthy water was making of her kitchen floor.

'I'd better be off to the office, then. Expect the lads later on today; you'll have fire and hot water by this evening, I promise, Olive.'

'I can't thank you enough, Frederick,' she reciprocated as she showed him out.

'Well, that's a turn-up for the books, Olive!' Nelly remarked as her friend came back into the cold kitchen. 'Him owning his own business and employing people, and asking you to call him Fred! Never been heard of before in this street!'

Olive grinned at her. 'I'll call him anything just as long as I get that damned boiler fixed!'

Nelly rolled up her sleeves. 'And I don't blame you, luv. Now, let's try and get some of this mess cleaned up before those blokes arrive and traipse it all through the house. And I have to say, I think Fred Garswood's taken a shine to you, Olive.'

Olive said nothing. There was no use him 'taking a shine to her', as Nelly put it. As far as he was concerned, she was a respectable married woman with two children and a niece to bring up. Nevertheless, she was very grateful for his assistance, and there was no harm in being on friendly terms with him. She'd try to find some little thing she could do by way of thanking him for his kindness; maybe she'd bake him a cake, or maybe she could invite him in for his lunch one weekend?

True to his word, the boiler was replaced that very afternoon, so when Charlie and Bella got home from school and Joan arrived home from work, the kitchen was warm and there was a pan of stew simmering on the range. Olive had determined to ask her neighbour in to share a meal with them on Sunday. After all, it was the least she could do to repay his kindness, and she suspected that beneath his dignified exterior he was often lonely.

# Chapter Fourteen

———◦◦◦◦———

Olive was even more grateful for Frederick Garswood's help as she glanced around her clean, tidy and warm kitchen the following afternoon when Lily called on her, bringing a small bunch of early daffodils. 'I thought they'd cheer you up, Olive. It's been a long, miserable winter all right, but finally spring is here.'

Olive smiled at her sister as she took off her hat and tweaked a curl into place with the aid of the small mirror on the wall, its frame made of coloured seashells – one of the souvenirs Billy had brought over the years. 'It's not often I get flowers! I'll root out a vase – you're right, these will brighten the place up no end. It was thoughtful of you, Lily.'

Lily opened her handbag, took out a small enamelled cigarette case and extracted a cigarette, before offering the case to Olive.

'You know I haven't smoked for years, Lil. I can't afford to,' Olive reminded her sibling, placing a little beaten-copper ashtray on the table as Lily produced a book of matches, lit her cigarette and inhaled.

'So, how are things now? How is Bella? Has she settled, or is she causing you trouble and upset?' Lily probed, through a cloud of smoke.

Olive put the kettle on and took two mugs down from the dresser. 'Thank God, she's really settled well, Lil. She seems to have got over that terrible journey and losing her mam, and she likes school. She follows our Joan around like a little lap dog. I have to say, Joan's very good with her, and I think that's helped the child a lot. I know that she still misses her mam, but that's only natural. She's not that keen on our Charlie, though,' she added.

'Well, you can't blame her for that, Olive. I know he's my only nephew, but you have to agree, he can be very . . . trying, at times. Has he still got that flea-bitten mongrel?'

'Oh, yes. But despite my misgivings, he does look after the animal.'

Her sister sniffed. 'I suppose that's something.'

Olive put the two mugs of tea on the table as Lily stubbed out her cigarette in the ashtray.

'I want to show you something, Lil,' Olive announced, delving into the cupboard in the bottom half of the dresser.

Lily looked on, a bemused smile playing around the corners of her lips as her sister placed the garment carefully on the table in front of her. 'Yes, it's a blouse, Olive,' she stated. 'One of yours, or is it Joan's?'

'Joan's – and just take a look at the collar,' she urged.

'It's embroidered. It's very nice; she must have paid quite a bit for it, she's got good taste. So?' Lily queried, raising her finely pencilled eyebrows.

'Bella did the embroidery. She's done one for Monica Savage too.'

Lily's eyebrows went higher. 'That *child* did this?' She held the garment closer for inspection as Olive nodded, smiling.

'She's gifted, Olive. I mean that.'

'I know, Lil, and I was thinking that maybe when she leaves school she could get a job in the likes of Henderson's or the Bon Marché or Cripps, doing alterations and the like.'

'And be paid a pittance and ruin her eyesight into the bargain! She could do better than that, Olive.' Lily took a sip of her tea, looking thoughtful. 'Maybe I could get her a job, working with me. Train her up as a wardrobe mistress; she could get a job in any theatre in the land then, and the pay's not bad. But it's all a bit premature, love. She's got years yet before she leaves school, and she might be better doing something else, training to be a tailoress or dressmaker . . .' She paused meaningfully. 'Now, have you decided what you are going to say to *him* when he gets home? How long is it now?'

Olive sighed heavily, the pain of betrayal twisting again in her heart. 'Three weeks, and I'm not going down to meet him this time.'

'Won't he think that's odd? You usually do.'

'I'm not starting a row in public and making a show of myself,' Olive replied firmly. 'Things are bad enough, without that.'

Lily nodded her agreement. 'Was the ship – what was it, the *Hubert*? – calling into Lisbon on the way home?'

'No. I made sure of that; I went down to the office to find out.'

'So, he won't know Bella's here or that the child's mother died?'

'No,' Olive replied firmly, 'and I don't think anyone in Lisbon would have thought to notify him – why would they? – Bella insists she has no relatives there. Would anyone even know how to contact him?' For nights now, she'd lain awake, turning over in her mind just what she'd say to Billy, wondering how he would react.

Lily finished her tea. 'Oh, I'd love to see his face when he's confronted with Bella, I really would, Olive. But just you remember, luv, it's his responsibility to provide for that child – and to try to make it up to you and the kids for what he's done.'

'I know, Lil, but I don't think I'll ever be able to really forgive and forget. Once he's away again, I'll be wondering . . . how will I ever trust him again?'

Lily nodded solemnly, thinking her sister was mad to even think about trying to forgive Billy Copperfield, particularly considering the position he'd left her in, although she was the only one nowadays who knew about that. But then what else could Olive do? She now had another kid to bring up, as well as her own two.

It was a subject that was playing on Joan's mind too, and she knew it was also troubling Bella, for the girl had asked when her father would be home and Joan had seen her looking anxious and biting her lip when she thought no one was watching her. 'Don't worry, Bella. Everything will work out

135

just fine,' she'd said, trying to allay the girl's fears. 'There might be some arguments and a bit of shouting at first, but things will soon calm down.' Joan had sincerely hoped her words would prove to be true, but she didn't hold out much hope of the next few months being serene and worry free.

'What will you say to him?' Monica asked as they sat in Nelly's parlour with a copy of the magazine Lily had left on her last visit to her sister. Monica had begged her mother to let them sit in there for a bit of privacy, intimating that Joan wanted to talk to her about her father's return, and Nelly had agreed, knowing the girl would need all the support she could get.

'I don't know, and that's the honest truth, Mon. I've been thinking about it a lot and . . . I suppose it depends on just what Mam intends to say to him. I've got a feeling she's not going to mince her words, and I don't blame her.'

'So there will be a huge row? Will she throw him out, do you think?'

Joan bit her lip. 'I don't know, but I don't think so. How would we manage without his wages? But you never know. I'm trying not to think about that. So, what do I say? Mam will have given him down the banks, and I really don't want to make matters worse. But he's *got* to know how I feel too.'

Monica could see her friend's position, and she didn't envy her. 'And poor Bella will be stuck in the middle of it all. She'll think it's all her fault.'

'I know, but it's *not*! Poor kid, what else could she do but come to Liverpool, like her mother told her to. She's been through enough.'

'She's bound to get involved – he is still her da, Joan.'

Joan sighed. 'Oh, it's all such a flaming mess, Mon! Why did he have to do it?'

Monica could see her friend was getting very upset. 'Oh, he'll have learned his lesson, Joan,' she replied confidently. 'I'm sure he wouldn't be such an idiot again.'

'Oh, I hope so! Sometimes I can forget about it all for ages, usually when I'm at work. But then when I get home and see Bella . . . I remember, and then I start torturing myself again with the questions. Why did he do it? Why carry on like that for all those years – and all the secrecy? Would he ever have told us if Bella hadn't come to Liverpool? Didn't he love Mam and me and Charlie enough that he had to have another family? Was he not happy when he was home with us? He certainly wasn't at Christmas, Mon. You remember?'

It was Monica's turn to nod. Yes, Billy Copperfield hadn't seemed at all happy to spend Christmas with his family and had only seemed to liven up when another sea voyage was in the offing. 'How is your Charlie taking it? Does he fully understand?'

'I think so. Mam tried to explain it all to him as best she could, and he didn't say much, he didn't cry or shout or anything. He's been a bit quieter, but he seems to get on all right with Bella. I sometimes wonder if he really understands she's his half-sister, or is he just ignoring the fact? I don't even know if he'll start on Da too, though I doubt it. He never really tells you what he's thinking, Mon. He's deep is our Charlie.'

'I've thought that myself, Joan, but he's not dense. I'm sure he realises Bella's related to him, and he's just kept his mouth shut about her not being his cousin. So has our Eileen – which is nothing short of a miracle. I don't know what Mam threatened her with, but it's certainly working.'

Joan managed a bit of a grin. 'Maybe she bribed her.'

Monica didn't reply but continued to look serious. 'Perhaps after all the shouting's over, Joan, you could get a few minutes on your own with your da and tell him how you feel – without yelling at him, I mean. He'll have had enough of that.'

'I don't know if I could keep my temper with him, Mon.'

'At least give him a chance to try to explain, Joan.'

'What is there to explain?' Joan demanded hotly. 'He wasn't happy with Mam – so he went and found someone else!'

'But he might not have wanted to hurt your mam, or you and Charlie, so that's why it's all been a secret for so long.'

'Why are you standing up for him?' Joan demanded indignantly.

'I'm just trying to help – to help you, Joan.'

Joan tossed the unopened magazine aside. 'Oh, I know, but I really don't think anyone can help. It's done. He's hurt us all terribly – including Bella. He left that poor kid alone with a sick mother – she must have been terrified, but he obviously didn't care.'

'All I'm saying, Joan, is give him a chance to explain.'

'Oh, I'll be so glad when it's all over and done with – whatever the outcome – and he's gone back to sea again. He'll be out of sight, and at least then we might be able to pick up the pieces and try to be like a normal family.'

'I hope so, Joan. I really, really do,' Monica replied sincerely, before getting to her feet. 'Come on, let's go back into the kitchen. It's cold in here, and we could both do with a cup of tea.'

As they drank their tea, nothing more was said about Billy's imminent return. Instead, Monica confided to her friend her progress with the serious and complicated art of cutting hair, which she assured Joan was far from easy.

'What I really need is some practice.' She glanced surreptitiously at her mother, who was, as usual, knitting. 'I've sort of hinted to Mam about me having a go on our Eileen's hair – I mean, it won't matter so much if I make a mess of it. It already looks as if someone stuck a basin on her head and cut around it.'

'I thought that's exactly what your mam did,' Joan hissed back, a look of mischief in her dark eyes.

Monica was glad to see her friend's spirits seemed to have revived a bit. 'You know full well she doesn't! But anyway, she won't let me. "Not yet," she said. How am I ever going to improve, with attitudes like that?'

Joan could see Monica's point, and an idea had begun to form in her mind. 'What if I ask Bella if she would like you to cut her hair? You've already trimmed it, and it was all right. What if she lets you take a few more inches off it? It would make it so much easier for her to manage – as it is, it takes ages to dry.'

'Would you, Joan? I'd do my best, I promise. Maybe she'd like it a bit shorter . . . it might make her look a bit older. And what with your da coming home, surely she'll want to look . . . decent?'

Joan silently dismissed this part of her friend's thinking. It struck her as a little tactless, although she wouldn't have said so for the world. Monica was her friend, and in her book you didn't go out of your way to upset friends. 'I'll see what she says, but don't go getting all upset and disappointed if she refuses.'

'Oh, I won't, but it would be a great help,' Monica replied brightly.

To Monica's delight, Bella agreed to the friends' plan. Joan brought her round to Nelly's a week later, after they'd had the evening meal and she'd helped Olive tidy away.

Nelly eyed them both sceptically. 'You're sure about this, the pair of you?' she queried. 'I don't want any hysterics if she makes a right mess of it, Bella.'

Bella smiled, her dark eyes sparkling. 'I no have hysterics, Mrs Savage. I like the way Monica cut my hair before. She is good hairdresser, yes?'

'See, Mam, someone's got faith in me! Right, Bella, I'm going to wash your hair in the scullery and then we'll come in here while I cut it.' She shot a quick glance at Nelly. 'It's all right, Mam, I'll put newspaper down on the floor.'

Bella nodded her agreement. Maybe she would look much nicer for when her father got home, for she was looking forward so much to seeing him again and wanted him to be happy that she had made it safely to Liverpool. Thanks to both Olive and to Monica's mother, she now had nice warm clothes and stockings and boots. She was doing well at school, and everyone thought her embroidery was nothing short of miraculous – which amused her, for she saw nothing unusual in it. All the girls of her age at school in Lisbon had been reasonably good at needlework, but it made her feel glad when people praised her. She so wanted her papa to be proud of her – and hopefully, with her hair cut, she would look really nice for him, even though she realised that her arriving in Liverpool would probably cause great trouble.

Monica worked slowly and methodically, as she was being taught, careful not to cut too much off at once. 'Remember, Miss Monique, work slowly. You can't stick it back on again!' was the mantra Helen Marshall had instilled in her. When she'd finally finished, both Joan and Nelly agreed that those few inches made all the difference, but to cut more off would probably make it difficult for Bella to manage herself. Monica towel-dried it and then set the damp strands in large, loose pin curls.

'It already curls naturally, so does she need it pinned?' Joan asked.

'Yes, left to dry on its own it will just fly everywhere. Pinned, it will at least be curly but with some shape to it,' Monica replied firmly. That much she did know.

They all had a cup of tea while Bella sat on the rug in front of the range to dry her hair. When Monica judged it was dry enough to brush out, Joan and Nelly sat back to admire the result. Bella, her cheeks flushed from the fire, looked a little apprehensive.

'It . . . it is good?' Bella asked tentatively as Monica fiddled with the curls around her face.

'Joan, pass me that mirror off the dresser, would you, please?' Monica asked, feeling very pleased with herself at the results. Bella's hair now came to just above her shoulders and fell in soft curls around her face. It did make her look older, but it also made her look very, very pretty. She could see that Eileen, who had watched the proceedings avidly from her seat at the other side of the table, was very impressed by her sister's handiwork.

Joan passed the mirror to her half-sister, and Bella gazed at her reflection and gasped. 'Monica! It . . . I . . . look wonderful!'

Monica smiled around at her friend, mother and sister. 'She does, doesn't she? I told you, Mam, I could do it! Now will you believe me?'

Nelly nodded, impressed. Of course, Bella had naturally curling hair. She wondered how Monica would manage on someone with hair as straight as Eileen's.

'Good,' Monica said triumphantly, 'perhaps now you'll let me cut our Eileen's hair, and maybe even yours?'

Eileen jumped off her chair in delight. 'Will you, Monica? Will you make me look like Bella?'

'I can't promise that, but I'll try and give you a decent haircut,' Monica said as Joan got to her feet.

At least Bella was happy with her new image, Joan thought, as she at last managed to prise the mirror away from the girl. 'You look lovely, Bella. Let's go home now and show Mam.'

Bella beamed at her. 'Joan, you think she will like it too?'

Joan nodded. You couldn't help but warm to Bella. Looking at her, she realised that the girl must resemble her dead mother. She wondered how her da would react on seeing his younger daughter, and hearing the woman he seemed to have loved alongside his wife was dead. Bella was looking forward to his return – she'd told her that – even though the rest of the family were not. She wondered if the girl knew what the return of Billy Copperfield might bring.

# Chapter Fifteen

———◆·◆··◆·◆———

Olive had cleaned the house from top to bottom on the Saturday prior to the Sunday when Billy was due home. It had given her a much-needed outlet for her nervous energy; she was so consumed with apprehension and simmering anger she couldn't sit still. She'd ascertained from the Journal of Commerce that the MV *Hubert* would come upriver on the morning tide and dock at approximately eleven o'clock. That meant Billy would arrive in Mersey View at about noon, having been paid off and made his way home.

She took rather more care with her appearance than usual. Did she really look as old as she felt? she wondered, as she examined her features in the dressing-table mirror. It was as if a huge cloud of butterflies were dancing manically in her stomach. She just wished the whole ordeal over. No matter the outcome, she surely couldn't feel any worse than she did now. Slowly, she dressed herself in the skirt of her red costume and her best black taffeta blouse, and put on the pair of red earrings Lily had lent her.

She had prepared the meal, as she usually did on a Sunday, and then left Joan downstairs in charge of keeping her eye on the joint of mutton cooking slowly in the oven and finishing off seeing to the vegetables, while Bella had dutifully begun setting the table, leaving Olive free to go up to dress. They'd all need something to eat at some time today, she'd told Joan. Both Joan and Bella were already dressed in their best clothes and while Joan seemed far calmer than she herself did, Bella was obviously both excited and apprehensive. As they worked in the kitchen, she stayed close to Joan, her large dark eyes following her half-sister's every movement.

When Olive went downstairs she found only the two girls were there. 'Where's Charlie?' she asked, a little sharply, for she'd had the usual battle to make him get a decent wash, comb his hair, make sure his socks were pulled up and that the much-hated, starched Eton collar was not twisted and sitting under one ear.

'He's gone out, Mam. He's taken Rags for a long walk, he said he hoped you wouldn't mind, but he'd sooner not be here when Da gets home!' Joan replied, peering intently at the pan of potatoes that were coming up to the boil and wishing she was anywhere but here.

'Well, I do mind! I wanted you all here when . . .'

Joan looked sadly at her mother. 'I know, Mam, but well . . . maybe our Charlie just couldn't face it all. I . . . I think he feels more deeply upset than he's letting on.'

Olive frowned as she tied an apron over her good clothes and prepared to make a start on the gravy. Perhaps Joan was right. Charlie hadn't said much on the subject of his da at all. Who knew what he was feeling?

'Do you think he'll stop off for a pint, Mam?' Joan asked tentatively, thinking that, not finding the usual welcoming party at the dock gates, her father might celebrate his return with a pint or two in The Baltic Fleet before catching the tram home, particularly as it was a Sunday.

'I don't know, luv, but I hope not.'

Joan sighed; all they could do now was wait. Her nerves felt as if they were strung out like piano wires.

Just after the clock on the mantel had finished striking twelve noon, they heard his key in the lock and the sound of the front door opening, then his footsteps on the lino of the lobby floor. Joan cast a quick smile of support at her mother and stood up, taking Bella's hand in her own. This was the first time in her life that she had not been happy and excited to see her da.

He looked the same as usual, she thought, as he dumped his sea bag on the floor and grinned around at them.

'I thought at least one of you might have come down to meet me,' he remarked. But as he caught sight of Bella the grin vanished, to be replaced by a look of surprise that instantly turned to recognition and concern. 'What the hell is . . . she . . . doing here?' he at last managed to get out.

Olive folded her arms and glared at him. 'Well might you ask, Billy Copperfield! I take it you never intended me to find out that you had taken up with someone else . . . and had another family in Lisbon? No wonder you know the place so well and can even speak some of the language. I should have flaming well known, especially after our early days together!'

Billy was frantically trying to gather his thoughts. 'Olive, let me . . . let me . . . explain!'

145

'Oh, please do! Joan and I can't wait for you to explain why you've betrayed and humiliated us without a thought for our feelings!' Olive shot back sarcastically. 'Do tell us, Billy, why you preferred to spend your time, money and affections on Maria Isabella Ferreira Silva – or did she call herself Copperfield – and little Bella here?'

Before Billy had time to try to reply, Bella rushed to his side and grabbed his hand, gazing up at him and smiling. 'Papa, are you glad that I come to Liverpool? Are you happy to see me?'

Instantly Billy shook off her hand. 'For God's sake, Bella, shut up! Now is not the time to be asking things like that!'

Bella drew back, looking shocked and hurt.

'Da! That's downright cruel!' Joan cried, outraged, rushing to put her arm around Bella, who had dissolved into tears.

'I didn't mean that!' Billy blustered.

Olive was further incensed by his behaviour. 'Joan's right! She's just a child, Billy! Her mother died and she did what Maria had told her to do – came to Liverpool to find you – but she had no money for her fare, so she stowed away. Yes, she actually stowed away! Twelve years of age, alone with no money, terrified and prey to that filthy swine who tried to molest her. She arrived in the middle of winter, with hardly any clothes on her back! So, don't you dare try to tell me you care anything for her! You care as much for her as you do for us, Billy! Not a jot!' She was shaking with pent-up fury and humiliation as she turned to Joan. 'Take her up to Nelly's, luv, and stay there until I come up for you. What I've got to say to *him* isn't fit for her ears – or yours either, come to that.'

Without a word, Joan guided the still-sobbing and confused

Bella towards the door, wondering if, when her mam came up to Nelly's, her da would still be a part of this family.

Billy had sunk down in a chair by the table and had covered his face with his hands. He was still trying to recover from the shock. He'd never intended things to get to this stage. He'd thought he had everything neatly organised up until now, but he'd not envisaged Maria dying – she was still young – and it was another blow he'd not expected. He'd spent as much time as he could with both Olive and Maria and gave them both as much money as he could afford. After all, he was fond of all his children, and it hadn't bothered him a great deal that what he was doing was morally wrong. The two women lived worlds apart, and at the end of the day everyone had been happy, until now . . .

Olive faced him squarely, her hands on her hips. 'Right, Billy, I want an explanation. A proper explanation – not a pack of lies dressed up in fancy words. I know how long this . . . this state of affairs has been going on! Ever since our Charlie was a baby – he's the same age as Bella! What did I do wrong? What did I say? Did you just fall out of love with me? Was that it? God knows you chased me for long enough; you swore I was the best catch in the whole neighbourhood, and you worshipped the ground I walked on, said you'd always be faithful because you knew I was the only one you truly loved! And fool that I am, I bloody believed you! When did all that end?'

Billy looked up at her, his face haggard. 'Olive, it was nothing like that, luv!'

'Don't you "luv" me! Don't you bloody well dare, Billy!'

'I . . . I . . . love . . . loved you both. It's not easy to explain, but I did . . . do. Oh, you've no idea what it's like, Olive, being away at sea for months on end. No wife, no family, no home life or comforts . . .'

Olive's temper, which she'd been struggling to hold in check, finally got the better of her. '*I* have no idea what it's like, being on my own!' she screamed at him. 'Scrimping and saving, having to be mother and father to two kids with no support from you when I needed it. When they were sick or I was sick, you were never around! *I* got little love or care from you when *I* needed it! I can't find the words to tell you just how much you've hurt and humiliated me! How can you possibly love two women at the same time, Billy? I don't understand that! How could you live with all the lies and secrecy? It was bad enough for me, but you left that poor woman to die alone! Did you even know or care that she was ill? Did you ever think how that poor child was coping? How can you say you loved her? Loved them? The only person you love, Billy Copperfield, is *you*!'

Wrapping her arms around herself, she began to pace the floor as waves of pain, bitterness and humiliation washed over her. 'Oh, my mam warned me! She begged me not to take up with you and disgrace her and the entire family, and so did our Lily! Can you not understand what you've done to me, Billy? How you've destroyed my life, never mind my trust in you? How much you've hurt Joan and Charlie? I don't know how that lad feels about it all, but I shouldn't wonder if it's scarred him emotionally for life! He always looked up to you, Billy. He idolised you – you were always his wonderful da, who could do no wrong! Well, not any more! Joan's in pieces too, though she's trying not to show it. How the hell are we all going to cope in the future? We'll not be able to believe a single thing you say. Oh, it's going to take a long, long time for those kids to get over this, if they ever do! What have you done, Billy Copperfield?'

'Olive, I'm sorry! Truly I am! I never meant . . .' Billy pleaded.

She turned on him. 'Oh no! You never meant to get found out, did you? You're not sorry you did it; you're just sorry you got caught! And how many more are there, Billy? Do you have a woman in every port, and more families? I swear to God, I wish you'd just gone to the brothels, like most of your shipmates, if you were that desperate!'

'No! No, I swear there's no one else. There's no more!'

'And you expect me to believe you?'

'Olive, you're so upset that you're not thinking straight! It's impossible! I couldn't afford it, for one thing – and I've not the time or inclination, for another.'

'You managed the time in Lisbon!' she snapped back.

Billy reached out and grabbed her hands, although she tried desperately to twist out of his grip. 'Olive, I'm sorry. I really mean that. Can't we put all this behind us and try to sort things out?'

Some of her anger was fading as she stared at him. She'd loved him – maybe she still loved him, even now – but she couldn't believe him, and every instinct was urging her to throw him out. But how could she? There was the kids' future to think of. 'It's not as easy as all that, Billy. It . . . it's a terrible thing you've done to us all.'

Billy let out his breath slowly, seeing the anger fading in her eyes. 'I know it will take you time, Olive. But I swear I never meant to hurt anyone, and I swear I didn't know that

Maria was dead . . . or even ill. I never expected Bella to come here.'

Olive nodded. That much was probably true. 'The child was alone; she didn't want to go into an orphanage. She told us so.'

Billy frowned, still feeling as if the foundations of his world had been rocked. He was deeply uneasy and unsure of himself, but at least Olive was starting to be reasonable. Maybe, just maybe, he could salvage something from the situation, although he doubted he'd be welcome in his wife's bed for a long time to come – if ever again. But he only had himself to blame for that. 'Bella does have relatives, Olive, two aunts and two uncles. But the family cut Maria off when –'

'Can you blame them?' Olive snapped, although this she hadn't known. Obviously, Bella's mother had come from a decent family, which meant there were more lives that Billy's loose morals and selfishness had blighted. 'It took a lot of guts for her to come all this way with no money, and I wasn't exaggerating when I said she was molested. She fought him off – the brave little soul – and then the Captain and the rest of the crew looked after her well enough until she got here.'

Olive felt suddenly utterly exhausted and sat down wearily at the table. It was as if all her emotions had completely drained away.

Billy sat beside her. 'You've been good to her, Olive. Thank you.'

'What else could I do? I couldn't turn her away, and she's a nice child, well brought up. She's bright and loves school, and she's really taken to our Joan – and Joan is very good with her, despite the age gap and the . . . situation.'

'And you'll be happy enough to keep her here?' he probed. All this sounded promising.

Olive remembered Lily's words. 'As long as you increase the allotment, Billy. We can't live on fresh air.'

Billy nodded his agreement. Well, he wouldn't have money stopped out of his wages and sent to Portugal now. At least he'd have a bit more in his pocket to spend on himself. He worked hard enough for it; he deserved a bit of pleasure in his life, and he could see that now there would be little of it either here or in Lisbon.

With a huge effort Olive stood up and took off her apron. She'd had her say, and she felt utterly spent. They'd all just have to try to put the past behind them and make the most of the future – there was no other course open to her. 'I'll go up to Nelly's and get the girls. And I've a good idea where our Charlie is too – helping Arthur with his pigeons, he often does. It seems to be the lad's bolt-hole these days, and at least Arthur's good enough to spend the time with him.' She sighed heavily. 'Everyone must be starving by now – if I leave it any longer, that joint will be ruined.' She herself had no appetite, the food would taste like sawdust, but kids were always hungry and no doubt he'd had nothing decent to eat for hours either.

'I suppose the Savages know . . . everything?' He grimaced at the thought of the 'happy families' charade he'd have to play in front of the neighbours.

Olive nodded. 'Yes, and so does our Lily. I . . . I had to tell them! Nelly's been very supportive, and generous too, where Bella's concerned, I couldn't have managed without her. Everyone else in the street and at the school thinks Bella is my niece.'

'Your Lily's child?'

'Don't be a fool, Billy! How could that possibly be believable? No, a fictitious sister, now deceased. It was Nelly's idea, and it's saved both my reputation and Bella's. And yours too, if that matters at all to you, which I doubt!'

Billy didn't reply. He resented Nelly Savage's part in all this. In his opinion that woman had far too much to say about things that were no concern of hers. This was between himself and Olive. Despite the fact that, for now, Olive had calmed down and seemed willing to try to forgive and forget, he could see life in the next few weeks didn't look very rosy at all in Liverpool, not for him. Maybe it would be best if he were to go down to the 'Pool' in the morning to see if he could get a ship. If he were away, Olive and the family might view things in a different light, given time, and a period away would help him adjust to the new situation. He certainly hadn't bargained for all this drama as he'd made his way up to Mersey View a few hours ago, looking forward to his Sunday lunch.

# Chapter Sixteen

———◆◆◆———

Joan had been deeply disappointed that she'd been given no opportunity to speak to her father alone about the situation. The rest of that awful Sunday had passed like a bad dream. Everyone had been quiet and she had taken her cue from her mother and been polite – frostily polite – on the few occasions she'd spoken to her father. She'd caught Charlie casting surreptitious but suspicious and hostile glances at his da, and as soon as the meal was over her brother had sidled out and gone back up to Nelly's, or so she'd assumed. She wished she could follow him, but she wouldn't desert either her mam or Bella. Bella hadn't spoken to Billy again after his awful entrance, and he'd not said a word to her. She'd said very little as she'd helped Olive clear away and wash up, but Joan had quietly wiped away the tears from the child's cheeks and squeezed her hand in a gesture of comfort.

When Billy had announced his intention to go to the Pier Head first thing in the morning to try to get another ship, his words had been met with silence. 'It's for the best! For everyone!' he'd said bitterly, before informing them curtly he was going over to The George and Dragon.

'Maybe him going *is* for the best, Mam,' Joan had remarked to her mother once the front door had banged behind him. Olive had said nothing, and neither had Bella, and so she'd let the subject drop.

They'd all gone to bed by the time Billy came back. And next morning, before Joan had left for work, he'd gone – although she noted his sea bag was where he'd dropped it the previous day, so that meant he would have to come back at some stage during the day.

He did return and at least had seemed a bit happier when Joan got home that evening, although the atmosphere was still terrible – you could almost cut it with a knife, she'd thought miserably. He'd managed to sign on to the *Hubert*, which was leaving again tomorrow for South America.

'A ship lying idle makes no money for its owners,' he'd remarked curtly. 'As soon as she's loaded we'll be away.'

Her mam had nodded slowly but said nothing. Joan knew that while he'd been out Olive would have gone up to see Nelly, to inform her of how things stood. She wondered how long it would be before her Aunt Lily would call to be apprised of the situation; probably not until she judged that Billy would have sailed again. She desperately wanted to go and unburden herself to Monica but knew she would have to stay in the house; after all, it would be her da's last night at home for quite some time. She had hoped to maybe get some time to talk to him, but sadly that hadn't happened; before she, Charlie and Bella had gone to bed he'd said his subdued goodbyes, and in the morning he'd gone.

* * *

The following Sunday afternoon Lily called, knowing her brother-in-law never remained home for very long. In these circumstances she was sure he'd be anxious to be away as soon as he could, and she didn't want to miss him. She was determined to leave him in no doubt as to what she thought of him.

'So, I take it you got things sorted out, Olive?' she enquired as Joan took her coat and hat. It was the first time Lily had seen Bella; she'd been at school when she'd called previously, and she was quite surprised to see that the child was very pretty indeed. 'And you must be Bella? I'm Lily, Olive's sister. So you must call me Aunt Lily.' She smiled down at the child. She was already aware that Bella addressed Olive as 'step-mama'.

'I thank you, Aunt Lily,' Bella replied shyly, rather overawed by this glamourous person to whom it now appeared she was related.

'Why don't you show Aunty Lil the embroidery you're doing on my blouse,' Joan suggested, wanting to give Bella something to do as well as to include her in the conversation. She'd already resolved to take her half-sister with her up to Nelly's, so Bella could play with Eileen, while her mam and Aunty Lil chatted in private – and she could bemoan the whole situation to Monica.

Olive smiled gratefully at Joan as Bella dutifully showed Lily her handiwork while she put the kettle on.

'You are very clever, Bella, dear. That is beautiful, it really is,' Lily enthused, even though she'd already seen the half-finished work.

'Joan and Monica buy me the pretty coloured threads,' Bella replied, relaxing a little under Lily's praise.

As Olive poured the tea, the two girls left them to it, and Olive was grateful for Joan's tact.

'So?' Lily probed, sipping her tea. 'Where is he?'

'He's gone again. Signed on the following day – and I can't say I'm sorry, Lily. There was a huge row and I told him exactly what I thought of him. After that, the atmosphere was shocking. Everyone was upset. Oh, he swore he was sorry but . . . well, I don't know if I believe him or not. I was quite relieved when he announced that he'd be going back to sea as soon as possible.'

Lily nodded sagely. 'So, you're happier with the situation now? Well, what I mean is . . . more settled.'

'I don't think I'll ever be what you could call "happy" or "settled" with him again, Lil. But life has to go on, and we have to make the best of things. We'd all have suffered if I'd thrown him out.'

'How are the kids taking it, now they've actually seen him, even if it was only for a few hours?'

'Joan is being sensible and Bella, although hurt at first by the reception she got from him, seems to have settled down again. But I'm worried about our Charlie. He doesn't seem to want to be in this house at all. He spends most of his time with Arthur and the pigeons.'

'Leave him alone, Olive. He'll get over it, and maybe messing about with those birds will help to take his mind off things.'

'I hope so. Oh, I just don't want him getting into trouble with the law again, Lily.'

'He won't, Olive,' Lily replied firmly. She sniffed. 'You never know, he might prefer Arthur's company to that of his da. At least Arthur Savage takes an interest in the lad – and he's around, which is more than Billy ever was. Arthur's a far better person for Charlie to look up to than his da.'

'All I know, Lily, was that Charlie *did* look up to his da, he could do no wrong in his eyes – until now. But you're right, maybe it is better if he starts taking Arthur as an example, rather than Billy. Oh, I just don't know!'

'What you need is taking out of yourself, Olive. I'm off on Wednesday night, so we'll all go into town for a drink in the Stork or the Bradford – you, me and Nelly. Get your glad rags out, Joan and Monica can look after the kids, and it will do you the world of good.'

Olive smiled tiredly at her sister. 'I'll take you up on that, Lily. I feel as if I really need something to cheer me up, something to look forward to; and maybe by the time he gets home again, I'll feel better about everything.'

Lily smiled back at her. 'I've got to hand it to you, Olive, you've always had guts and you could always find a way to look on the brighter side of things. He doesn't deserve you!'

Olive managed a smile. 'I try, Lil. I really do, but I'm going to need all my ruddy backbone to get on with my life now.'

As the weeks went by and the weather turned warmer, it seemed to Joan that life had actually gone back to something like normal. Her da had never been one for writing letters, neither had her mam, and as he was seldom mentioned there were times when she actually forgot about him.

She'd said this to Monica one warm June evening as they sat in the gardens of St George's Church at the top of the hill, where there was always a light breeze and from where you got a good view of the river and the city.

Seeing the turgid grey waters of the Mersey far below turned to molten gold by the rays of the slowly setting sun, gilding the wake of the ferries still criss-crossing the river, Joan was reminded of him.

'I wonder where exactly he is now?' Monica pondered aloud.

'Somewhere in South America, I suppose. Or maybe he's actually on his way back.'

'Don't you know just when he'll be back?'

Joan shrugged, tucking a stray wisp of hair, dislodged by the breeze, behind her ear. 'I don't think any of us are that interested to actually find out. In the past, Mam used to go down to the shipping office a few weeks before, but I can't see her doing that this time. Oh, I know it seems as if he's been away ages, but it's not that long – and no one's really got over all the upset yet.'

Monica nodded sympathetically. 'That's understandable. Both Bella and your Charlie seem to spend a lot of time at our house. Da says that Charlie's got a real way with the birds, that he's a bright lad and quick to pick things up.'

'Well, he's never shown much sign of that at home. Although when Mr Garswood came in to sort out the back door for Mam – it was sticking – and even knocked together a sort of kennel for Rags out of a couple of old packing cases, Charlie seemed interested in how it was all done,' Joan replied, thinking that Arthur Savage obviously saw her brother in a very different light to herself. 'How are your Eileen's embroidery lessons coming on?'

Monica cast her eyes skywards. 'Oh, Bella has the patience

of a saint with her, but Eileen's little better than useless at it! Bella is always unpicking it, and I don't think Eileen'll ever master the skill. She's learning to knit, though. Mam's teaching them both – and our Eileen is better at that than Bella is, I have to say.'

'Well, at least it keeps the pair of them occupied, and now summer's here they can play out more after school. Get out from under everyone's feet, as it were,' Joan commented, although her mind had moved beyond the subject of Bella and Eileen's accomplishments, or lack of them.

She glanced at her friend and smiled to herself before she spoke. 'Have you seen anything more of that Richard Eustace?' she enquired with an innocent expression on her face.

Monica blushed and proceeded to fan her cheeks with her handkerchief, as if the warm evening were the cause of her heightened colour. Richard, or 'Rick' as he preferred to be called, was the salon owner's son and she'd first met him three weeks ago, when he'd come to see his father, Claude, one afternoon. She'd not got him out of her mind since. He was about eighteen or nineteen, she judged, tall and athletic-looking with fair hair and the bluest eyes she'd ever seen. In fact, in her opinion he was the best-looking boy she'd ever met. He'd smiled at her as she'd been shampooing a client's hair and she'd smiled back at him in the mirror. Then, after he'd left his father's office, he'd come over to her.

'You're new here, aren't you?'

She'd blushed and nodded. 'Well, fairly new. I'm the youngest apprentice,' she'd replied, trying to concentrate on sorting the correct waving clips and pins Miss Marshall would need.

'And I have to say, the prettiest by far. What's your name?'

The colour had deepened in her cheeks. 'Here I'm called Monique, but my name is Monica. Monica Savage.'

He'd laughed. 'Dad and his crazy notions!'

She'd smiled but said nothing; it was not her place to criticise her employer.

'I've got a few errands to do for Dad but then, if you'd like, I can run you home?' he'd offered. 'It must be terribly hot and stuffy on the tram.'

She'd been completely taken aback. 'Oh . . . I . . . that would be great, thank you, er . . . Mr Eustace.'

'Less of the formality, it's Richard – Rick – to my friends. I'll wait in the mews at the back of the shop for you.'

For the rest of that afternoon she'd worked in a daze. She'd noted how her companions had looked at him, and Nora had actually said how jealous she was of her – he'd never offered to take any of the girls home before. When she finally took off her overall and draped her cardigan around her shoulders she'd been shaking with what she assumed was excited anticipation. She wished she'd put on a nicer dress but took comfort from the fact that she did dress far more smartly these days; her hair was always styled and her nails polished, as the manicurist had taught her.

The sun had still been strong as she'd stepped out into the mews and she'd had to shade her eyes with her hand. He'd been waiting for her, sitting in a very smart, dark green sports car with the hood down. She'd felt her excitement rise; she'd never been in a car in her entire life – and this one, she was certain, was a very expensive model. He'd got out and opened the passenger door for her and she'd settled into the comfortable leather seat. This was sheer luxury!

'Right, then, Miss Monique, where to?' he'd asked, smiling at her.

She'd given him the directions and they'd driven at what she considered to be high speed through the city streets. It was an exhilarating experience, and on the journey he'd managed to extract quite a lot of information from her about herself. In turn, she'd learned that he had two younger sisters, that he lived in Woolton and that his father had two other salons, one in New Brighton and one in Chester – both in good areas – and that he helped his father to manage them.

She'd liked him, liked him a great deal. He was open and friendly and amusing, and she was sorry when they'd finally drawn up outside number fifteen Mersey View. Their arrival had caused quite a stir for, as was usual on summer evenings, most kids were playing in the street and many of their mothers had escaped the uncomfortable heat of their kitchens to stand on their doorsteps gossiping – although her ma wasn't one of them, she was thankful to note. Very few cars were seen in these streets, and such a one as this caused everyone to stop and stare, and many of the kids to point. As he'd helped her out, she'd seen the speculative glances and noted the whispering behind hands. She was aware that she wasn't of his class, but that hadn't bothered her. But sadly, she thought now, it appeared it did bother him, for she'd not seen him since.

Nelly had not been very impressed, demanding to know what she was doing 'running around' with the likes of him? Surely, she must realise that that car would have cost more than her father earned in years? She should stick to her own class – and furthermore, she was not yet sixteen, far too young to be taking up with lads.

'Oh, Mam! Don't be so old-fashioned!' she'd replied, but now she was wondering if her mother was right. She'd not heard a thing from him since – she'd obviously been just a brief amusement for him, on a dull afternoon.

Now she shrugged and smiled at Joan. 'No, I haven't seen him – I've not given up hope, though.' And as she spoke the words she knew she hadn't.

# Chapter Seventeen

─◆─◆─

As summer progressed, the weather became more and more sultry. Some days, the heat in the salon was unbearable despite the fact that all the windows were open, as were the back and front doors, but what little breeze wafted through was rendered ineffectual by the heat from the hairdryers.

It wasn't much better for Joan in the factory either. She complained to Monica as they walked home from the tram stop. 'And then when you finally get out, the tram is just as sweltering – it's like being jammed into a tin of sardines!'

'I don't know how Mam sticks that kitchen. I know we have to keep the range in for cooking and hot water, but I think I'd sooner just have a bit of salad than put up with that furnace – and I certainly wouldn't mind getting washed in tepid water,' Monica said.

'And the jigger absolutely *stinks*!' Joan complained. 'I think Mam must have cleared out Ethel's entire stock of fly papers,' she added, alluding to the strips of brown paper coated in glue which everyone hung from the ceilings and light fittings to try to combat the hordes of flies that came in through open windows and doors, attracted by the ashcans and privies in the yards.

'I know, all you can smell in our house and yard is Jeyes Fluid! Mam's fanatical about flies and germs. I wish it would cool down, though. It's just no fun at all having to work in this heat. A good thunderstorm might help.'

'The only one in our house who doesn't seem to mind the heat is Bella. But then, I suppose she was brought up in weather like this – even hotter, probably. Remember how she really felt the cold?'

The girls fell silent as they turned the corner into Mersey View, both feeling hot and listless, but then Joan gave a startled cry and nudged Monica. 'Who's that parked outside your house? Is it *him*? It's got to be – you said he had a posh, dark green car.'

Monica's heart turned over and her hand went instinctively to pat her hair. 'I never thought I'd see him again.'

'Well, he's obviously still interested in you. Go on, hurry up! Don't keep him waiting any longer or your mam will be out, asking him what he wants, and then the whole street will be up!' Joan urged, grinning at her friend, for she knew how badly Monica had been smitten by him.

As Monica drew level with the car, he got out and stood smiling down at her. 'I was passing through Everton, so I thought I'd call and see you – it's such a lovely evening. Then I realised I was a bit early so I sat and waited. I didn't want to intrude or inconvenience your mother. Would you like to come for a drive? We could go over to New Brighton – it doesn't take long now through the new tunnel – and we could get something to eat there. There are a couple of nice little places away from the promenade.'

She beamed up at him, her heart pounding. 'Oh, I'd love that . . .' But then her features clouded. 'Can I get changed first? It's been like a Turkish bath in the salon today.'

'I know – I'm fortunate, I can get out for a few hours in the afternoons. There's plenty of time, I don't mind waiting.'

'I can't leave you sitting out here; will you come in and wait for me? Though I have to warn you, it's probably cooler out here in the street.' She wasn't sure how her mam would react but it was only manners to ask him in, she thought. He could wait in the parlour – at least it would be cooler there. She could scarcely believe he'd not forgotten about her, after all, and he was actually going to drive her through the new tunnel under the Mersey, opened by the King and Queen only two years ago. And he was taking her to what sounded like a proper restaurant! He certainly knew how to treat a girl. Even if her mam didn't put out the welcome mat for him, she was too happy to care. After all, it wasn't her mam he was taking out.

She changed quickly, but with care, into her best pale pink cotton dress. She liked the new style of clothes that were coming in, the dropped waists of her mother's era long gone. Skirts were still short, but her dress was fitted at the waist and had what was termed a 'sweetheart' neckline, and fashionably short cap sleeves. She chose a pair of pale pink earrings that matched almost exactly the shade of the dress, and she changed her flat shoes for a pair of white courts with a heel and a strap across the instep. She found her small white clutch bag, wrapped in tissue paper, which normally resided in the top of the wardrobe, and took out her white cotton gloves, kept in the top drawer of the chest, but decided against wearing a hat. It was too hot – and it would be hard to keep on in an open car. She glanced at her reflection in the dressing-table mirror and smiled – yes, a quick splash of Yardley English Lavender Water and she was ready.

She found Richard sitting rather stiffly on the edge of the sofa in the parlour, with her mother sitting facing him and looking decidedly unimpressed. He stood up immediately as she came into the room.

'Ah, ready, then, Monica? You do look lovely, and your mother has very kindly been keeping me company.'

She smiled at him. 'I hope I've not been too long. Thanks, Mam. I won't be late,' she promised, kissing Nelly lightly on the cheek.

Nelly just nodded curtly. She wasn't at all happy with this situation, but she had to admit the lad had perfect manners and seemed nice enough. Far too old for Monica, of course, and from a very different background. But still, she didn't think it would last. These first romances usually didn't. In time, her daughter would no doubt find someone of her own kind and settle down – until then, she had other things on her mind to worry about. Olive's situation, for one thing.

Her neighbour had called in to see her that afternoon, as she often did. It seemed to Nelly she confided in her far more than she did her own sister – but then Lily Cooper had never been married, so she didn't really understand what it often entailed.

'Oh, this heat really is getting me down now, Nell,' Olive

had stated, fanning herself with a piece of cardboard she'd torn off a box.

'I know, luv. It wouldn't be so bad if you could get a decent night's sleep, but the bedrooms are like ovens, and if you have the windows wide open you're tormented with the blasted flies! Roll on autumn!' she'd replied, and then realised that she'd inadvertently brought the subject around to Billy's return. 'Isn't Billy due home soon?'

Olive had nodded. 'The end of the week, but I've no intention of going down to meet him, Nell. I know it's a terrible thing to say, but . . . well, I wish he was away for longer. We've all been better lately, and now it'll bring it all back to us.'

Nelly had reached over and patted her hand. 'I know, luv. But I'm afraid it's just one of those things you've all got to live with, especially you. We all took our vows. At the end of the day, your Joan and Charlie and even Bella will get married and leave, then there will be just you and him.'

Olive had sighed heavily. 'I know, Nell. But that's a long time in the future, I hope. Until then . . .'

'You'll all just have to put up with him when he's home. I'm sure things will get easier as time goes on, Olive, luv. He's only been away for one trip – after all, he's not getting any younger, and there might come a day when he actually *wants* to stay at home. And perhaps, by then, you'll be glad to have him back. At least then you'll have time to come to a better understanding with each other.'

Olive had looked very sceptical. 'I very much doubt that, Nell. Oh, once I did want him here for longer. Before . . . before all this happened. Our family's not going to stay the same, you know. The kids won't be kids forever. Our Joan getting herself a feller may not be all that far off in the future. Your Monica seems to have landed one.'

Nelly had tutted. 'Oh, I hope that doesn't last. He seems nice enough, Olive, but did you see that car? It must have cost a fortune. He's her boss's son and they've a house in Woolton, no less! No, she'll be better off with someone not so far above her station. She's not been brought up with fancy ways and airs, as no doubt he and his sisters have been. We're plain, ordinary working folk.' Nelly had sighed and passed a hand over her forehead. 'You know, she's changed ever since she started working in that place.'

'I agree, Nell. She's looking a lot better, I have to say, in her appearance, like. She dresses with far more style, our Lily commented on it.'

'That's part of it, but she . . . well, she seems to have become more mature, more confident in herself.'

'Is that such a bad thing?' Olive had queried.

'I suppose not, but I don't want her getting ideas into her head.'

'Nelly, she's not sixteen until the end of this month. I know the pair of them are still trying to decide what they'll do to celebrate. It's nice their birthdays are within a few days of each other.'

'I just hope our Monica hasn't got any plans to celebrate it with *him*,' Nelly had said gloomily. 'Perhaps we should organise something that everyone can be a part of, Olive,' she suggested on a brighter note. 'Billy included – he'll be back then. It might help things. What about a day out, or an evening out? I wonder, with the weather being so good, will the ferry company do a couple of special evening trips? They've done them before – it's not really a cruise. They just sail up and down the river – out as far as the Bar and back – and they put a band on board, so I heard.'

'That sounds promising. How much do they charge? It might be too expensive for us all.'

'It might, I suppose . . . and it could be a bit tame for Billy, just up and down the river, and with no drink on board.'

Olive nodded, suspecting she was right, but it was something to think about for when he got home. It just might help lighten the atmosphere.

Monica was a bit apprehensive when Rick opened the door of the Café de Normandie for her. The restaurant was situated in one of the quiet streets up the hill and away from the shops on the promenade selling souvenirs, sweets, brightly coloured rock, and fish and chips. It looked very classy, she thought. She'd never been to a proper restaurant before – and in fact, if she were really honest with herself, she'd have preferred a fish and chip supper. The room he ushered her into was small and the walls were decorated with prints of scenes from French life. The tables were covered in red-and-white-gingham cloths and boasted both candles and small vases of fresh carnations. Even the waiter who approached them, smiling and ushering them to a table, looked foreign. She felt decidedly out of her depth but determined not to show it. To her relief the waiter, when he spoke, was as scouse as she was.

She smiled at Rick over the top of the menu. 'I think I'll let you choose. I'm not familiar with any of this,' she admitted honestly.

'Well, I usually have the *poulet* – chicken – it's very good;

they do it in a sauce with white wine and garlic. Or the *moules marinière* – mussels – are good.'

'I think the chicken sounds great,' she enthused, although she wasn't sure about the sauce. But the mussels certainly didn't appeal – for a start, how on earth did you go about eating them?

'So, what did you think of the tunnel?' he asked when he'd ordered for them both. 'It's a tremendous feat of engineering.'

'It's fantastic, it really is. It's a bit scary, though, when you think of all those gallons and gallons of water above and around it.'

'They wouldn't have let the King and Queen be driven through it if it wasn't safe, Monica,' he chided gently.

She smiled at him, thinking just how good-looking he was. He was so nice too. 'I'm just being a bit silly, I suppose. It's much quicker than the ferry – and in winter it will be a lot more comfortable too.'

'Oh, definitely. It makes my life easier, having to travel to both Chester and here.'

'Do both those salons have a manageress, like La Belle Coiffure, or do you have to oversee everything?' she wondered aloud.

'They have a senior stylist, like Helen Marshall, to oversee the actual work, and I see to the ordering, the books, general maintenance, things like that. I suppose it's good training, because one day the three salons will be mine.'

He wasn't boasting, she thought. He was simply stating a fact, that he would one day be a wealthy man. But she wasn't really interested in that, she just liked him. She liked him a lot and hoped that this relationship would blossom – particularly if he brought her to places like this, where she was being made to feel so special. She'd have a lot to tell Joan tomorrow, she thought.

# Chapter Eighteen

———◦✦◦———

Joan was avid to know all the details of Monica's night out. She met up with her friend as they both left the house for work the following morning.

'So, did you have a fabulous time? Where did you go? Did he try to take liberties? Did he kiss you goodnight? And are you seeing him again?'

'Oh, for heaven's sake, Joan! I'm barely out of the door!' Monica laughed, and then proceeded to tell her friend most of the details of the previous evening

'Well, he certainly doesn't seem short of cash,' Joan remarked as they neared the tram stop.

'And he doesn't mind spending it either. I don't know what that meal cost, but it wouldn't have been cheap, and it's obvious that he's used to eating in places like that. It was all a bit fancy for me but I really did enjoy myself. The sensation of driving through that tunnel is so exciting, and when we got home I told him to park the car around the corner. He asked to walk me to the door but I said no, I didn't want

Mam peering through the curtains in the parlour at us – or worse still, appearing on the doorstep and demanding I go in immediately.'

'And I don't imagine he would have wanted all the kids in Northumberland Terrace climbing all over his car,' Joan added dourly. 'I suppose there is a bit more privacy there than outside your own front door – although not much, I suspect. That car will always cause a stir around here.'

Monica didn't reply, remembering the feel of Rick's lips on hers and his arms around her. The way her heart had hammered, she'd even felt a little dizzy.

'So, are you going to see him again?' Joan probed. He was clearly a good catch; she'd certainly be eager to be asked out by the likes of him. If the truth be told, she was a little envious of her friend.

'I don't know. We didn't make any definite plans. He just said he'd like to take me out again but he's not sure when he'll be free, as there are some hairdressing events coming up he'll have to attend.'

'And are there?' Joan asked.

'Actually, there are. Competitions and demonstrations mainly, but also a couple of what they call "trade events" where they show off new products. You know, the very latest in setting lotion, and stuff like that.'

'Can't you go too?'

'I'm the youngest apprentice, don't forget, Joan. Maybe in a year or two they'll let me go, but for now . . .' She shrugged. She'd been disappointed herself that Rick had made no definite plans, but she'd hidden her feelings. He was older than her, more experienced and worldly-wise, and she didn't want to appear childish – or even worse, forward and pushy. No, she'd just have to bide her time and hope he would call again.

As the day of Billy's arrival drew closer, Olive became more and more anxious. Joan had commented on the fact she seemed tense; she'd tried to shrug it off, but she knew her daughter was no fool. She sensed that all the children were very apprehensive too, so she'd gone with Nelly down to the Pier Head to enquire if the Mersey Ferries had any plans for forthcoming events – something they could all look forward to.

They'd been informed that there were, indeed, two evening river excursions planned for the next two weeks, providing the weather held. The *Mountwood* would sail from the Pier Head out to the Mersey Bar and back, and the *Overchurch* would sail from Seacombe to the Bar and back. The cost would be a shilling per adult, and sixpence for a child.

'That's daylight robbery! It only costs tuppence to cross from one side of the river to the other,' Nelly had protested to the official behind the counter.

'You're forgetting that this is a special excursion that goes out to the Bar – quite a distance – and that there will be music provided for your entertainment too, madam,' had been the rather imperious reply.

'Well, four shillings is a bit too steep for my purse,' Olive had remarked as they turned away, disappointed.

'It's a scandal, that's what it is!' Nelly had added, loudly enough for the other people at the enquiry desk to hear. 'There's the tram fare on top of that, and I'm not paying three and six for my lot just to see the streets and warehouses in Bootle, Litherland and Seaforth on one bank and Cammel

Laird's shipyards on the other. And then what is there to see out at the Bar? Nothing! We'd no doubt be half deafened by some second-rate band into the bargain. Come on, Olive, let's go and get a cup of tea at Lyons Corner House, at least that won't cost a fortune!'

Olive had noted in the Journal of Commerce when the *Hubert* was due to dock – in the morning, at eleven – but by mid-afternoon on Friday she was sure that Billy had stopped off at some pub or other, and would no doubt finally arrive home drunk. Maybe it was the only way he could cope, she thought, but it made her feel even more on edge. By the time Charlie and Bella arrived home from school, her nerves felt cut to ribbons. When Joan got in, herself full of apprehension, she instantly noticed that her mam was looking drawn and tense, her brother and half-sister were subdued, and there was no sign of her father.

'The ship *has* docked, Mam?'

Olive nodded curtly. 'This morning. He's probably propping up the bar in some pub on the dock road.'

By this time, he'd more than likely be unconscious in a gutter somewhere, Joan thought bitterly, but she said nothing. There had been a few times in the past when he'd been spectacularly drunk but had at least managed to make it home. The excuse was usually the fact that one or other of his shipmates had become a father again, or some such tale. It was quite obvious her mam had no intention of going looking for him. 'Did you enquire about the ferry trip?' she asked, to change the subject. She liked the idea of celebrating both her own and Monica's sixteenth birthdays next week with a short trip on the River Mersey.

175

'I did, and it's much too expensive, Joan. They're charging a shilling each for adults – which will no doubt include you – and sixpence each for Charlie and Bella.'

'I don't mind paying for myself, Mam. But that *is* expensive – the usual fare is only tuppence.'

'I wouldn't mind if it was anything really special, but it's not – and if the weather's not great, it could be uncomfortable to say the least! No, luv, we'll have to think of something else to do.'

Joan nodded, disappointed. Maybe they could take a picnic to Calderstones Park, in the south end of the city; it was a bit posher than either Sefton Park or Stanley Park. She'd see what Monica had to suggest, for no doubt Nelly too would have ruled out an overpriced ferry trip. But they had to get over the weekend first – and it looked like her da would have a monumental hangover for most of it.

By early afternoon the following day Olive was getting seriously worried, for Billy still hadn't arrived home. Oh, there had been times in the past when he'd been late – occasionally very late when there had been some event to celebrate with his mates – but nothing like this.

Joan was just as concerned. 'Mam, do you think we should report it to the Police? Something could have happened to him.'

'Oh, I don't know, Joan! I'd look such a fool if he turned up, or if they've got him locked up for being drunk and disorderly.'

'He wouldn't be disorderly. He's never been violent – more like drunk and incapable, Mam. But shouldn't we do *something*?' Joan urged.

Olive bit her lip and nodded. 'I'll go down to the shipping office to see if there's any light they can shed on it – if not, then I'll just have to start and ask in the pubs. I *am* worried, Joan. He's always managed to get home in the past.'

'I'll come with you, Mam. If . . . if we have to ask in the pubs, at least we'll be able to try more of them. Our Charlie's up with Mr Savage's pigeons. Will I send Bella up too, to Eileen? I know she's anxious as well, even though she hasn't said anything.'

'That would be best, luv. Perhaps she could tell Nelly what's happened and where we've gone,' Olive suggested as she went to get the only hat she possessed. She wasn't going down to the offices of the Booth Line Shipping Company looking as if she hadn't two halfpennies to rub together, even if there really wasn't much more than that in her purse at the moment – there never was, at the end of Billy's trips.

When they arrived at the shipping office, the clerk sitting behind the long polished wooden counter looked bored and didn't seem very interested at all, Joan thought irritably, noting the frayed and grubby cuffs of his shirt. He was probably peeved he had to work on a Saturday afternoon, and on what was probably one of the hottest days of the summer so far.

Olive was of the same opinion. How old was he? she wondered. Nineteen, twenty? 'It might not seem like a very important matter to you, young man,' she said, when he told them he didn't see how he could tell her where her husband was, 'but it is to us! Before I go to the police station to report him missing, I'd like you to check for me that he was actually paid off when the *Hubert* docked yesterday morning. His name is William Copperfield, he's employed as a stoker,' she snapped. She was already feeling a little faint with the heat and anxiety, and she wasn't going to put up with this supercilious attitude.

'I don't have that information, madam,' was the sullen reply.

'Well, then, I'd like to speak to someone who has!' Olive demanded.

'And don't tell us that there's no one else here, and to come back on Monday, or I'll be telling them at the police station that you were very unhelpful. I'm sure your boss will be delighted to hear that!' Joan added, wanting to shake him.

'If you'd like to sit over there, I'll go and see if I can find Mr Hayes. He's the shoreside superintendent,' was the ungraciously muttered reply.

They both sat on the leather-covered bench seat set against the wall, and Joan stared unseeingly at the posters on the wall depicting the various ships of the company against a background of exotic-looking ports. Who knew what went on in those far-off places? she wondered grimly.

After what seemed to Olive like at least half an hour, the clerk returned. He was accompanied by a small sandy-haired man dressed – despite the heat – in a neat, dark three-piece suit and carrying a large leather-bound ledger.

Both Olive and Joan stood up as he beckoned them to the end of the counter furthest away from the now openly curious young clerk.

'Thank you, sir, for seeing me . . . us. My husband, William Copperfield, was working aboard the *Hubert* as a stoker and I . . . I'm very worried about him. I know they docked yesterday and that it –' Olive was trying to choose her words carefully –

'is ... possible that he got caught up in some sort of ... celebration. But you see, sir, he's still not home and I thought, before I go to the Police, that maybe you could at least tell me if he was actually paid off? He ... he's never done anything like this before, sir, I assure you, not in all the years we've been married.'

The man looked at her with some sympathy; the wives of seafarers didn't have it easy. It certainly wasn't unknown for a man to drink or gamble away most of his wages before he got home, which was why wives would often wait at the dock gates when a ship was due in port. 'Let me just check for you, Mrs Copperfield, it won't take long and hopefully it will be of some help to you.'

They both watched as he opened the book and ran his finger down the page over what appeared to be a long list of names, with titles and figures written beside them. When he reached the bottom of the column he frowned and turned back a few pages.

'Is there something wrong, sir?' Olive asked tentatively.

'It does seem a little strange. His name doesn't appear on the page for yesterday as being paid off but ... if you'd have a little patience, I'll delve into the matter. I'm sorry to keep you waiting.' He closed the book and left the room, so there seemed nothing left for them to do but go back and sit down on the bench. 'Maybe it's just a mistake, Mam. An ... oversight or something,' Joan said quietly, although her stomach was churning. Had he been paid off or not? And if not, where on earth was he?

When Mr Hayes returned, they were both disturbed to see that he was looking rather grim.

'I'm afraid it's not good news, Mrs Copperfield. I've checked thoroughly and he wasn't on the *Hubert* for the return voyage. He signed off – and was also paid off – in Recife, Brazil.'

Olive stared at him, stunned. She was unable to take in what he was telling her.

'You mean . . . he . . . he didn't come home at all?' Joan cried.

'I'm afraid that it looks like that, Miss Copperfield. Unless, of course, he intended to get another ship home at a . . . later date.' Something Mr Hayes thought highly unlikely. He was beginning to feel very sorry indeed for the woman.

Olive clutched the counter for support as the reality of it all hit her. 'Recife! Brazil! No! No, he . . . he's not coming home! He . . . he's deserted us, Joan! He . . . he's left us all! Bella included. Oh, my God! No! No! How could he do this?'

The colour drained from Joan's face as she grasped what her mother was saying. This news was terrible. 'Mam, no! He . . . he wouldn't have, he *couldn't* have! Not after . . . !'

Olive's eyes had filled with tears and Mr Hayes gently escorted them both to the bench seat. 'I'm so, so sorry. Do sit down for a few minutes,' he urged, realising that obviously the poor woman had been deserted. Quite possibly the errant husband had another family in Recife. It certainly wasn't all that unusual amongst the seafaring community.

Olive turned to Joan. 'What . . . what will we do now? He . . . he's not coming back, Joan, and what money he left has almost gone.'

Joan too was fighting back tears. She could never have believed that he could do this to them in a million years. All the hurt and humiliation they'd suffered when they'd found out about Bella was as nothing compared to this. That he'd thought so little of them that he'd just walked out of their lives without a backward glance. Not even a note posted through the Agent. He didn't care if they were sick with worry about him, not knowing if he were alive or dead. He didn't care how they'd manage without his support. He just didn't *care*! That's what hurt the most. Through her tears she clutched Olive's cold hand tightly. 'We . . . we'll manage, Mam. Come on, let's go home.' She got to her feet, slowly pulling her mother up with her. 'At least now we know. And we . . . we've still got each other.'

Olive nodded, although Joan's words really didn't register. She was too shocked to even try to think straight. Yes, she wanted to go home. Home to Mersey View – but what kind of a home would it be now? How long would they be able to afford to stay there? These were questions she couldn't cope with now but, in the days to come, she knew she would have to.

# *Chapter Nineteen*

—◦◦◦◦◦—

A ll the way home on the tram neither of them spoke, totally wrapped up in their own emotions. As they began the journey from the tram stop neither of them noticed that the tall figure of Frederick Garswood had also alighted and was walking just behind them.

He could tell there was something very wrong, for both were always friendly towards him. Joan, in particular, was invariably very chatty, but both were silent now. He'd caught a glimpse of Olive's pale, drawn face and thought he'd detected tears in Joan's eyes. Because the walls of the houses were very thin, he'd heard the row between Olive and Billy a few months ago, just after the child Bella had appeared on the scene, and then he'd heard that Billy had gone back to sea almost immediately. He'd said nothing about it all, as it was none of his business, but his opinion of Billy Copperfield had hit rock bottom. After he'd gone off to sea, Olive, Joan and Charlie had all seemed to get on with life. Bella had settled in well and was very polite. She was also very pretty and obviously of foreign parentage. He, like everyone else, accepted the story that she was Olive's niece – at least, on the face of it – but he knew the truth. Obviously now something else had happened that had upset both Olive and Joan dreadfully. Something concerning Billy.

He hastened his steps. 'Joan, Olive. I got off the tram just behind you. Is something wrong? You both look very upset. Is there anything I can do to help?'

Joan shook her head, and he could now clearly see that she'd been crying. Olive remained silent; she just looked down at the pavement as if she hadn't even heard him speak and didn't know who he was.

'I . . . I wish there was something you could do, Mr Garswood, but thanks anyway,' Joan managed to reply.

They had reached his house but he didn't want to just leave them thinking he didn't care. 'I don't want to pry, Joan, but has something happened to your father?'

Joan nodded miserably, her head lowered, as if she daren't meet his gaze. 'You could say that, but we . . . we'll manage. We'll be all right.'

He was still reluctant to leave them, certain now that something terrible had occurred, and he wondered if he should ask them in for a cup of tea. Olive particularly looked as if she needed one.

Suddenly Joan looked decisively up at him. 'We're going on up to Mrs Savage's house now. I . . . I think it's best, and the kids are there. But, thanks. Thanks for your concern.'

'Well, if there's anything I can do to help, Joan, just knock,' he repeated, sighing to himself. There was something very wrong here; he knew it, and he determined to help if he could.

Nelly's front door, like most of those in the street, stood wide open. Shafts of bright, hot sunlight lit up the entire length of the lobby. Nelly, who had been supervising Arthur in the placement of a new fly paper, took one look at both their faces, abandoned the task and quickly eased her friend and neighbour down on to the bench beside the table while Arthur, equally perturbed, got down off the chair he'd been standing on.

Glancing around quickly, Joan was relieved to see there was no sign of Charlie, Bella or Eileen, and that Monica had quietly put the kettle on to boil.

'Olive, what's happened, luv? Oh, it's not bad news, is it? Did you go to the shipping office?'

Olive could only stare at Nelly in silence as the tears slowly welled in her eyes and then began to trickle down her cheeks.

Nelly looked quizzically at Joan; she'd never seen Olive as upset as this before, not even when she'd found out about Bella. 'Joan, luv, what the hell is wrong?'

Joan took a deep breath and the colour rushed to her cheeks as hurt and anger both began to rise in her. 'He . . . he wasn't on that ship when it got home yesterday. He . . . he was paid off . . . he left it – voluntarily – in Brazil. Some place called Recife, I think they said. He . . . oh, this is worse than last time, Mrs Savage! He's not coming back. He . . . he's abandoned us!' Joan dissolved into sobs.

Monica rushed to her friend's side and put her arms around her, unable to believe what she'd just heard.

'Oh, dear God! Olive, you poor, poor luv!' Nelly cried, taking Olive's cold hands in her own. 'Arthur, go and get that bottle of brandy,' she urged, and he left the room, as shocked as his wife at this revelation. 'Joan, are you absolutely sure about all this? They couldn't have got it wrong at that office?'

Joan was beyond words, sobbing on Monica's shoulder and wondering how both Charlie and Bella were going to take this disastrous news.

'No, Nell. They . . . he . . . checked,' Olive managed to get out. 'The man, I think he was some kind of manager, he checked in a book. I . . . I never thought he . . . he'd do this to us, Nell!' The tears and emotions she'd been holding in check suddenly burst forth and, like Joan, she was overtaken by sobs.

Gently, Nelly urged her to try to sip the brandy Arthur had poured. What kind of a feckless, selfish, useless excuse for a man was Billy Copperfield? she fumed inwardly. How could any man who considered himself to be in any way decent simply abandon his wife and his three children? Just get off a ship in some godforsaken foreign country, half a world away, and walk off, without a thought for them or how they were going to manage now? It didn't bear thinking about. She for one couldn't take in the enormity of it, let alone poor Olive.

'Nell, will I go and try to break this news to young Charlie?' Arthur suggested. 'He's out in the back with the birds,' he added, feeling helpless in the face of all this grief and shock.

'Would you? It would save poor Olive – and perhaps, coming from you . . .' Nell's words trailed off.

Maybe it would be better coming from him, he thought, as he moved towards the back door, but just what he was going to say to the lad he didn't know. There was nothing that could lessen the pain of this.

'Mam, where's Bella?' Monica asked quietly as Joan's sobs began to subside.

'Out with our Eileen in York Terrace, at Lizzie McBride's, I think,' Nelly replied, a little relieved to see that Olive was sipping the brandy and that some colour was coming back into her ashen cheeks, although her hands were still trembling.

'I'll go and bring them . . . her . . . back,' Monica stated. She'd offer to take on the burden of telling Bella, for neither Joan nor her mother were in any fit state to do it, and she couldn't put her best friend through any more traumatic experiences. Joan would no doubt bear the scars of her father's callous treatment for years to come.

Nelly was desperately trying to remain calm and to try to think practically, aware *someone* had to. 'Olive, would you like us to send for your Lily? She is family, luv, and I don't think any of you should be alone just yet.' She was wondering how Olive would be able to face going back to that house. Maybe if her sister was with her it would help in some way? Nelly had no room to put them all up – and she doubted that Olive would want that – but she would insist that they all stay here until Lily could get away. It was Saturday, and the theatre would be busy both this afternoon and evening, but there was no help for it. She had to try to calm everyone down, get them all to eat something, try to find some measure of 'normality'. Although she doubted she could work such a miracle.

Arthur duly went into town to find Lily while Joan, Monica, Bella and Eileen huddled in a miserable little group in Nelly's kitchen. Nelly and Olive sat quietly together in the parlour,

Nelly giving what small measure of comfort she could to her friend. Charlie had taken the news almost in silence, insisting on staying out in the loft with the pigeons, and Arthur hadn't pushed him. He was concerned about the lad, he thought, as he sat on the tram. But maybe if Lily were to come to stay for a few days, or even a week, things might improve? He sincerely hoped so.

After a few heated words, followed by some persuasion, the uniformed individual in charge of the stage door of the Empire let Arthur in and directed him to a door that bore the title 'Wardrobe Department'.

'You'll likely find 'er in the side room, sewin' or somethin'!' was the curt instruction.

He did indeed find Lily in a small room with a rail of very ornate costumes covered in sequins and feathers, which she appeared to be checking carefully.

'Good God! Arthur Savage! What's wrong?' she demanded, her heart sinking as she realised it must be something to do with Olive and that it would be bad news.

In a few words he told her, adding his own opinion of her absconding brother-in-law and finishing with the request that, if at all possible, she accompany him back to Mersey View as her sister needed her badly.

Lily nodded, her dark eyes flashing with anger. 'Wait here, I'll go and speak to the manager, then Maisie. She's the assistant wardrobe mistress, and she'll just have to manage tonight's performance on her own, providing the boss gives his approval – although I can't see why not, in this case! Oh, I could murder that Billy Copperfield, I really could!' she exploded. 'If I could get my hands on him I'd wring his bloody neck! Our Olive's too good for him and always has been! And now look at the mess he's left her in!'

'I couldn't agree more, Lily,' Arthur replied curtly, relieved she would be accompanying him home.

Frederick Garswood, walking home from his workshop, almost collided with Arthur and Lily as they turned the corner into the street. He was instantly alert, having not been able to get the thought of Olive and Joan out of his mind, and now . . . Lily was here and with a face like thunder.

'Arthur, mate, what's wrong? I saw Olive and Joan earlier and, well, they looked very distressed. Is there anything at all I can do to help?'

'Not at the moment, Fred, but thanks,' Arthur replied, not really wanting to discuss Olive's predicament.

Lily had no such reservations. 'You might as well know, sooner rather than later, Frederick, that . . . that *no mark* Billy Copperfield has jumped ship in Brazil and abandoned them! God knows what our Olive's going to do now, what with all the kids and not a penny to her name! I'll be staying for a while, but after that . . . He's one selfish, useless, untrustworthy, cowardly little rat!'

Arthur pushed his cap further back on his head. 'I'm afraid Lily's right, Fred. Obviously Nelly and I will do what we can but . . .'

Frederick Garswood was shocked to the core. At first he'd thought them a happy family – that was at Christmas, when he'd been welcomed into their home. Then Bella had appeared on the scene and he'd heard the row and learned about Billy's transgressions . . . and now . . . well, Lily had hit the nail on the head. The man was an out-and-out rat! In fact, there were other far less savoury names he could think of to call Billy Copperfield. 'As if she hasn't had enough to put up with lately,' he said sadly, thinking of Bella's sudden appearance.

Lily stared at him shrewdly. He was no fool – and the walls of these houses were paper thin. 'Then I take it you didn't fall for that fairy tale about Bella?'

'No, I didn't. She's a nice enough child, but it must have been a terrible shock and . . . a betrayal for Olive.'

'It was. She should have thrown him out then. She should have thrown him out years ago – in fact, she should never have got involved with him in the first place! No one in the family ever trusted him. Too big for his boots, thinking he was God's gift to women, and then to mislead her . . . make her think she was his one true love and that he would always be faithful to her!' Lily shrugged her elegant shoulders. 'Well, all this isn't going to help her. If we find there is something you can do, Frederick . . .'

'Just ask, Lily. That's what friends . . . and, er . . . neighbours are for.'

'You might be able to help her with Charlie, Fred,' Arthur suggested. 'The poor lad is taking it badly, I know, I had to break the news to him. He comes up to me to help with the birds but . . .' He lapsed into silence.

'He could come and help me around the yard after school – he likes to find out how things work, and I'd give him some pocket money,' Fred offered, glad to be of some assistance to the family. Maybe when the lad was older and had left school he could take him on as an apprentice, if he was up to it. Give him a trade; he was sure Olive would be relieved.

'Thanks, I'll suggest it to him later,' Arthur replied.

'It might help to take his mind off things.'

Lily had listened to this in silence. At least Olive had good neighbours, people only too willing to help her when she needed it – and she'd certainly need all the help she could get in the weeks and months ahead. 'Well, we'd better get on, Arthur,' she said briskly. 'It's up to us to try to pick up the pieces. Our Olive's always been strong, but how she's going to cope with all this, I just don't know. Maybe, in time, she will – personally, I think she'll be better off without him in the end! I hope he gets some horrible jungle fever and rots! There'll be no tears shed for him, I can assure you!'

Frederick Garswood mused on her words as he watched them walk up the street towards Nelly's house. He wanted to offer something more practical than just giving Charlie a few pence to help tidy the office and the yard. He'd admired Olive Copperfield from the day she'd moved in, and now she'd be virtually penniless. He would have to think of something he could do to help, otherwise the workhouse would be the only option for the whole family, and he couldn't stand by and let that happen.

# Chapter Twenty

———◆◆◆———

Lily had decided to stay with Olive until the following Monday but one week soon lengthened to three. Between Joan and herself they had managed to pay the rent and keep food on the table – and thankfully the weather was still warm, so there was no need for huge amounts of expensive coal. But autumn was just around the corner, and poor Olive didn't have a single penny to bless herself with now. God help them all when winter was upon them, she thought bitterly.

She travelled by tram to work each day, which was an added expense, often inconvenient because of her hours, and of course she still had her own lodgings to pay for. She had a small amount of money saved in the Post Office, but that wouldn't last forever, and there was no way a family of five could live here on her and Joan's wages. She valued her independence and enjoyed living on her own, but at the same time Olive needed both her financial and moral support. She was worried sick as to where it would all end.

It was a predicament that was causing sleepless nights for

Joan and anxiety for Nelly, Arthur and Monica too. As Nelly had said sadly to Arthur, it was terrible to see a family fall apart, and through no fault of their own. Her heart went out to Olive, and each day she counted herself very fortunate to have a reliable, loving husband with a good job, who cared for his family.

Down the street, Frederick Garswood had undergone a great deal of soul-searching but had finally come up with what he considered a solution that would benefit everyone concerned. But quite how he was going to broach the matter to Olive he wasn't sure.

Each evening he'd spent long hours walking the length of the waterfront, deep in thought. The summer evenings were warm and the sun didn't set until almost ten o'clock, and he'd always loved to walk beside the river, so he considered it the ideal place to try to work through the implications of his idea, to think through the answers to all the questions and objections that Olive might come up with. At last he was satisfied and intended to put the matter to her in the next couple of days. On his way home that evening he bumped into Lily, obviously returning from the corner shop, for she was carrying a hemp shopping bag and, as usual, was looking smart and fashionable in a cream skirt and navy-and-cream blouse.

'Good evening, Lily. Have you got a few minutes to spare? There's something I'd like to talk to you about before I mention it to Olive. I've got an idea . . .'

Lily was intrigued; she'd thought for a while that Frederick Garswood had a soft spot for her sister, and his concern lately had reinforced that view. 'If it's something constructive, I'd be very relieved to hear it, Frederick,' she answered as, at his suggestion, she followed him into his house.

She'd never been in there before, so she gazed around curiously. Despite the fact that he lived alone, she noted that everything was very clean, neat and tidy. The furnishings were old-fashioned but good and obviously well cared for; she recalled Olive saying he'd lived here with his mother for many years before she'd died. It was a big house by comparison to the others in the street; the rooms had high ceilings and wide sash windows which let in plenty of light, and there was a very ornate fireplace in the room Lily was ushered into. Obviously, it was the parlour and rather grand – if somewhat cluttered in decoration, she thought. But the paintwork was unchipped, and the windows and curtains were pristine. He indicated that she should sit on the deep blue brocade sofa while he sat in a matching chair opposite.

Lily placed the bag on the floor and smoothed down her cream knife-pleated skirt. 'So, have you managed to come up with something practical to help, Frederick? If you have, then I certainly commend you. It's more than we've been able to do, although our Olive's state of mind isn't up to sorting out problems yet.'

He leaned forward, his hands clasped tightly together, and she was a little perturbed by the serious expression on his face. 'I have . . . and I've given it a great deal of thought, Lily. I just . . . well, I just couldn't see them all ending up in the workhouse!'

'Oh, God forbid!' Lily exclaimed in horror. It was everyone's nightmare, and one she hadn't allowed herself to contemplate; she knew her sister would go out and scrub every office floor in the entire city to avoid that fate.

'So, what if Olive and the children came to live here? As you can see, this is quite a big house –'

Even though taken aback, Lily could see the first obstacle. 'Our Olive is too proud for that, Frederick. She'd view it as charity,' she interrupted.

'No, I didn't explain that properly, Lily. I mean . . . if she took over this house and turned it into a boarding . . . lodging house. The place is too big for me, I only need a couple of rooms – and the smaller ones would suit. My father paid off the mortgage before he died, which was years ago. If Olive ran it, it would provide her with an income, so she could keep the family together and at the same time have a decent home. She could offer the lodgers room and board, breakfast and dinner – and clean bedding and towels.'

'But it's your *home*, Frederick. Would you want it full of strangers? And in all fairness, shouldn't what they pay come to you?' Lily protested – even though she could see that it could work, and felt the stirrings of relief.

He shook his head. 'No. I don't need the money, Lily, and it would be a lot of work for Olive, all that cooking and cleaning and washing. She'd more than earn it.'

'The girls could help her with that, and Charlie could do his bit too,' Lily mused aloud. 'Of course, you'd have to expect certain standards from the lodgers, you wouldn't want to take in any riff-raff.'

'Of course, but it would be *her* business Lily, not mine. I've got the plumbing to keep me going,' he smiled. 'And if truth be known, it would be very pleasant to come home to a decent meal on the table and convivial company and children's laughter.'

Lily smiled back. 'And noise and cheek and tantrums too! You might not feel that way after a few weeks. And don't forget that fleabag of a dog of our Charlie's, he's bound to insist on bringing it. You could be turning the place into a menagerie!'

'Do you think she'll agree, Lily? I mean, it's the only feasible solution I can think of, and it would take the pressure off you and the Savages too. But would people . . . talk? I know that'd upset her, and she's been through enough.'

Privately, Lily thought Olive would be utterly mad not to take him up on this offer. But she knew her sister, she could be obstinate. However, at the moment her pride was at rock bottom, and she was worried sick about the future. She'd do everything she could to persuade her sister. She smiled brightly at him. 'Olive will be very grateful to you, I'm sure,' she said. Especially if I've got anything to do with it, she added to herself. 'As for people gossiping, it will be a nine-day wonder, Frederick.'

He shook his head. 'Maybe, maybe not. I wouldn't want her reputation to suffer. Would . . . would you consider moving in too, Lily? I know it's further for you to go to work, but with both of you here . . .'

She was taken aback, she hadn't thought of that. 'Well, I suppose I could. As long as I have my own bit of privacy. I'm used to being independent, you see.'

He could fully understand that and so he nodded his agreement.

'I could, of course, find plenty of lodgers too, should we need to. People in the entertainment business spend months on tour and are always looking for good theatrical digs.' Lily stood up and picked up the bag of shopping. 'It could work very well – for everyone concerned. Thank you, Frederick.'

'Indeed, it could,' he replied, feeling relieved and somewhat hopeful that she could persuade her sister to agree and that she would move in too. She would certainly liven life up.

She smiled at him, her eyes sparkling with mischief. 'I think you've got a soft spot for our Olive, Frederick.'

He was instantly serious. 'Whether I have or not, it's of no matter, Lily. As long as *he's* alive, she's beyond my reach. There's no question about that.'

Lily studied him thoughtfully. He was a decent, hard-working, kind man, not short of money, generosity or gentility, and was about Olive's age. He was educated and knowledge-able and, in his quiet way, not unattractive. He would make a good husband and she was sure now that he *did* care some-thing for Olive, and in more than a neighbourly way. Over the months, he seemed to have helped Olive out in numerous small, practical ways. 'I wouldn't be too sure, Frederick.'

He looked puzzled. 'What exactly do you mean, Lily?'

She shrugged. 'Oh, let's leave that for now, shall we? Let's get our Olive to agree to move to start with.'

It was as if she never had a single minute's peace of mind, not since Billy had left them, Olive thought wearily. Everyone had been so good, so kind, so sympathetic – and she was grateful, really she was – but it didn't help how she felt, or the terrifying predicament he'd left her in. The numbing daze that had clogged her mind for the first few days had given way to a tension that filled her mind and body, and for the first time in her life she felt as if she could no longer cope, that she just didn't know where to turn or how she would find the strength to carry on. Lily was doing what she could, Joan was proving to be her strength instead of the other way around, and as for poor Bella and Charlie she didn't know where to begin. How should she try to comfort them? How could she explain to them something she didn't understand herself? The reason or reasons why their father had abandoned them.

Joan had told her Bella was taking it very, very hard.

'I have no one now, and no one really wants me, Joan. My mama is gone and even my papa doesn't want me,' the child had confided.

Joan said it had almost broken her heart. 'Mam, I could kill him, I really could, for what he's done to that poor child! It's bad enough for us, but for her . . . this is twice he's abandoned her!' What Joan didn't tell her mother was that she herself had confessed all this to Monica in floods of bitter tears.

All Olive had been able to do was nod in reply. Her heart was too heavy and she was too sick with worry about the future. Charlie seemed to spend very little time at home, which added to her upset and concern, but she hadn't the heart to reprimand him, not after she'd found him one evening sitting in the yard with his arms around the dog's neck, sobbing. She hadn't even felt able to try to comfort him then; she'd had to turn away and go back indoors, too numbed by her own despair. Oh, one day she hoped to God this awful feeling would leave her, this feeling of utter uselessness and despair.

She didn't look up when Lily came into the kitchen and dumped the shopping bag on the table. 'Stir yourself, Olive, and when I've put these bits away we'll have a cup of tea.'

Reluctantly Olive got to her feet. 'Then I hope you've got the tea, Lily. The caddy's empty.'

'I have . . . and I've been next door, talking to Frederick Garswood. I met him on the street and he asked me in. And what's more, Olive, he's come up with a solution that could be the answer to all your prayers.'

'God, Lily!' Olive snapped wearily. 'Isn't my position bad enough, without it being gossiped about all over the neighbourhood?'

'Oh, get off your high horse! People only want to help, Olive, and you were aware he knew what's happened.' She watched in silence as her sister made the tea. 'Now, sit and listen to what I've got to say. And then think about it – just think!' she instructed, before relaying to Olive Frederick Garswood's offer.

'So, you see, it's just what you need. A decent roof over your head; a way of earning a living and yet staying at home to care for the kids. And no more worries about the future,' Lily finished.

Olive didn't reply; a million and one thoughts were whirling around her head. Move in next door! Take in lodgers! Cook and clean for strangers – and what kind of people would *they* be? And she barely knew him! How would the kids react? What would people say? Whatever would Nelly think of her? What if . . . what if Billy came back? It was these latter thoughts that she finally focused on. 'What . . . what will people say, Lily? I mean, me moving in with him! I . . . I've always striven so hard to be respectable, as you know well.'

'And where did thinking like that get you, Olive? Into this predicament, that's where. Oh, it will be a nine-day wonder!

When they see that you're running a decent boarding house, they'll soon shut up and find someone else to talk about.'

'But . . . but Billy?' It hurt to even speak his name.

Lily's expression hardened. 'Billy's got no claim on you, Olive! Don't be a bloody fool, luv. Think of yourself for once – not him! You won't have to worry about money ever again; you'll be earning your own living. The kids will have a good home, a steady, reliable future, and Frederick . . . well, I think he'll be very glad of the company, to be part of a family. He's been on his own for so long, it must be lonely, and he told me he doesn't want or need the money. The house is paid for, he's got his own business, and he's a pleasant, generous, reliable man with sober habits who won't be walking out on you – which is more than can be said for some! Just think about it all . . .' She paused for a second, then continued. 'And I might even move in with you too. My own lodgings, although very convenient for work, aren't all that great, and I could easily find you boarders. I'd vet them, so no worries there.'

Olive began to nod slowly as Lily's words sank in, and gradually it all seemed to make sense. It was very unorthodox, she knew that, and the risk to her reputation – and his too – still worried her.

'What will we tell people?' she wondered aloud.

'We'll tell most people nothing! I'm certain Nelly will think it's a godsend for you, and she's more than capable of telling the likes of Ethel Newbridge to keep her mouth shut. If people are so rude as to ask outright, we'll tell them that *he* has decided to go on very long trips from now on – away for years, not months – and there are shipping lines who operate like that. The lease on this house was up and this opportunity came your way, so you took it. End of the gossip!'

Olive was still cautious. 'Do you think people will *believe* that?'

'Does it matter, Olive? They all seemed ready to accept the story that Bella's your niece. Forget about convention, you've got to think of yourself and the kids' future now. Where are the kids, anyway?'

'Where do you think?'

'At Nelly's',' Lily judged correctly, getting to her feet. 'I'll go up and give them all our wonderful news, while you go and thank Frederick for his offer and tell him you accept – gratefully.'

Olive got to her feet, feeling suddenly as if every single worry had just drifted away, although the bitter hurt remained. 'Do you mind not going up to Nelly's just yet? Do you think we should wait until I can tell her myself – and the kids, of course.'

Lily smiled at her. 'All right, I'll wait until you've been next door and then we'll go together.'

For the first time in days Olive glanced at her appearance in the mirror over the mantel. 'I think I should at least do something with my hair, Lily.'

'And put a bit of lipstick on, Olive, you look as washed out as a sheet,' Lily advised, smiling.

Olive felt nervous, apprehensive and a bit tearful as she knocked on Frederick's door. She'd never been inside his house but she'd known from the outside it would be large. She could see that it was three storeys high and with a cellar too, so plenty of rooms for lodgers. It was one of the original early

Victorian houses, built before the rest of the street, before the area started to become run-down. At the end of the last century there had been people with money and status who were happy to live in Everton. Things had changed, she thought, ruefully.

'Olive, do come in,' Frederick Garswood greeted her pleasantly. As he ushered her inside he could see she was still upset, but somehow that distracted look seemed to have disappeared.

'Lily told me what you are so kindly offering me, Frederick,' she began nervously as she sat on the edge of the sofa in the parlour that was so unlike her own. 'And . . . and it's so very generous of you.'

'And I hope you've come to a decision, Olive. A . . . a favourable one?'

She nodded. 'I have. I would very much like to accept your offer for us to move in here and for me to start a lodging-house business. I . . . I know that –' she twisted her hands together in her lap nervously – 'you know about Billy, and I just didn't know where to turn . . .'

'Don't distress yourself, Olive, please. I hope life will be more comfortable for you in future.'

She smiled at him, thinking Lily was right. He wouldn't walk out and leave any woman destitute. It wasn't in his nature. 'It will, I'm sure.' She was still unhappy about the money side of things, though. 'I'd feel happier if you would at least let me give you part of what the lodgers will pay.'

He shook his head resolutely. 'No, Olive. You won't be getting a great deal – and there will be the costs of the food and washing and heating to take into consideration. And don't forget, it will be hard work for you too.'

'I don't mind that. But I suppose you're right, when I've taken out the expenses . . .'

He nodded slowly, then got up and poured them both a small glass of brandy from a cut-glass decanter on the sideboard. He handed her one, and proposed a toast. 'To our new venture. And if it's not too soon, perhaps we should get down to the more practical matters?'

She took a small sip, hoping it wouldn't cause her to catch her breath or cough, but she was already feeling much better. 'I definitely think we should, Frederick. There's so much to discuss, but if we can decide how we're going to arrange things, at least I'll have something definite to tell the rest of the family.' She glanced around. 'This is a lovely house, Frederick, and such nice furnishings too. It will be a joy to live here.'

'And I hope you will all be very happy here, Olive,' he replied with a smile.

# Chapter Twenty-One

'Oh, that wind is bitter!' Monica remarked, pulling the collar of her coat up higher around her ears.

'It's what Mam calls a "lazy wind". Goes straight through you,' Joan remarked, grimacing against the icy sleet-laden blast which stung her cheeks as they both got off the tram that Friday evening, a week before Christmas.

It was already dark and the dull, yellowish glow of the street lights added very little brightness to the December evening. They had met up after work in town to finish their Christmas shopping. Most of their purchases had been made in Woolworths or St John's Market but they'd also gazed into the brightly lit windows of the more fashionable stores in Church Street and Bold Street, which were way beyond their means.

'Where does your Aunty Lil get her clothes, Joan? She's always so smart, and she seems to have so many different outfits,' Monica had asked as they'd both enviously gazed at a fitted black velvet cocktail dress in the window of Cripps in

203

Bold Street. It was just the sort of thing that would look stunning on Lily.

'Not from here, you can be sure, but she's very good at altering things and adding different trimmings – I suppose from being a wardrobe mistress. Between you and me, I think she buys some from second-hand shops and alters them. You know, she shortens the sleeves or changes the neckline, adds a bit of fancy braid around the hem. I think she goes to the better-class second-hand shops, mind. But I'd never have the nerve to ask her,' Joan had added.

Monica had said nothing, but her friend's words had set her thinking. All the staff of the salon were being taken out in the evening next Thursday by Mr Eustace – his annual treat – and she'd wanted something that would really make her stand out from the other girls, all of whom she was sure would be dressed up to the nines. And she definitely wanted to impress Rick Eustace, for he hadn't taken her out for a while. But on her meagre wages she didn't hold out much hope of being able to afford anything remotely impressive.

The lights were shining from the windows of the houses through the curtain of sleet. They looked warm and welcoming, Joan thought to herself, as they hurried towards home. 'I hope Mam's got something hot and tasty for supper, I'm starving hungry. You know, Mon, I would never have thought we'd all get on so well, but we do. I was very dubious at first. I mean you know how relieved I was – we all were – in the beginning, but I thought that with him being so quiet and used to being on his own, and the place so nicely furnished and tidy, he'd soon get fed up with us all, and there'd be rows.'

'We all wondered about that too,' Monica divulged.

Frederick had converted two small bedrooms into his private sitting room and bedroom, but they'd all wondered if that would be enough to insulate him from the hurly-burly of Copperfield family life. 'Mam says that your mam told her he still does spend quite a lot of his spare time reading or listening to the wireless in his room. That he seems to like his privacy.'

'He does, but he enjoys sitting in the parlour some evenings with the others after supper. And on a Saturday afternoon, you know, he often goes to the football match with Mr Barnard and your da – and sometimes they take our Charlie too.'

Like Lily, Mr Barnard, a bachelor who worked as a supervisor in the packaging and despatch department of George Henry Lee's, one of the more prestigious shops in Church Street, was one of the new regular lodgers. He'd been unhappy in his last lodgings and now often thanked Olive for the clean, comfortable and warm rooms she provided; the pleasure of sitting in the spacious parlour with the other lodgers after supper was a luxury he'd not had for a long time, he'd explained. The second regular lodger was a Mr Arnold Taylor – again a bachelor – who was some sort of clerk in a city office. The other guests consisted of acquaintances of Lily, who seemed to come and go quite regularly as they moved from theatre to theatre and town to town.

Lily herself rented a large bedroom at the front of the house. It was big enough to double as a small sitting room too, which gave her privacy when she needed it, and it was an arrangement which worked well.

Under the care and guidance of both Frederick Garswood and Monica's father, Charlie Copperfield seemed to have overcome the shock of his father's abandonment. He still helped her da with the pigeons and really seemed to enjoy it – to her mam's disgust – but most of his spare time was spent down at the plumbing yard. Privately, Monica thought that Charlie was happier being with Frederick and her da than with Billy. They took him to football matches and spent far more time with him than Billy had ever done when he was home. Joan sometimes asked if she thought Charlie was still missing his da, but she always bolstered her friend's spirits by answering honestly that Charlie seemed far more content these days. Even the dog was well catered for, having a proper, roomy wooden kennel in a sheltered corner of the yard, lined with straw and then an old blanket. And nowadays, with the help of the lodgers – some of whom were very fond of him – the animal was very well fed.

They had nearly reached Joan's home, so Monica decided to ask her friend the favour she'd had in her mind most of the way back. 'Do you think your mam and Aunty Lily would mind if I came down later on?' she asked, slightly hesitantly.

'When have you ever needed to ask that, Monica Savage? Isn't the door always open to you – not literally, in this weather, of course!'

'Well, there's a favour I'd like to ask your Aunty Lil, about what I should wear for this big night out?'

Joan grinned and nodded. 'I take it someone tall, blue-eyed, fair-haired and not short of money will be going too?'

'Of course, and I want to look . . . well, as gorgeous as your Aunty Lil looks when she's all dressed up. I want to ask her advice on what to wear, my make-up, things like that.'

'She does look gorgeous when she's going out somewhere special, I'll give you that,' Joan replied, chaffing her cold hands together as they stood on the step.

'I . . . I've actually been thinking about having my hair lightened . . . bleached,' Monica confided cautiously.

'God! Monica! Your mam will kill you!'

'Not if it looks like Lily's hair,' Monica shot back.

'Don't bank on it, Mon. Come down about eight. I'm going in now, it's freezing out here!'

Monica nodded and continued her journey home. Even if she couldn't afford an elegant new dress, at least she could do something with her hair. She could have it done at work so it would be professional and wouldn't cost a fortune. She really did want to look special for Rick. She'd seen him a few times over the past months, but not on a regular basis, and nothing that could be termed 'courting', much to her mother's relief. But she had become fonder of him each time they'd gone out. Maybe, in part, it was because he always took her somewhere different – not just to the cinema or a dance – and he managed to make her feel very special, as if she were someone to be treated like a queen. If they did go dancing, it was usually to a place where you could get a meal too, and he often bought her a corsage for her dress, no expense spared. Of course, the cocktail lounges of the big hotels were out of bounds, for her at least. Although since Rick had turned twenty-one, he could legally drink in such places. She longed to be able to go to those places with him and was sure that if she had her hair bleached and adopted a new style, she'd look older. Then maybe she would indeed be able to join him.

She sighed as she opened the back door, then sniffed

appreciatively; if she wasn't mistaken, that was a meat pie cooking in the oven. Life did hold its consolations.

Joan peeled off her gloves, scarf and hat and then her coat. She hung her coat on a hook on the hallstand and put the accessories into one of the shallow drawers in the base. Mam always insisted they hang things up, as it was tidier. And at least they did have a hallstand now, and a very fine one too, so there was no excuse. They also had a runner of Axminster carpet down the length of the lobby, which meant it wasn't nearly so draughty as in their old house. She noticed, as she glanced at her reflection in the small hall mirror, that Mr Taylor's bowler hat was placed neatly on the shelf above it. He'd no doubt already be in the parlour, reading his newspaper and waiting for the sound of the gong. She grinned as she went down the hall towards the kitchen. Lord, how they'd come up in the world since they'd moved in here! It had been her Aunty Lil, of course, who'd suggested they place the small brass gong – which her mam had found when she'd been tidying out the dining room's heavy mahogany sideboard – on the table in the hall.

'Get one of the kids to use it to summon our guests for breakfast and dinner – it will give the place a bit of class!' Lily had instructed, aware that such things were a regular feature in boarding houses and small hotels where she herself had often stayed. It had also been her idea to address the lodgers as 'guests' for the same reason.

Within a couple of days, the task of sounding the gong had fallen to Bella, as Charlie had undertaken it with such vigour that Mam said it could be heard all the way down to Ethel's shop. And Aunty Lil had said he'd deafened them all and that there was nothing 'classy' about that! So now Bella did the honours. Joan smiled as she caught sight of her half-sister coming from the kitchen, her dark curls tied back with a red ribbon.

'I take it everyone is at home now, Bella?'

The girl cheerfully brandished the small felt-covered hammer. 'I beat the gong now.'

Joan nodded. She and Bella would help Mam serve the meal and later clear the table, but the whole household – including Charlie – ate together in the evenings in the dining room, which she thought was a bit on the dark and gloomy side, being at the back of the house. Sometimes her aunt ate with them, sometimes she didn't, depending on her work schedule. But on the days she joined them, Lily often regaled them all with tales from the Empire Theatre, which she knew both Mr Barnard and Mr Taylor enjoyed, and she was sure Frederick did too. In the mornings everyone went out at different times, so breakfast was a more informal affair, although her mam cooked them all a full breakfast. Olive didn't hold with going to work with just a few slices of toast and a cup of tea inside you, especially not when her guests were paying good money for a meal.

Leaving Bella to her task, Joan went into the kitchen.

'I'm home, Mam, are these ready to take through?' she asked, indicating a pile of plates stacked on the side of the cooking range that filled up nearly one complete wall and gleamed dully with black lead.

'Yes, luv, take them through, I'll bring in the potatoes and veg and then Bella can bring in the pie. I wouldn't trust our

Charlie with it, he'd likely drop it!' Olive answered, wiping her hands on her apron before removing it and dropping it on a kitchen chair.

Joan smiled at her, thinking how different her mam looked now from the thin, pale, worn and worried woman she'd been when they'd first moved in here. Then Olive had been almost broken, but in the five months since she had bloomed. Her hair was glossy, her eyes bright, and the lines of care around her mouth and eyes and the furrows in her forehead had faded and she'd put on a little weight. She knew that, deep down, her mam was still very hurt, but these days she didn't let it show, at least not very often, though as Christmas approached she wondered how Olive would cope with the holiday. Last year, her da had been home – reluctantly, even then, she thought bitterly – and they'd known nothing of Bella's existence. But she was determined to try to forget all about last year and make an effort.

She and Bella had agreed they would try to make this Christmas a good one. They would make paper chains to hang across the ceilings and get holly from the market to brighten up the hall and dining room, and they'd have a tree in pride of place in the parlour window. Bella was already engaged in making decorations for it, using silver and gold paper from cigarette packets, pipe cleaners, cardboard, knitting wool and the like, and everyone agreed her creations were as good as anything you could buy. There were some customs and festive food that Joan had had to explain to Bella, for from what she could gather, Christmas was celebrated a bit differently in Portugal, but she was sure they would all have a good time. Even though Billy had gone, they were still a family.

When everyone was seated, and the meal had been served, Olive glanced around the table at her family and guests. Tonight there were no theatrical people, apart from Lily, just Frederick, Arnold Taylor and Gerard Barnard, as well as herself and her family.

She couldn't help feeling a sense of satisfaction. She worked hard but at least that kept her mind off everything to do with Billy and her former life, and for the first time in years she was earning her own money. She'd even begun to put a few shillings away once a fortnight in a Post Office account, for she had sworn she would never again allow herself to be put into such a dire predicament. Each day after breakfast was over, she cleared the table and washed up, then cleaned the kitchen and raked out the fire in the range and reset it. She then made beds and cleaned and tidied rooms, cleaned the bathroom, went shopping and prepared the evening meal. The towels were changed every three days and the beds once every ten days – unless one of her theatrical guests only stayed a couple of nights, in which case the bed was stripped and remade. She gave the parlour and the dining room a thorough clean every Saturday morning, with Bella's help. With all that work and washing and ironing, when she fell into bed at night she was exhausted. But she found she enjoyed having the company, enjoyed providing some home comforts for people who had seldom had them in their lives, especially their benefactor, Frederick Garswood.

Like Joan, she too had wondered how they would all get on at first, but she was at ease with everyone now – and what's more, to an extent, was enjoying being independent. She found Frederick an easy man to get on with, there was seldom a cross word between them, and he was very good with Charlie and the girls. It was helpful to have someone around when things went wrong too – like bursting back boilers, dripping taps and doors that became warped and stuck. Billy had never been around to help with things like that.

'I'm glad you are not out tonight, Aunty Lil,' Joan addressed her aunt as she handed her the dish of carrots and peas.

'So am I, Joan. It's freezing outside, and backstage in that place is like being in a barn. I'd much sooner sit by the fire in the kitchen or the parlour.'

'Could it be the kitchen tonight, do you think? Monica's coming down later and I think there's something she wants to . . . er . . . discuss with you.'

Lily passed the dish on to Frederick and raised an eyebrow quizzically. She enjoyed the company of her young niece and her friend. 'I take it it's . . . personal?'

Joan nodded.

'I think it best if we all sit in the kitchen tonight – that's if you don't mind, gentlemen? Charlie, you can wrap up well and take Rags for his walk,' Olive added, glancing first at Frederick then at the two other men.

They both looked a little disappointed, she thought, at not having Lily to entertain them. However, she wanted to talk to her sister about Bella and her future. Oh, she knew the child still had some time left at school, but she couldn't afford to keep both the girl and Charlie in education until they were fourteen, let alone fifteen, and they would both be thirteen next year. Come next year, she would have to help them find jobs. She needed the money, so they would need to work too.

Certainly, Charlie got on well with Frederick. Her son

made no complaints about going down to the yard after school or at weekends, and the comics he bought with his pocket money helped keep him quiet during these long winter evenings. But lately she'd begun to hope that maybe, just maybe, Frederick would give Charlie the chance of a lifetime – an apprenticeship, a trade, something that would set him up for his future. She couldn't afford to pay indentures but she could still hope that her son would have better chances in life than his father could have afforded to give him, had he deigned to stay around long enough, not that he'd ever seemed to care much about how Charlie might make his way in life.

For the moment Joan, at least, was settled; she enjoyed her job and had even been given a little promotion and a raise. There were no boyfriends on the horizon but there was plenty of time for that, and from a few things Joan had said lately she had begun to realise that Billy's actions had had an effect on her daughter. Joan, she was sure, would be very careful who she gave her heart and her trust to, which was maybe no bad thing.

Olive had to admit to herself that life was better now than she had ever envisaged it would be, and maybe someday she herself would even get over what Billy had done to her and her family.

# Chapter Twenty-Two

———◆·»◆«·◆———

Whance Monica arrived, windblown and cold, even though she'd run the short distance down the street, Joan made a pot of tea and passed the mugs around.

'This should warm you up, Mon.'

Monica smiled her thanks, cupping her icy hands around the mug.

'Do you think you should take one in for the Three Musketeers in the parlour, or would that be spoiling them? They might come to expect it every night,' Lily remarked with a mischievous smile.

Olive laughed. 'Oh, honestly, Lily, you're so irreverent! I'll take them one in later, seeing as it's so cold tonight.'

Lily turned her attention to Monica. 'Right, then, Monica, I believe you want some advice?'

The two girls had pulled the bench from beside the table closer to the fire and Bella had settled herself at the side of the hearth. Of them all, Bella hated the cold weather the most.

'Well, I'm going on the works' night out next week. It will

be my first time, and I want to look really special, but I can't afford an expensive new dress . . .'

'And there will be someone there she wants to impress,' Joan added, raising an eyebrow.

Lily looked thoughtful. 'It doesn't have to be expensive, Monica.'

'Something really eye-catching is bound to be,' Monica replied gloomily.

Lily glanced at Olive and then made up her mind. 'There's a shop I sometimes go to, run by a woman who used to be in the theatrical business, like me. I know her well – she has some very chic clothes and sells them at a fraction of their original price.'

'Second-hand you mean?' Joan queried, thinking she'd been right about her aunt's extensive wardrobe.

'If you like, but there's nothing tatty about her stuff and it's not a run-of-the-mill second-hand shop. She takes dresses, coats, costumes, blouses – sometimes haute couture – and even hats and handbags – to sell for ladies, and I mean proper *ladies*, and she keeps a percentage of what they sell for.'

'Really?' Even Olive was curious now.

'Oh, you'd be surprised at the likes of the people who go to her. There are a lot of well-off ladies in this city who are careful with their money, and also particular about who's seen in clothes they no longer have use for or are just tired of. And plenty of women and girls who aspire to be seen in something very upmarket but can't afford the price, who are happy to buy and wear them.'

Monica was trying to work this out. 'So, it's more like a dress . . . exchange?'

'I suppose you could call it that, although money does change hands; that's the whole point of the exercise,' Lily replied.

Felicity's Wardrobe was a well-kept secret, situated above one of the smaller shops in Bold Street, but in certain circles it was becoming more and more popular. Lily had worked with 'Fliss' McKenzie years ago, and they'd remained in touch ever since.

'She quite often gets clothes that have come from Henderson's and Cripps, or Liberty and even Harrods in London, Galeries Lafayette in Paris too. Clothes you will never see on women in the dance and music halls and cocktail lounges of Liverpool,' Lily added.

'Oh, that sounds just great! Could . . . could I go and buy something?' Monica begged enthusiastically. 'I do have a bit of money saved.'

'I don't see why not. You could both come, and I'll introduce you. That's the way Miss McKenzie usually likes to meet her clients – not "customers", you'll note.'

'It all sounds a bit too posh and fancy for the likes of these two, Lily,' Olive put in. In her opinion her sister was filling the girls' heads with ideas. And was Lily forgetting that they were both only sixteen, didn't have much money and wouldn't want to look like a child who'd raided her mother's wardrobe.

'Oh no, Mrs Copperfield, don't say that! It sounds as if I'll get just what I'm looking for there!' Monica cried.

'But I don't want you bandying the name of the place all over, at either Crawford's, Joan, or the salon, Monica,' Lily impressed upon them. 'Miss McKenzie would like it to remain exclusive. She doesn't want half of Liverpool parading through her establishment.'

They both nodded, then Joan spoke. 'And, Mam, now don't go off the deep end, but Monica's thinking of having her hair lightened too.'

Lily clapped her hands delightedly. 'What a good idea, Monica! You have beautiful hair – but nothing too drastic, though. You don't want to look brassy. Sometimes on young girls very bleached hair can look . . . well, just like that.'

Olive had a good idea what Nelly would have to say about this – she definitely *would* look on it as being 'brassy', possibly something even worse – but she said nothing. Nelly was well able to take care of Monica and her fads.

'You must have seen pictures of Veronica Lake, the new American film star. She's very glamourous and her hair is lovely. I think you'd suit her style, Monica, especially if your hair were kept in excellent condition and set properly, something you'll be able to do.'

Monica and Joan nodded. Veronica Lake famously wore her ash-blonde shoulder-length hair in a pageboy style which curled under but fell in a shiny curtain covering almost one half of her face. It was very glamorous and quite seductive, but you needed thick hair with a slight natural wave and nothing too curly. It was not an easy style to maintain, Monica knew, but she was excited about Lily's suggestion . . . and if she could find a fabulous dress at a good price, well, all to the good. Things were certainly looking up. She hoped Lily would be able to take her to this 'dress exchange' place on her day off, although she realised that Joan would be working. They had this problem often, she mused. Saturday – Joan's half-day – was Monica's busiest day of the week.

'Why don't you girls go on up to my room and, Monica,

you can see how your hair would look with that new style in my dressing-table mirror,' Olive suggested. Maybe if Monica could manage to recreate this film star's hairstyle she'd think twice about having her hair bleached – and besides, she wanted to talk to her sister about Bella.

'Can I go too, please?' Bella asked, looking eagerly up at Olive as the older girls left the kitchen. She was growing up and keen to be included in Joan and Monica's exciting plans.

'Later, luv. I need you to stay here for a little while.' Olive turned to Lily. 'I need some advice from you too, Lil, about Bella here.'

Both Lily and the child frowned but Olive smiled encouragingly at Bella. 'Next year you will be thirteen, Bella, as will Charlie,' she started.

Lily instantly realised what was coming but remained silent.

'I know it is usual for children to stay at school until they are fourteen, like Joan did, but I'm afraid that . . . well, both you and Charlie will have to leave next year and find work. I . . . I don't have enough money to feed and clothe you and keep you both at school. And I won't treat you differently, Bella, because you're a girl. That's not fair, and you've had too much unfairness in your life already. I know that, one day, Charlie will have to provide for a wife and family.' She smiled. 'At least, I hope so. But I've been thinking about all the things that have changed in my life over the last year, and how I now have to work to keep my family, so I want to give you the chance, Bella, to learn to do something that will be useful for you if ever . . .' She didn't finish.

Lily leaned forward. 'Bella, you are excellent at sewing, is that something you would like to do, or is there something else?' She glanced up at Olive. 'I don't mean in the workroom of a shop doing alterations, but learning the trade properly. You could train as a tailoress or seamstress, maybe. There are some very good bespoke dressmaking establishments in Liverpool – Gladys Drinkwater's, for one.'

Bella looked thoughtful, trying to take everything in. 'They would teach me to make clothes for people to buy?'

'They would. It will take you years to learn everything but . . .' Lily spread her hands expressively. She was certain the girl would be a willing pupil and would prove to be very successful.

'And they would pay me?'

'Of course. Not much to start with, but then Monica doesn't earn much now. But in years to come she will, and it is something she will *always* be able to do to support herself, should she ever need to. It would be something that you would always be able to do too.' Neither of them would find themselves beholden to a man, Lily thought, although she didn't voice this.

Slowly Bella nodded. 'Yes. I would like to do that, Aunt Lily. But how . . . how will I . . . ?'

Olive looked questioningly at her elder sister. At least they had ascertained that Bella would be happy to learn to be a seamstress, yet employment from the likes of Gladys Drinkwater would be almost impossible to achieve.

'Leave all that to me, Olive. I have friends and acquaintances I can speak to – Felicity McKenzie, for example. She has a sister who has been in charge of the workroom at De Jong et Cie for many years, and another at Wetherall's. I'm sure she'll be able to help.'

Olive smiled at Bella. 'So, that's you more or less sorted, Bella, for when you leave school.'

'Thank you, Aunt Lily, that French place sounds very . . . posh.'

Lily shook her head. 'Don't go calling it that, Bella, luv. Say it's a very "exclusive" establishment.'

Bella nodded and smiled. Slowly, and with some effort, she repeated the rather long words. It was a little daunting to think that soon she would be going out to work amongst many, many new people. But then she remembered she'd known no one when she first arrived here, and the thought cheered her.

'You can go on up to Joan now that's settled, Bella,' Olive urged, getting to her feet.

'I go and tell them I am to work making clothes in an *exclusive establishment*,' the girl replied, trying out the new words and grinning as she left the room.

'She really is very obliging, Olive, and she's going to be quite a looker, as they say, when she gets older. You'll have your work cut out keeping the suitors at bay.'

Olive nodded. 'I'll certainly try and make sure she doesn't take up with anyone like her father!'

Lily looked at her sceptically. 'I seem to remember Mam saying something like that.'

'Thank you for that, Lily! Now, I think I'll make a pot of tea and take it into those Three Musketeers, as you call them.'

'I think you'll find Frederick's gone up to his sitting room. I heard him saying goodnight to the others a few minutes ago,' Lily informed her, unperturbed by Olive's sarcasm.

'Then I just hope those girls won't disturb him. I'll take

him a cup up and make sure there's no noise going on up there to annoy him,' her sister replied.

'I'll have my tea and then go up myself, Olive. I've a busy day ahead tomorrow; we've the pantomime starting in a couple of days, and Christmas is always a bit of a chaotic time,' Lily confided.

'Don't remind me,' Olive replied as she poured the tea.

After checking that Joan, Monica and Bella were not turning the bedroom into an impromptu hairdressing salon, Olive went along the landing to the room Frederick used as his sitting room. She had no intention of disturbing him, for she respected his privacy, and so was surprised when he insisted she come in and sit down.

'Is everything all right, Frederick?' she asked cautiously after handing him his tea.

'Perfectly, Olive, thank you,' he replied, thinking that the warm, pale blue-and-yellow paisley-print blouse and dark mustard-coloured wool skirt she wore suited her. 'And it's very thoughtful of you to bring me up a drink.'

She smiled at him, relieved there was nothing he was going to complain about. 'We'd made one for ourselves and the others, so it was no bother.' She began to relax; it was very pleasant in here, she mused. 'You know, Frederick, I have to say it's been a long time since I've been so content with my life. I did have some reservations about moving in but . . .' She waved a hand expressively.

'And it's been a very long time since I have experienced having such comforts – good meals and pleasant company, I mean. We have Lily to thank for some of the company but we were also extremely lucky to find men of the calibre of Arnold and Gerard.'

'I know, Frederick,' she agreed. She'd advertised in one of the morning papers and the men had answered almost by return post, and she'd liked them both. 'It's all working out well – I think everyone is actually looking forward to Christmas.'

He looked at her closely. 'And are you, Olive?'

She nodded. In fact, she was. 'It . . . it's strange to think that last year you were our guest for Christmas dinner, and now . . .'

'I know, but I have the feeling that this year – because we have such good company – we'll enjoy it more.' Last year Billy Copperfield had made an effort to be convivial but it had been obvious that it *was* an effort, he recalled, as he set his tea down on a side table.

'The girls are insisting we decorate every room downstairs.'

'Really? That's splendid, and if I remember rightly, Olive, at the back of the sideboard cupboard is a box of crockery my mother only ever used at Christmas.'

'I'll look it out; it will certainly add style to the table. You've seen Bella's tree decorations?'

He nodded. 'That girl's a marvel with a needle and a bit of glue. Will she be all right, do you think? All her Christmases until now must have been spent very differently.'

'I think so, but she does hate the cold weather. Lily and I have just been discussing her future with her.'

'Isn't that a bit early?' he queried, leaning forward to hear her explanation.

But when Olive had told him of the situation, and their

subsequent plans, he nodded slowly. He admired her for the care and consideration she'd given the girl and her future. She had no need to be so thoughtful – after all, Bella was not her flesh and blood. Some women would view bringing up Bella as a trial and do very little to help her at all, just be glad to get the girl off their hands.

He finished his tea and Olive got to her feet. 'Well, I'll leave you in peace, Frederick, and I'll take those girls down with me too. It's time Bella was getting ready for bed, and I'd better make sure our Charlie's got that dog bedded down for the night.'

'You wouldn't consider letting the dog sleep by the kitchen fire on a night like this, Olive?'

'I would not! Both that animal and our Charlie would come to expect it, and you just never know what that dog has picked up. No, as Nelly is always saying about Arthur and his birds, give them an inch and they'll take a mile!'

He grinned and then became serious. 'Sit down again, Olive, please?'

She was puzzled but did as he asked.

'Talking about how Arthur helps Charlie, and Bella leaving school, has reminded me of something I want to discuss with you and about which you must be anxious. Now is as good a time as any. My question is, what will Charlie do for a job? As he's leaving school too, would you consider letting me take him on as an apprentice plumber?'

Olive gave a little gasp. She'd hoped and prayed he might offer something like this, but she would never have dared to presume. 'I . . . I couldn't pay for his indentures, Frederick.'

'There would be no need for payment, Olive.'

'There would, if you were to pay him a wage.'

He shook his head. 'The pay would be not much more than I give him now, and he's very good around the yard. He grasps things quickly. I'd say he'll make a good tradesman in time, Olive. He'll have to attend evening classes, of course, at the Mechanics' Institute but . . .'

Tears were pricking Olive's eyes. Was there ever a more generous man than Frederick Garswood? 'I . . . I can't thank you enough, Frederick. You've done so much for us all, and now . . . this. Oh, I know he'll be so grateful and I'll make sure he works hard. A tradesman! Oh, our Charlie a proper tradesman! He'll never be short of work in his life. How can I ever thank you enough?'

He got to his feet and took her hands in his, feeling his heart beat a little faster, until he remembered Billy. 'You're thanking me just by being you and making this Christmas one for three middle-aged men to remember.'

She managed a smile. 'I can certainly do that, by forgetting the past – the bad bits, at least! And you've helped me with that. It will be a great Christmas, Frederick, I promise!'

# Chapter Twenty-Three

There had been hell to pay when she'd arrived home last Monday evening, Monica mused, a little smile hovering around her lips. She'd spent her day off with Lily, buying a dress at Felicity's Wardrobe and then they'd gone into the salon where Helen Marshall had opened up specially, supervising Madelaine who'd done her hair. When she emerged, her hair had been bleached three shades lighter, and set and then brushed out in the much-admired style of Veronica Lake, as Lily had suggested. Monica had been delighted with it and when they returned, triumphant, Lily had commented that they'd had a very successful day indeed. It had not been a view shared by her mother.

Nelly was far from impressed, despite the fact that it was the latest fashion, that it had been done professionally and that everyone, but *everyone*, had said it was gorgeous and really suited her.

'It makes you look brassy, Monica! Really bold and brassy! In fact, I'd go so far as to say it makes you look like one of those women you see dressed up to the nines and parading up and down on Lime Street!'

'Oh, Mam, don't say that!' she'd cried in horror at the images her mother's words conjured up of Lime Street's infamous 'ladies of the night'.

Even Arthur was taken aback by the remark. 'I think that's a bit harsh, Nelly, luv,' he'd remonstrated. 'It suits her, and it's been done professionally. I don't think it's at all brassy.'

'It's not as if I've just gone mad with the bleach bottle, Mam, and ended up with it like straw or platinum! I wanted it done so I'd look more grown-up and elegant for my first big function. I've never been to anywhere as grand as the Excelsior!'

'And you will look great, luv. You'll look lovely,' Arthur had soothed, frowning at his wife, who was still muttering under her breath about girls of her daughter's age even being let through the door of places like the Excelsior.

Her mother hadn't changed her attitude over these past days, but Monica had realised now that she didn't really care. She was a child no longer; she was grown-up and working, and determined to be fashionable and elegant like Lily. In her opinion both her mam and Joan's mam were old-fashioned and dowdy in the way they dressed.

She'd got a gorgeous dress from Felicity's Wardrobe and Lily had done some minor alterations to it. And now, she thought, as she checked her appearance in the full-length mirror on the door of her parents' bedroom wardrobe, it fitted her as perfectly as if it had been made especially for her. It had cost a bit more than she had intended to pay, but she hadn't been able to resist it – and it was very obvious that it was a cut above what you could get in the cheaper shops in Liverpool. It was made of a very dark navy lace over a pale blue satin, which made the lace stand out like a gossamer overskirt. It had a fitted bodice and a full skirt and cap sleeves, and Lily had lent her two diamanté clip brooches to adorn each corner of the square neckline and a matching pair of earrings. It was all the jewellery she needed, Lily had advised. Anything else *would* make her look brassy and overdressed, which was definitely not the desired effect. She recalled the very famous French fashion designer Coco Channel, who'd advised, 'Each time, before you go out, take off one piece of jewellery.'

Now, she was convinced that she looked years older than sixteen, and was thrilled with her appearance. When she'd had a 'trial run' of the whole outfit Joan had said she'd never seen anyone their age who looked so utterly glamorous – which had pleased Monica no end. Lily had been so generous and helpful too, Monica thought. She had such style, something her mother was definitely short on! She had even lent Monica her precious imitation Persian lamb coat to wear over the dress, as her own plain wool one would have ruined the effect. On condition, of course, that she take great care of it.

Tonight, Joan had come round to help her dress and do her make-up, and now she grinned approvingly at her friend's appearance.

'Well, if he doesn't dance attendance on you all night, Mon, I think he must have gone blind or mad or both! You'll be turning heads all night. Definitely the belle of the ball!' she added, a little enviously, for her friend certainly looked stunning.

'Really, Joan? You are telling me the truth? You don't think it's all a bit – too much?' Monica probed. She felt that she did look really good, but . . .

'Would I say something like that and not mean it? What are friends for but to tell you the truth – even when it's not what you want to hear? But you look fabulous, Mon, you really do! Just let him do all the running tonight, don't be too eager. This is the new grown-up Monica Savage. And make sure he drives you home; you don't want to be standing at tram stops at this time of year, and in this weather, with everyone falling out of the pubs half cut.'

Monica grinned at her. 'I'll have Lily's lovely coat to keep me warm. Oh, she's been so good to me, Joan!'

Joan grinned back. 'I know. Just make sure you don't lose the damned coat!'

When Monica came downstairs, Arthur smiled and told her she looked like a princess – a grown-up princess – and even Nelly managed a nod and a muttered 'very smart', while Eileen was lost for words at the sight of this elegant, sophisticated vision that apparently – and unbelievably – was her elder sister.

Monica had never been into The Excelsior Hotel and Ballroom before. As she entered the carpeted foyer, she felt a little daunted by the heavy gilt-framed mirrors on the walls and the side tables laden with huge arrangements of Christmas greenery. She searched the faces of the people milling around but, seeing none of the familiar faces from the salon, began to feel panic rising. Had she got the right place? Oh, it was all so very grand, and she'd be utterly mortified if she had to walk out again.

Thankfully, she was spotted by a uniformed porter and directed to the Ladies Cloakroom where she handed over her coat and received a ticket in its place, which she carefully tucked into her evening purse. Quite a few women and girls were crowded around the very large mirror which covered one wall, all applying lipstick and face powder and adjusting hairstyles, and it was with some relief that she spotted Francine, the manicurist, resplendent in a full-skirted taffeta cocktail dress of emerald green.

'Lord above! Monica! I didn't recognise you! You look . . . fabulous!' Francine cried, with genuine admiration.

'Thanks! I'm hoping that I look older and that I sort of . . . fit in, here.'

'Oh, believe me, you do!'

'I've never been here before.'

'Just wait until you see the dining room and then the ballroom. I have to say, it's really good of Mr Eustace to treat us all to a dinner and dance here once a year. There's not many would do that, I can tell you.'

Helen Marshall had appeared beside them. 'And let's hope no one disgraces themselves! Just watch what you drink, girls – remember neither of you are legally old enough, though I suppose one small glass of wine or sherry won't hurt.' She smiled, then added, 'Just be careful – and don't accept drinks from strangers, we aren't the only Christmas celebration party here tonight.'

They followed her through into the vast ornate dining room with its huge crystal chandeliers and large circular tables all set with white damask clothes and napkins and gleaming cutlery and glasses. It was already packed with fellow diners and revellers, and Monica felt her spirits rise. She'd never imagined places like this even existed. She caught sight of Mr Eustace and her colleagues, seated around a large table, and then she smiled delightedly as she saw Rick get to his feet, looking incredibly handsome in his dark evening suit and black tie. She couldn't help but notice that he was looking at her with open admiration and some amazement.

'Monica! You look stunning! That dress, your hair . . .'

Her heart turned over with joy and excitement as he took her hand and led her to a place at the table beside his. Everyone was staring at her – mostly with admiration, but some envy too. She smiled shyly at Mr Eustace as Rick helped her sit down, holding out her chair.

'You do indeed look very different tonight, Miss Savage. I compliment you,' her employer commented.

'Thank you, Mr Eustace. It . . . it's very generous of you to invite me.'

'Well, we couldn't leave the juniors out now, could we? Enjoy your evening – but no strong drink, or I'll be in trouble with the management.' He smiled before turning his attention to Helen Marshall, seated on the other side of him.

She had enjoyed her evening, she thought to herself, as she joined the queue to collect her coat. The meal had been wonderful, and she'd had just one small glass of a fizzy wine that Rick had told her was something called 'sparkling perry', not real champagne, which was far too expensive in places like this.

When the meal was over, everyone had gone through into the ballroom. It seemed vast to her, and – like the other rooms – was very ornate with lots of gilded mirrors and picture frames, and delicate-looking chairs and tables set around the dance floor. Rick hadn't been able to dance with her very often, for she had been in great demand, her new elegant look causing many heads to turn when she'd walked in on Rick's arm. Now, if she were honest, her feet were really hurting her but she had immensely enjoyed being swept around the dance floor by different young men and had revelled in their admiration and flattery.

'At least I'm taking you home, Monica!' Rick had impressed upon her when he'd claimed her for the last waltz.

She'd smiled up at him. None of the others were quite as handsome, she thought. 'Thank you. I've had the most wonderful night of my life, Rick!'

'But it's not over yet,' he'd replied, winking.

She'd laughed, thinking that maybe Joan had been right when she'd said to let him do all the running. He was being very attentive, and she really hadn't been short of partners, but now she was more than content to get her coat and let him escort her out to wherever it was he'd parked his car, and drive her home.

It was a short but chilly ride and she pulled the collar of Lily's coat up around her ears. The cold brought colour to her cheeks and a sparkle to her eyes so that when Rick pulled up outside her home in Mersey View he was struck by how radiant she looked.

Gently, he put his arms around her and drew her close to him, nuzzling her neck and feeling her soft, silky hair against his cheeks. 'How come I've never noticed before just how utterly gorgeous you are, Miss Monique Savage?' he whispered.

She stifled a little giggle but her heart was pounding. 'Probably because you haven't really seen all that much of me lately, Rick.'

'And I'm realising just what a fool I've been for neglecting you, Monica!'

He kissed her with increasing passion. It was true, he thought, he hadn't really taken her out for a while – and yet somehow she'd suddenly changed. She'd grown up, she'd become a real stunner. Why had he not noticed that? She'd had blokes buzzing around her all night, so much so that he'd barely got a look-in on the dance floor. Well, from now on he'd see her more often, he promised himself. It didn't matter to him that she lived in a small terraced house in Everton, and was just an employee – and a junior one at that. He was becoming very attracted to her, and the feeling was obviously mutual.

It was the end of a perfect evening, Monica told herself, as she finally disentangled herself from his embrace and kissed him goodnight, noting the parlour curtains twitching. She was certain now that they were becoming closer – hadn't he told her so? And she would be seeing him again on the night after Boxing Day. He'd promised to take her to the Cocktail Lounge of The Stork Hotel – he was certain no one would have the temerity to ask how old she was. Not if she looked as glamorous and gorgeous as she did tonight. Oh, she felt as if she were walking on clouds as she went indoors. She did indeed feel so grown-up and sophisticated, and everything was beginning to work out just as she wanted it. Christmas would be wonderful this year!

It was a sentiment Joan endorsed the following day after Monica had finished telling her every detail of the wonderful evening she'd had with Rick Eustace at the Excelsior.

'Well, after the year we've had, Mam is determined Christmas is going to be great, and all the guests are looking forward to it too. She's been baking mince pies, and even a Christmas cake, and Bella and me have got the place done up like Lewis's Grotto,' she enthused. 'There's just the tree to finish off tonight.'

Monica sighed happily. 'Will it be all right if I come down late afternoon on Christmas Day with your presents and to hear how it all went?'

'Of course! I bet they'll be so stuffed with food that they'll all be asleep by then. Aunty Lil is going out, though – there's some kind of do at the theatre for everyone who works there.'

'And do you think Bella will be fine with everything?'

Joan shrugged. 'She seems happy enough. She's really looking forward now to leaving school and earning her own money – not that it will be much – but it's all a big novelty for her, so I think she's thinking more about that than the past. She's even started to sing – Christmas carols, I think, in Portuguese – and she's got a really good voice too, which surprised everyone.'

Monica got to her feet. 'Shall we go to yours and help her finish off the tree?'

'I think she was going to ask our Charlie to help her.'

'Charlie!'

Joan nodded and grimaced. 'I know, but she said he could do all the high bits she can't reach, and I think Mam was encouraging her. It'll help keep him occupied for a while at least. And anyway, I'd like you to try and do something different with my hair. I'm sick of this style.'

Monica smiled, happy to practise her skills on her friend.

* * *

Olive looked around the parlour door and smiled to herself at the sight of Charlie, balancing on a stool to attach the silver star to the very top of the Christmas tree. They'd done a good job, the pair of them, she thought, before she went back to the kitchen to her baking.

'It will not fall off, Charlie?' Bella asked, a little concerned that it looked lop-sided.

''Course not, Bella! When I fix something, it stays fixed!' he replied firmly. He was actually looking forward to starting work. He liked being down at the yard and got on well with the two men Frederick employed. He'd been over the moon when Mam had told him that he was being taken on as an apprentice. The only fly in the ointment he could see was the fact that he'd have to go to evening classes at the Mechanics' Institute. But as Joan had said, was that really so bad? As he climbed down off the stool he stood beside his half-sister to admire their handiwork.

Bella smiled and nodded. 'I think it looks very . . . grand now, Charlie.'

'Did you have a tree at home in Lisbon?' he asked a little awkwardly. He was curious, and she seldom spoke about her life in Portugal.

'Yes, we did, but we never had so much food,' she replied a little wistfully. All the customs that had been explained to her were different, as was the food that was to be eaten.

'Sometimes *we* never had all the stuff Mam's been making lately. Sometimes, there wasn't much money.'

Bella understood that. 'For us too there was not much. But we always had a *berço*, I think here you call it a "crib" and you have it in the church. We have it in the house and it has figures and I made a lake from a piece of mirror and hills from pebbles and moss. We went to church on Christmas Eve to the *Missa do Galo* – the Mass – and then we go home to our supper – *consoada*. The cod fish and potatoes and green vegetables; not the goose, the stuffing and the sprouts, parsnips, carrots and the roasted potatoes. Then the plum pudding, then the cake. But we had sweets too sometimes. *Rabanadas* and *azevias*, which would have a tiny gift inside, and *pasteis de nata*. Then I would leave out a *sapataho* – my shoe – for the Christ child to fill, if He could. We did not have this Santa. But sometimes He had no gifts left for me.' She smiled sadly at Charlie. 'You see, we . . . my *mãe* had only what . . . Papa left us.' Bella smiled sadly. The pain of her mother's death wasn't so bad these days, but she still missed her and probably always would do.

Charlie looked down at his feet, feeling embarrassed and bitter, as he always did when he thought of Billy. Quite often, in the past, Mam had struggled to get them the toy they'd asked Santa for – he remembered the football he'd got last year, when his da had been at home. 'Do . . . do you miss him, Bella?'

She reached out to gently straighten a bauble she'd made. 'Now . . . not so much. When I think – really think – I did not know him very well, Charlie. He would be away for such a long time and then he would come, just for a day or two, and then – gone again. I miss my mama more.'

'It was pretty much the same for us, until . . .'

Bella reached for his hand and squeezed it, instinctively feeling the depth of his hurt. 'But now I have you and Joan. I did not have a sister or a brother. Now I have . . . everyone! I have this – you, Charlie, my family and . . . Christmas!'

He managed to smile back at her, thinking that she had suffered far worse than he had at Billy's hands but she was trying to make the most of her new life. He couldn't help but admire her. 'Happy Christmas, Bella,' he said, warm with pleasure at the idea that she was there to share it with them.

'*Feliz Natal*, Charlie!' she replied, her dark eyes bright with tears of joy. She did have a family now, and she could look forward to a future she was sure would be better than anything she could have hoped for in Lisbon. Softly she began to sing the words of the carol '*A Todos um Bom Natal*' – 'A Merry Christmas to You All'.

# Chapter Twenty-Four

———◆·━◆·◆·━◆———

*1938*

'Is your mam still fussing?' Monica asked Joan as they walked slowly along Northumberland Terrace towards Mersey View, taking advantage of the warm sunlight of the September evening. Christmas and New Year had gone so well, and over the spring and summer months everyone had seemed to be very settled.

Joan raised her eyes skywards. 'Thankfully, no. She's been driving everyone mad, you'd think it was the King who was coming to stay.'

Monica smiled at her. Olive was expecting a new permanent lodger to move in that day. Poor Mr Taylor had had a heart attack at work and had died last month, which had been a shock for everyone. Frederick Garswood had taken charge of all the 'official' things, for apparently the poor soul had no relatives at all, but he'd paid into a life insurance policy so all the expenses were covered by that. Olive had then found herself with a spare room, and it had been Lily who had found their new guest, a newly employed member of the theatre orchestra, from Glasgow, so he needed permanent lodgings.

Olive had cleaned Mr Taylor's old room from top to bottom, and a different bedspread and curtains had been found in a bedding chest. 'So it gives the room a new look and feel,' she'd told her sister, anxious to make the new member of the household welcome.

'I don't think he expects The Adelphi Hotel, Olive,' Lily had replied. 'From what I can gather, he doesn't come from a very salubrious part of Glasgow, and he's not a senior member of the orchestra. He plays the trumpet, not that he'll expect to be practising much at home – though he will need to practise every day. He'll do that at the theatre each day before the matinee,' she'd added hastily, in case her sister changed her mind.

'What's his name?' Olive had asked.

'James McDonald – he's twenty-two, and people call him Jim.'

All this had been imparted to Joan and the rest of the family – and she, in turn, had passed the information on to Monica.

'At least it will be good to have someone young as a lodger; he won't go having heart attacks and dying on you.'

'There's that to it, but I do wonder what he'll be like. I mean he's quite young to be in an orchestra, and one in Liverpool. You would have thought he'd have wanted to stay in Scotland, they must have theatres up there,' Joan mused aloud.

'Maybe he actually *wants* to get away from Scotland.

Mam was saying that parts of Glasgow are as bad as parts of Liverpool – worse, in fact, what with all the violence – those "razor gangs".'

Joan nodded; she'd heard of them too, though Liverpool had its own violence to contend with. 'It could be out of the frying pan et cetera, if you ask me.'

'Still, he must be all right, or your Aunty Lil wouldn't have suggested him.'

Again, Joan had nodded. 'I'm quite looking forward to meeting him. I'm curious.'

Monica grinned at her. 'You never know, you might really take a shine to him.'

It was certainly about time Joan found herself a steady boyfriend, she thought. They were both now eighteen. Oh, there had been a few, for Joan was a very attractive girl, but she knew her friend was wary. She seemed not to want to get too involved with any of the young men she met. She herself was very happy with what she termed her 'love life'. Ever since that Christmas dance at the Excelsior, now nearly two years ago, she had seen Rick on a regular basis. She was almost certain that she was in love with him, and he with her. Of course, her mam still did not fully approve; she wondered if Nelly would ever get over what she called 'the class thing'. But she'd relaxed around Rick a bit more, since they'd often stayed in – especially during the winter months, when the weather had been really miserable – and, apart from moaning about having to heat the parlour, Nelly hadn't been too vocal about his existence.

He'd taken her home twice to meet his family, which had been daunting but interesting occasions. They had a large house in a quiet leafy road in Woolton, one of the city's more fashionable and expensive suburbs. It even had a garage for the cars, and they actually owned the house, not rented it. It was furnished in a far grander and more modern style than her own home and had all the most up-to-date appliances. She'd liked his mother, a small, quiet woman, with light brown hair and grey eyes, who dressed in twinsets and expensive skirts and dresses, and wore pearls. His sisters hadn't been too bad either – she'd thought they might be stuck-up and offhand with her, but they were friendly enough.

Monica realised that, if she and Rick eventually got married, she could have a lifestyle like his mother's, which was a very appealing thought. She'd have no need to work then, and would have all the luxuries she wanted. It was very tempting. But then she would ask herself, did she really love him enough to spend the rest of her life with him? Mam was very clear on what marriage entailed. It was for life, there would be no question of divorce or separation. That was only for the rich and famous – or infamous – she'd stated on numerous occasions, and it wasn't always a bed of roses. But, whatever the future might bring, Monica was enjoying her life at the moment. She loved her job, and she was earning more so could therefore spend more, and thanks to Lily and Felicity's Wardrobe she was always very smartly dressed. Rick took her to all the best places and bought her flowers and chocolates, so was she ready to stay at home and just keep house?

There was also the small fact that he hadn't yet asked her, she reminded herself, but she was sure he would, for they had become very close – sometimes too close for comfort for both of them. It was getting harder and harder for her to refuse his increasingly intimate advances. And then there were all the terrible things going on in the world. Everyone was saying there would be another war; that Hitler and Mussolini had to be stopped. Schoolchildren had been issued with gas masks, and there was much talk of bomb shelters being erected. Would the likes of Rick and Joan's new lodger be called up? It was all very disturbing, although she tried not to think too much about it all – and it certainly hadn't affected her trade. But she knew her mam and dad were seriously worried, as were most of their generation. A generation who had lived through one war and were aware of what it all meant.

They parted company, as usual, at Joan's house, with Joan promising to come up to tell her friend all about what the new lodger was like after their meal.

Joan found her mother in the kitchen with Bella, who was helping her put the final touches to the meal. Bella had grown up, this last year, she thought. She was almost as tall as herself now, had filled out and wore her hair much shorter, in a style Monica had recommended for her. She appeared to be doing well enough at work, being an apprentice seamstress at De Jong et Cie, although she didn't seem to have made many friends there and sometimes complained about Miss Whitworth, her supervisor, being difficult.

'So, has he arrived, Mam?' Joan queried.

Olive nodded. 'He has indeed. I've shown him up to his room and instructed him on what few rules and regulations there are, and he'll join us all for supper. I left him unpacking. He seems a nice enough young man, although I do have a bit of difficulty with his accent at times. Lily says I'll get used to it and it's not as broad as some she's known.'

241

'What do you think of him, Bella?' Joan asked her half-sister.

Bella shrugged. 'He is all right. He doesn't talk much and he's like me – foreign.'

'You're not foreign, Bella!' Joan protested. Sometimes she thought Bella could be a little difficult, but then she was nearly fifteen; her moods were just part of growing up. No one ever mentioned Billy these days, and Joan wondered sometimes if both Bella and Charlie had forgotten all about him. They'd heard nothing from him, of course, but she still thought about him, as she knew her mother did, although they both now looked on Frederick as the head of the household. She suspected her mam was growing rather fond of Frederick Garswood, and he of her. Nothing untoward had been said or done, of course, for Olive was a stickler for respectability, but Joan thought that her mother's life was far more comfortable and settled than it had ever been. After all, they'd been in Mersey View for over three years now – longer than they'd ever stayed anywhere else.

When the dinner gong had sounded, and the guests were assembled in the dining room, Joan had an opportunity to study the new lodger. Jim McDonald was a very ordinary-looking young man, she thought, as she passed the plates around the table. When he'd come in she'd noticed that he was tall, over six foot, with light sandy-coloured hair and blue eyes, and was obviously a bit daunted by being in the presence of strangers.

She smiled at him. 'It must all take some getting used to, moving here to Liverpool and the orchestra and then . . . us, a house full of strangers – except Aunt Lily, of course.'

He nodded, smiling back shyly. 'I'll be all right when I've settled in, both here and at the theatre. It's a lovely house, as I've already told your mam. I'm lucky, for I never expected to find anything as comfortable.'

'Well, it shouldn't take long to settle in at the theatre, Jim, we're a friendly lot,' Lily put in. 'Were you in your last job for long?' she queried, passing him the vegetable tureen.

'Two years, but I decided I'd like a change, and to travel a bit.'

Joan smiled at him. 'Well, you've not travelled far, Jim.'

'Not yet, Joan, but I intend to see some of the world – when I've managed to save up enough money, that is.'

Lily raised her eyebrows. 'With what they pay you, I should imagine it'll take quite a while.'

'And with the state the world is in, it might not be advisable . . . or possible,' Frederick remarked. 'I'm not alone in hoping that this "peace in our time" Mr Chamberlain's just agreed with Herr Hitler lasts.'

Jim nodded his agreement, as his mouth was full of Olive's shepherd's pie – the best he'd ever tasted. They all seemed very friendly, he thought, and he particularly liked Joan, whom he thought very attractive and confident. Of course Bella was very pretty – in a dark, exotic sort of way – but she was much younger. Miss Lily Cooper was a very glamorous and sophisticated lady, but very nice too, and he was very grateful to her for finding him a place here. From what he'd seen of the other two men so far, they were not stand-offish or old fuddy-duddies. They were a rather mixed lot, he concluded, but no doubt he'd find out more about them all as time went by. But for now he was just happy that he'd found a decent, comfortable place to stay. Only time would tell if he would come to call it home, but he hoped so, for he'd not had a very happy or secure childhood. The only thing in his life he'd really enjoyed so far was his music, and he'd been trained in that courtesy of his da's maiden sister, Aunt Isabelle, who had had virtually nothing to do with her family and had lived in a small house near to the Necropolis. She was dead now, but he would be eternally grateful to her for paying for his tuition. His music had been his escape route from a life of poverty and unhappiness.

'If you are interested in football, Jim, you're welcome to come to a match with me and Arthur Savage and Charlie here,' Frederick offered. 'Football is almost a religion in this city.'

Jim grinned back. 'Aye, I'd say it's the same in Glasgow. I was brought up Protestant but I sort of fell by the wayside, so I'm a Rangers supporter.'

'And I'd say football and religion are responsible for most of the trouble in both cities,' Lily put in succinctly.

Joan got to her feet to collect the dirty plates. 'Well, we hope you'll settle in and be happy here, Jim.'

He grinned up at her. 'Thanks, Joan, I hope I will too.'

Olive glanced thankfully across at Lily. It seemed as if her new guest would fit in very well, and obviously Joan thought so too. It was a relief, for she'd wondered if he might be a bit on the 'loud' side, but it seemed he wasn't. She smiled across at Frederick and he smiled back. They were all at ease with one another now – she knew he'd been anxious about their new guest too. She never forgot that this was his house – his home – and that they were all, in fact, *his* guests. Nor did she forget how much she owed him, especially now that Charlie was doing so well. He was capable of doing small plumbing jobs by himself now, and Frederick had told her that he was a neat and tidy workman, and she was pleased he was applying himself at his evening classes. Charlie and Bella had the occasional bust-up but that was only normal, she thought. They were both growing up, and apparently Nelly was having similar problems with Eileen. Since she'd started as a clerk in the offices of the London and North Western Railway, she'd become a right little 'know-it-all', according to her mam.

At least Bella and Eileen had remained friends, though there did seem to be a bit of jealousy between them, mainly owing to the fact that Eileen earned far more than Bella and had found new friends at work, and she wondered if they were perhaps growing apart. Olive sighed as she got to her feet to fetch in the dessert – sponge pudding and syrup. She knew she really didn't have much to complain about, these days, and her savings in the Post Office were growing. That was something she was proud of, for there would come a day when she'd be past undertaking all the work involved in running this boarding house and would need that money. But she pushed that thought to the back of her mind. Like everyone else, she was relieved that another war could be averted, or so it appeared. The Prime Minister's negotiations seemed to have been successful, otherwise the future didn't bear thinking about.

# Chapter Twenty-Five

———◆·❋·◆———

On a mild, misty morning in the middle of October Olive had finished her morning chores and was sitting having a cup of tea with Lily, whose day off it was, when the kitchen door flew open and Bella rushed in, immediately bursting into floods of tears.

'Bella, child! What on earth is wrong? What's happened?' Olive cried, jumping to her feet and gathering the girl into her arms. She'd never seen Bella so upset before.

'I not go back there! Never! Never!' Bella sobbed.

Olive looked at Lily over the top of Bella's head, noting that her sister too was concerned.

'Bella, sit down and calm yourself, and tell us what this is all about,' Lily instructed gently. Over the years she'd grown fond of the girl and now really did think of her as her niece and possibly the daughter she'd never had. She always advised Bella on her hair and clothes, and she enjoyed keeping the little confidences the girl trusted her with – like how she wished she looked like Monica, or even Eileen Savage, with their fair colouring and peachy skin.

Olive eased the still-sobbing girl down on to a chair, wondering what on earth had happened to make Bella leave work, and in such a state. 'Try to calm down, Bella, luv,' she urged.

Lily got up and fetched a glass of water. She pressed it into Bella's hands, which she noted were shaking.

Bella took a gulp, spluttered and then took a deep breath. 'She . . . she never like me, Miss Whitworth, never, but this morning I was finishing my *toile*, it had taken me two whole days to sew, and I sew most carefully and neatly and she . . . she . . .' Bella took another gulp of water while the expressions on both Olive's and Lily's faces became grim. 'She take it from me and she say . . . it's not right – again!' Bella swallowed hard to fight down the tears of anger and frustration that were threatening to overwhelm her.

'So, did she say why it was not right?' Lily asked. Any sewing Bella did was always perfect.

Bella shook her head and then with one hand brushed a curl that had fallen across her forehead, back behind her ear. 'No. She . . . she pulled it apart! She ripped it into pieces and throw it in the bin . . . and say I must do it again, and it is not the first time she do this to me . . .' Bella broke down again.

Lily's expression hardened. Olive knew very little about sewing, let alone dressmaking, but Lily did. She knew that if Bella had taken two days to make a *toile* – a garment made in cheap cotton, and to exact measurements, which would be used as a pattern to cut out the final garment – then it wouldn't have had a fault in it.

247

'I say no, I will not! I say she is always picking on me. Then she say I am rude and insolent and she call me names and the . . . the other girls they . . . laugh.'

Lily felt her temper rising. Young girls could be nasty little cats and this lot definitely sounded that way inclined. 'What names, Bella?' she probed.

'She say I am stupid! I am a stupid foreign . . . *dago*? That I will never be good enough or clever enough to be a seamstress and I should go back to where I come from! I hate her! I *hate* her! I not go back there!'

'No, you will not!' Olive reassured her, her dark eyes flashing with anger.

'Indeed you won't, Bella!' Lily added, getting to her feet, her face like thunder. 'But *I* will! This Whitworth person is not going to be allowed to get away with behaviour and language like that! She is a vindictive bully who is obviously jealous of your skills, Bella!'

Both Bella and Olive looked at her quizzically. 'You mean you're going there to . . . to confront her, Lily?' Olive asked. It was all terribly unfair on Bella but what Lily was proposing was unheard of. There were bullies in all walks of life and all jobs; you put up with it or you got another job.

'I am! It was me who asked Fliss McKenzie to put a word in for Bella to her sister Julia, so it's down to me to sort this out. But one thing is certain, Olive – she's not going back there. At least not while *that* woman's still there.'

Olive bit her lip. She could fully understand Lily's feelings. But was there any point in going to an establishment like that and confronting a woman who was obviously a senior and valued employee? No doubt this Miss Whitworth's superiors would back her up; bosses always did. Bella would just have to look at finding another position.

She set about calming Bella down and bathing her tear-blotched face while Lily went upstairs to change. When she came back downstairs, she was resplendent in her very best russet wool costume with a cream crêpe de Chine blouse underneath. It had been a real find; it had initially come from Harrods, and anyone could tell from its style and cut that it had cost a small fortune. Over her carefully arranged blonde hair Lily wore a matching russet velvet hat with a small brim, around which curled creamy-coloured egret feathers. Lily was pulling out all the stops, Olive thought, and by the look on her face she knew her sister meant business.

'Right, then, I'll be off. Bella, you just leave things to me, luv.'

The girl looked at her with admiration mixed with appre-hension. 'I not go back there, Aunt Lily!'

'No, you won't, but I intend to have my say, and I will insist they give you a good reference – despite this . . . this woman and her opinions!' Lily also intended to demand they hand back the money she and Olive had managed to scrape together for Bella's indentures. It was money the girl would need until she was able to get another job.

Neither Olive nor Bella replied as Lily picked up her bag and gloves and left the house.

All the way into town on the tram Lily fumed. That poor girl had suffered enough in her short life, and she for one was not going to stand by and see her hurt and humiliated – again! She could just imagine what Bella had been going through; no wonder she'd said she wished she looked like Monica. Although as a port Liverpool was a very cosmopolitan city, and always had been, there was still a lot of fear and suspicion of anyone who was perceived to be foreign or foreign-looking.

She worked out her plan as the tram trundled through the city streets. She did have some influence herself, she was aware of that. She was known throughout the entertainment business in the city because of the position she held at the Empire, and she counted amongst her friends and acquaintances quite a few journalists who worked for the Liverpool *Echo* and *Daily Post*. She doubted that the management of such a prominent fashion establishment would take kindly to the behaviour of this Miss Whitworth being printed in the daily papers for the population of Liverpool and beyond to read. Once she'd met her, confronted her, she'd have a far more personal insight into the woman's character.

She walked confidently into the rather dimly lit reception area, which Lily noted was furnished in quite an avant-garde fashion, and asked the girl sitting at the desk if she could possibly see Miss Julia McKenzie, a senior member of management, so she believed.

'May I ask what it is about, Miss . . . ?'

'Cooper. Miss Lillian Cooper, and it is concerning my niece and a woman you employ . . . a Miss Whitworth? I am the wardrobe mistress at the Empire Theatre and, I might add, a friend of Miss McKenzie's sister, Felicity.'

The girl nodded and got to her feet. 'If you would wait here, Miss Cooper.'

Lily had never met Julia McKenzie before and was surprised to see that, compared to her younger sister, Fliss, she was rather staid in her dress and looks, but she appeared friendly enough.

'Miss Cooper . . . Lily? How nice to meet you at last.' She smiled as she extended her hand.

Lily smiled back. 'Thank you. May I call you Julia?

'Of course. Now what is the reason for your visit? Something to do with our Miss Whitworth, I understand.'

'It is, and I would very much like to meet her, if it is not too much of an inconvenience. I have heard a lot about her and would like to make her acquaintance. And of course, being involved with costume and fashion, I would love to pay a visit to your workrooms. Perhaps we could kill two birds with one stone?'

'Excellent,' Julia replied. If Julia McKenzie thought the request to meet Phyllis Whitworth was a little strange, she said nothing but politely escorted Lily down a long corridor and then opened a door to a very large, light room filled with huge work surfaces. There were girls of various ages, all engaged in some stage of the dressmaking process. Despite the low buzz of talking, all seemed focused on their work.

'This is all very industrious, Julia,' Lily commented, searching the room for the woman who had treated her niece so badly. Her gaze finally alighted on a tall, thin woman of about forty who Lily could only describe as dowdy, with her sallow skin, pale eyes and light brown hair scraped back into an unbecoming chignon. 'And I take it that is Miss Whitworth?'

'Yes, that's Phyllis, our senior and most experienced seamstress.' Julia beckoned the woman over, smiling at her. 'This is Miss Lillian Cooper; she's the wardrobe mistress at the Empire Theatre.'

Phyllis Whitworth's thin, pale eyebrows rose a little in surprise, and she gave a half-smile.

'And aunt to Annabella Copperfield,' Lily said curtly. 'I would like to see the *toile* my niece made recently, Miss Whitworth.'

The woman's eyes hardened but her gaze went fleetingly to Julia McKenzie. 'Is . . . is she allowed to ask this, Miss McKenzie?'

Julia was clearly puzzled and turned to Lily. 'Lily, what is all this about?'

'My niece – Bella – came home in floods of tears this morning, Julia. Apparently she had taken two days making the required *toile* only for this person here to tell her it was not good enough and then to rip it apart! My niece is a gifted embroiderer and spends endless time and effort on any piece of work she undertakes, so I would like to see this garment which was apparently so badly made. I gather this is not the first time Bella's work has been destroyed.' Lily looked around the room, which had now fallen silent, and raised her voice. 'And why did its destruction cause so much amusement and laughter amongst your other apprentices?'

Phyllis Whitworth was clearly shocked, but she wasn't going to give up without a fight. 'It was not fit for purpose, and the girl is . . . insolent,' she snapped, although two bright spots of colour had appeared on her cheeks.

Lily turned on her. 'Bella is never insolent! At school she was always commended for her excellent manners – you may contact Miss Forshaw, her headmistress, if you do not believe me. And, Miss Whitworth, I think it is *you* who need to learn some manners and how to speak to people, especially those in

252

your charge. You called my niece,' she turned to Julia, 'who is a girl of fourteen, "a stupid foreign . . . *dago*". Bella is half Portuguese,' she explained. 'She also said she was someone who would never be clever enough to become a seamstress at all and that she should go back to Portugal. Now, I would like an explanation, please?'

The expression on Julia McKenzie's face had hardened.

'I would be obliged if you could explain this, Miss Whitworth. Please fetch the *toile* – or the remaining pieces of it.'

Phyllis Whitworth's face was now scarlet. But with tightly clenched lips she turned away and went to fetch Bella's work from the bin where she had consigned it. When she returned, she handed over the various pieces of material to Julia for inspection. Both she and Lily examined them closely.

'I'm afraid I can see very little wrong here, Phyllis. The stitching is even and neat – though of course it makes it difficult, it being in so many pieces,' Julia at last commented.

'Which just shows the amount of force that was used to tear it apart. And like you, I can see nothing wrong with it either,' Lily stated, glaring around the room at the silent, watchful and now decidedly uncomfortable-looking apprentices.

'I will speak to you later in my office, Phyllis,' Julia stated, before waving a hand to dismiss the woman. 'She is very senior, has been with us for years, and has never acted like this before, to my knowledge. She will be severely reprimanded, if all you say about her outburst is correct, but I would be very, very loath to dismiss her, Lily.'

'I understand your position perfectly, Julia, but Bella is refusing to return – and I have to say, I agree she shouldn't.

But I at least expect her to be given a good reference and, if possible, whatever money from her indentures that you may see fit to refund. I think that is only fair. The girl's work is excellent, as you've seen for yourself – De Jong is losing a girl who will one day be an outstanding seamstress, and I can assure you that she is far from insolent. In my opinion the fact that she has been forced to put up with such treatment, so that her working life has become unbearable, is scandalous. And from a woman I deem unfit to supervise young girls in any manner whatsoever. She is a jealous bully. If such vindictive behaviour were more widely known, it would be most unfortunate for the company's reputation. She is certainly not a good example to the young.'

Julia McKenzie nodded, her lips tightly pursed. 'If she spoke to your niece in the way you suggest, I can only apologise. It should never have happened. And I think we can accommodate your requests, Lily. Providing there will be no further mention of the matter. I'm so sorry this has happened.'

Lily smiled pleasantly. She'd got exactly what she'd set out to get for Bella. A reference, an apology and the residue of her money. 'Of course not, Julia. Annabella will put the matter behind her. I can assure you that I will be in a position to make sure of that, as I intend to train her myself. She'll be working with me in the Wardrobe Department at the theatre.'

Julia McKenzie smiled back, thankful that Lily wasn't going to make an almighty fuss. 'An excellent profession for her, I'm sure. I hope she'll be happy there.'

But, as Lily took her leave, she wondered just what she had done. She hadn't meant to say that. She didn't know if Ben Stoker, the manager, would even entertain the idea of an extra member of the wardrobe staff, or if Bella herself would be content to work with her. She patted her hat and tucked her bag firmly under her arm. Well, she'd said it now, and she wouldn't go back on it. Bella deserved all the help she could get in life from now on, and she would do her best to make sure she got it.

When Lily got home, she was relieved to see that Bella was more her usual self and was helping Olive to make a meat and potato pie for supper.

'So, how did you get on?' Olive asked, rubbing the flour from her hands on to the rolling pin.

Lily took off her hat and jacket and smiled. 'Very well. You're going to get a good reference, as well as what's left of your indenture money. Julia McKenzie had to agree with me that there was nothing wrong with your work, Bella, and that *that* woman should never have spoken to you in such a manner or behaved the way she did. She apologised, and I wouldn't like to be on the receiving end of the dressing-down Julia McKenzie will dole out to Miss Phyllis Whitworth – and most probably all the apprentices too.'

'Lord, Lily! How did you manage that?' Olive asked, while Bella smiled at her aunt.

'If I'd had my way she would have been sacked! There is far too much injustice in this world. But I could see Julia's point. She is senior, and she says this is the first complaint she's ever had against her. Though I imagine she must have some idea of what she's like, if she's been there so long.'

Bella wiped her hands on her apron and proceeded to make a pot of tea. 'Thank you, Aunt Lily. It was very good of you to go and see them. What . . . what will I do now? I have to work. Step-Mama cannot afford to keep me, I know that.'

'With a good reference you shouldn't have too much trouble getting work, Bella. After all, you've more than a year's experience now too, you're not a complete beginner,' Olive reminded her.

Lily took a sip of her tea and looked pensive. 'I was thinking, Bella. If, and it is quite a big if, Mr Stoker at the theatre agrees, would you like to come and work with me? I could train you to be like me eventually – a wardrobe mistress. There are plenty of theatres in the country, so in the future there would be prospects. The pay will only be what you have been getting, I'm afraid, but . . .' Lily spread her hands expressively.

Bella's dark eyes lit up. 'I will be like you? I will work in the theatre, with all the famous people?'

Lily smiled and nodded. 'Oh, yes we do get some famous people – Arthur Askey, Rob Wilton, Ted Ray, Gracie Fields and many more.' At least the girl was interested, but she didn't want to raise her hopes too much. 'It is hard work, Bella. Just like learning to be a seamstress, and the hours are not regular. In fact, they can be very irregular. You might not like that as you get older. You will be working when all your friends are out enjoying themselves.'

'I not mind that at all, Aunt Lily, truly.'

'Oh, you might, Bella, in time. But let's just wait and see, shall we? I have to speak to Mr Stoker first.'

Bella beamed at the two older women. 'I'm glad now that I leave. Things will be better now.'

Olive looked concerned. 'Did you really not like it that much, Bella? Why did you not say something?'

'No, I did not like it because of *her* and the other girls. They did not want to be friends with me but I said nothing because I did not want you to think I am ungrateful. I had a job like Joan and Charlie; I bring money into the house like them.'

Olive and Lily exchanged glances. Well, from now on she'd make sure Bella would be happier in whatever work she found, Olive thought, while Lily was more determined than ever to get Ben Stoker to agree to Bella working with her. Bella deserved some success and happiness.

# Chapter Twenty-Six

To everyone's relief – and Bella's delight – Mr Stoker agreed, and so Bella duly accompanied Lily to work the following week and seemed to settle in very well.

'It's as if she's found her niche in the world, Olive. She loves it and everyone loves her, she's getting quite spoilt,' Lily confided after Bella had been at the theatre a week.

Olive smiled back. 'Well, I think she deserves a little spoiling, Lily, don't you? And she does seem to have come out of her shell more. She's far . . . livelier, more confident.'

'She's bound to be, because she's not being bullied – far from it,' Lily replied firmly. She was fast coming to the conclusion that it was the best thing Bella could have done, to walk out of that dreadful workroom and away from that vindictive, spiteful woman.

Like her mother and aunt, Joan too had been furious when she'd learned of Bella's treatment but had calmed down when the entire situation had been explained to her.

To her surprise Jim McDonald asked her if everything was

all right after supper that night. 'You haven't seemed your usual self recently, Joan.'

She smiled up at him. 'I am now, Jim. I was upset about Bella, that's all, but now everything's sorted out and you'll probably be seeing more of Bella than I will in the future.'

'Why?' he asked, puzzled.

Joan told him the whole story and he listened in silence, nodding occasionally. 'I've been called a few names myself since I've been down here,' he confided when she'd finished. 'And for some reason folk seem to think everyone from Scotland's called "Jock".'

'That's not as bad or as hurtful as what Bella was called – or is it?' She'd already cleared the table, so she sat down opposite him in the dining room; everyone else had gone into the kitchen, the parlour or to their own rooms.

'No, I don't suppose so, but she'll be happier now – and it's important that she's happy, she's barely more than a bairn.'

Joan nodded and smiled at him, it was nice of him to be so interested. 'She's fourteen – she didn't have much in life until she came to us. She's my half-sister, in case you didn't know.'

He leaned forward across the table. 'I didn't have much in life either – except my music – until I started work. My mother died when I was only a young bairn and my da, well . . . he didn't cope with it very well. He . . . he was a hard-working, hard-drinking man.' He smiled at her; he didn't want it all to sound like one long moan. 'But I managed, and my Aunt Isabelle paid for my music lessons and then I got a bursary and went to the Edinburgh School of Music and then I got work and . . . here I am.'

Joan nodded. 'Bella's mother was Portuguese; she died when Bella was twelve. She had no brothers or sisters in Lisbon, where she lived.' She wondered why she was telling him all this, for she hardly ever discussed Bella's past with anyone, but somehow she trusted him. She felt easy, talking – confiding – in him.

'I don't want to pry, Joan, but I take it your father is Bella's father too. Is he . . . dead?'

Joan looked down at her hands, folded on the top of the polished table that gleamed softly in the glow from the wall lights. 'Yes, he's Bella's father too but . . . but we don't know if he's alive or dead.' She took a deep breath. 'He went away to sea, was away for months at a time, and then, just after Bella's mother died and she came to us, he . . . he . . .' Her voice cracked with suppressed emotion, but she was annoyed with herself. Why in God's name should she cry over him now, when she barely thought of him these days?

Jim reached across the table and took her hands in his and she looked up at him through her tears.

'I'm sorry, Joan, really I am! I didn't mean to upset you . . . forgive me?'

She nodded, his hands were warm and his grip felt comforting. She took a deep breath. 'He never came back from his last trip to Brazil. He stayed in a place called Recife, according to the shipping company's records. He . . . he abandoned us, all of us, Mam, me, Charlie and Bella.' He squeezed her hand and she managed a smile. 'But like you, Jim, we managed and here we are.'

He smiled back. How could any man treat his loved ones like that? he asked himself. The answer was that obviously he didn't love them, not truly. 'How could any man do that? It must have been hard for you all, Joan.'

'It was, because Mam had no other means of support then. That's when Frederick stepped in. This is his house, but Mam runs the boarding side of it.'

'And she does it very well.' He hadn't known that. He'd actually wondered if Olive and Frederick were related in some way, because they got on so well together. They were obviously not husband and wife . . . but perhaps cousins?

Joan could see his mind working. 'We are all strangers here, Jim . . . well, we were to start with, except for Aunt Lily. Now we're all more like friends, and Mam hopes everyone looks on the place as home, because that's what she wants it to be.' She withdrew her hands slowly and got to her feet, preparing to leave him to his own devices, for she knew she should be helping in the kitchen. She was planning to go up to Nelly's house after her chores were done, to see her friend and impart the latest news.

Jim stood too. 'It already feels like home to me, Joan.'

'Thanks. I'm glad – Mam will be too.'

'I . . . I know I've not been here long, but would you . . . would you come out with me next week? I'll be doing the matinee, but I have a night off.'

She didn't hesitate. 'I'd love to, Jim. Which night?'

He grinned at her, delighted. 'Friday. I'll look forward to it!'

Nelly had been down to see Olive the afternoon of Bella's abrupt departure from De Jong et Cie, and Olive had regaled her with the whole story of Lily's part in it, which had then been relayed in detail to Nelly's family over the evening meal. During the following days, they had shared Olive's relief that Bella seemed to be settling in well at the Empire. But when Joan arrived this evening, Monica was delighted to hear there was more news of a different kind – that Jim McDonald had asked her friend out.

'So, you've got a date,' she stated, examining her eyebrows critically in a hand mirror. She was sitting at the dressing table and Joan had seated herself on the edge of the single bed Eileen slept in. At least the weather was still warm enough for them to have the small luxury of sitting in Monica and Eileen's bedroom and not the kitchen. 'What will you wear? Did he say where he was going to take you?'

Joan shrugged. 'He didn't say, and so I haven't really thought about what I'll wear.'

Monica frowned. 'That's a bit inconsiderate of him. Rick always tells me where he's taking me. He knows how much I care about wearing the right thing.'

'So do I, but . . . well, I haven't got that much to choose from.' Joan didn't spend as much as her friend did on clothes or make-up, she preferred to have some money saved up: she'd never forgotten how distraught her mam had been about their desperate financial situation before they'd moved in with Frederick.

'Do you like him? I mean *really* like him?' Monica probed. 'You know what you're like. I've never known any lad to last more than three dates with you, and if you decide you don't want to see him any more . . . well, that's going to be a bit awkward this time, isn't it?'

Joan had already thought about that, but she instinctively

felt that there was something different about Jim McDonald. 'Yes, I think I do really like him, Mon . . .' She paused and smiled as Monica brushed her shining, shoulder-length hair. 'You see, he was asking me about our Bella and Da, and I . . . well, I opened up to him, and I've never felt able to do that before. He did tell me a bit about himself too, and I don't think he's had a very happy life.'

'Up until now, I hope,' Monica put in. 'I thought you said he'd settled in well.'

'Oh, he has. He told me tonight that he's looking on our place as home already.'

'So, when is the big night out?'

'Friday. He's got the evening off, for once. I suppose with Aunty Lil being in the theatrical business, I'm used to the odd hours they all work.'

Monica put down the hairbrush and turned around to face Joan. 'Rick's taking me to the Royal Court on Friday to see a play, *Lady Windermere's Fan* by Oscar Wilde. It's very famous and quite amusing, so I've heard. Why don't you and Jim join us? I'm sure Rick won't mind, and I imagine you'll still be able to get tickets. We could all meet up for a drink somewhere before we go, perhaps the Bradford or the Stork or the Imperial?'

Joan frowned, unsure of how much all this would cost and not wanting to embarrass Jim, knowing he didn't earn much and had to pay for his board and lodgings. Neither did she have anything to wear that was suitable for the likes of the Lounge Bar in The Imperial Hotel – one of Liverpool's grandest venues – although she was sure Lily would help out there. 'I don't know, Mon. I mean he might be a bit embarrassed, it being our first date, like.' A thought occurred to her. 'And it might be a sort of busman's holiday, going to a theatre.'

'It's a play, Joan, not a musical show, but I see your point. It was just a thought.'

Joan changed the subject and grinned. 'Has Rick hinted at anything yet?'

It was Monica's turn to frown. 'No. I was hoping he might, but . . .' She shrugged.

'It's not that far off to Christmas. He could . . .' Joan suggested.

'That's true. Maybe he's waiting. Oh, it's getting harder and harder to say no to him, Joan. Especially as I . . . well, I want to too. I love him so much that I'm sure it can't possibly be wrong.' Monica's cheeks flushed pink. 'Joan, the last time we were alone, well . . . I very nearly did.'

Joan sat up straight. 'Your mam would absolutely kill you if you did and found yourself in the family way, you know she would.' It was the very worst thing that could happen to a young, unmarried girl. The disgrace would taint the family for years to come, and Monica's reputation would be absolutely ruined.

Monica nodded. 'I know. Honestly, Joan, I swear that is the only thing that stops me.'

'Lord, Mon! You'd be wise not to be alone with him too often – not until he pops the question. At least you'll know he's serious then, and that you'll be getting married.'

'Why do you think I suggested that we all go out in a foursome?'

Joan had nodded. '*That* bad?'

'I'm really frightened that I'll just . . . give in, Joan, and once it's happened . . .'

'Oh, all right. I'll have a word with Jim.'

Monica had smiled at her with some relief. She wasn't the most strong-willed person in the world, she knew that, and she could feel herself being tempted more and more. 'Thanks, I'm really grateful.'

Joan grimaced at her. 'I just hope you don't expect us all to go out together every single time you and Rick want a night out until you walk up the aisle, Monica Savage. I think that would be stretching our friendship a bit too far!'

Monica laughed. 'I won't, but I'd do the same for you, Joan, you know that.'

Luckily, it turned out that that particular play was one that Jim McDonald had been wanting to see for a while, and he was quite happy to go along with the plans for a drink prior to the performance. Joan had been relieved, and also glad that the tickets he'd bought were in the dress circle, as she knew Rick and Monica's were – although she and Jim would be sitting in the less expensive seats, further back.

'It's different to being down in the orchestra pit, if you ken what I mean,' Jim remarked to Rick as they escorted Joan and Monica into the Lounge Bar of The Stork Hotel, which was near to the Royal Court Theatre. 'For one thing, you get to see more.'

'I don't suppose you get to see or hear much usually, do you, Jim?' Rick asked as they sat down and ordered the drinks.

'No, too busy concentrating. But this is supposed to be a good play.'

Rick laughed as Monica's eyebrows rose. As always, she looked so glamorous and elegant. Her sapphire-blue fitted velvet dress suited her slim figure, and she wore matching evening gloves, a diamanté clip holding her hair in place. You could take her anywhere and be certain she would not only stand out but be suitably dressed for the occasion. He was very proud of her and now, after nearly two years of courtship, he was certain that she was the one for him. Even his mother – a very difficult woman, at times and especially where girlfriends were concerned – had said as much. His father liked her and said she would make a very good hairdresser. He advised his son not to underestimate her – he was sure she wasn't just a pretty face. And Rick really wasn't bothered about what his sisters thought, though they seemed to quite like her too.

'It will make a nice change for us all, I'm sure,' Joan stated firmly, sipping her drink and smiling at Jim. He looked different tonight, she thought. He was sporting a tartan waistcoat underneath his suit jacket; he'd told her it was the tartan of Skye's Clan McDonald, of which his family was a very minor and insignificant branch. He'd commented on her appearance too, saying she looked 'right bonny', which she'd taken as a big compliment. Lily had loaned her a black-and-white-brocade cocktail dress, which suited her colouring, and she'd also found a pair of long jet earrings and a bracelet. She wore black court shoes and carried a small black evening bag, and even though she knew she couldn't compete with Monica's elegance she was quite happy with how she looked and felt. It was going to be an evening she was certain she would enjoy. And perhaps the first of many – who knew? But she liked Jim far more than she'd liked any of her other suitors, so that was a start.

# Chapter Twenty-Seven

————◆◆◆————

Although it was only mid-November, Lily was busy with the costumes for the chorus for the Christmas season shows. She had sent Bella to see if Maisie – her assistant – would be free to give her a hand this afternoon but was wondering what was keeping the girl, for she'd been gone for over twenty minutes.

She frowned and looked up as the door to the sewing room opened, but instead of her niece it was Maisie herself who stood in the doorway. 'Where's Bella?'

Maisie shrugged. 'Mr Stoker has sent me to fetch you. He said to tell you to put down whatever you're doing and go to see him,' she announced, looking rather mysterious, or so Lily thought.

'Do you know what he wants?'

Maisie shrugged again and Lily got to her feet.

'I take it he's in his office?'

'No. He's standing in the wings – stage left.'

Lily stared at her, wondering what on earth the manager

was doing in the wings of a deserted stage at this time in the morning – and, more to the point, what it had to do with her. 'Can you carry on with this for me, Maisie, please, while I go and see what nonsense he's got into his head now?'

The girl nodded and took the garment Lily had been mending.

'Oh, is there anyone else around out there? Any of the musicians?' Lily enquired. She knew Jim McDonald was in the theatre; for Jim, Bella and herself had all three of them travelled in to work together this morning.

'Not that I know of, but there is a rehearsal just after lunch, so if you're looking for Jim McDonald he'll be around then.'

Lily walked through the maze of narrow and chilly corridors towards the stage. The theatre was quite dimly lit and she knew that both the curtain and the fire curtain would be down – and there would be even less light on the vast stage, so she'd not see Jim even if he were already in the orchestra pit. She was at a loss to know why Ben had summoned her, and had hoped that maybe Jim could have thrown some light on it. From their seats beneath the stage the musicians tended to see most of what went on with the cast and backstage workers.

She found Ben standing with his arms folded, leaning against a large piece of scenery and looking out from the wings, watching what she could now discern was a small figure standing in the centre of the stage.

'Bella, what on earth . . . ?' she exclaimed.

'Shush, Lily!' Ben Stoker admonished in a loud whisper.

Lily looked up at him, puzzled. He was a big man, middle-aged now, but had been in the business all his life, and she respected both his judgement and the way he ran the theatre.

'Ben, what . . . what's she doing?' she whispered back, her gaze following Bella.

'Just watch and listen, Lily.'

Her eyes were becoming more accustomed to the gloom now. As she watched, Bella began to move slowly forward, her hands on her slightly swaying hips, and tossing her dark curls. But then Lily felt a shiver run down her spine as the girl began to sing, softly at first but then increasing in volume. Oh, she'd heard Bella sing before, usually when she was at home doing her chores, and usually strange songs with foreign words, but this was very different and she instantly recognised it. 'My God! Isn't that from *Carmen*? Where the hell did she learn that?' she hissed, but then she remembered they'd had a touring opera company here two weeks ago.

He nodded. 'The "*Habanera*", and never mind where she learned it, Lily. It's her voice that matters.'

Lily nodded slowly and they both stood in silence for a few more minutes, watching and listening in awe, before he took her arm and pulled her further back and away from the stage while Bella continued to sing and act out the gypsy girl's aria to the empty auditorium.

'I've never heard a girl that young sing like that, Lily.'

Lily shook her head, dumbfounded. 'I had no idea . . . she sings at home . . . ditties, but . . . she's picked that up from the company who were here two weeks ago.'

'From what I heard, she's picked it up very well, she's almost word perfect – and just watching her, I'd say she can act the part. She's got the looks too. All that talent is too good to waste, Lily.'

She frowned. 'What do you mean, Ben?'

'She's half Spanish or something, isn't she?'

'Portuguese.'

'Well, some of the greatest operatic sopranos and mezzos are Italian or Spanish, Mafalda Favero for one, so . . .'

Lily gasped, utterly astounded. 'You mean . . . ? You think Bella . . . ?'

'She needs to be trained – professionally, Lily.'

'That would cost a fortune!'

'Well, at the very least she needs to be assessed by someone who knows far more than either of us. But we can't let a talent like that just go to waste. Are you sure you had no idea?'

Lily shook her head vehemently. 'No! None whatsoever! She certainly doesn't take after her father, though; Billy Copperfield couldn't hold a tune to save his life.'

'Must be her mother, then.'

'She's dead and buried in Portugal, so we'll never know.' Lily looked thoughtful. 'So, what do we do now, Ben?'

His brow creased in a frown of concentration as he ushered her towards the corridor and the back stairs. 'First of all, we'd better actually ask Bella a few questions.'

'Yes, she might be quite happy to just be trained as a wardrobe mistress; she might not want to sing publically at all.'

He ignored her pessimism. 'But if she does, I think we should seriously think about sending her to be assessed. I'll make enquiries, but I think there's someone who has a studio in Crane Buildings, on Hanover Street. Frances . . . David Frances, I think his name is.'

'Let's not rush things, Ben. Let's talk to Bella first,' Lily advised.

'Right, when she finally comes back into the real world, will you bring her to my office, Lily?'

She nodded and they parted company, he to his office and she back to her workroom.

Bella looked at her aunt with some trepidation when she finally returned and Lily imparted Ben Stoker's instructions.

'I do something wrong, Aunt Lily? I'm sorry, I should have come back when I could not find Maisie but . . . but I . . .' Her dark eyes were filled with fear. She didn't want to lose this job, she was so happy here. She shouldn't have been so silly as to wander on to the stage and start singing. But she just hadn't been able to resist. It was something she'd been dreaming about, night after night, an idea that she felt she needed to get out of her head.

'You've done nothing wrong, Bella. Mr Stoker just wants to ask you a few questions, that's all,' Lily explained, examining her appearance quickly in the long mirror on the wall.

'Questions?' the girl probed, still very uneasy.

'Don't look so terrified, Bella! Trust me, you have done nothing wrong – far from it.'

When they reached the manager's office, which was rather on the small side for a man of his position, Lily always thought, he indicated that they should both sit down.

Lily smoothed down the folds of her skirt as she settled herself but Bella perched on the very edge of the chair, her hands clasped tightly in her lap, her dark eyes wary.

'Both your aunt and I watched you, Bella, just now when you were singing on the stage – it was the "*Habanera*" from the opera *Carmen*, wasn't it?'

Bella's eyes widened further. 'I not know what it was called. I not know that you were . . . watching. I'm sorry . . .'

He held up his hand to stop her, for he could see she was getting upset. 'No, Bella, no! You were very good; in fact, you are much, much better than good. Your voice is . . . exceptional.'

Bella calmed down and looked quickly at Lily, who smiled encouragingly at her. 'Mr Stoker thinks that maybe one day, Bella, you might be able to sing in an opera.'

'Me? I . . . I . . . only copy the girl who was Carmen. I watch her, I listen and I like her very much. And . . . and when I sing I can forget everything . . . unhappy!'

Ben Stoker leaned forward across his desk, his hands clasped in front of him. The girl clearly had no idea that she was very talented – or that she was well on the way to growing into a beautiful young woman. 'I'm sure that with training, Bella, you will one day be as good as that mezzo-soprano who sang Carmen. Would you like to have a singing career?'

Bella just stared at him, shaking her head in disbelief. All her life she had been singing, but no one had ever said there was anything special about her voice.

Lily leaned towards her. 'Was there anyone in your other family, Bella, who could sing?'

The girl nodded. 'My *mãe* – my mother – she sang. Before I was born she was a famous singer of the *Fado* but after . . . she just sing at home.'

Lily looked at Ben, a little mystified.

'The *Fado* is the music of Portugal, Lily. It is particularly popular in Lisbon,' he informed her – and a bit morbid it was too, in his opinion, although he didn't say that aloud.

'Yes, my mother sang in all the best places in Lisboa!' Bella added, with pride shining in her dark eyes.

'Then you have inherited her voice, Bella. Would you like to sing professionally? When you are older?' Lily asked gently.

'I could do that, Aunt Lily? Really?' Never in her life had Bella envisaged such a future, not even in her wildest dreams. It had never occurred to her that a girl born in the Alfama district of her native city could ever – in reality, rather than just her dreams – appear on the stages of the world's great opera houses, perhaps even at the Teatro Nacional de São Carlos in Chiado, an important district of Lisboa. But now both her aunt and, more importantly, Mr Stoker seemed to think she could. She felt almost delirious with excitement.

'First of all, Bella, I will make arrangements for you to see a Mr David Frances. He is an experienced and respected voice coach, with a studio here in Liverpool. He will listen to you and then tell us what he thinks and what he advises. Will you be happy with that?'

Bella nodded delightedly, not trusting herself to speak. Oh, how proud her poor mama would have been, and how proud Olive, Joan and Lily would be. She refused to think of her father.

Lily got to her feet, smiling. 'Right, we'll leave all that to you, Ben. Now, I think it's time we both got on with what you pay us to do, don't you?'

'I'll go over there at lunchtime. Maybe I'll be able to see him then. If not, I'll make an appointment, but I'll most definitely let you know,' he promised them.

Ben Stoker doubted Bella would ever sing on the stage of his theatre, unless it was with an opera company. She'd certainly be wasted in stage musicals, he mused ruefully, but he wondered if she had the determination, ambition and stamina for the years of training that lay ahead – and even more to the point, did her family have the money? He doubted it. But there were bursaries and scholarships for such talented people as Bella Copperfield, though that surname would have to go. It just wasn't exotic enough for the world she might be about to enter.

Bella couldn't concentrate on her tasks for the rest of the day; her mind was in a whirl and she was impatient to get home and tell everyone her news. News she could hardly believe herself.

Olive, Joan, Frederick and Charlie all listened in total silence as, between them, Bella and Lily told them of the day's events.

'I'd never have believed it myself, Olive, if I hadn't seen and heard her,' Lily finished as her sister shook her head in disbelief.

'And your mam was a famous singer of this *Fado*?' Joan cried, hugging her half-sister in delight.

'But I not know how famous. And then after she have me, she did not go to sing in public again.'

'And you'll go on the stage and be famous too?' Charlie could barely take it in, but he was pleased for her all the same.

'And this man – this voice coach – he'll train her?' Olive asked Lily.

Lily shrugged. 'I suppose so, although Ben didn't say he would. It's just what I suppose you'd call an audition, to start with.'

Olive bit her lip. 'If he takes her on . . . it won't be cheap, Lily.'

'I dare say it won't be. These things never are.'

'But it would be criminal not to pursue it. Don't let's worry about it, Olive, we'll find the money somehow,' Frederick put in gravely.

'I'm sure there must be some form of financial help. Jim told me he got what he called a "bursary" to go to the Edinburgh School of Music. His family had no money,' Joan added.

'There's bound to be. I'll look into it,' Frederick promised. He was delighted that Bella was going to be offered such a chance. She really must have an exceptional talent – and that must never be disregarded, whatever the circumstances, he thought.

The question of finance was the one little dark cloud in Bella's otherwise clear blue sky of pure happiness, but she took courage from both Joan's and Frederick's remarks. Perhaps she could carry on working with Lily in the theatre while she trained? That way, she could partly fund her fees. It was something she would ask her aunt later, after she'd gone with Joan up to Nelly's house to impart the news to them. She was certain it would be received rapturously for, as Joan had already said, no one from this area of Liverpool had ever climbed so high on the ladder of success. Did she even dare to hope that she, Bella Copperfield – the little orphan waif who had stowed away because she had no money for her fare – could ever be a star?

# Chapter Twenty-Eight

Both Bella and Lily were nervous as they sat with Ben Stoker in an anteroom outside David Frances's studio. There was just one tiny window overlooking the soot-blackened buildings opposite. The floors below were taken up by the Crane Theatre, one of the city's many small venues, and the showrooms where musical instruments of all kinds were displayed for sale. It was a building dedicated to music and the arts. The whole family had been nervous when Bella left Mersey View that morning but had expressed their hopes for her success.

'Just do your best, Bella, that's all you can do,' Olive had urged as she'd smoothed a wayward curl from the girl's forehead.

Lily absolutely hated this waiting around, knowing how nervous Bella was. 'I can't hear anything coming from in there,' she whispered to her employer, while Bella bit her lip in nervous anticipation.

'That's because the studio is soundproofed, Lily,' Ben Stoker answered.

'So we won't be able to hear Bella sing . . . or what he has to say to her?'

'I'm afraid not.'

Lily was disappointed; she'd been aware that they would probably not be allowed to be in the same room while Bella had her audition, but she had hoped they'd at least be able to gauge how her niece was getting on.

'Perhaps that is a good thing, Aunt Lily, because I will be so nervous. And if you were both there too . . .'

Lily reached over and patted her hand. 'I just thought we could have given you some moral support, Bella, by simply being there.'

Bella smiled back at her, and then the door to the studio opened and a tall, middle-aged man appeared, dressed in a well-cut charcoal-grey suit. He was sporting a red-and-white-spotted bow tie, and looked rather natty, Lily thought. He had a shock of unruly brown hair, and the hazel eyes that looked out from behind wire-rimmed spectacles were kind. Lily rather liked him; he did not look in the least bit intimidating, thankfully, since Bella was white with nerves.

He smiled around at them all. 'Good morning, Mr Stoker, Miss Cooper . . . and you, young lady, must be Miss Annabella Copperfield?' He shook hands with Ben Stoker and Lily before turning his full attention on Bella. 'So, you have come to sing for me, Bella?'

She nodded – looking rather like the proverbial rabbit caught in the headlights of a rapidly advancing motor car, he thought.

'There's no need to be afraid. I don't bite! Now, let's go on into my studio and we can begin. I have high hopes of you after what Mr Stoker has told me.'

Bella glanced quickly at Lily, wishing her aunt could accompany her. 'I try to do my best.'

'That's all we can ask of you, Bella,' Lily replied as Bella was ushered inside and the door closed firmly behind her.

As Ben had foretold, they could hear nothing of what was going on in the studio. Lily was so apprehensive that she couldn't sit still but began to pace up and down the small room. What would they do if he said Bella only had a mediocre voice and could not hope for a singing career? What then could she say to the girl? She hoped they hadn't built her hopes up too high. Was Bella going to have another great disappointment to cope with, when she'd already had so many to contend with in her life so far? Oh, she hoped not. The girl was due some good luck, she was so sweet-natured. She was not demanding, petulant or arrogant, as many girls of Bella's age could be, nor did she throw tantrums over the least little thing. Oh, she wished David Frances would hurry up with his assessment! She was a bag of nerves, but common sense and experience told her that he would take his time – and of course she didn't want it to be a rushed job.

'Lily, for God's sake sit down, you're making me jumpy!' Ben Stoker instructed irritably, for he too was impatient to hear the results. After all, it was at his instigation that they were there.

'Oh, what if he doesn't think she's as exceptional as we do?' Lily asked, resuming her seat beside him and taking her compact from her bag to examine her reflection in its small mirror.

'Then we'll know, won't we? She could still have a good

career on the musical stage when she's old enough. Great opera stars only seem to emerge every one or two generations, and then I suppose a lot of their success is down to luck as well as talent.'

Lily nodded, glancing at her wristwatch. Bella hadn't been in there long but it seemed like ages. 'Frederick Garswood was looking into bursaries and scholarships for her, because even if Olive and I scraped together what we could, we know it won't be enough – it's a long-term expense.'

'You do realise that if she were to get a scholarship she would have to go to London, to somewhere like the Royal College or the Royal Academy of Music?'

Lily frowned; she hadn't realised that. 'Yes, I suppose she would, but let's just wait and see. Bella can't go to London on her own; she's far too young and naive,' Lily mused aloud. Someone would have to go with her as a chaperone until she was at least twenty-one. 'But how could we stand in her way?' she asked Ben Stoker.

He shrugged. 'We couldn't, Lily. But we're running ahead of ourselves. Let's see what the verdict is today.'

To her relief, a few minutes later the door opened and a smiling Bella emerged, followed by an also-smiling David Frances.

Ben Stoker and Lily both got to their feet, anxious to hear the verdict.

'Oh, how did she get on, maestro?' Lily asked, her hands clenched together and her heart beating faster. The fact that her niece was smiling was surely a good sign.

'Well, Miss Cooper, you were both right to bring her to me. She has the basis of an excellent mezzo-soprano voice, which will need to be trained of course.'

Lily clapped her hands in delight. 'And – dare I ask – can you . . . will you be prepared to do that?'

He smiled back at her; she was a very attractive woman and clearly very fond of the girl. 'Of course, Miss Cooper, it will be a pleasure and, I must say, a delight, for from what I have seen so far, she has not a hint of the diva in her, thank God!'

Lily put her arm around Bella's shoulders. 'Are you happy about that, Bella?'

'I am so very, very happy, Aunt Lily, and thank you . . . thank you all! But thank you especially . . . sir.' Bella beamed up at the man who was going to be her teacher and mentor.

'Maestro,' Lily corrected. 'You must give Mr Frances his correct title – and your respect, of course.'

He smiled down at her. 'You are very formal, Miss Cooper.'

'In some things, I suppose I am.'

'I like that. Now, I suggest you and Bella go back to work while Mr Stoker and I discuss a strategy for Bella's future training and the costs involved – if you will be happy with that? I do think that we should get started very soon; in a perfect world I would have started her training at the age of twelve or thirteen. Everyone knows that boys' voices break at about that age, but few people realise that girls' voices do too, although the results are generally not very noticeable.'

'I didn't know that either, but Bella only came to this country at that age, and we . . . well, we didn't know she could sing,' Lily informed him. She was thankful that Ben would do the financial negotiations and pass the information on to her. It wasn't as though she wouldn't be able to comprehend what it all entailed; she just didn't want David Frances to think she was mercenary in any way. She liked him and hoped that in future she might see more of him, for he was an interesting man and she was sure they would have a lot in common. And she'd noticed there were no rings on any of his fingers.

Bella began her training at the beginning of December, and from the very first she loved it. Neither Olive nor Lily had ever seen her so happy before: she would religiously practise the exercises she'd been set, so her voice soared through the rooms of the house. To help pay for her lessons it had been decided by Ben Stoker and Lily that she would continue to work in the theatre, but as time went on and she progressed then her hours would be reduced. In one respect Lily was thankful, for Christmas was always chaotic and she needed all the help she could get. David Frances's fees were far from cheap, but between them all – and with contributions from Frederick – they managed to afford them. Lily was determined that Bella was going to have the best that money could buy, for her fondness and pride in the girl were growing daily.

Lily had also begun to see more of David Frances. She made it her business to call at his studio to pick Bella up whenever she was able to, and to chat to him about the girl's progress. Occasionally they would go to a small café just across the road for a cup of coffee, while Bella struggled with the exercises she'd been set in music theory, which she was now learning and was essential for every classically trained artist.

He was very impressed with her niece, he told her on one such occasion. 'It is always so amazing, Miss Cooper, when out of the blue, and so unexpectedly, comes a girl like Bella with such a voice – and looks, ambition and a lovely temperament to boot. That combination is very rare, believe me. She is dedicated to her music, I can tell already.'

Lily smiled. 'Yes, she really is special – and to think that we had no idea at all.'

'You seem very fond of her, Miss Cooper.'

'I am . . . and please will you call me Lily? All this "Miss Cooper" makes me feel so old and staid!'

He laughed. 'Two things you most definitely are not . . . Lily. And please call me David.'

'I do almost look on Bella as a daughter. I never married – I was happy with my career, friends and independence – and so never had any children of my own, unlike my sister. But Bella has been quite a blessing.'

'She told me your sister is her stepmother, that her mother is dead, and about her being a *Fado* singer – not an easy medium to accomplish well, either,' he continued, slowly sipping his drink.

Lily sighed heavily. 'And has she told you about her father?'

'No. When I asked, she seemed to withdraw into herself and would say very little.'

'That's not surprising, but he certainly wasn't musical in any way. One day I'll tell you all about the infamous Billy Copperfield, but not now. She doesn't look like him; Bella must take after her mother.'

He nodded seriously, his curiosity roused by her description of the man as 'infamous', but he wouldn't press the matter. She'd tell him – eventually. 'That is something that she will have to address in time, Lily. Her surname, it's rather . . . ordinary for the stage – as I'm sure, with your experience, you'll agree?'

'I do. Yes, names are very important. Hopefully, it's the first thing people remember about you, but it's not something I'd thought about, and I don't think Bella has either.' Privately, Lily thought that Bella wouldn't be unhappy about dropping her father's name at all.

'Do you know what her mother's maiden name was? She was Portuguese, I believe?' he probed.

'Ferreira Silva,' Lily replied promptly. She'd always had a good memory for names, and none of them would ever forget the day Bella arrived with her baptismal certificate.

'Oh, excellent!'

Lily sipped her own drink and smiled. 'Bella Ferreira Silva?'

'No. Annabella Ferreira Silva.'

Lily nodded. 'You know, David, that sounds just perfect!' Lily spread her hands in an elegant gesture. '*Voilà* – and a star is born.'

# Chapter Twenty-Nine

———

As Christmas approached, amidst the ever-growing tensions in the country, life in both Olive's and Nelly's households was busier than ever with all the shopping and baking and planning. But for Nelly there was one event she hadn't planned for – Monica had informed her that she and Rick Eustace were getting engaged.

She'd realised that over these past months they'd been seeing more and more of each other, but she still wasn't at all happy about the situation, although she had nothing personally against the lad. He just wasn't their kind, and she felt in her bones it was a marriage that wouldn't work.

'Well, we'll just have to wait and see, Nelly, luv. She'll be nineteen next year, and you know our Monica – she knows her own mind, and always has done,' had been Arthur's response to her worries when Monica, with a mix of excitement and defiance, had delivered her news.

'Well, that's as may be, but she can't get married until she's twenty-one, not without your consent,' she'd replied curtly.

But Arthur had only shaken his head and reminded her that it looked very likely that another war was on the horizon and that Rick Eustace might very well be called up to serve. And who knew what might happen then?

Monica had confided in Joan that Rick would be coming round to the house later that evening to speak formally to her father. It was the very day Bella had been accepted as a pupil by David Frances, and Joan and Bella had come up to their house with the news.

'What a wonderful day! So, what did he say? Did he go down on one knee and all that?' Joan asked, her eyes wide with happiness and excitement for her friend.

Monica was sitting at the foot of Joan's bed, having been dragged away from the kitchen where both Nelly and Eileen were fussing over Bella. She hugged her friend, and her eyes were shining as she nodded. 'Oh, we went to that little French restaurant in New Brighton, the one he took me to on our first real date, and I sort of had a feeling it was going to be a special evening because he ordered champagne – the real thing, not a sparkling perry. Then he took this box out of his pocket and opened it! It was a Boodle's box and . . . oh, Joan! It's fantastic and I can't wait until I can wear it!'

'Well, go on, then, tell me what it's like!' Joan demanded.

'It's a solitaire diamond surrounded by smaller diamonds; it was a bit big so he's taken it to be made smaller. I was so excited, and a bit embarrassed, when he got down on one knee and asked me. Thankfully, the restaurant wasn't really crowded. Oh, after I'd said yes, and he stood up and kissed me, everyone clapped and congratulated us, and the maître d' came over with a bouquet of roses Rick had ordered to be delivered.

It was such a magical moment, Joan, I'll never forget it!'

'So, I take it you're not going to wear the ring until he's asked your da properly, and it's been announced – all official, like?'

Monica nodded.

'How do you think that will go?' Joan was more serious now, knowing Nelly's strong misgivings.

Monica shrugged. 'It'll be all right, if Mam doesn't stick her oar in. I'm going to say to them it's not the "done thing" for her to be included in the conversation, as I won't be either. Hopefully, we'll just leave Rick and Da to it – fingers crossed.'

Joan wasn't too worried for her friend, for she knew that Monica was determined to marry Rick, whatever her mam's misgivings. And why not? she reasoned. She loved him, he loved her – and Joan for one couldn't understand why Nelly was so opposed to it. Her own mam had said she couldn't understand Nelly's views either, for if it had been Joan, she'd have been delighted she was making such a good match. Olive had wondered, was there something Nelly knew about him or his family that no one else did? But Joan couldn't see what on earth that might be. No, it was just Nelly being awkward with her ideas on 'class'.

'So, have you thought about when you'll get married, or is it too soon for that?' she asked.

'I think it will be June or September next year. I like both months, but the weather is usually better in June. You *will* be my bridesmaid?'

'Of course! I'll be delighted to!'

'I'll have to have our Eileen too, of course, and his sisters – and I was wondering about Bella. I don't want to leave her out, but will five be too many? And then what should I do about Charlie? Shouldn't he have some part?'

'Oh, you can forget about him. He'd die of embarrassment if you asked him to get all dressed up like a dog's dinner to be an usher or something.' Joan frowned as she thought about this situation. 'I'm the only grown-up bridesmaid, the others are all younger, and you don't want it to look like a May procession . . .'

'I certainly do not! I want it to be elegant and tasteful. I'm not having them looking down their noses at me.'

'Do they?' Joan queried. Monica hadn't said very much yet about her new family.

'Well, not so far, but I don't want too "showy" a wedding. Nothing in bad taste.'

'Then I don't think five is too many. You don't want them to think you can't muster up enough friends and relations either, do you?'

Monica nodded her agreement but then bit her lip and frowned. 'What if they are expecting a proper engagement party? Mam will go mad. She'll be mortified if she has to invite everyone to our house and . . .'

'Mortified if she has to go to their posh house in Woolton,' Joan finished for her.

'Oh, why on earth can't people just get on together, no matter what they do or where they live? I thought all that "social class" thing was finished off by the last war?'

Joan shrugged. 'Some people just won't move with the times and never will, even though it looks as if there's going to be another war. Hardly anyone believes in this "peace in our time" promise. Frederick says Hitler certainly doesn't, that he's just a nasty, arrogant, two-faced little dictator.'

'Oh, I hope there won't be a war, Joan! If there is, you do realise that both my Rick and your Jim will probably have to go and fight?'

Joan smiled at Monica calling Jim McDonald 'your Jim', because that's how she'd begun to think of him lately. But the smile disappeared as she realised that Monica was right. Lads as young as sixteen had volunteered in the last conflict – and some, even younger, had lied about their ages and gone. Rick Eustace was nearly twenty-two and so was Jim McDonald. She shook off the disturbing thoughts.

'Well, when your engagement is all official, like, we'll go out in a foursome to celebrate – somewhere posh!'

'That'll be great. As it's Christmas in a few weeks, things should be livening up in the city.' Monica stood up. 'I'd better be getting changed, Joan. Rick's coming over at half past eight and I've some serious coaxing to do with Mam.'

Joan grinned, also getting to her feet and reaching for her coat. 'Best of luck. And first thing tomorrow I want to see this fabulous ring – providing we don't have to wait for an official party.'

Monica grinned back. 'That's something else I'm going to have to negotiate my way around!' she remarked as they both went back down to Nelly's kitchen.

Rick arrived promptly, bearing flowers for Nelly and a bottle of good Scotch for Arthur. He kissed Monica and then patted his pocket and whispered, 'I picked it up this afternoon,' which filled her with excitement. Things had not gone too well with her mam when she'd broached the subject of who should be there when Rick came round, but at least her da had agreed with her, that after the initial greetings he and his future son-in-law should discuss the matter together in the parlour.

'After all, luv, I've got to give him my permission – formally. I'm her father,' Arthur had stated firmly.

'And I'm her mother! Am I to have no say in any of this?' Nelly had protested.

Monica had gazed pleadingly at her father.

'It's going to be a hard enough experience for the lad as it is, Nell. We don't want to make things worse – embarrass him – now do we?'

'I know he's already nervous, he told me so,' Monica had added, and Nelly had reluctantly refrained from pressing the matter any further.

When the two men finally emerged from the parlour, both smiling happily, Monica's heart leapt with joy. 'Now can I wear my ring?'

Rick laughed and took the box from his pocket as both Nelly and Arthur looked on, Arthur with undisguised happiness and Nelly with grudging acceptance, which changed to utter astonishment when Rick slipped the ring on to her daughter's finger. Never in her life had she seen such a magnificent ring, and certainly not on the finger of anyone who lived in this part of the city. Most women were lucky to get a wedding ring; hardly anyone got an engagement ring too. Her own was seldom worn and consisted of only two small – very small – stones.

Rick kissed Monica on the cheek. 'Well, there you are, it's all official now,' he turned to Arthur. 'And I'll put the notice in the paper tomorrow, shall I? I've more time than you; I know how early you start work.'

Arthur nodded gratefully, as he'd no idea how these things were worded.

Rick then turned to Nelly. 'Mrs Savage . . . er . . . mother-in-law to be, my parents would be delighted if you – and the family, of course – would come up to our house on Sunday evening. Just for a drink and a few bits to eat? Nothing formal, but they'd like to get to know you all.' He beamed around at Monica's small family, which now included Eileen, who had returned from Olive's house where she'd gone to show Bella the new shoes she'd bought.

Monica swallowed hard. She'd been expecting something like this, so before her mother had time to speak she clutched Rick's arm and smiled up at him. 'Of course, we'll all be delighted to come. It's only right that everyone gets to know everyone else, after all, we'll all be "family" soon. Isn't that right, Mam?'

Nelly knew when she was beaten and nodded slowly. Indeed, they all would be related by marriage soon, but that didn't mean they had to live in one another's pockets. 'That's very kind of them, Rick.'

'When you get married, where will you live?' Eileen asked bluntly, thinking that she would get a bedroom all to herself – unless of course they were going to move in here. But she couldn't see that happening, there wasn't room for a start.

Monica laughed. 'Oh, for heaven's sake! I've only just got the ring on my finger, and you're asking questions like that . . .'

'It's early days yet, there's plenty of time for you both to discuss everything,' Arthur put in.

'Well, can I be bridesmaid, then?' Eileen was not to be deterred.

Rick grinned at her. 'We wouldn't dream of not having you. Or my sisters, either,' he added.

'And Joan and Bella too,' Monica put in.

Rick squeezed her hand. 'As many as you like, darling! It's your big day.'

Nelly said nothing, wondering how they were going to pay for what was obviously going to be quite a big wedding.

They were all rather quiet on the journey to Woolton on the Sunday evening. Arthur and Nelly were filled with apprehension at what faced them, Eileen with suppressed excitement at being invited to what was obviously going to be a very 'posh' house, and Monica hoping that her sister would behave and her parents wouldn't feel too out of place. She remembered the first time Rick had taken her home, how she'd been very overawed, but she was sure that both Mr and Mrs Eustace would make them all very welcome.

To her great relief she was right. Claude opened the door to them as they stood in a subdued little group on the front step, having negotiated the long, neat path through the garden. 'Mr and Mrs Savage, lovely to welcome you to our home. Do come in,' he beamed as he ushered them into the wide hall, ablaze with light.

Nelly managed a smile and tried, surreptitiously, to take in her surroundings before being introduced to Rick's mother.

'Hello, I'm Nancy. This is such an occasion, isn't it, er . . .'

'Ellen . . . but Nelly to my friends,' was the rather clipped reply.

Rick's mother wasn't what she'd been expecting at all. She'd envisaged a tall, stout, well-corseted woman with iron-grey hair perfectly set in a Marcel wave and wearing an elegant dress and pearls. Well, she had been right about the dress and the pearls, but Nancy Eustace was the same height as herself, and slim, with light brown hair that waved softly and naturally around her face, and kind but intelligent grey eyes. Nelly found herself beginning to relax a little as she was introduced to Nancy's two daughters, both of whom seemed quiet, polite girls, and she was thankful that Eileen seemed to be on her best behaviour.

She had to admit that the lounge they were ushered into was very comfortably furnished, and in such delicate shades of eau de Nil and cream. No serviceable dark browns and dull beiges here in Willow Gardens, unlike the houses in Mersey View. There were delicate china ornaments and vases of flowers and winter greenery on the side tables dotted around the room, and a roaring fire in the very elegant cream marble fireplace, over which hung a huge gilt-framed mirror.

Everyone had a drink – Claude had seen to that – and Arthur seemed to be getting on very well with him, she thought, as she watched the two men chatting – which surprised her, for she was sure they would have little in common. Monica and Rick were obviously wrapped up in each other, but Beverley and Ruth had been instructed by their mother to pass around the plates of small sandwiches and cakes.

'Eileen, don't just sit there, get up and help the girls,' Nelly instructed.

Eileen, who was the same age as Ruth, duly did as she was told and it wasn't long before all three girls were making attempts at conversation, interspersed by giggles.

'Well, at least they seem to be trying to get on,' Nancy remarked, seating herself beside Nelly on the cream-and-pale-green chintz-covered sofa.

Nelly nodded as she sipped her drink, a pale, rather dry sherry, served in a beautiful crystal glass.

Nancy Eustace watched her closely. She could tell that the woman was far from happy about the entire situation – Rick had confided that to her.

'These are beautiful glasses, Nancy,' Nelly remarked, feeling she should try at least to appear at ease.

'They are. I haven't had them long; they weren't a wedding present or a family heirloom. No, nothing like that. They're Stuart crystal and I buy them from Stoniers, in Clayton Square.' She leaned a little closer to Nelly. 'Twice a year they have a sale of what they call "seconds". Almost perfect glasses, but half the price, and you really have to look very closely indeed to find the fault, which could be a tiny chip or a bubble in the glass. I do like a bargain, I think every woman does.'

Nelly nodded and took another sip, and then held the glass up to the light. She could see no fault in it herself. She wasn't quite sure what to make of Nancy Eustace yet. She'd anticipated someone stand-offish and maybe even a bit of a snob, and had dreaded the woman looking and talking down to her – or even not talking to her at all!

Nancy continued, lowering her voice a little. 'And I can tell you, Nelly, that it was far from crystal glasses and fine china where I was reared. I doubt we even had a glass in our house when I was growing up, and certainly no china cups.'

Nelly stared at her in surprise and then relaxed a little. 'You don't come from Liverpool, do you, Nancy? You've hardly any accent, but it's definitely not a scouse one.'

Nancy smiled at her. 'No, it's Lancashire, and I'm proud of it. I was born and raised in Blackburn. Both my parents worked in the Britannia Street Mill – cotton. I did too, from the age of twelve – and bye, it was damned hard work, Nelly, and long hours. We lived in a two-up two-down terrace just around the corner from the mill, and there were seven of us crammed into that little house.'

Nelly was both taken aback and intrigued. She'd never expected this. 'How . . . how did you get here?'

'Ah, that's a long story, and I'll tell you one day how and where I met Claude, but suffice to say that when we got married we moved here. Claude's mother was from France, the Picardy region. When she married his father, at the end of the Great War, she came to live here – she was a hairdresser.'

'Really? So, that's where . . . ?'

Nancy nodded, smiling fondly at her husband. 'Yes, but he wasn't into salons when we got married. He'd trained as a barber but saw the opportunities ahead in high-class ladies hairdressing. His mother's hairdressing services had been very popular with the ladies of Blackburn even then, when times were very bad for returning soldiers. But there were quite a few who still had money – mill owners' and overseers' wives and daughters, those of solicitors and doctors and members of the Council – and she being a French hairdresser was a bit more exotic than the local lasses, so she did well. After a couple of years, Claude decided there was bound to be far more business in a big city like Liverpool, and there was.' Nancy smiled again at Nelly. 'It was from his mother that he got the idea of having all his stylists adopting French Christian names, although she was dead by then.'

Nelly was very impressed. 'He . . . you've both done very well.'

Nancy reached over and patted her hand. 'I know you have reservations about this marriage, Nelly, but don't worry. I'm sure they will be very happy. Claude and I came from very different backgrounds. Rick confides a great deal in me, and I know he loves Monica deeply. I like her, she's pleasant, kind and with some ambition – and that's not a bad thing. I do admit that I was a little cautious at first, having met two of the others he'd brought home.' Nancy rolled her eyes. 'Thankfully, they were not serious, and I'm sure Monica will make him an excellent wife. She's a lovely girl. A credit to you and Arthur.'

Nelly finally smiled, genuinely relieved. Nancy Eustace had been an ordinary girl, like herself, and she and her husband had done well for themselves – as she and Arthur had done, to a much lesser degree of course. So why shouldn't Monica also have a good future? What more could she wish for, for her elder daughter? She would have a loving husband, no doubt a beautiful home, no shortage of money, and one day Rick would be the owner of three very successful salons. She pushed away the one dark thought that came to mind. The fact that another war seemed in the offing – and that could change everyone's futures.

# Chapter Thirty

When spring at last came to Mersey View the situation in the country was even more sombre, Nelly thought. In February it had been reported in the newspapers and on the wireless that air-raid shelters were being provided free to every household if you earned less than £250 a year, which included the vast majority of the population.

'Where in heaven's name will we put one? There's hardly room to swing a cat in that yard,' she had protested when Arthur had read the article aloud.

He'd shaken his head. 'It says there'll be public shelters for people like us who have no room for one of our own.'

Nelly hadn't replied. The need to use one was a circumstance she didn't want to contemplate, but things were clearly getting worse. The Government obviously expected that towns and cities would be bombed, and then no one, rich or poor, air-raid shelter or not, would be safe.

In March, Hitler marched his army into Prague, the capital of Czechoslovakia, to the great consternation and anger of many of the countries in Europe, especially those that bordered Germany.

'I said you can't trust that Hitler feller, he doesn't want peace!' Frederick said as he sat after supper one evening with Olive, Lily and Joan, together with Jim McDonald and Gerard Barnard, in the parlour of the house in Mersey View. Bella was upstairs practising her scales and Charlie was out with the dog.

'I think you're right, Frederick. It makes you wonder which country he's got his sights on next,' Gerard replied gloomily.

'Well, it's obvious the man is so full of himself that he thinks he and his armies can conquer the world – him and that Italian feller. Every bit as bad as Kaiser Bill, that Hitler is – and the Kaiser was as mad as a hatter,' Olive put in curtly. These events put everyone on edge, although the young ones like Joan and Jim, and Bella and Charlie, didn't fully understand the consequences of war – and how could they? They'd not lived through one, as she, Lily, Frederick and Gerard had.

'I read that there's speculation it will be Poland next, and then that's going to make Mr Chamberlain think again about this "peace in our time", as he's pledged to defend Poland, in accordance with some treaty or other,' Frederick said sombrely.

Jim had glanced at Joan and was perturbed to see she looked a bit pale. 'Ah, it may not happen, Joan,' he whispered to her.

She managed to smile back. 'I just hope not. But I've got a nasty feeling it will, and then . . . ?'

He squeezed her hand by way of support but at the same time he was wondering just when conscription would be announced, for he too had a nasty feeling that it would take a war to stop Adolf Hitler and his minions.

He'd grown very fond of Joan, he mused to himself, as the

rest of the household chatted of other things, rather than the current situation, and Joan had risen to collect the tea cups. They went out as often as he could afford, given their limits of time and money, and he was now certain that he loved her. He'd never felt like this about any of the other girls he'd been out with – not that there had been many. He'd not had either the opportunity or the inclination to be escorting girls about in Glasgow or Liverpool. Joan was different, and she always had been, from the very first moment he'd set eyes on her. He saw her every single day and so he'd got to know her really well, and they just seemed so suited to each other. Well, if things got any worse, he'd definitely ask her to marry him, he decided. There was no use shilly-shallying at a time like this. Of course there wouldn't be an expensive engagement ring from the likes of Boodles – he only had what little bit he'd managed to save – but she would have the best he could afford, providing she accepted him. That was a sobering thought. But why wait, if there was going to be another war and he'd have to go and fight?

It was a sentiment Rick and Monica agreed with, for they'd decided to get married in June; September seemed so far off when things were getting worse with each passing day. Both families had agreed, although Nelly would have liked a bit more time to save up for the wedding. Despite Nancy Eustace's revelations about her humble beginnings, she wanted to give her daughter a good day – a day to remember.

Monica, Joan, Rick and Jim met up in town for a drink on Jim's night off, and as the April evening was fine and fairly mild they sat for a while in St John's Gardens, behind St

George's Hall, where the golden heads of the daffodils and the varied colours of the early primulas contrasted with the bright green of the new grass. Despite the noise of the traffic, there was an illusion of tranquillity, added to by the statues and sculptures dotted around the gardens, an oasis of colour and peace in the heart of a bustling and soot-blackened city.

'So, what was the house like, then? Did you like it?' Joan asked of her friend, for she was full of curiosity.

Monica and Rick had been to see a house in Allerton, a district quite near to Woolton where the Eustaces lived, but not as prestigious or as expensive. Joan had been amazed when Monica had told her that as a wedding gift Claude Eustace was giving them the deposit for a house of their own. Rick would have to get a mortgage to pay the rest, but Monica had been over the moon, and Joan could understand why. She'd never known any young couple who started married life in a house they were actually *buying* – and neither had her mam or Monica's mother. Nelly and Arthur had been dumbstruck by the gesture.

Monica smiled at her and nodded. 'We both liked it, didn't we, Rick? It's in a quiet street – Garthdale Road – and it's a semi-detached, not a terrace. And with three bedrooms, a bathroom and toilet inside, oh, pure luxury! A modern kitchen, a sitting room and dining room, it's just perfect.'

'It's got a nice bit of garden both front and back, and room for me to park the car at the side of the house,' Rick added.

'And it's not too far for us to get to work.' A little frown creased Monica's brow. 'Heaven knows what we're going to do for furniture, though. Mam's promised to let me take a few bits from the bedroom, but when I think of all those rooms . . .'

Joan turned her attention away from a couple of pigeons strutting across the grass, their feathers a myriad colours in the late sun. 'You won't be using all the rooms at once, so you can start off with second-hand stuff, Mon, until you can afford to replace it with new and furnish the empty rooms. There's plenty of second-hand shops in the city, some with good-quality stuff too.'

'I know – and I really can't expect any expensive wedding presents either. Mam's determined that my dress and yours and the rest of them are going to be bought from Lewis's; she's having nothing home-made or second rate, so she says.'

Joan raised her eyes skywards. 'That's not going to be cheap.'

'Don't I know it, but Rick's mother is adamant that she'll pay for Ruth and Beverley's outfits, so that will help, and I'm determined that I'm not going to spend a small fortune on mine either. I mean it will never be worn again, will it? I want something elegant but not too expensive. It's such a pity Felicity's Wardrobe doesn't do wedding dresses.'

It had been decided Monica would be married in her local church, St George's, at the top of the hill, for like Olive and her family, the Savages were Protestants by upbringing. Even now, Nelly was engaged in writing out invitations and making lists of all the things that had to be done before the big day, on 30th June – which, the vicar had informed her, was the feast of Saints Peter and Paul, and therefore a good choice.

'It will be tea towels and pillowcases, if I ever get married, and a couple of rooms in someone's house too,' Joan stated, without any touch of envy. There were very, very few brides in this city who would do as well as Monica Savage.

'So, have you told them you'll be taking the house, then?' Jim asked Rick as he stretched out his long legs, which were getting a bit cramped sitting on the small bench.

'I told the bloke who showed us around that I'll go into their offices tomorrow morning to finalise it all,' Rick replied, getting to his feet. It was growing a bit too chilly now to sit in the rather exposed gardens. 'Shall we make our way down to Exchange Street and the Bradford?'

The others also rose; Joan was shivering a little. 'That's a good idea, it's really cold here now. Have you finally decided what colours we're going to wear, Mon?' she asked as the little group left the gardens and crossed into the Haymarket, where the soot-blackened buildings threw one side of the street into shadow.

'Well, I thought that for you I'd like apricot – it will suit your colouring and make you stand out. For the rest I'd like a very pale sort of creamy peach, which would suit all of them.'

Joan nodded her agreement, wondering what style and material her friend would choose and what kind of headdresses they'd wear. She hoped Monica wouldn't opt for a hat, although the large-brimmed 'picture' hats were very fashionable for weddings. Not for the bride, of course; she was sure Monica would have the traditional veil.

'Has Bella said anything more about being a bridesmaid?' Monica queried, for there was some doubt about it. It had been obvious to everyone for a while now that Bella would have to go to London where, hopefully, she would obtain a place at the Royal Academy of Music. David Frances was enquiring into all of it – apparently, he had contacts down there – and both he and Lily were very much involved in

301

Bella's future now, or so it seemed to Joan.

'She'd like to be, of course. In fact, she'd love it, for she's never had the chance to "dress up", as she puts it, but it all depends on what happens in the next few months. Aunty Lil and Mr Frances are desperately trying to get her both a scholarship and a bursary to study in London, but who knows?' Joan shrugged. 'Of course, if she does get a place, she won't be able to go there on her own, she's too young. So, it looks like Aunty Lil will go with her. Mam can't go; she's the house to run.' Joan privately thought her aunt was getting quite fond of Bella's voice coach. She seemed to be seeing rather a lot of him. Bella was naturally the excuse her aunt used, but Joan thought there was more to it. She'd be sorry to see them both go to London but realised it was selfish of her – Bella's future was what really mattered.

'Oh, that's a shame. I was hoping your Aunty Lil could advise me on my dress and your outfits – and even Mam's. I want her to look every bit as stylish as Rick's mother.'

'Well, we'll just have to wait and see, Mon. I know it's not the ideal situation, you really need to know one way or the other about Bella, but . . .' Joan shrugged.

'I know. It can't be helped – I've got so much on my mind at the moment, Joan, that I'm not going to get in a state about it. If she has to go to London, then she must go, that's all there is to it. It's just one bridesmaid less.'

Joan smiled at her friend, thankful she wasn't going to make a huge song and dance about it. Other things, she was sure, would crop up which would put Bella's likely absence into perspective. She knew weddings often reduced the bride and those closest to her to the state of nervous wrecks. Personally, she thought it was not worth getting into a state about, but then she wasn't the one getting married in two months' time.

They had barely seated themselves in the quiet, comfortable if slightly old-fashioned Lounge Bar of The Bradford Hotel, and ordered their drinks, when the barman called over to the lads.

'I'd make the most of being out enjoying yourselves, lads, it's not going to last much longer.'

Both Jim and Rick looked at each other, and the girls frowned.

'Why? What's up now?' Rick called back.

'Conscription. Just been announced that men, twenty and over, are going to be called up. You'll all be getting your papers in the post in the weeks ahead.'

Monica bit her lip and glanced anxiously at Rick, while Joan glared at the barman. 'There's always *someone* happy to spoil people's enjoyment! A proper killjoy you are! Couldn't you have kept that to yourself for a few hours longer?'

The man shrugged and went on polishing a glass. 'You'd have seen it in the papers or heard it on the wireless anyway.'

'At least Charlie's too young,' Jim reminded Joan, for he could see she was shocked, as they all were. They'd been expecting it, but it had never quite seemed real. Now it was. There was no doubt about it. They would have to go and fight, and they'd need to be ready when war was declared – whenever that might be.

Monica felt cold fingers of fear tighten around her heart. Oh, when things were going so well for her and Rick . . . and now soon they would be parted. 'So, what will happen next?' she asked him tentatively.

He shrugged, trying to appear unconcerned, for he could see the fear in her eyes. 'I don't really know. I suppose we'll get some kind of form, and a letter telling us what we've to do.'

Jim nodded. 'One thing that won't happen is hordes of laddies and men rushing to the recruiting offices as if they're off to a picnic.'

'Aye, that's what happened last time. "All over by Christmas" my foot – or so they tell us!' Rick added. As the drinks arrived, he patted Monica's hand. 'Don't worry, luv. I'm sure they won't be sending us away before the wedding. I'll still go to the Estate Agents in the morning and tell them we'll have that house.'

Joan nodded her agreement. 'That's the spirit, Rick. Life has to go on, and we'll make the best of it while we can.'

Jim smiled at her. As soon as they got back to the house in Mersey View he'd ask her to marry him. They wouldn't have as grand a wedding, or a house of their own, but he was determined that they would be together in the days and months that lay ahead.

# Chapter Thirty-One

A s soon as they got home, Joan could tell by her mother's face that the family had heard the news. They hadn't stayed at the Bradford very long after they'd finished their drinks for, as Rick had remarked, the atmosphere hadn't exactly been conducive to enjoyment. She and Jim had parted company with the other two at the bottom of Exchange Street. Rick was driving Monica home and unfortunately there wasn't room in the car for them all, so they'd got the tram.

'I take it you've both heard the news?' Frederick enquired.

'Yes, the barman at the Bradford told us, and it's all over the newspapers, so I wonder we didn't see or hear it before we got there,' Jim replied as Joan put the kettle on, unsettled by the strange, tense atmosphere in the kitchen.

'So, I suppose, Jim, you'll be going back to Scotland to join a Scottish regiment?' Olive queried.

Joan was so startled by this that she almost dropped the tea caddy. She'd not thought about him going back to Scotland.

Jim frowned; he'd not given that a thought either. 'I don't

think so, Mrs Copperfield. I mean I don't even know if we get the option of which regiment we want to join. Maybe they just tell us where we're to go.'

Joan sighed with relief; that sounded more plausible, she thought. The last thing she wanted now was for Jim to be going so far away that she wouldn't be able to see him for months. Maybe that would happen in the future – in fact, she was sure it would – but she didn't want to lose him just yet.

'Monica and Rick are taking that house,' she supplied, to change the subject and hopefully lighten the atmosphere.

'I thought they would. Nelly's getting a bit frazzled. And what with this latest news, she's going to be worried sick that maybe they'll have to put the wedding off, and that Rick won't be able to afford the mortgage on army pay, after all. You know what she's like.'

That was something else Joan hadn't thought of – and she was sure Monica hadn't either. 'Oh, I hope not, Mam. She's very taken with the house, and who wouldn't be? Maybe they'll bring the wedding forward if . . . if things get worse, not put it off.'

'That will only upset Nelly more! And if things do get worse, then I'm going to have to have a talk to our Lily about Bella.' They weren't home from the theatre yet, but Olive was sure they wouldn't be very late. She wasn't at all happy about the prospect of them going to London now that war seemed inevitable.

Frederick nodded his agreement as Joan passed around the tea, thinking that Lily would be foolish to think of taking the girl there now.

It wasn't until Olive had gone up to bed, and Frederick had

banked down the fire for the night and then taken his leave of them, that Joan and Jim were finally alone.

'Come and sit here by me, lassie,' Jim urged, smiling up at Joan.

'I thought they'd never leave us in peace,' Joan replied as she sat down beside him by the range. 'I'm glad you don't think they'll let you have a choice of regiment. I . . . well, I don't want you to go away at all. I know that eventually you'll have to, but . . .'

Jim put his arms around her and held her close. 'I don't want to go either. But I've no option . . . but before . . . before that happens, will you marry me, Joan? I love you, I think I've loved you from the day I first met you, I knew then that you were the one for me.'

Joan felt her heart swell with joy as she gazed up at him, her dark eyes shining. 'I love you too, Jim McDonald – you've always been . . . special to me, ever since you came to live here.'

'I can't offer you anything like Monica's having –'

She cut off his words with her lips, but after a few minutes she drew away and smiled at him. 'You're all I want. Of course I'll marry you!'

'You don't think your mam will object at all?'

'Why on earth should she? She knows you well enough by now, and she likes you. And she knows that I . . .' She frowned.

'What?'

'She knows that after . . . Da, I'd be very . . . careful who I married.'

'Does that still bother you, Joan . . . what happened?'

She leaned her head against his chest. She'd sworn she

would never be used and humiliated the way her mother had been, but she'd also instinctively known that Jim McDonald was a very different kind of person to Billy Copperfield. 'No, I don't really think about him much at all now. I don't think anyone does.' She sighed heavily.

'That sounds ominous,' Jim teased her.

'Not really. I . . . I just wish that he hadn't just gone. I mean if we knew he'd died, then Mam . . .' She looked up into Jim's eyes and saw understanding there.

'Then your mam could wed again – to a better man who would look after her and cherish her?'

Joan nodded. 'Yes . . . I know Frederick cares for her, and I also know she's fond of him – she's told me so – but . . . but she's not free, and won't be while *he's* alive.'

Jim looked thoughtful as he drew her to him again. 'Well, let's not dwell on that, Joan, at the minute. I'm just so happy you've agreed to become Mrs McDonald.'

Joan kissed him, thinking 'Mrs Joan McDonald' sounded strange but very nice, very nice indeed.

Everyone was delighted by the news, particularly Monica. 'Have you any idea when?' she asked after she'd hugged her friend.

'It won't be the same day as you, so don't worry about that – and it will be very quiet too. Jim has no close relatives, so there will be just Mam, Charlie and Frederick, and Bella of course, if she's still here.'

'Well, I'll be your bridesmaid – or matron of honour, depending when you decide – and I'm sure Rick will be happy to be best man.'

'I'm not much of a one for the church, Mon, as you know. I don't really believe in it all, and neither does Jim. It will probably be at the Registry Office, and I'll get something from Felicity's Wardrobe that I can wear again.'

Monica rolled her eyes. 'Oh, honestly, Joan, you're so . . . practical! Whatever happened to romance?'

Joan grinned. 'I have enough romance with Jim, thank you – I never did have dreams of walking down the aisle in a long white dress and veil, with masses of flowers and music. No, something smart will suit me fine.' She'd discussed all this with Olive, who'd agreed and suggested that they go on living in the house after the wedding, but that she'd sort out a bedroom for them.

'There's no need to turn the house upside down, Mam, surely I can just move in with Jim?' Joan had stated, and Olive had nodded.

No one seemed to know how long it would be before both Jim and Rick Eustace would have to leave for training at least, if not full deployment, but plans had to be made and the weeks were going on. Soon it would be May.

Lily was rather surprised when, that evening, she found David Frances waiting for her as she left the theatre, by the back entrance in Lord Nelson Street. She'd sent Bella home just before the evening performance began, for she would seldom allow Bella's work here to interfere with her musical training. Bella needed to practise, just as Jim McDonald did.

'This is a nice surprise, David!' She beamed at him, tucking her arm through his. They had become very much at ease with one another over the last weeks, particularly as the news had grown graver by the day.

'I didn't want you to be on your own when you heard the news, Lily,' he replied.

She looked up at him, concerned. 'What news?'

'They're bringing in conscription for all men over the age of twenty.'

'Oh, my God!' Lily cried, startled. Although she shouldn't be, she told herself. It had only been a matter of time. 'Oh, will that include you, David?'

He looked grim. 'I expect so, Lily. They haven't said yet what the upper age limit will be, and of course there will be those in "reserved occupations" like the Ambulance, Police and Fire Brigade. But I don't fall into those categories, and there is very little wrong with my health.'

Lily felt her heart sink at his words. She didn't know exactly how old he was, but she assumed he was about the same age as Frederick Garswood – in his late forties. They had turned the corner into Lime Street and he ushered her towards The Imperial Hotel, on the corner near the station.

'Let's go in here for a drink, Lily,' he suggested.

She nodded her agreement; she could do with something stiff to bolster her spirits, she thought.

When they'd found a seat in an alcove decorated in rich shades of plum, maroon and gold, and their drinks had been served, David broached the subject that had been foremost in his mind since he'd heard the latest news. 'So, obviously now the Government thinks events are escalating, we need to talk about Bella's future, Lily.'

She sipped her pink gin and looked seriously at him. 'You

think this will change everything, David? Are things really getting *that* bad? They've virtually accepted her, there's just the audition and interview, and I'm sure she'll sail through both. You've been marvellous, sorting absolutely everything out for us – I really do feel as if I should have done more to help.'

He smiled at her. 'It's been a pleasure, but now I'm wondering if it's all going to have been wasted.'

From the start Lily had been determined that Bella was not going to be disappointed – the girl had been working so hard towards her dream, and now she was more certain than ever about Bella's future potential. 'Surely, she can still audition? Oh, she'll be so disappointed if she can't, David! She's suffered so much in her short life that she *must* have this chance at least!'

'I understand that, but she's so young, Lily. There's a war coming and everyone's futures are uncertain. There's no point in her auditioning if she couldn't possibly take up a place.'

'I know – but I'm quite prepared to go and live in London with her if she gets accepted, as you know. War or no war, Bella is going to have her chance! That bloody Hitler isn't going to stand in her way!'

He smiled at her. 'Lily Cooper, you are the most determined – not to say obstinate – woman I've ever met.'

She smiled back. 'I believe in Bella, David. I would go to the ends of the earth for her and her career, so London's not that far, is it?'

He could see he was wasting his time trying to get her to change her mind. 'If you put it like that, then I suppose not, but neither of you are going alone. I'm coming with you, Lily.'

She stared at him in astonishment. 'But . . . I don't understand . . . you'll have to give up everything here . . .'

'I may not have my work here for much longer, and in London I have friends we can count on to find us suitable accommodation, hopefully near to the Royal Academy of Music, and help us to get settled. That's if you don't mind putting up with me, of course.'

Lily's eyes widened further. 'I . . . I . . . do I understand exactly what you are saying, David . . . or am I being an utter fool?'

He laughed, his eyes sparkling. He'd decided on this a couple of months ago, when they'd realised Bella would have to go to the capital to continue her training. 'I hope so, Lily. I can't . . . won't let you go there alone under the circumstances, and I'm old-fashioned enough to want to protect your reputation, so we'll go as a married couple – Mr and Mrs Frances . . .' He paused, smiling. 'Oh, and I happen to be very fond of you too, Miss Cooper.'

Lily was utterly speechless. She had never even contemplated getting married – and certainly not now, at her age. But if she were brutally honest, there were times when she did feel as though there was *something* missing from her life – and she did care for him. The feeling had grown and then intensified over the months, and they had a great deal in common: he was an interesting man, with a background she admired and respected. He also had a sense of humour that matched her own – and then, of course, they both were so involved with Bella and her career. So, why not? She was truthful enough to admit that she wasn't wildly in love with him. Not as Olive had been with Billy, but look how that had ended! She took another deep swig of gin and said nothing, but she placed her other hand over his and smiled. They'd do well together, she was certain: herself, David and Bella. And then they would be a little family themselves, and both she and David could guide Bella's career. It was a novel thought – she as a wife and surrogate mother!

'I'll take that as a "yes", then?'

Lily nodded, feeling both excited and content. She had no intention of telling Olive about this development – not until Bella had had her audition and hopefully succeeded in obtaining a place at the Royal Academy of Music. But she was looking forward to seeing the expression on her sister's face when she did.

A week later, both Jim and Rick's call-up papers arrived, to the consternation of both Joan and Monica.

'At least they won't be too far away. They're both training in Cheshire, so they'll be able to get some leave, I'm sure. So the wedding can go ahead, Mon, don't get upset,' Joan comforted her friend.

She and Jim had decided to wait until after Monica's wedding before they too tied the knot, but with the provision that, should the situation escalate, it would be easier for them to be married by special licence in a Registry Office, rather than go through the ceremony in a church, nor would they have to arrange a big reception. There would be just a small wedding breakfast with the close family, in the dining room of the house in Mersey View. The meal would be cooked by her mother and served by Olive, Lily and Bella – for she was certain that her aunt and Bella would no longer be going to London. How could they, at a time like this?

# Chapter Thirty-Two

Three weeks later, Bella received the letter from the Royal Academy giving her the date and time for the most important interview of her life – her audition for entry.

She was so excited that they all found it hard to keep her feet on the ground, let alone remind her that there was a war on the horizon and the world would be bound to change, with the result that the best-laid plans and the most cherished hopes could well be shattered.

'Oh, see, Joan! It is not until July the third. I can be Monica's bridesmaid, after all!' Bella cried, excitedly waving the letter.

Joan looked across at her mother, who just shrugged her shoulders.

'It's a good job you are going for the dresses this week, then,' Olive replied laconically. Personally, she thought Lily was mad to still be going along with this London plan – but then she didn't want Bella to be disappointed either. Maybe there would be no harm in the girl going for the audition – who knew what the future held? A war could change everything.

'Shall I go up and tell Monica now?' Bella queried, running her fingers through her dark curls, a habit she had when excited or upset.

Joan grinned at her. 'I'll come with you. She'll be delighted – no doubt her mam will be very relieved that the decision has finally been made.'

Their news was greeted with delight by both Monica and Eileen but with more reserve by Nelly, who was of the same opinion as Olive – that it was madness for the girl to even think about London now, for the capital would surely be the prime target for the enemy.

'Oh, isn't that just great news, Mam?' Monica cried when Bella had shown her the letter. 'Then you can come with us to Lewis's at the weekend. We've already been in, and they showed us the most gorgeous dresses, didn't they, Mam?'

'And did they show you anything for yourself, anything special, like?' Joan queried.

'There were two I really liked. Oh, it's all getting so exciting now!' Monica could hardly contain her feelings. Before he'd left for the training camp in Cheshire, she and Rick had gone to a couple of good-class second-hand shops and bought a sofa and two chairs, a bed and a bedroom suite, and a small dining table and chairs. She was beginning to feel that her new home was taking shape. Of course, there was so much else she'd need, not least some curtains – but well, she'd have plenty of time for all that after the wedding, for Rick would have to go back to camp then.

'Monica, there is something special I want to do for you and Rick, if you permit it?' Bella said rather shyly.

'What?' Monica asked, wondering what the girl meant.

315

'I like to sing at your wedding. I know it is at the church, but even though it is not the religion I had in Portugal, I want to do it, so I ask Maestro Francis for something special . . . something that is not a hymn but is still . . . sacred.'

Tears pricked Joan's eyes, for this was something she hadn't expected at all, and neither had Monica. She hugged Bella tightly and Joan caught the glimpse of tears in her friend's eyes too.

'Oh, Bella! Oh, that is . . . that will be so . . . wonderful!' Monica enthused.

Bella smiled as she disentangled herself from the bride-to-be's embrace.

'I sing "*Panis Angelicus*" for you – it means "Bread of Angels". Maestro Francis, he teach me, and it is so very beautiful! And sacred too.'

Monica looked across at Joan and smiled. She doubted anyone had ever heard it before, but she had no doubts at all that it would indeed be beautiful, as well as fitting.

'Thank you, Bella.' Monica smiled at the girl. 'It is so kind and generous of you.'

'I want to do it, Monica, for perhaps soon I will be going away. As you know, I have little else I can give to you for a gift, so this will be my special offering to you.'

'And one that I'm sure we will all remember for a very long time, Bella,' Nelly said firmly, with a slight catch in her throat.

If what Olive had told her about the girl's voice was true, this solo piece would be the finest St George's had heard in its entire history.

As the day of the wedding drew nearer so did the pace of activity – and the pressure on stretched nerves. All the girls had been pleased with the dresses Monica had chosen, and to Joan's relief they were to wear wreaths of silk mock-orange blossom on their heads. In the end Nelly had been quite adamant about her outfit, insisting on accompanying Olive and Lily to Felicity's Wardrobe. There had been nothing that had really taken her eye in Lewis's – nothing that she was prepared to pay the price for anyway – and after Joan had informed her that she was going to Felicity's to look for something for her own wedding, Nelly had made up her mind.

With the help of Lily and Fliss McKenzie, she'd picked out a dusky-pink moiré dress and coat trimmed with silver-coloured braid, and Joan had found a smart hat that matched almost exactly. They had all agreed that she looked extremely elegant: as she gazed at herself in the long mirror attached to one wall, Nelly could scarcely believe the transformation. She'd never had anything as stylish as this in her life before, not even for her own wedding. It obviously had been very expensive when new, which pleased her, as did the fact that she was getting something of far better quality for the price she would have had to pay in Lewis's. This Miss McKenzie certainly had a good business head on her shoulders.

To her disappointment Joan had found nothing for herself but, as Lily remarked, business was brisk and there were clothes coming in each week – and as the wedding wasn't until July, there was still plenty of time for her to find a special outfit. Fliss would keep her eye out too, she was certain.

Lily herself had gone through Fliss's stock and had more or less settled on a very well-tailored navy dress and jacket, trimmed and piped with white piqué braid and finished with gold buttons, a style that was becoming synonymous with the

French fashion house of Chanel. She'd had a quiet word with Fliss, who had agreed to put it aside for her and suggested both a hat and handbag that would complement it. Lily's long-time friend had merely raised an eyebrow when Lily had whispered to her that it wasn't for Monica's wedding nor Joan's, but for her own, although that probably wouldn't be for some weeks yet.

'I've got a couple of outfits already, so let's just get these two married and settled first,' she'd finished with a smile as Fliss carefully covered the dress and jacket to take them through to the back room.

Felicity McKenzie always respected her clients' confidences, Lily knew that.

Thankfully, June that year seemed to be starting well, so Monica thought, as she walked home from the tram stop with Joan. She wasn't seeing Rick tonight; he was going to a hair-dressing products supplier's exhibition in Manchester with his father and the senior stylists from all three salons.

'I do hope this weather holds, Joan, sometimes June can be cloudy and chilly,' she stated, gazing up at the sky which was just beginning to take on a faint hint of pink as the sun slowly slid lower. The light that flooded the narrow street seemed golden and somehow luminous, making all the windows of the houses sparkle. It was a beautiful evening, no doubt about that.

'Stop worrying, Mon, it will be gorgeous, and if not . . . well, there's not a lot anyone can do about the weather, is there? Everyone will make the most of the day, I'm sure.'

Monica sighed. 'No, you're right. No good getting into a state about something you can't change. I've got enough on my plate thinking about how I'm going to get everyone's hair done in time, and that's not including my own.' Rather foolishly, she now thought, she'd agreed to do Nelly, Eileen and Olive's hair the night before the wedding and then comb them all up in the morning. She'd offered to do Joan and Bella's too, but Joan had been adamant that they were quite capable of doing their own.

'Why don't you ask one of the girls from the salon if they can help?' Joan suggested.

'On a Friday morning? It's almost as busy as a Saturday – which is one of the reasons I'm getting married on the Friday. No, I'll just have to manage. I'll get up early.'

Joan smiled ruefully at her friend. 'So, no lie-in and leisurely breakfast for you, then?'

Monica shook her head but grinned. 'No, but I think I'll be too excited and nervous to lie in bed anyway.'

'There'll be no lying in bed in our house either. I'll have my work cut out trying to keep Bella calm.'

Monica frowned. 'She's not having second thoughts about singing, is she?'

'Lord, no! She's been practising so much I think we all know the words by heart, even though they're in Latin and we haven't a clue what they mean. No, she's just so excited about her dress and headdress and bouquet – she's never had anything like it before, not even when she made her Communion in Portugal. They didn't have the money for such finery, so she told me. No, she's not worried about singing, I really think she's looking on it as a sort of rehearsal for her audition.' It was Joan's turn to frown. 'You know, Mon, I really don't want her to go to London to study – not now. Both Mam and

319

Frederick think it will get very dangerous down there. I mean they're not giving everyone air-raid shelters and gas masks for nothing, and there's talk that all the young kids will have to be evacuated to the country soon.'

Monica said nothing, although she agreed with Joan. But it seemed as if Lily was intent on Bella at least attending the audition. 'Does . . . does this . . . hymn, or whatever it is, sound good?'

Joan stopped and stared at her but then smiled. 'It's supposed to be a surprise, Mon, but I'll say this much. If she doesn't pass that audition with flying colours then that lot down there at the Royal Academy must be tone deaf – and that's all I'm saying! Now, let's get a move on, I'm starving!'

Nelly was preparing to serve the meal when Monica entered the kitchen. She knew her sister would be in any minute from work, but there was no sign yet of her father.

'Will Da be late this evening, Mam?'

Nelly nodded, wiping her forehead with the back of her hand. The kitchen was stiflingly hot, for she needed the range to cook. 'Oh, how I envy Rick's Mam and that fancy new gas cooker she's got! It must be a real pleasure to cook in her kitchen. It's certainly not in this damned inferno! And she's got some kind of gas heater for hot water – or was it electric, I can't remember – but I do remember thinking how fortunate she is. And you will be too, luv, when you move into that house.'

Monica smiled at her as she began to set the table. 'Sometimes, Mam, I still can't believe it. A house of my own! My own home – mine and Rick's! And with a proper bathroom and gardens too!'

Nelly smiled tiredly back at her as Eileen appeared, complaining about the heat and the stuffiness of the tram, but she wondered just how much time her future son-in-law would actually get to spend in his own home.

The meal was ready when Arthur got back from his work, looking tired and shaken.

'What's wrong, luv?' Nelly asked, helping him off with his uniform jacket and taking his guard's cap from him and placing it on the dresser.

He handed her the newspaper. 'It's not good news, Nelly. Read the headlines.'

Nelly sat down at the table, as did they all, but the food was ignored as she scanned the bold headlines and her eyes widened. 'Oh, my God! Why . . . why has no one heard about this before?'

'Probably it was forbidden by the Admiralty,' Arthur answered, while the girls looked at each other in alarm.

'Mam, what is it?' Monica asked in hushed tones.

It was her father who answered. 'There's a submarine out there in Liverpool Bay – the *Thetis*. It was built at Laird's and they were testing it and something . . . they don't know what – or at least that's what they're saying – went wrong and . . . and they couldn't get it to the surface again.'

Nelly began to read slowly from the paper. 'They sent twenty-one warships out to try to help, and four men managed to escape through a hatch, but then those left inside couldn't get the hatch closed again and the water poured in. The warships then sent out small boats to the submarine to tap out messages in Morse code on its side but . . .' She stopped and shook her head sadly.

'But after being underwater for so long, seventy-one men died. Drowned or suffocated, I suppose. God rest them!' Arthur finished grimly.

'Oh, and to think how I was complaining about being stuck in the kitchen in the heat just for a couple of hours! Dear Lord above, how they must have suffered!' Nelly was fighting back tears.

Eileen looked down at her plate; she didn't feel in the least bit hungry now.

Monica bit her lip and looked fearfully at her father. 'Oh, Da! That . . . that's . . . terrible.'

'I know, luv. But I suppose the worst part was that their wives, mothers and girlfriends waited outside the gates of the shipyard for three whole days before they could get any news . . . and then it was too late.'

'It's a tragedy but it's also a disgrace!' Nelly put in. 'An utter disgrace to make those poor women wait that long without telling them a single thing about what was happening.'

Arthur nodded his agreement. 'I know, but I suppose they had their reasons, Nell. It was a new type of sub and I don't imagine they wanted that plastered all over every newspaper – not nowadays. The country could be full of German spies, for all we know.'

Monica aimlessly pushed the mashed potato around on her plate. This seemed to have brought the threat of war and death closer to home, and she desperately hoped that it wasn't an omen – a bad omen for her wedding and her future.

# Chapter Thirty-Three

The tragedy of the *Thetis* remained in everyone's mind but at least on the day of Monica's wedding the sun was shining in a clear blue sky, Nelly thought thankfully, as she drew back the bedroom curtains. Her new outfit, covered with tissue paper, was hanging on the back of the door, and the hat, also carefully wrapped in tissue, reposed in pride of place on the dressing table. She felt a little thrill of pleasure at the sight.

When she went to rouse her daughters, she found Monica up and in her dressing gown but Eileen still in bed.

'Right, miss, get out of that bed this minute!' she instructed Eileen, before turning to her elder daughter and smiling. 'It's you who should be having a lie-in this morning, luv.'

Monica smiled back. 'I know, but does that really matter, Mam? I've a lot to do before we'll all be ready to go to the church.'

Nelly nodded. 'You can say that again! Now, come down, both of you, breakfast is ready.'

'I don't want much, Mam, I'm so nervous I just don't feel hungry.'

'Well, you'll have to have something; we don't want you fainting at the altar, now, do we?' Nelly chided.

Monica turned to her younger sister, who was sitting on the edge of the bed, pulling a face. 'What's the matter with you?'

'I've hardly slept a wink with all these damned pins sticking into my head!' Eileen complained, pulling at the metal clips that held the carefully wound pin curls in position.

'Well, you had a choice. Sleep in the clips or look a mess this morning. I wasn't having you spoil the look of everything.'

Eileen managed a smile. 'I know – don't think I'm being ungrateful, I'm not. I just wish I had hair like Bella's.'

Monica smiled back. 'No one is ever satisfied with their hair. If it's straight, they want it curly – that's why perms are so popular – and if it's curly, they want it straight.'

Eileen grinned. 'I know. Bella complains often enough. I think she's going to be great today, Mon. She's not even a bit nervous, so she told me.'

Monica frowned. 'I just hope she's not overconfident.'

'Oh, don't start worrying about that now. I'm sorry I mentioned it. Come on, we'd better go down and get things started. I've to help you dress later on, don't forget.'

In a rare show of affection, Eileen hugged her sister. 'It will be the most wonderful day of your life, Mon. I know it!'

After what seemed like a morning of complete chaos, with people coming and going and calling to wish Monica every happiness, they were all finally ready. Eileen and Bella, their hair stylishly curled under the wreaths of creamy white mock-orange blossoms and dressed in the pale peach crêpe de Chine dresses with long full skirts and slightly puffed sleeves, went through into the scullery to bring out the flowers from where they had been resting in buckets of cold water since their arrival earlier.

Joan looked around Nelly's small and crowded kitchen and smiled to herself. Everyone looked gorgeous. She was very happy with her dress, the same style and material as the others, but a vivid shade of apricot. Rick's sisters, Ruth and Beverley, having been dropped off earlier by their father, were trying their best not to look uncomfortable in what felt to them like a cramped and rather stuffy room. Nelly looked so smart and proud in her new pink moiré outfit and wide-brimmed hat, but she still felt nervous that *something* was bound to go wrong.

Joan smiled at her. 'Stop worrying, Mrs Savage. It's going to be a great day, one we'll all remember. What can possibly happen? You've organised everything and we all look the bees knees, and Monica . . . well, she looks gorgeous, doesn't she?'

Joan and Eileen had helped Monica to dress and when she was ready Nelly had been summoned to see the result. She'd been so overcome by emotion she hadn't been able to speak but had just wiped her eyes with a handkerchief and carefully hugged her daughter, afraid she'd crush the dress or disturb the veil. Monica was a vision to behold – Nelly had not looked like that on her own wedding day to Arthur, she knew. She smiled back at Joan, thinking it had all been worth every penny. No one could possibly find fault; it would be one of the nicest weddings ever to be held in St George's, she was certain of it, and with the sun shining . . . what more could she ask?

After Nelly had gone, Arthur, wearing his best suit, his starched white shirt with its winged collar and a sober tie, guided Monica down the stairs and into the narrow lobby where the bridesmaids were assembled, to await the return of the car. The church was only around the corner, and he supposed they could have walked the distance; a lot of brides did, he'd reminded his wife, but Nelly would have none of it. They would have a car – for wouldn't the Eustaces be arriving in their own car?

'Oh, Mon, you look . . . gorgeous! Doesn't she, Mr Savage?' Joan cried, taking her friend's hands in her own and smiling happily.

Monica smiled back as Arthur, with a lump in his throat, agreed with Joan.

'You're sure my hair looks all right?' Monica queried. Her own hair had been the last to get done, for she'd spent most of the morning titivating her mother's, her sister's, Olive's and that of Rick's sisters.

'Just perfect,' Joan assured her, thinking that the small wreath of white silk rosebuds set the long tulle veil off to perfection. Monica's dress was of white lace – not handmade lace, of course, that was much too expensive – over white satin, with a high neck and long tight sleeves fastened at the wrists by tiny pearl buttons. It was fitted into the waist but then flowed out and into a short train at the back. It was a simple design that relied on the fabric for its elegant effect, and it did that to perfection. Monica reached up to pat a curl as Joan handed her the large bouquet of peach carnations and white stocks, which smelled wonderful, interspersed with green sprigs of myrtle and trailing fronds of smilax. 'Right, here's the car back for us, girls!' she instructed Bella, Eileen, Ruth and Beverley, ushering them towards the front door.

Monica took a deep breath as she turned to look up at her father. 'My turn next – I'm so nervous, Da.'

He smiled down at her. 'Everyone is, luv, on their wedding day. I know I was shaking – and your mam could hardly get the words of her vows out, she was so full of nerves.'

'Mam was really *that* nervous?' Monica couldn't imagine her redoubtable mother ever being in such a state.

Arthur nodded. Maybe he'd stretched the truth a little but, ah well . . . 'Just remember a couple of things that make for a good marriage, Monica. Sayings my old mam had, but they seem to work. "Do as you would be done by" and "Never let the sun set on your anger", although I hope there won't be *any* anger, luv. He's a good lad and I'm sure you're both going to be very happy.'

She smiled as they heard the sound of a vehicle coming slowly down the street, accompanied by the whistling of all the small lads who were out to watch the spectacle, and she slipped her arm through her father's. It was going to be the most wonderful day of her life.

Olive glanced curiously around the church as she stood with Frederick, Lily, David, Charlie and Jim McDonald in a pew off the centre aisle. She'd never been in this church before – in fact, she'd been in very few churches if the truth were told. She had little time for religion, any religion. The church was very grand, she mused, watching the rays of the bright sunlight from outside turning the colours of the huge stained-glass window above the altar into a veritable rainbow of vivid

327

dancing lights. There was an upper gallery that ran along both sides of the central aisle, supported by delicate wrought-iron pillars and arches and fretwork that stretched right to the high Gothic ceiling, all painted white, which gave the illusion of lightness and airiness. The interior was not what you would expect from looking at the exterior, she thought. Outside it was a large, square and fairly plain building of red sandstone, with a square bell tower that crowned the hill and looked down on the rows and rows of narrow cobbled streets that ran down to the city and the river beyond.

The thought of the river made her think briefly of Billy, something she seldom did these days. She glanced sideways at Frederick and gave a little sigh. He was very fond of her, she was almost certain of that by the glances, the little tokens and the subtle hints. And she . . . well, she'd grown fond of him too, and today, with Nelly looking so smart and proud and soon to have Arthur at her side as their daughter was married, she suddenly wished that when Joan was married, she could have a husband at her side to share the moment with – but certainly not Billy!

Joan had looked absolutely stunning in her bridesmaid's dress, she thought, remembering the evening her daughter had tried on the entire ensemble for the family's benefit. That shade of apricot really suited her colouring, and the fairly simple style emphasised the fact that her daughter had a very good figure, something she was sure Jim had noticed too, judging by the look of stunned admiration in his eyes. Joan had already told her that she was going to have the dress cut short so it could be worn again, and that for her own wedding there would be no long white dress and veil. It hadn't surprised her, for Joan was like herself, practical and down to earth – although Lily had commented that it would be a shame, because she was certain her niece would look every bit as beautiful as Monica Savage, if not more so. She could definitely look stunning when she put her mind to it.

Olive's deliberations were cut short by the thundering of the organ as it burst into life with the opening bars of the 'Bridal Chorus' from Wagner's opera *Lohengrin* and she knew that Monica had arrived. As Nelly turned a little to try to catch a surreptitious glimpse of her daughter, Olive caught her eye and smiled. From the first days of her arrival in Mersey View, Nelly Savage had proved to be a good friend and neighbour to her, and she wished her well, today of all days.

Monica felt as if she were walking on a cloud – in fact, everything seemed to be so unreal – but as she looked up at Rick, resplendent in the dark, neat dress uniform of a sergeant in the South Lancashire Regiment, and with his cap under his arm, she realised with a jolt that she was now to become his wife. All of a sudden, her nerves left her and she felt grown-up. She was an adult, a woman – no longer a girl. As he smiled down at her, she felt a wave of pure happiness engulf her.

She passed her bouquet to Joan and Rick took her hand in his.

Joan smiled happily as she returned to the front pew beside Nelly and Arthur. Jim looked every bit as handsome and smart as Rick, although she couldn't see why Rick Eustace had been made a sergeant at all – perhaps because he'd been better educated than Jim? They were not actually even in the same branch of the services now, for after the initial call-up and a couple of weeks in Cheshire, Jim had been sent to Skellingthorpe in Lincolnshire and was a lowly aircraftsman at the RAF base there. They hadn't yet set a date, but although she knew her own wedding would be nothing like this, she was content. This was what Monica had wanted; she too would soon have the day she desired.

It was a beautiful service, Nelly thought, as the vicar continued with his short sermon. Soon she and Arthur would have to stand and go up to sign the register, with Monica – now Mrs Richard Eustace – Rick, Jim and Joan, and of course Nancy and Claude. She had managed a quick word with Nancy before Monica arrived and the service had begun, complimenting her on her sage-green-and-cream dress, coat and matching hat, although being rather superstitious Nelly wasn't sure about the colour green. Everything was perfect, she reflected, and the final piece of perfection would be Bella's recital while the register was being signed. She was so looking forward to it.

When the time came and the vicar gave her the prearranged signal, Bella left the pew and climbed the narrow, winding wrought-iron staircase to the organ loft, holding the folds of her long skirt high so as not to trip. She wasn't nervous; she was looking forward to her very first public appearance since she'd started her training. Training that would, she fervently hoped, continue at the Royal Academy of Music in London next month. She handed her music to the organist, who nodded and smiled at her, for they'd had a rehearsal two days ago and he was delighted to be able to accompany her.

Monica had just finished signing her name when Bella's voice rang out through the church, so pure and clear that she heard both her mother and mother-in-law gasp aloud and she felt the hair on the back of her neck stand up. She couldn't see Bella but that didn't matter; what mattered was that the girl was singing to make her day so special – Bella truly had the voice of an angel, and this church set it off magnificently.

Olive turned in her seat to look upwards to where the small, slim figure with the cloud of dark curls was standing, filling the church with a voice so beautiful it brought tears to her eyes. Oh, she'd heard Bella sing this before but never 'full voice', as Lily had informed her it was called. This . . . this was so different . . . so utterly entrancing. She felt Frederick's hand on her own and she looked up at him through misted eyes.

'She has a remarkable voice, Olive,' he whispered. 'We're doing the right thing, sending her to London.'

She nodded her agreement as she dabbed her eyes delicately with a handkerchief.

Lily leaned towards her as the last silvery notes died away. 'I told you so, Olive. She's a star, no doubt of that. And no thanks to a certain person we know, who hopefully is living in poverty and squalor in Brazil.'

Olive smiled grimly. 'I hope so too, Lily!' she replied, before wondering was it right to be thinking such thoughts in a church? But somehow she really didn't care what had happened to Billy. He was no longer a part of her life, no longer a part of any of their lives, especially not Bella's.

Five days later, Bella, Lily and David stood outside the grand facade of the Royal Academy of Music, Bella shaking with nerves. They had all travelled down on the train the previous day and stayed in a small bed-and-breakfast hotel in Marylebone, close to the academy on Marylebone Road.

Bella's eyes travelled upwards over the red-brick-and-white-stone edifice, built in the Georgian style with wide steps going up to the double doors, flanked by two squat pillars on top of which were copper urns filled with flowers and adorned with what looked like ladies with outstretched arms holding the bowls.

When they had arrived in London, they had all been taken aback by the obvious preparations for war – the signs directing the way to the public air-raid shelters, propaganda and recruitment posters on almost every building, and everyone carrying gas masks. But as she gazed up at the entrance, Bella forgot all that. 'This is . . . it?' Bella asked Lily, her dark eyes wide and fearful.

Lily nodded and took her hand. 'It is. Now, don't go getting in a state, Bella, luv. It all looks very grand, but you weren't nervous in St George's, were you? And this is just the same size, if not smaller.'

Bella nodded slowly. 'I was happy to sing there . . . for Monica and Rick.'

David took the situation in hand. 'Right, well there's no use us standing here like a group of tourists, let's go in and get this over with. And then we're all going for tea at Harrods. I've promised your aunt,' he added, smiling for Bella's benefit, hoping to dispel some of her nerves with the thought of the treat.

Inside was just as grand, Lily thought, glancing around as David ushered them up a wide ornate staircase of wrought iron above which a large stained-glass window flooded the stairs with light.

'It . . . it looks a bit like a church, yes?' Bella stated hesitantly.

'It does, so just think of it as being like Monica's wedding. One of your pieces is "*Panis Angelicus*",' Lily reminded her.

Bella nodded as they reached the first landing and David directed them to a door beside which was a desk where a middle-aged gentleman sat sifting through papers.

Lily and Bella stood back and let David approach and do the talking. It appeared they knew each other, judging by the smiles, handshakes and nods. Lily nodded politely as David's companion looked across towards her and Bella.

'Right, Bella. You are to go with Mr Simmonds. Everything is ready for you, and he will bring you back here to us when you've finished,' David instructed, smiling encouragingly at her.

She nodded slowly. 'They . . . they tell me . . . today?'

'I'm afraid not, Bella. They will make a decision and then, because we are staying on for a few days, they will contact us here, in London. They have the address and telephone number of where we are staying.'

Both Bella and Lily looked a little perturbed, but Lily took the girl's hand and held it tightly. 'You'll be fine, Bella. You really will. You have nothing to be afraid of – just remember how you came to this country. You are a brave girl, Bella, so go in there and sing as you've never sung before, luv. Sing for Olive and Joan, and me and David. Sing for your mama, Bella – but most of all, sing for yourself! This is your chance, grasp it with both hands.' She placed her hands on the girl's shoulders, turned her in the direction of the door and gave her a gentle push, smiling.

She and David watched Bella as she walked slowly across the marble floor clutching her music. 'Will she be all right,

Lily? She won't succumb to her nerves?' David was anxious for he'd known singers whose voices had cracked with nerves – or worse, dried up completely.

'She'll be fine, David. That girl is special. As I told her, she's brave – and by God, she deserves this chance after how that rat of a father treated her and her poor mother,' Lily replied. Then she smiled up at him. 'Sit down, and while we're waiting – and to take our minds off things – I'll tell you all about Billy Copperfield and how Bella came to us.'

He sat and patted her hand. 'I've often wondered, Lily, but I knew you'd tell me – one day.'

# Chapter Thirty-Four

———◆◈◆———

When the trio returned from London, it was with the news that Bella had been accepted and her training would begin in the new term, in September.

Olive could see that the girl was completely overawed and looked excited but slightly dazed. She hugged her tightly. 'Oh, I'm so pleased for you, luv, even though I'll really miss you. We'll all miss you!'

'I miss everyone too – but I still have some time with you all,' Bella replied, smiling happily. 'And Maestro Frances will continue to teach me while we are still here in Liverpool.'

Lily nodded. 'Why don't you go up and see Eileen? I'm sure they will all be dying to know how you got on and to hear about all the places David took us to see,' she urged Bella. There were practical things she now had to discuss with her sister.

When the girl had left, Olive made a pot of tea and settled herself down in an armchair. 'So, do I get to hear all about the places you've seen? The Palace, Westminster Abbey, the

Tower, the Houses of Parliament and, of course, what I'm sure was the most interesting of all to you – Harrods and afternoon tea!'

Lily smiled as she examined her nails, wondering how to start. 'You're right there. Oh, Harrods was absolutely amazing, Olive, but very expensive! I'd have liked to have bought you something from there, but even a small box of embroidered handkerchiefs cost an arm and a leg – and Bella's embroidery is as good as theirs.' She settled herself more comfortably in the chair. 'There's plenty of time for me to tell you every single detail, but the first thing I need to report is I'm going to London with Bella.'

Olive nodded as she sipped her tea. 'I knew you'd already decided that, Lil, and I'm grateful that she'll have someone to keep an eye on her. She's so young to be in such a big city.'

'I'll have to get a job, of course, but I'm hoping with my experience and with so many theatres in London that it won't be too difficult. We'll have to find somewhere to live too – not too far from the academy, to save on fares – but London is an expensive place to live and work, so money will be tight –'

Olive started to protest. She was sure Lily would soon get a job – but rooms or a flat?

Lily held up her hand. 'It's not fair that you and Frederick keep on helping out. You've both done enough, Olive.'

Olive looked concerned; she didn't want Lily and Bella having to live in a couple of run-down rooms. 'Then will David be able to help you? He does seem to know people down there.'

Lily smiled and nodded. 'Yes, he's got so many acquaintances and friends from when he was studying – and of course he lived there himself for a few years too.' She paused. Well, there was no use shilly-shallying about the matter. She took a deep breath. 'Actually, Olive. David is . . . he's coming with us.'

Olive was so surprised that she slopped her tea in the saucer. 'He . . . he's going too? What about his work? What will you . . . ?'

'We'll be going as a family, Olive. David and I will be getting married.' She smiled and reached over and took her sister's hand. 'I know. I was rather taken aback myself. I never expected . . . at my age . . . and after years of independence . . .' She shrugged. 'Oh, don't worry, we'll get married down there, probably at Caxton Hall, so there will be no overshadowing Joan's wedding. I really do think that Mersey View will have had its fair share of weddings by then. And I'm certain that no one wants to see the spectacle of a middle-aged spinster as a bride,' she finished drily, with a small grimace.

Olive was stunned. 'Lily . . . I . . . don't know what to say! I never thought . . . you always said . . .'

'Neither did I . . . but we suit each other, and he's not in the least demanding – I couldn't stand that! David is confident he too will find work; there are always opportunities for voice coaches, even if he has to do private tutoring, and we . . . we want to try to provide a stable and happy home life for Bella. To give her all the help and support we can in the difficult years ahead – for they will be difficult, Olive. She's going to have to work very hard indeed. Places in the more prestigious opera houses are hard to obtain and harder still to keep.'

Olive nodded slowly, trying to take everything in. It was by far the best thing for Bella to have two such loving and dependable people as Lily and David guiding her career, but although she was delighted for her step-daughter she was also afraid. 'You know I still don't want her – any of you – to go, Lily? Oh, the last thing I want to do is to put a damper on things and upset Bella, but what happens if there really is another war? What will happen to Bella's career then? Times are just so uncertain and . . . dangerous.'

Lily pursed her lips with determination. 'I don't know, Olive. Does anyone know what will happen? But I do know one thing, and that is that Bella is going to have the opportunity to become one of the greatest opera stars of our time – and I for one am not going to let that jumped-up little toerag with that ridiculous moustache and delusions of grandeur stand in her way!'

Olive just stared at her sister, thinking that if every woman in the country adopted Lily's attitude then Adolf Hitler might as well pack up his army and crawl back to Austria and his job as a house painter.

'Right, then,' Lily continued. 'I've plenty of things to do, starting with writing to the theatres David has suggested. I'm going to have to break the news to Ben Stoker, and that's not going to make him happy. But at least we've got a couple of months to get everything sorted out – she doesn't start until the second week in September – and I want us to be settled into a flat or something by then, and for us all to have become used to the area.'

'I've plenty to do myself, Lil. Joan and Jim have set the date. It's Saturday the twenty-second of July, just over two weeks' time.'

Lily's eyebrows rose. 'That soon?'

'It's the only time Jim can get leave – and even then, it's only for a long weekend. They're training him to be some sort of aircraft mechanic.'

Lily grinned. 'I thought they'd have put him in the band, but maybe not at a time like this. If it's that soon then we'd all better be going to see what Fliss McKenzie's got in stock,' Lily remarked, although her own outfit was already picked out. It just needed to be paid for. A thought struck her. 'You'll have to find a couple more lodgers, Olive. My room will be empty, and Bella will be going too . . .'

Olive mused on this. 'I could give your room to Joan and Jim; he's bound to get leave at odd times in the future, and they would enjoy the space. But that leaves the room Bella and Joan share, and Jim's room. You're right, I'll have to look into it.'

'I wonder, will Monica stay on in that house on her own? I mean, with Rick away, it's big just for one person.'

Olive thought about this. 'I don't know, Lil, but I suppose she will. It's not that far from her mother-in-law, I expect she'll visit her – and of course she's bound to come back to see Nelly at least once a week. She'll manage, will Monica Eustace, you can bank on it.'

Lily sighed as she finished her tea, thinking about the future when she would no longer be here in Liverpool. 'And what about you, Olive, luv?'

Olive looked startled. 'What about me?'

'Well, with so many weddings in the offing . . . what about Frederick?'

Olive pursed her lips and frowned; she knew what her sister

was getting at. 'What about Fredrick, Lily?'

'Oh, you know what I mean, so don't tell me you don't! The man worships the ground you walk on – any fool can see that.'

Olive sighed heavily. She really didn't want to discuss this with Lily but she could see no way round it – and anyway, Lily would be going to London soon enough so the subject wouldn't be brought up again if she could help it. 'I know and I . . . I'm really very fond of him, Lily. He's a good, caring man, but I've got the kids to think about. Well, our Joan and Charlie anyway, as you'll be looking after Bella from now on.'

Lily was exasperated. 'Olive, your daughter is a grown woman – and in two weeks will be a married woman to boot – and Charlie, well, the lad's almost grown, and you know how he looks up to Frederick. I'm sure he looks on him as a father. For God's sake, Olive, you deserve some happiness in life! You've had to put up with so much . . . just tell Frederick the truth!'

Olive shook her head slowly. 'I . . . I can't, Lily. I . . . I'm too proud and I wouldn't want him to think I'm . . . I couldn't bear to see the look on his face if I told him, Lily! I've always tried so hard to be a respectable woman, you know I have!'

'You're too damned obstinate, Olive! Why throw away the chance of a happy and secure life for the sake of your misguided pride and sense of respectability?'

'I have a happy and secure life now, Lily.'

'Yes, thanks to Frederick Garswood! You are being such a fool, Olive!'

Olive managed a sad little smile. 'I know that, Lily. I know. But it doesn't change things.'

Lily said nothing but an idea was forming in her mind. She would be leaving Liverpool in a matter of weeks and she wasn't prepared to stand by and do nothing to help her sister improve her life.

Two weeks later on a warm though overcast Saturday morning the little group walked up the steps of the grim-looking, soot-blackened building in Brougham Terrace, not far from Everton Brow and the church where Monica had been married a few weeks ago.

Monica stood with Bella, Lily and David, together with Olive and Charlie, as they waited for Joan and Frederick to arrive by taxi. Jim was with them, looking very smart in his RAF uniform, but Monica couldn't help feeling a little sad for her friend. Joan deserved better than this, she thought. The building faced a busy main road and there were certainly no gardens, or greenery of any description, in sight. The building was used for the registering of births and deaths, as well as marriages, and she wondered what it would look like inside. She doubted there would be flowers of any kind, let alone music. She smiled as she caught Olive's eye, not wishing to appear downcast. Both she and Bella wore identical outfits; the dresses had actually been worn by Monica's bridesmaids, but Bella had shortened her own and Eileen's, which Monica was now wearing. They both wore wide-brimmed 'picture' hats adorned with a large single artificial bloom, to give some semblance of occasion. Lily, as usual, looked very elegant but had toned down her outfit so as not to overshadow either Olive or her niece. Monica stared around a little anxiously, for her mother and father had yet to arrive, and Nelly was seldom late.

Lily had taken a small lace fan from her handbag and proceeded to fan herself. 'Oh, it's so sultry. I just hope we're not going to have a storm, a downpour would ruin all our hats.'

'There's no rain or storms forecast,' David reassured her, smiling. He was pleased with how things were progressing with the London project. They'd managed, through the influence of one of his friends, to find a small but nice part-furnished flat above offices in Great George Street, just off Marylebone High Street, which was just about affordable, providing Lily got the job she'd applied for in the wardrobe department of the Theatre Royal and he was offered enough work by both the Royal Opera House and the Royal College of Music. Lily had even started to pack up what he considered to be her quite extensive wardrobe and numerous possessions.

'Oh, thank goodness for that!' Monica said, with considerable relief, as Nelly and Arthur alighted from a taxi cab, although she could see her mother looked far from pleased as Arthur paid the driver.

Nelly adjusted her hat. 'Doesn't your father insist on making sure his damned pigeons are all right just as we're ready to leave? I could kill him sometimes!' she hissed to her daughter, while Arthur just looked skywards, a slight smile hovering about his lips.

Monica smothered a grin. 'Well, at least you both got here on time,' she hissed back, just as the black hackney drew up alongside the kerb and Frederick got out, looking sober and neat in his best suit and carrying a bowler hat. He held open the door and Monica stepped forward to help Joan out. Even though there was no traditional dress or veil, her best friend looked stunning, she thought. As soon as Joan had set eyes on the bright fuchsia-pink silk suit trimmed with navy braid she'd gone into raptures. 'It's exactly what I was looking for but didn't really hope to find!' she'd exclaimed as Fliss McKenzie had taken it off the hanger. Its extremely well-tailored lines had suited Joan perfectly, and she'd also bought the large-brimmed hat in the same colours, complete with its two long feathers. The outfit had been worn at a very exclusive wedding held at the Anglican Cathedral, no less, Fliss had confided. She'd bought navy shoes from Timpsons in Church Street and Monica had lent her a navy leather clutch bag – her 'something borrowed'.

'You look so elegant, Joan!' Monica complimented her, meaning it. 'Are you nervous?'

Joan shook her head, which made the long feathers of her hat waft a little. 'No, truly I'm not! This is what I want . . . he's exactly what I want.' She smiled up at Jim, thinking the smoky blue of his uniform suited his colouring.

Frederick ushered the little group towards the doors. 'Let's be getting inside. I'm sure they will be waiting for us, and these officials don't like to be kept waiting,' he urged.

Monica's heart dropped like a stone when they finally all entered the small room where the ceremony would take place. It was dark and drab and utterly cheerless, there wasn't even a window. It was totally suited to the sombre business of registering a death, but certainly not holding a wedding, she thought. There was a plain wooden table upon which were the official forms, a couple of pens and an inkpot, with a couple of rows of chairs set around it, obviously for the guests. She glanced quickly at her friend and her future husband, who were standing in front of the table, but neither looked upset or even perturbed. In fact, she'd never seen Joan look so happy, she positively glowed with joy. Monica let out a sigh of relief. After the ceremony they were all going to The Bradford Hotel where a buffet had been arranged, to be paid for jointly by Frederick and Jim. At least that was something to look forward to, Monica thought, as a small man wearing gold pince-nez, an old-fashioned tail coat and pinstriped trousers came into the room and nodded to everyone before taking his place behind the table.

David surreptitiously took Lily's hand in his and she smiled up at him, sincerely hoping that Caxton Hall would not be as gloomy or forbidding as this dire place.

Olive too felt slightly disappointed with the venue, mingled with anxiety, for one small worry nagged at her. Joan's marriage certificate. She kept Joan's and Charlie's birth certificates safe in a small tin box, so perhaps she could persuade Joan to add her marriage certificate as soon as it was signed. These things were important documents – and with Jim stationed away, and her daughter not the most methodical of people, she didn't want it to get lost. She shook her anxiety away as the registrar cleared his throat.

It was a very short ceremony and, before Joan had time to realise it, the ring was on her finger, Jim was kissing her, and she was officially now Mrs James McDonald. She felt so happy that she could even have kissed the dry little registrar, who was smiling thinly at them and wishing them well. She didn't care about the room, the lack of flowers and music, or the fact that there was no sunlight streaming in through a stained-glass window – or any window. She didn't care that there would be no honeymoon, that after they left the Bradford they would be going back to the house in Mersey View. She had her family and friends around her, and she had Jim – at least for the next forty-eight hours – and he was all that mattered to her.

# Chapter Thirty-Five

---◆◆◆◆◆---

Very little seemed to have changed since she'd got married; she didn't feel as if she had changed much at all, although she did feel sort of older, more mature, Joan thought, as she walked home from the tram stop on the last evening in August. She still went to work and she still lived in the house in Mersey View with all the same people, except for Jim, and she missed him terribly. The time they'd had together had been so short, but so happy and so utterly marvellous. She comforted herself with the thought that while he was stationed at RAF Skellingthorpe they were unlikely to send him overseas any time soon – if at all – unlike Rick Eustace.

She missed Monica too, she mused, feeling the warm rays of the evening sun on her back. She missed their chats and the gossiping and the laughter. She wondered if her friend missed her too, living alone in that house on the other side of the city and not knowing when she would see Rick again, with only the weekly visit to his mother and to Nelly. Neither of the men seemed to get much leave, she thought sadly, but that was only to be expected, the way things were. She caught sight of Ethel Newbridge outside her shop, sweeping the dusty pavement, and waved to her. The current situation didn't seem to be affecting Ethel or her business, at least.

The news each day just seemed to be worse, and so that dampened everyone's spirits. France, Poland, the Netherlands and Russia had all mobilised their forces, and everywhere you went there seemed to be men in uniform of one kind or another. To her mam's relief Frederick had not been called up, and neither had Arthur Savage or Harry Newbridge, partly because they were considered too old to fight but also because Frederick and Monica's da had what were considered 'reserved occupations': jobs necessary to keep public life going. And to Lily's relief David Frances's eyesight had kept him out of the army. They had all been allocated civic duties, however, mainly as air-raid wardens, but so far all they'd received in the way of a uniform was a tin hat with the letters ARP painted on the front. With all this going on, the house seemed to be in turmoil as the preparations went ahead for Lily's and Bella's move to London, much to everyone's growing consternation.

As she reached the corner and turned into the street, Joan frowned. It seemed very quiet; there were no kids out playing as there usually were. No shouting and squabbling, no laughter, no games of cricket with the stumps chalked on someone's wall, no grid fishing, no cherry wobs or marbles, no one kicking a football, no one swinging from the arms of the lamp post by a rope. She'd have thought that the children would have been making the most of these last warm days and fairly long evenings before autumn came, but as she pushed open the scullery door and went through into the kitchen she discovered why.

She found herself walking into a full-blown argument between her mam and Lily. She'd passed Charlie out in the yard, trying to teach the dog a trick, obviously getting out of the way, but Bella was sitting white-faced and biting her lip on the bench by the table. Frederick sat there too, the newspaper spread out before him, looking decidedly concerned.

'Oh, Joan! Will you for God's sake try and talk some sense into your aunt!' Olive greeted her, looking distracted and worried. 'We've been trying for the last half an hour but . . .'

Joan looked from her mother to her aunt. 'What's the matter now?'

'She's still insisting on taking Bella and them all to London!' Olive cried, infuriated.

'We know that, Mam, and . . . well, while no one wants them to go . . .' Joan pointed out resignedly, wondering how many times they'd had this argument.

'Joan, today they've been sending all the children away. Didn't you notice there was no one in the street? They're evacuating them! They were all taken around to the school late this morning, and there were women in this street in floods of tears, seeing them go. Bless them, they all went off with their names and details on labels attached to their coats and clutching their gas masks, like little parcels! It . . . it was heartbreaking to see! They're sending them off by train out to live in North Wales, in the countryside, to be safe from the bombs.' She turned to Lily, whose face was like stone. 'And still this one here is determined to take Bella by train, right into the heart of a city that's bound to be the first to be bombed!

But will she listen to us? Will she hell! She's mad! Stark, staring mad!'

'We've tried to make her see the sense of not going just yet,' Frederick stated quietly.

'Well, it's too late now, as I've told you umpteen times already!' Lily interrupted angrily. 'Everything's arranged, we're moving straight into the flat, and Bella will start her training next week! I really don't understand you, Olive! We've been over this, time and again, and you've agreed that you don't want to deny her a future. Yes, there *is* a risk – a big one. No, no one knows what the future will bring, but that's not going to stand in her way! I'm determined she's going to have her chance! I thought you'd understand that too? Both David and I are willing to risk everything –'

'Well, I don't understand, Lily! Things in the world have got so much worse since Bella went for her audition and, as she's got no one else, I feel responsible for her and her safety, which you seem to be forgetting – conveniently! I wonder, is it really Bella that you're thinking of, or is it yourself and David? Are you both too wrapped up in a new life for yourselves in London that you're blind to the dangers?'

Lily's face drained of colour and her dark eyes flashed dangerously. 'How dare you, Olive! How bloody dare you suggest that we don't care about Bella! You know how hard David's worked with her, and we're both prepared to give up good jobs so we can look after her and guide her! She's like a daughter to me! How dare you say such a thing!'

'Yes, a very talented daughter – and isn't that the nub of the matter, Lily? Do you want to live the rest of your life through her, basking in her success?'

Frederick laid a hand on Olive's arm, thinking that now she'd gone too far. 'I don't think she really meant it to sound like that, Lily.'

Lily glared at them both, deeply hurt by her sister's remarks. 'I just want the best for Bella – not for myself or David. If she's a success, then we'll be happy – that's all we want. So, we *will* be going to London on Saturday, as planned, whether you're happy about it or not, Olive!'

'And what makes you think you'll even be able to get on a train to London? There's so many servicemen on the move,' Olive shot back, still desperate to try to make her sister change her mind.

'Because David's got the tickets and has had the presence of mind to reserve seats, that's why, Olive! He doesn't leave things to chance. And we have the keys to the flat too, and most of the luggage has gone on ahead, as well you know!'

'Oh, just stop it! Stop it, both of you!' Joan shouted, losing her temper and causing both her mother and her aunt to look a little startled. 'Aren't you both forgetting about the one person in all this who matters most? Bella! Does she want to go or not? Is her opinion of no importance at all? Is it all just about what you two want?' Joan turned to her half-sister, who was twisting her hands together in her lap. 'It's up to you, Bella.'

Suddenly Bella jumped to her feet, the tears streaming down her cheeks. 'I no want to go at all if you all . . . fight over it!' she cried, before rushing from the room, slamming the door behind her.

'I understand that you all want what is best for her. But now look at what the pair of you've done!' Joan berated them, yanking open the door and following the girl upstairs, leaving Olive, Lily and Frederick looking angry, hurt and worried.

Joan found Bella sitting on the edge of the bed beside her half-packed suitcase, crying. She sat down beside her and took Bella's hand. 'Oh, take no notice of them, luv. Everyone's nerves are on edge just now, it's only to be expected. Mam is thinking of your safety – all of you – and Aunty Lil is thinking of your career.'

Bella wiped away her tears and nodded. 'I know this, Joan.'

'What matters most is what *you* want to do, Bella. It's your life, your future – not theirs.'

The girl didn't reply for a while and Joan had begun to think that she wasn't going to answer her at all, then Bella began hesitantly. 'I . . . ever since I come here you have all been so good . . . so kind to me – especially you, Joan – and I feel so sad to go away and leave you, but . . . but I feel here –' she pressed a hand to her chest – 'that I have been given such a gift, a blessing . . . that I should not waste it if I can help it. I . . . I cannot let my mama down. When I sang at Monica's wedding it made me realise that . . . that this is what I must do. This is my *life*. Unless I can sing I will not be properly . . . alive. When I sing, I forget about all the bad, unhappy things that have happened to me in the past . . . and I can remember and be glad of all the good and wonderful things. Yes, I will be afraid in London. I will be afraid of the bombs, but as long as I have my music and I can sing . . .'

Silently Joan nodded. She understood how Bella felt, and it was useless to say now that there would be no war: it was obvious to all but complete idiots that, any day now, hostilities would be declared. 'Then you must go, Bella. I'll miss you –

351

we'll all miss you – and I'll miss Aunty Lil, and so will Mam, no matter what she says now.' She smiled. 'Sisters always fight, just look at Monica and Eileen.'

Bella managed a smile, twisting a necklace of cheap plastic beads between her fingers. 'No. *We* don't, Joan.'

Joan smiled too. 'No, we don't. I'll go down and tell them . . . and try to calm things down. And you'd better get on with your packing if you're going to be ready to go on Saturday.'

Bella looked up at her, her dark eyes still misty with tears. 'I think I have too many things. When I come here I have nothing, now I seem to have so much and too many beads and trinkets.' She twisted the coral-coloured string of beads around her neck.

Joan smiled at her. 'I love you dearly, Bella, and I'm certain that one day you will have pearls and diamonds around your neck – not plastic – when you sing in all the great theatres in the world.'

Bella smiled back. 'I will be happy with plastic, Joan.'

She had half-heartedly started packing when there was a tapping on the door and Charlie appeared, looking a bit embarrassed.

'Have they stopped shouting at each other down there?' Bella greeted him.

He nodded. 'That's why I stayed in the yard with Rags. Are you still going to London, Bella?'

'Yes, that is why I keep on with my packing, Charlie. I do not want Aunt Lily to be even more cross.'

Charlie crossed to the window and looked down into the

yard where the dog was now dozing in the last rays of the sun, no doubt thankful that his master had given up trying to train him for today. 'Are you scared, Bella?'

She looked at him frankly. 'I would tell a lie if I said no, Charlie. Yes, I am very afraid but . . . but I have been afraid before . . . and everything, it was good in the end. So, I trust in myself. Are you scared of what will happen?'

He'd admit it to no one else – but he had grown fond of her, and she was going away the day after tomorrow – so he nodded his answer. 'Yes, I'm scared too.'

'At least you are not old enough that you will have to go and fight like Jim and Rick,' she reminded him, trying to cheer him up and allay his fears.

Charlie smiled at her grimly. 'Not yet, Bella, but the Great War went on for four years – and in four years I'll be turning twenty.'

There was nothing she could say to that.

Charlie dug into his pocket and brought out a small object wrapped in a piece of white cloth, which he handed to her. 'I made it for you . . . to keep.'

Carefully, she unwrapped it, revealing a tiny ornament, a cockerel made of highly burnished copper standing on a little base of polished wood. 'Oh, Charlie! It is beautiful and it is one of the symbols of my country. In Portugal the Barcelos Rooster is special, it is a symbol of the Portuguese love of life! Thank you!'

'I know. I looked it up in a book in the library. I made it from a bit of copper piping that was left over. I know it's usually painted in bright colours, but I didn't have any paint.'

'That doesn't matter! I keep it with me always, I promise.

He will be my lucky charm, Charlie! Thank you.'

Charlie's cheeks were turning pink as he turned for the door. 'You won't need a lucky charm, Bella. Not if you sing like you did at Monica's wedding. Everyone loved it. You were amazing.'

Bella stared after him, still holding the little ornament in her hand. It was so kind of him to go to so much trouble for her, and she *would* keep it. She'd keep it forever.


Joan's news of Bella's decision was met with grim satisfaction by Lily, apprehension by Frederick, and downright exasperation by Olive.

'Oh, I'm going up to see Nelly before I explode!' she announced, leaving the kitchen and going into the lobby for her jacket. Joan followed; she had no desire to stay here to be questioned by her aunt, and she hoped that maybe Monica would have decided to visit her mother that evening, although she didn't hold out much hope. Still, the atmosphere couldn't be nearly as bad as in their house, she mused, even though the news about the evacuation of the children hung like a black cloud over everyone.

When they'd gone, Lily sat at the kitchen table for a while, deep in thought. She assumed Bella was still packing, and Charlie had gone through into the yard with the muttered excuse of taking the dog for its evening walk, so she had the kitchen to herself. At last she made up her mind. She was leaving on Saturday and she didn't know when, or even if, she would ever come back to Liverpool. Of course she wouldn't leave without making her peace with Olive, but it was Olive and her future that concerned her most at this precise moment in time. She got to her feet slowly. Frederick had gone up to his sitting room to listen to the wireless although she didn't think that was such a good idea. There would be nothing cheering on the BBC tonight – there never was, these days.

She hesitated for a moment before she knocked and heard him inviting her to go in.

She smiled at him as she closed the door behind her. She hoped she was doing the right thing and that it wouldn't turn out to be the biggest mistake of her life – one for which her sister would never forgive her.

'What is it, Lily?' Frederick asked, indicating she should sit down.

'Something rather important, Frederick, which I hope you will be very pleased to hear,' she replied, smoothing down her skirt before finally embarking upon what she had to say.

# Chapter Thirty-Six

———◆•※•◆———

Joan had said her goodbyes the evening before, for she had to work that Saturday morning, and neither Olive nor Charlie were going to the station to see Lily and her party off. Olive had breakfasts to cook, and Charlie had a couple of small jobs to do for Frederick.

Joan had hugged Bella tightly after she'd helped her to close her suitcase, and Charlie had taken it downstairs to put in the lobby with Lily's cases. 'You remember to write when you can. I know you'll be very busy, and things might be hectic, but everyone will want to know how you are getting on and what living in London's really like,' she'd urged her half-sister.

'I promise, I write when I can, Joan. I know Step-Mama will worry. And you, you will write to me and tell me all the news?'

Joan had brushed a stray tendril of dark curly hair away from Bella's brow. 'I will, although I can't see anything of much interest happening here in Mersey View.' She'd brightened up. 'Of course, Jim might be able to get some leave.'

'I hope so, Joan,' Bella had replied as Joan had turned away to go to the room she shared with Jim, whenever he managed to get home.

On Saturday morning, Olive had tears in her eyes as she hugged her sister and Bella – and David too, when he arrived in the taxi to take them to Lime Street.

'Oh, Lily, take care! Please don't take any risks? You know how much you mean to me. I didn't mean those awful things I said! I was just so frantic with worry.'

Lily blinked away her own tears. 'Of course, I know you didn't mean it all, Olive. And I promise, we'll not be foolish. We'll take good care of Bella. I only regret that you won't be there when David and I get married. You are all the family I have.'

Olive had nodded. 'I wish I could, Lily, but . . .'

Lily pulled herself together, it was time to go. It was no use everyone getting maudlin. The meter on the taxi was running, and the city streets would be busy on a Saturday morning. 'Right, it's time we were on our way.'

Olive hugged Bella tightly, one last time, wishing with all her heart that she could keep the girl safe. But she wouldn't stand in Bella's way now. She kissed her forehead and wiped the tears from Bella's cheeks. 'Off you go, luv. Look on it as another new chapter in your life, but this time you have Lily and David with you. You're not setting out on your own any more.'

Bella managed a smile and followed Lily and David, as well as Frederick, who was accompanying them into the taxi, for Olive felt that *someone* should see them off at the station. She waved until the vehicle turned the corner into Northumberland Terrace.

The concourse of Lime Street Station was crowded with people, even for that early hour of the morning, Lily thought a little anxiously, as she held on tightly to Bella with one hand and to David's arm with the other.

'Goodness, I didn't think it would be as bad as this, David! Thank God you booked seats.' She stared around at the crowds.

David and Frederick seemed to be the only men not in uniform. Khaki, Airforce blue, Navy blue and the very dark indigo of Police officers made the concourse look like a dull, heaving sea, she thought. The only bright colours were those of the women and girls who were obviously here to see their menfolk off.

'Oh, it is so busy, Aunt Lily!' Bella remarked, looking around her with some apprehension.

David smiled at her. 'Ah, Bella, wait until you see Euston Station. And then all the streets of London. Everywhere will be busy and crowded, it always is. You'll soon get used to it.'

Bella looked doubtful as Frederick propelled them towards Platform Seven, where their train would depart from. At the gate a porter took their luggage, and David handed over both tickets and reservation slips to the official on duty. Then he turned to Frederick. 'Well, we'd better get on board, I don't think they'll be very happy if we hold things up. Take care of yourself, Frederick.'

They shook hands as Frederick nodded. 'Good luck, David.

And to you all.' He bent down and kissed Bella on the cheek and then Lily. 'Lily, take care of yourself and . . . thank you. Thank you for everything.'

She looked up at him quizzically. 'Did I do the right thing, Frederick?'

He smiled. 'Of course you did. All I've got to do now is convince her. And, Lily, you know that if ever you need to come back, there will always be a home for you – for you all – in Mersey View.'

Lily reached up and patted his shoulder before David hustled her and Bella through on to the platform.

Frederick stood back to let people pass and watched the little group until they were out of sight, swallowed up in the clouds of steam issuing from the huge black engine that stood waiting to start its long journey. He wondered if he would ever see any of them again. He hoped so, especially for Olive's sake. Lily was her only sister, and despite their differences, he knew they were extremely close.

The house seemed very quiet when Frederick returned, but according to the clock on the mantel in the parlour it was still only half past ten. Joan was at work, as was Gerard Barnard, and Charlie was occupied with changing the washers on the taps in Ethel's kitchen and scullery. There was no sign of Olive but he hoped she hadn't gone out shopping, for there was something of great importance he wanted to talk to her about; something that would affect both their futures.

He went through into the kitchen and put the kettle on. The room was tidy and smelled of fresh bread; Olive had obviously been baking. He was restless as he poured himself cup of tea and sat down at the table to read the newspaper he'd bought on leaving the station. He'd barely glanced at the headlines on his way home; for once the imminent war took second place in his thoughts.

It was fifteen minutes before Olive returned, her laden hemp bag over her arm; she must have been down to Ethel's.

'Frederick, I didn't expect you back so soon!' Olive smiled as she placed the bag on the table. 'Is that tea fresh? If so, I'll have a cup, please. Lord, but Ethel does go on sometimes! Did they get off all right?'

He nodded as he poured the tea. 'Yes, but the place was absolutely heaving! I've never seen it so crowded, Olive. And everyone was in uniform.'

'Well, Ethel was saying that all the naval reserves have been told to report for duty, that's in addition to the territorials. It's as if the whole country is on the move. It was a good job David thought to reserve seats.'

'If they'll be allowed to use the reservations,' he observed.

'Yes, there's that. Arthur says that when things are really crowded, quite often it doesn't matter if you have booked a seat or not, you don't get to use it. They even get people having to sit on the floor. I just hope that doesn't happen to our Lily, she'll be mortified. Knowing her, she'll create a scene something shocking. Although much good that will do her,' she finished, putting her cup down on the table and preparing to unpack her shopping.

'You'll miss her, Olive, won't you?'

Slowly she nodded. 'I'll miss them both.'

Frederick stood up and gently took her hands in his. 'You ill have me, Olive.'

She smiled, he was always so considerate and kind to her. 'I know, and I'm grateful.'

'I don't want you to be grateful. I want you to marry me, Olive? I know I should be down on one knee with a bunch of flowers, but well . . .'

She stared at him, her eyes wide and uncomprehending. 'Frederick . . . I . . . how can I?' she stammered, taken aback, though a part of her wanted to say yes immediately, and to fling her arms around him. But she couldn't do that, she knew.

Frederick held her gaze steadily. 'I know, luv. I know all about you and Billy Copperfield. Lily told me before she left.'

Olive felt as if she had been punched in the stomach. She sat down suddenly on the bench by the table and stared up at him, her eyes wide, her cheeks drained of all colour. 'She . . . she had no right!' she gasped. 'It was not her secret to tell!'

'You must have loved him to distraction, Olive, and I envy him that much,' Frederick carried on gently, still holding her hands.

She pulled them away and covered her face with them. 'I did! God help me, I did, and I'll regret it for the rest of my life, but I had my pride, Frederick! My stupid, misguided pride! It was Lily who found out he was already married and that his wife was . . . expecting. I refused at first to believe her, and when I finally confronted him, he swore he'd never loved her. It had been a quick "fling" and he . . . he'd been forced to marry her by her da, who was known as a terrible, violent man. It was either marry her or suffer a beating that might well have killed him – or meet with a fatal accident on the sh'

361

or the dockside. What choice had he had? He swore that it was me he truly loved, and always would, and he promised that we could still have a life together, if only I would give him a second chance to prove his love. We could live as man and wife, he would buy me a ring, and no one need ever know. We could start afresh, I would be his wife, for he loved no one else. I . . . I gave in, even though I suspected I was being a fool, but I loved him so much. We moved away from the Dingle area so no one would know, but it broke my mam's heart and she . . . she never forgave me, and I never saw her again.' A shuddering sob ran through her. 'I heard that his wife and the child went to live with an aunt in Birmingham . . . and no one ever seemed to hear of them again.' She dabbed at her eyes. 'Things weren't so bad, to start with. I was happy, even though he was away at sea for most of the time. But then, when I had the kids, I was so terrified someone would find out we were not legally married and tell them the awful truth – and also that they were illegitimate – that I felt we had to keep moving. And . . . and the rest you know, Frederick, although you now know how hard I've tried to keep that secret, tried to make us all appear to be a respectable family. I just couldn't bring myself to confide in anyone, Frederick. Not even Nelly, who is the closest friend I've ever had. Oh, there were times when I wanted to tell her, but you know just how much of a stigma it is, and I didn't want to risk losing her friendship and respect, so I just couldn't! Lily is the only one who knew.'

Frederick shook his head. He did know how much of a stigma it was, and society would not have been kind to her or her children, so he understood how she'd tried so hard to protect them at the expense of her own happiness. All she'd been guilty of was once being a young girl who'd foolishly given her heart to a man who so patently did not deserve it. 'There surely is nothing for you to regret, Olive. It was he who lied and cheated.'

Olive groaned. She could kill Lily for bringing this shame on her. 'I . . . I was young and pig-headed and besotted. I wouldn't listen to anyone! I loved him. I wouldn't believe the things Lily said about him. So I . . . I was happy just to have him.' She broke down completely, sobbing.

Frederick gently pulled her to her feet and, wrapping his arms around her, drew her close to him. 'I don't understand him, Olive. How could he do all that to you? He'd a wife already and one he deserted! Your parents ostracised you. Only Lily stood by you. He treated you as no man should treat a woman he loves, but he seemed not to care at all for any of you. His legal wife, or you, or Bella's mother – and God knows who else!'

Olive raised a pale, tear-streaked face. 'And that hurt me most of all, Frederick. My mam. I missed her so much. Oh, I tried so hard to keep everything from people. I tried desperately to appear to be a respectable married woman, but I was so afraid that someday, someone would find out that I was living like a . . . a whore, with two bastard children!'

The sobs tore her apart again. Oh, what would he think of her now? He'd been so kind, so generous, so loving. He, a respectable man from a decent family, with his own business and some standing in this neighbourhood, what would he think of her? And what about her children? Oh, how hard she'd fought to save them from finding out that they wer illegitimate. It was one of the worst sins in society, a stigma they would always bear. They would be looked down upon, despised because of it, and it was all her fault for being so stupid! So blindly stupid! Joan had only to look closely at her marriage certificate, something she'd so far not done, having been happy to pass it over to her mother for safe keeping.

'Olive, my love, I won't have you speaking . . . thinking of yourself like that. You *are* a decent, respectable woman who made the mistake of loving the wrong man. A man who obviously loved no one but himself, had no morals at all and who ruined your life.'

'Until I came here. Until you took me . . . us in, Frederick. But . . . but I can't marry you. I'm so, so sorry.' She couldn't look at him; she was already hurting so much she thought her heart would break in two.

'Why not, Olive?'

'I . . . I've just told you.'

'I don't care about any of it, my love. None of it is your fault; to me you are the most wonderful woman on earth. From the day you moved in next door I have admired you, but I never thought that I could dare to love you – even from afar – because of *him*. I'd even begun to hope that if you never heard from him again, after seven years he would legally be considered deceased . . . and then . . . maybe; but now! Oh, Olive, please don't deny us both the chance of a full and happy life. Forget about convention! Who knows about all this, apart from Lily? No one, so it doesn't matter. There's going to be a war, Olive, no one can deny that now, so please let's face whatever the future brings together?'

Slowly she raised her eyes to his, and she saw there the love and adoration she'd never, ever seen in Billy's eyes when he'd looked at her. Oh, why not say yes? She loved him. Not as blindly or as obsessively as she'd once thought she'd loved Billy, but he wasn't remotely like Billy. Why deny herself happiness, contentment and peace of mind? Why deny him? He had given her so much already, so why couldn't she give him her heart and her love? She could stop the pretence and put down roots. The past was finally behind her.

At last she nodded. 'Yes, Frederick. I . . . I'll marry you.'

His heart felt as though it were about to burst as he held her and kissed her as he'd dreamed of so often doing in the past.

When she at last pulled away, her eyes were bright with tears – tears of happiness. 'There's only one thing, Frederick.'

'What, my love?' he asked as he traced the outline of her cheek with his forefinger, thinking he was the luckiest man in the world.

'What am I going to tell Joan and Charlie? It's going to be a terrible shock and an awful blow to them . . . to learn that they're . . .'

'Olive, Joan is a married woman, so it really doesn't affect her now. Jim took her at face value and he loves her. And besides, if she ever looks closely enough at her marriage certificate, she'll see that her father's name is entered as "William Copperfield" and her mother's as "Olive Mary Cooper". She will find out eventually, so it may as well be now. And as for Charlie, we get on well together and he talks to me a lot – he always has done, ever since Billy left. I don't think he has ever really got over Billy's relationship to Bella and his desertion of you all. Forgotten, maybe – forgiven, no! If Charlie wants to take my name legally, I'll be happy with that. So if there are no more obstacles, Olive, shall we take ourselves off to Brougham Terrace as soon as is convenient?'

Olive nodded. She'd think about Nelly and the children's reactions later. It was as if a great weight had rolled off her shoulders. All these years of trying her utmost to keep her secrets and appear to be a respectably married woman were over. Now she would indeed be that person. Mrs Frederick Garswood.

Monica gave her best sherry glasses a final polish and held them up to the light to check there were no smears. She'd made some sandwiches when she'd got in from work and there were some scones her mam had given her on her last visit, all laid out on a tray on her kitchen table. Joan was coming this evening – Monica's first proper visitor.

She'd put out a small table and two deck chairs in the garden, for it was a gorgeous evening even though it was now September. She missed her friend and wished she would visit more often. She did get lonely in this house, even though she loved every room and every stick of furniture she possessed – which, she had to admit, wasn't a great deal, yet.

She put down the glasses and checked her hair as she went through into the hall to answer the bell.

Joan stood on the step, a large bunch of Michaelmas daisies in her arms.

'I went into Clayton Square and I bought these off the flower ladies,' she announced, thrusting the flowers into Monica's arms.

'Oh, you shouldn't have! I'll get my one and only vase;

they'll look gorgeous in the middle of the dining-room table.'

Joan grinned at her. 'Fine for some to actually have a dining table! Are we eating off it?'

Monica shook her head. 'No, I thought it might seem a bit stuffy. I thought we'd sit in the garden as it's a lovely evening. I've made some sandwiches. Come on through.'

When Joan had settled herself in her chair and Monica had handed her a glass of sherry and brought out the bottle and plates of food, she looked around at the dappled sunlight on the lawn and flower beds. 'It's really lovely out here, Mon. We neither of us could sit out in Mersey View, could we? Not much fun sitting in the yard with the ashcans and the privy!'

Monica laughed. 'No. Have you heard from Jim?'

'He writes as often as he can. They're starting to censor letters now, though,' she said with a shrug.

'I know; Rick wrote saying it's hard to get hold of good writing paper too.'

'My last from Jim was in pencil and on paper so thin you could almost see through it. "Government Issue", I suppose.' She took a sip of her drink. 'Do you get lonely here, Mon? I mean, it's so quiet. Not that that's a bad thing.'

'It is quiet, and as I'm out all day I hardly know the neighbours. It . . . it's not like Mersey View, Joan. Everyone knows everyone there. I was thinking . . .' She paused and took a sip of her drink.

'What?'

'Well, would you like to come and stay with me for a couple of nights each week? While Jim is away, I mean. There's plenty of room.'

Joan considered this. There was plenty of room; it wa

lovely house in a nice area, with a bathroom and gardens, and fairly near to her work. And with Lily and Bella gone . . . 'I don't see why not, Mon. It would make a nice change, and I'll still be with Mam for most of the time. And now she has got Frederick to keep her company . . .' Joan smiled to herself.

It had been quite a shock when her mam had enlightened her about the entire situation, but she'd got over it. All she wanted was for Olive to be happy; she couldn't care less about Billy, and this news only deepened that feeling. She wanted her mam to be as happy as she herself was with Jim. Mam deserved to be loved and cherished. She grinned now at her friend. 'You know, Mon, I've never looked out of my bedroom window and seen a garden. Do you know much about gardening?'

Monica shrugged. 'Not a thing really, but I suppose I can learn.'

Joan grinned at her as she took another sip of her drink, thinking that it was so lovely to be able to sit here in peace, with her closest friend. 'You can learn to cut grass, then, as well as hair.'

Monica grimaced. 'I hope it won't take as long to learn.'

Joan turned her face up to the evening sun. 'Oh, this is very . . . civilised, Mrs Eustace.'

'It is, isn't it, Mrs McDonald? It's just a pity the rest of the world isn't!'

Joan frowned and sat up in her chair. There was little warmth in the September sun now. 'What do you think will happen to us, Mon, the girls from Mersey View? You, me, Bella, Eileen – even your mam and mine, and Lily?'

'I don't know, Joan. If you think too much about the future, it's frightening. And sometimes it's as well we don't know what's going to happen. But one thing I'm sure of is that, no matter what, we'll always be friends.'

Joan smiled and leaned across, holding out her glass. 'A toast to friendship, Mon.'

Monica raised her glass. 'To friendship and the girls from Mersey View.'

# *Afterword*

On Sunday 3rd September 1939, Britain issued an ultimatum demanding that Adolf Hitler cease his attack on Poland and withdraw his forces.

After two hours, when there was no response, Britain and her Empire declared war on Nazi Germany.

For the second time in less than twenty-five years, the world was at war.